THE
FOURTH
PROTOCOL

ALSO BY FREDERICK FORSYTH

The Day of the Jackal
The Odessa File
The Dogs of War
The Shepherd
The Devil's Alternative
No Comebacks (short stories)

THE
FOURTH
PROTOCOL

FREDERICK
FORSYTH

VIKING

VIKING
Viking Penguin Inc.,
40 West 23rd Street,
New York, New York 10010, U.S.A.

First Published in 1984

LIBRARY OF CONGRESS CATALOGING IN PUBLICATION DATA
Forsyth, Frederick, 1938–
The fourth protocol.
I. Title.   II. Title: 4th protocol.
PR6056.O699F6   1984   823′.914   83-40646
ISBN 0-670-32637-2

Printed in the United States of America
Set in Plantin
Designed by Roger Lax

FOR SHANE RICHARD
AGED FIVE

*Without whose loving attentions this book
would have been written in half the time.*

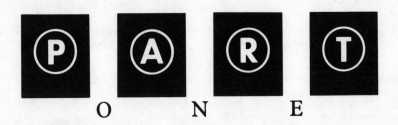

PART

ONE

CHAPTER

The man in gray decided to take the Glen Suite of diamonds at midnight. Provided they were still in the apartment safe and the occupants away. This he needed to know. So he watched and he waited. At half past seven he was rewarded.

The big, wide limousine swooped up from the subterranean parking area with the powerful grace implied by its name. It paused for an instant in the mouth of the cavern as its driver checked the street for traffic, then turned into the road and headed toward Hyde Park Corner.

Sitting across from the luxury apartment building, dressed in a chauffeur's uniform at the wheel of the rented Volvo Estate, Jim Rawlings breathed a sigh of relief. Gazing unobserved across the Belgravia street, he had seen what he had hoped for—the husband had been at the wheel, with his wife beside him. Rawlings already had the engine running and the heater on to keep out the cold. Moving the automatic shift into Drive, he eased out of the line of parked cars and went after the Jaguar.

It was a crisp and bright morning, with a pale wash of light over Green Park in the east, and the streetlights still on. Rawlings had been at the stakeout since five o'clock, and although a few people had passed down the street, no one had taken any notice of him. A chauffeur in a big car in Belgravia, richest of London's West End districts, attracts no attention, least of all with four suitcases and a hamper in the back, on the morning of December 31. Many of the rich would be preparing to leave the capital to celebrate the festivities at their country homes.

He was fifty yards behind the Jaguar at Hyde Park Corner and allowed a truck to move between them. Up Park Lane, Rawlings had one momentary misgiving; there was a branch of Coutts Bank there and he feared the couple in the Jaguar might pause to drop the diamonds into the night safe.

At Marble Arch he breathed a second sigh of relief. The limousine ahead of him made no turn around the arch to take the southbound carriageway back down Park Lane toward the bank. It sped straight up Great Cumberland Place, joined Gloucester Place, and kept on north. So, the occupants of the luxury apartment on the eighth floor of Fontenoy House were not leaving the items with Coutts; either they had them in the car and were taking them to the country or they were leaving them for the New Year period in the apartment. Rawlings was confident it would be the latter.

He tailed the Jaguar to Hendon, watched it speeding into the last mile before the M1 motorway, and then turned back toward central London. Evidently, as he had hoped, they were going to join the wife's brother, the Duke of Sheffield, at his estate in north Yorkshire, a full six-hour drive away. That would give him a minimum of twenty-four hours, more than he needed. He had no doubt he could take the apartment at Fontenoy House; he was, after all, one of the best safecrackers in London.

By midmorning he had returned the Volvo to the rental company, the uniform to the costumiers, and the empty suitcases to his closet. He was back in his top-floor flat, a comfortable and expensively furnished pad atop a converted tea warehouse in his native Wandsworth. However he prospered, he was a South Londoner, born and bred, and though Wandsworth might not be as chic as Belgravia and Mayfair, it was his "manor." Like all of his kind, he hated to leave the security of his own manor. Within it he felt reasonably safe, even though to the local underworld and the police he was known as a "face," underworld slang for a criminal or villain.

Like all successful criminals, he kept a low profile around the manor, driving an unobtrusive car, his sole indulgence being the elegance of his apartment. He cultivated a deliberate vagueness among the lower orders of the underworld as to exactly what he did, and although the police accurately suspected his specialty, his "form book" was clean, apart from a short stretch of "porridge" as a teen-ager. His evident success and the vagueness about how he achieved it evoked reverence among the young aspirants in the game, who were happy to perform small errands for him. Even the heavy mobs who took out payrolls in broad daylight with shotguns and pickax handles left him alone.

As was necessary, he had to have a front business to account for the money. All the successful faces had some form of legitimate oc-cupation. Favored fronts have always been the taxi business (driving or owning), grocery shops, and scrap-metal yards. All these fronts permit a lot of hidden profits, cash dealing, spare time, a range of hiding places, and the facility to employ a couple of "heavies," or "slags." These are hard men of little brain but considerable strength who also need an apparently legitimate employment to supplement their habitual profession as hired muscle.

Rawlings, in fact, had a scrap-metal dealership and car-wrecking yard. It gave him access to a well-equipped machine workshop, metal of all kinds, electrical wiring, battery acid, and the two big thugs he employed both in the yard and as backup should he ever run into any "aggro" from villains who might decide to make trou-ble for him.

Showered and shaved, Rawlings stirred Demerara crystals into his second espresso of the morning and studied again the sketch drawings Billy Rice had left him.

Billy was his apprentice, a smart twenty-three-year-old who would one day become good, even very good. He was just starting out on the fringe of the underworld and eager to do favors for a man of prestige, apart from the invaluable instruction he would get in the process. Twenty-four hours earlier, Billy had knocked at the door of the eighth-floor apartment at Fontenoy House, carrying a large bou-quet of flowers and dressed in the livery of an expensive flower shop. The props had got him effortlessly past the commissionaire in the lobby, where he had also noted the exact layout of the entrance hall, the porter's lodge, and the way to the stairs.

It was her ladyship who had answered the door personally, her face lighting up with surprise and pleasure at the sight of the flowers. They purported to come from the committee of the Distressed Veterans Benevolent Fund, of which Lady Fiona was one of the patronesses, and whose gala ball she was due to attend that very night, December 30, 1986. Rawlings figured that even if, at the ball itself, she mentioned the bouquet to any one of the committee members, he would simply assume it had been sent by another member on behalf of them all.

At the door, she had examined the attached card, exclaimed, "Oh, how perfectly lovely!" in the bright cut-crystal accents of her class, and taken the bouquet. Then Billy had held out his receipt pad and ballpoint pen. Unable to manage all three items together, Lady Fiona had withdrawn, flustered, into the sitting room to put down the bouquet, leaving Billy unattended for several seconds in the small hallway.

With his boyish looks, fluffy blond hair, blue eyes, and shy smile, Billy was a gift. He reckoned he could work his way past any middle-aged housewife in the metropolis. But his baby eyes missed very little.

Before even pressing the doorbell, he had spent a full minute scanning the outside of the door, its frame, and the surrounding wall area. He was looking for a small buzzer no larger than a walnut, or a black button or switch with which to turn the buzzer off. Only when satisfied there was none did he ring the bell.

Left alone in the doorway, he did the same again, searching the inner side of the frame and the walls for the buzzer or switch. Again there was none. By the time the lady of the house returned to the hall to sign the receipt, Billy knew the door was secured by a shunt lock, which he had gratefully identified as a Chubb rather than a Brahmah, which is reputedly unpickable.

Lady Fiona took the pad and pen and tried to sign for the flowers. No chance. The ballpoint pen had long since had its cartridge removed and any remaining ink expended on a blank piece of paper. Billy apologized profusely. With a bright smile Lady Fiona told him it was of no account, she was sure she had one in her bag, and returned beyond the sitting-room door. Billy had already noted what he sought. The door was indeed linked to an alarm system.

Protruding from the edge of the open door, high up on the hinge side, was a small plunger contact. Opposite it, set in the doorjamb, was a tiny socket. Inside that socket, he knew, would be a Pye microswitch. With the door in the closed position, the plunger would enter the socket and make a contact.

With the burglar alarm set and activated, the microswitch would trigger the alarm if the contact was broken—that is, if the door was opened. It took Billy less than three seconds to bring out his tube of Super Glue, squirt a hefty dollop into the orifice containing the microswitch, and tamp the whole thing down with a small ball of Plasticine-and-glue compound. In four seconds more it was rock-hard, the microswitch blanked off from the entering plunger in the edge of the door. When Lady Fiona returned with the signed receipt she found the nice young man leaning against the doorjamb, from which he straightened up with an apologetic smile, smearing any surplus of glue from the ball of his thumb as he did so.

Later, Billy had given Jim Rawlings a complete description of the layout of the entrance, porter's lodge, location of the stairs and elevators, the corridor to the apartment door, the small hallway behind the door, and what parts of the sitting room he had been able to see.

As he sipped his coffee, Rawlings was confident that four hours earlier the apartment owner had carried his suitcases into the corridor and returned to his own hallway to set his alarm. As usual, it had made no sound. Closing the front door after him, he would have turned the key fully in the mortise lock, satisfied his alarm was now set and activated. Normally, the plunger would have been in contact with the Pye microswitch. The turning of the key would have established the complete link, activating the whole system. But with the plunger blanked from the microswitch, the door system, at least, would be inert. Rawlings was certain he could take that door lock within thirty minutes. In the apartment itself there would be other traps. He would cope with those when he met them.

Finishing his coffee, he reached for his file of newspaper cuttings. Like all jewel thieves, Rawlings followed the society gossip columns closely. This particular file was entirely about the social appearances of Lady Fiona and the suite of perfect diamonds she had worn to the gala ball the previous evening—so far as Jim Rawlings was concerned, for the last time.

■ A thousand miles to the east, the old man standing at the window of the sitting room in the third-floor-front apartment at Mira Prospekt 111 was also thinking of midnight. It would herald January 1, 1987, his seventy-fifth birthday.

The hour was well past midday but he was still in a robe; there was little enough cause these days to rise early or spruce up to go to the office. There was no office to go to. His Russian wife, Erita, thirty years his junior, had taken their two boys skating along the flooded and frozen lanes of Gorki Park, so he was alone.

He caught a glance of himself in a wall mirror, and the prospect brought him no more joy than he felt at contemplating his life, or what was left of it. His face, always lined, was now deeply furrowed. His hair, once thick and dark, was now snow-white, skimpy, and lifeless. His skin, after a lifetime of titanic drinking and chain-smoking, was blotched and mottled. His eyes gazed back miserably. He returned to the window and looked down at the snow-choked street. A few muffled, huddled *babushkas* were sweeping away the snow, which would fall again tonight.

It had been so long, he mused, twenty-four years almost to the day, since he had quit his non-job and pointless exile in Beirut to come here. There had been no point in staying. Nick Elliot and the rest at "the Firm" had got it all together by then; he had finally admitted it to them himself. So he had come, leaving wife and children to join him later if they wished.

At first he thought it was like coming home, to a spiritual and moral home. He had thrown himself into the new life; he had truly believed in the philosophy and its eventual triumph. Why not? He had spent twenty-seven years serving it. He had been happy and fulfilled those first, early years of the 1960s. There had been the extensive debriefing, of course, but he had been revered within the Committee of State Security. He was, after all, one of the "Five Stars"—the greatest of them all—along with Burgess, Maclean, Blunt, and Blake, the ones who had burrowed into the inner core of the British establishment and betrayed it all.

Burgess, drinking and buggering his way to an early grave, had been in it before he had arrived. Maclean had lost his illusions first, but then he had been in Moscow since 1951. By 1963 he was sour and embittered, taking it out on Melinda, who had finally quit to come here, to this apartment. Maclean had gone on, somehow, utterly disillusioned and resentful, until the cancer got him, by which time he hated his hosts and they hated him. Blunt had been "blown" and disgraced back in England. That left him and Blake, the old man thought. In a way he envied Blake, completely assimilated, utterly content, who had invited him and Erita for New Year's Eve. Of course, Blake had had the cosmopolitan background, Dutch father, Jewish mother.

For him there could be no assimilation; he had known that after the first five years. By then he had learned fluent Russian, written and spoken, but he still retained a remarkable English accent. Apart from that, he had come to hate the society. It was a completely, irreversibly, and unalterably alien society.

That was not the worst of it; within seven years of arriving he had lost his last political illusions. It was all a lie, and he had been smart enough to see through it. He had spent his youth and manhood serving a lie, lying for the lie, betraying for the lie, abandoning that "green and pleasant land"—and all for a lie.

For years, provided as of right with every British magazine and newspaper, he had followed the cricket scores while advising on the inspiration of strikes, looked at the old familiar places in the magazines while preparing disinformation aimed at bringing it all to ruin, perched unobserved on a barstool in the National to listen to the Brits laughing and joking in his language while counseling the top men of the KGB, including even the Chairman himself, on how best to subvert that little island. And all the time, deep inside, these past fifteen years, there had been a great void of despair that not even the drink and the many women had been able to blank out. It was too late; he could never go back, he told himself. And yet, and yet . . .

The doorbell rang. It puzzled him. Mira Prospekt 111 is a totally KGB-owned building in a quiet back street of central Moscow, with mainly senior KGB tenants and a few Foreign Ministry people. A visitor would have to check in with the concierge. It could not be Erita—she had her own key.

When he opened the door, a man stood there alone. He was youthful and looked fit, sheathed in a well-cut greatcoat and with a warm fur *shapka*, without insignia, on his head. His face was coldly impassive, but not from the freezing wind outside, for his shoes indicated he had stepped from a warm car into the warm apartment building; he had not trudged through icy snow. Blank blue eyes stared at the old man with neither friendship nor hostility.

"Comrade Colonel Philby?" he asked.

Philby was surprised. Close personal friends—the Blakes and half a dozen others—called him "Kim." For the rest, he had lived under a pseudonym for many, many years. Only to a few at the very top was he Philby, a full KGB colonel on the retired list.

"Yes."

"I am Major Pavlov, of the Ninth Directorate, attached to the personal staff of the General Secretary."

Philby knew the Ninth Directorate of the KGB. It provided the bodyguards for all the top Party personnel and for the buildings in which they worked and lived. In uniform—nowadays confined to duty inside the Party buildings and for ceremonial occasions—they would wear the distinctive electric-blue cap bands, shoulder boards, and lapel tabs, and be known also as the Kremlin Guards. Attached as personal bodyguards, they would wear beautifully cut civilian clothes; they would also be utterly fit, highly trained, icily loyal, and well armed.

"Indeed," said Philby.

"This is for you, Comrade Colonel."

The major held out a long envelope of high-quality paper. Philby took it.

"This also," said Major Pavlov, and held out a small square of pasteboard with a phone number on it.

"Thank you," said Philby. Without a further word the major inclined his head briefly, turned on his heel, and went back down the corridor. Seconds later, from his window, Philby watched the sleek black Chaika limousine with its distinctive Central Committee license plates, beginning with the letters MOC, slide away from the front entrance.

■ Jim Rawlings peered down at the society magazine photograph through a magnifying glass. The picture, taken a year earlier, showed the woman he had seen driving north out of London that morning with her husband. She was standing in a presentation line while the woman next to her greeted Princess Alexandra. And she was wearing the stones. Rawlings, who studied for months before he made a hit, knew their provenance better than his own birth date.

In 1905 the young Earl of Margate had returned from South Africa, bearing with him four magnificent but uncut stones. On his marriage in 1912 he had had Cartier of London cut and set the stones as a present to his young wife. Cartier had them cut by Aascher's of Amsterdam, then still regarded as the finest cutters in the world following their triumph in the cutting of the massive Cullinan stone. The four original gems emerged as two matching pairs of pear-shaped fifty-eight-facet stones, one pair weighing in at ten carats each, the other pair at twenty carats each.

Back in London, Cartier had set these stones in white gold, surrounded by a total of forty much smaller stones, to create a suite composed of a tiara with one of the larger of the pear-shaped gems as its centerpiece, a pendant with the other of the larger pair as its centerpiece, and matching earrings comprising the two smaller stones. Before they were ready the Earl's father, the seventh Duke of Sheffield, died, and the Earl succeeded to the title. The diamonds became known as the Glen Diamonds, after the family name of the house of Sheffield.

The eighth Duke had passed them on his death in 1936 to his son, and he in turn had had two children, a daughter born in 1944 and a son born in 1949. It was this daughter, now aged forty-two, whose image was beneath Jim Rawlings's magnifying glass.

"You won't be wearing them again, darling," said Rawlings to himself. Then he once again began checking his equipment for that evening.

■ Harold Philby slit the envelope with a kitchen knife, extracted the letter, and spread it on the sitting-room table. He was impressed; it was from the General Secretary of the Communist Party of the Soviet Union himself, handwritten in the Soviet leader's neat, clerkish script and, of course, in Russian.

Like the matching envelope, the paper was of fine quality and un-headed. He must have written it from his own apartment at Kutu-zovsky Prospekt 26, the huge building that since the time of Stalin had contained in its sumptuous quarters the Moscow homes of the very top level of Party hierarchs.

In the top right-hand corner were the words *Wednesday, December 31, 1986, a.m.* The text came below. It read:

Dear Philby,

My attention has been drawn to a remark made by you at a recent dinner party in Moscow. To wit, that "the political stability of Great Britain is constantly overestimated here in Moscow and never more so than at the present time."

I would be happy to receive from you an expansion and clarification of this remark. Put this explanation in written form and direct it to me personally, without retaining any copies or using secretaries.

When it is ready call the number Major Pavlov has given you, ask to speak to him personally, and he will come to your residence to collect it.

My felicitations upon your birthday tomorrow.

Sincerely . . .

The letter ended with the signature.

Philby let out his breath slowly. So, Kryuchkov's dinner on the twenty-sixth for senior officers of the KGB had been bugged after all. He had half suspected it. As First Deputy Chairman of the KGB and head of its First Chief Directorate, Vladimir Alexandrovitch Kryuchkov was the General Secretary's creature, body and soul. Although styled a colonel-general, Kryuchkov was no military man and not even a professional intelligence officer; he was a Party *apparatchik* to his bootstraps, one of those brought in by the present Soviet leader when he had been Chairman of the KGB.

Philby read the letter again, then pushed it away from him. The old man's style hadn't changed, he thought. Brief to the point of starkness, clear and concise, devoid of elaborate courtesies, inviting no contradiction. Even the reference to Philby's birthday was brief enough simply to show he had called for the file, and little more.

Still, Philby was impressed. A personal letter from this most glacial and remote of men was unusual and would have had men trembling at the honor. Years ago it had been different. When the present Soviet leader had arrived at the KGB as Chairman, Philby had already been there for years and was considered something of a star, lecturing on the Western intelligence agencies in general and on the British SIS in particular.

Like all incoming Party men set to command professionals of another discipline, the new Chairman had looked to put his own in key posts. Philby, even though respected and admired as one of the Five Stars, realized that a highly placed patron would be useful in this most conspiratorial of societies. The Chairman, infinitely more intelligent and cultured than his predecessor, had shown a curiosity, short of fascination but above mere interest, about Britain.

Many times over those years he had asked Philby for an interpretation or analysis of events in Britain, its personalities and likely reactions, and Philby had been happy to oblige. It was as if the KGB Chairman wanted to check what reached his desk from the in-house Britain experts and from those at his old office, the International Department of the Central Committee, against another critique. Several times he had heeded Philby's quiet advice on matters pertaining to Britain.

It had been five years since Philby had seen the new tsar of all the Russias face-to-face. In May 1982 he had attended a reception to mark the Chairman's departure from the KGB back to the Central Committee, apparently as a secretary, in fact to prepare for Brezhnev's coming death and to mastermind his own advancement. And now he was seeking Philby's interpretation again.

Philby's reverie was interrupted by the return of Erita and the boys, flushed from skating and noisy as ever. Back in 1975, long after Melinda Maclean's departure, when the higher-ups at the KGB had decided his desultory whoring and drinking had lost their charms (for the *apparat*, at least), Erita had been ordered to move in with him. She was a KGB girl then, Jewish (this was unusual), aged thirty-four, dark-haired, solid. They had married the same year.

After the marriage his notable personal charm had taken its toll. She had genuinely fallen in love with him and had roundly refused to report on him anymore to the KGB. Her case officer had shrugged, reported back, and been told to drop the matter. The boys had come two and three years later.

"Anything important, Kim?" she asked as he stood and pushed the letter into his pocket. He shook his head. She went on pulling the thick quilted jackets off the boys.

"Nothing, my love," he said. But she could see he was absorbed by something. She knew better than to insist, but she came over and kissed him on the cheek.

"Please don't drink too much at the Blakes' tonight."

"I'll try," he said with a smile.

In fact he was going to permit himself one last bender. A lifelong toper who, when he started drinking at a party, would usually go on until he collapsed, he had ignored a hundred doctors' warnings to quit. They had forced him to stop the cigarettes, and that had been bad enough. But not the booze. He could still quit it when he wanted, and he knew that he would have to stop for a while after this evening's party.

He recalled the remark he had made at Kryuchkov's dinner table and the thoughts that had prompted it. He knew what was going on, and what was intended, deep inside the heart of Britain's Labour Party. Others had received the mass of raw intelligence that he had studied over the years and that was still passed to him as a sort of favor. But only he had been able to put all the pieces together, assembling them within the framework of the British mass psychology, to come up with the real picture. If he was going to do justice to the idea forming in his mind, he was going to have to describe that picture in words, to prepare for the Soviet leader one of the best pieces he had ever penned. At the weekend he could send Erita and the boys to the dacha. He would start, alone in the apartment, at the weekend. Before then, one last bender.

■ Jim Rawlings spent the hour between nine and ten that night sitting in another, smaller rented car outside Fontenoy House. He was dressed in a beautifully cut dinner jacket and attracted no attention.

What he was studying was the pattern of lights high up in the apartment building. The flat he had targeted was of course in darkness, but he was happy to see that lights were on in the apartments above and below it. In each, to judge from the appearances of guests at the windows, New Year parties were getting under way.

At ten, with his car parked discreetly on a side street two blocks away, he sauntered through the front entrance of Fontenoy House. There had been so many people going in and out that the doors were closed but not locked. Inside the lobby, on the left-hand side, was the porter's lodge, just as Billy Rice had said. Inside it the night porter was watching his Japanese portable television set. He rose and came to his doorway, as if to speak.

Rawlings was carrying a bottle of champagne decorated with a huge ribbon bow. He waved a hand in tipsy greeting.

"Evening," he called, and added, "Oh, and Happy New Year."

If the old porter was thinking of asking for the visitor's identification or destination, he thought better of it. There were at least six parties going on in the building. Half of them seemed to be open house, so how was *he* to check guest lists?

"Oh . . . er . . . thank you, sir. Happy New Year, sir," he called, but the dinner-jacketed back had gone down the corridor. The porter returned to his movie.

Rawlings used the stairs to the second floor, then the elevator to the eighth. At five past ten he was outside the door of the apartment he sought. As Billy had reported, there was no buzzer and the lock was a Chubb mortise. There was a secondary, self-closing Yale lock, for everyday use, twenty inches above the Chubb.

The Chubb mortise has a total of seventeen thousand computations and permutations. It is a five-lever lock but for a good key man not an insuperable problem, since only the first two and a half levers need to be ascertained; the other two and a half are the same but in reverse, so that the owner's key will operate equally well when introduced from the other side of the door.

After leaving school at sixteen, Rawlings had spent ten years working with and under his uncle Albert in the latter's hardware shop. It was a good front for the old man, himself a notable safe-cracker in his day. It gave the eager young Rawlings access to every known lock on the market and to most of the smaller safes. After ten years of endless practice, and with Uncle Albert's expert coaching, Rawlings could take just about any lock in manufacture.

From his trouser pocket he produced a ring of twelve skeleton keys, all made up in his own workshop. He selected and tested three, one after the other, and settled for the sixth on the ring. Inserting it into the Chubb, he began to detect the pressure points inside the lock. Then, using a flat pack of slim steel files from his top pocket, he started to work on the softer metal of the skeleton key. Within ten minutes he had the first two and a half levers—the configuration, or profile, that he needed. In another fifteen minutes he had reproduced the same lever pattern in reverse. Inserting the finished skeleton key into the Chubb lock, he turned it slowly and carefully.

It went fully back. He waited for sixty seconds, just in case Billy's tamp of Plasticine and Super Glue had not held inside the doorjamb. No bells. He let out a sigh and went to work on the Yale with a fine steel spike. That took sixty seconds, and the door swung quietly open. It was dark inside, but the light from the corridor gave him the outlines of the empty hallway. It was about eight feet square and carpeted.

He suspected there would be a pressure pad under it somewhere, but not too close to the door, lest the owner trigger it himself. Stepping into the hall, close to the wall, he eased the door closed behind him and put on the hall light. To his left was a door, partly open, through which he could see a bathroom. To his right, another door, almost certainly the coat closet containing the alarm control system, which he would leave alone. Taking a pair of pliers from a breast pocket, he stooped and lifted an edge of the carpet. As the square of carpet rose, he spotted the pressure pad, in the dead center of the hall. Just the one. Letting the carpet fall gently back in place, he stepped around it and opened the larger door ahead of him. As Billy had said, it was the door to the sitting room.

He stood for several minutes on the threshold of the sitting room before identifying the light switch and putting on the lights. It was a risk, but he was eight floors above the street, the owners were in Yorkshire, and he did not have the time to work in a booby-trapped room by pencil flashlight.

The room was oblong, about twenty-five by eighteen feet, richly carpeted and furnished. Ahead of him were the double-glazed picture windows facing south and over the street. To his right was a wall containing a stone fireplace and, in one corner, a door that presumably led to the master bedroom suite. To his left the opposite wall contained two doors: one open to a hallway going to the guest bedrooms; the other closed, perhaps to the dining room and kitchen.

He spent another ten minutes standing motionless, scanning the walls and ceiling. His reason was simple: there could well be a static movement alarm that Billy Rice had not seen and that would detect any body heat or movement entering the room. If bells went off, he could be out of there in three seconds. There were no bells; the system was based on a wired-up door and, probably, windows, which he did not intend to touch anyway, and on a system of pressure pads on the floor.

The safe, he was sure, would be in this room or in the master bedroom, and it would be on an outside wall, since interior walls would not be thick enough. Just before eleven o'clock he spotted it. Right in front of him, in an eight-foot piece of wall between the two wide windows, was a gilt-framed mirror; it did not hang slightly away from the wall like the pictures, which cast narrow shadows at their edges, but was flat against the wall, as if hinged.

Using his pliers to lift the edge of the carpet, he worked his way around the walls, unveiling the threadlike wires leading from the baseboards to the pads, somewhere out toward the center of the room.

When he reached the mirror he saw there was one pressure pad directly beneath it. He thought of moving it, but instead lifted a large, low coffee table from nearby and placed it over the pad, its legs clear of the edges. He now knew that if he stayed close to the walls, or stood on pieces of furniture (no furniture can stand on a pressure pad), he would be safe.

The mirror was kept close to the wall by a magnetic catch, also wired. That was no problem. He slipped a flat wafer of magnetized steel between the two magnets of the catch, one in the mirror frame and the other in the wall. Keeping his substitute flat to the wall-based magnet, he eased the mirror away from the wall. The wall magnet made no protest; it was still touching another magnet, so it did not report that the contact had been broken.

Rawlings smiled. The wall safe was a nice little Hamber Model D.

He knew the door was made of half-inch-thick high-tensile hardened steel; the hinge was a vertical rod of hardened steel, going into the frame upward and downward from the door itself. The securing mechanism consisted of three hardened-steel bolts emerging from the door and entering the frame to a depth of one and a half inches. Behind the steel face of the door was a two-inch-deep tinplate box containing the three locking bolts, the vertical control bolt that governed their movements, and the three-wheel combination lock whose face was now staring at him.

Rawlings did not intend to tamper with any of this. There was an easier way—to cut the door from top to bottom on the hinge side of the combination dial. That would leave sixty percent of the door, containing the combination lock and three locking bolts, jammed into the safe's doorframe. The other forty percent of the door would swing open, giving him enough space to get his hand inside and the contents out.

He worked his way back to the hall, where he had left his bottle of champagne, and returned with it. Squatting on the coffee table, he unscrewed the bottom of the false bottle and emptied out his supplies. Apart from an electric detonator, ensconced in cotton in a small box, a collection of small magnets, and a reel of ordinary household electric cord, he had brought a length of CLC.

Rawlings knew the best way to cut half-inch steel plate was to use the Monroe theory, named after the inventor of the shaped-charge principle. What he was holding was called in the trade CLC, or charge-linear-cutting—a V-shaped length of metal, stiff but just pliable, encased in plastic explosive, manufactured by three companies in Britain, one government-owned and the other two in the private sector. CLC was definitely not available except under stringent license, but as a professional cracksman Rawlings had a contact, a "bent" employee in one of the private-sector companies.

Quickly and expertly, Rawlings prepared the length he needed and applied it to the outside of the Hamber's door, from top to bottom, on just one side of the combination dial. Into one end of the CLC he inserted the detonator, from which protruded two twisted copper wires. These he untwisted and separated widely, to prevent a short circuit later. To each wire he attached one of the strands from his domestic electric cord, which itself terminated in a three-pin household plug.

Unraveling the cord carefully, he worked his way backward around the room and into the corridor leading to the guest bedrooms. The lee of the hallway would give him protection from the blast. Making his way gingerly to the kitchen, he filled with water a large polyethylene bag he took from his pocket. This he fixed to the wall with thumbtacks to hang over the explosive on the safe's door. Feather cushions, Uncle Albert had told him, are for the birds and TV. There is no shock absorber like water.

It was twenty to midnight. The party upstairs was getting noisier and noisier. Even in this luxury building, with its accent on privacy, he could clearly hear the shouting and dancing. His last act before retiring to the corridor was to turn on the television set. Inside the corridor he located a wall plug, made sure the switch was off, and plugged in his electric cord. Then he waited.

By one minute to midnight the noise above was horrendous. Then, suddenly, it lessened as somebody roared for silence. In the quiet, Rawlings could hear the television he had switched on in the sitting room. The traditional Scottish program, with its ballads and Highland dancing, changed to a static image of Big Ben atop London's Houses of Parliament. Behind the clock's facade was the giant bell, Great Tom, which was often mistakenly called Big Ben. The TV commentator chattered away the seconds to midnight as people across the kingdom filled their glasses. The quarters began to sound.

After the quarters there was a pause. Then Great Tom spoke: *Bong!* the thunderous boom of the first stroke of midnight. It echoed in twenty million homes across the land; it crashed through the apartment on the ninth floor of Fontenoy House and was itself eclipsed by the roar of cheering and "Auld Lang Syne." As the first boom rang out on the eighth floor, Jim Rawlings flicked the electric switch to On.

The flat crack went unnoticed, save by himself. He waited sixty seconds, then unplugged his cord and began to work his way back to the safe, tidying up his gear as he went. The plumes of smoke were clearing. Of the plastic cushion and its gallon of water there was nothing left but a few damp patches. The door of the safe looked as if it had been cleft from top to bottom by a blunt ax wielded by a giant. Rawlings blew away a few wisps of smoke and with gloved hand pulled the smaller part of the door back on its hinges. The tin-plate box had been torn to pieces by the blast, but all the bolts in the other section of the door were in their sockets. The opening he had made was large enough for him to peer inside. A cash box and a vel-vet bag; he eased out the bag, undid the drawstring, and emptied the contents onto the coffee table.

They glittered and flared in the light, as if they contained their own fire. The Glen Diamonds. Rawlings had put the remainder of his equipment—the cord, the empty detonator box, the thumb-tacks, and the remainder of the CLC—back into the false cham-pagne bottle before he realized he had an unforeseen problem. The pendant and earrings would slip into his trouser pockets, but the tiara was wider and higher than he had thought. He glanced around for a receptacle that would attract no attention. It was lying on top of a bureau a few feet away.

He emptied the contents of the attaché case—wallet, credit cards, pens, an address book, and a couple of folders—into the seat of an armchair.

The attaché case was exactly right. It accommodated the Glen Suite and the champagne bottle, which might have seemed odd if glimpsed *leaving* a party. With a last glance around the sitting room, Rawlings switched off the light, stepped back into the hall, and closed the door. Once in the corridor, he relocked the main door and sixty seconds later strolled past the porter's lodge and out into the night. The old man did not even look up.

■ It was nearly midnight that first day of January 1987 when Har-old Philby sat down at the sitting-room table in his Moscow flat. He had had his bender the previous evening at the Blakes' party, but had not even enjoyed it. His thoughts were too locked into what he would have to write. During the morning he had recovered from the inevitable hangover and now, with Erita and the boys asleep in bed, he had the peace and quiet to try to think things out.

There was a *coo* from across the room; Philby rose and went over to the large cage in the corner and gazed through the bars at a pigeon with one leg in splints. Philby had always adored pets, from his vixen in Beirut through a range of canaries and parakeets in this very apartment. The pigeon waddled across the floor of its cage, the splinted leg impeding its passage.

"All right, old fellow," said Philby through the bars, "we'll have them off soon and you will be able to fly again."

He returned to the table. It had better be good, he told himself for the hundredth time. The General Secretary was a bad man to cross and a hard one to deceive. Some of those senior Air Force men who had made such a dog's breakfast of the tracking and downing of the Korean jetliner back in 1983 had on his personal recommendation ended up in cold graves beneath the permafrost of the Kamchatka. Racked by ill health, confined to a wheelchair part of the time he might be, but the General Secretary was still the undisputed master of the USSR. His word was law, his brain was still razor-sharp, and his pale eyes missed nothing. Taking paper and pencil, Philby began to rough out the first draft of his reply.

■ At just before midnight of January 1, the owner of the apartment in Fontenoy House returned alone to London. A tall, graying, distinguished man in his mid-fifties, he drove straight into the basement parking area, using his own plastic admission card, and, carrying his suitcase, rode up in the elevator to the eighth floor. He was in a foul mood.

He had driven for six hours, having left his brother-in-law's stately home three days prematurely, following a blazing row with his wife. She, angular and horsey, adored the countryside as much as he loathed it. Content to stride the bleak Yorkshire moors in midwinter, she had left him miserably cooped up indoors with her brother, the tenth Duke. Which was in a way worse, for the apartment owner, who prided himself on his appreciation of the manly virtues, was convinced the wretched fellow was gay.

The New Year's Eve dinner had been appalling for him, surrounded as he was by his wife's cronies, who talked hunting, shooting, and fishing the entire time, the whole being punctuated by the high, twittering laugh of the Duke and his too-handsome pals. That morning he had made some remark to his wife and she had gone off the deep end. The result was that it had been agreed he would drive south alone after tea; she would remain as long as she wished, which might be a month.

He entered the hall of his apartment and paused; the alarm system should be emitting a loud, repeated *peep* that should last for thirty seconds before the full alarm sounded, during which time he could reach the master control box and turn it off. Damn thing, he thought, probably out of order. He went into the coat closet and turned the whole system off with his personal key. Then he entered the sitting room and threw on the light.

He stood, with his bag behind him in the hall, and stared at the scene in openmouthed horror. The damp patches had evaporated in the warmth, and the television was not on. What caught his eye at once was the scorched wall and cloven safe door right ahead of him. He crossed the room in several strides and peered into the safe. There was no doubt—the diamonds were gone. He looked around again, saw his possessions scattered in the armchair by the fireplace and the carpet lifted from its smooth edge against the wall. He sank into the other fireside armchair, as white as a sheet.

"Oh, my God," he breathed. He seemed stunned by the nature of the disaster and remained in the chair for ten minutes, breathing heavily and staring at the disarray.

Finally he rose and went to the telephone. With a trembling forefinger he dialed a number. At the other end it rang and rang, but there was no reply.

■ The following morning, at just before eleven, John Preston walked down Curzon Street toward the headquarters of the department he worked for, around the corner from the Mirabelle restaurant, in which few of the department's employees could afford to dine.

Most of the civil service that Friday morning was being allowed to bridge over from Thursday, New Year's Day, which was a public holiday anyway, into the weekend. But Brian Harcourt-Smith had asked Preston to come in especially, so he had come. He suspected he knew what the Deputy Director-General of MI5 wanted to talk about.

For three years, more than half the time he had spent with MI5 since joining as a late entrant in the summer of 1981, John Preston had been in F Branch of the service, which dealt with surveillance of extremist political organizations of the Left and the Right; with research into these bodies, and with the running of agents within them. For two of those years he had been in F1, heading up D Section, which was concerned with the penetration of extreme left-wing elements into Britain's Labour Party. His report, the result of his investigations, had been submitted two weeks earlier, just before Christmas. He was surprised it had been read and digested so quickly.

He presented himself at the front desk, proffered his card, was vetted, checked out with the DDG's office as an expected visitor, and allowed to proceed to the top of the building.

He was sorry he would not be seeing the Director-General personally. He liked Sir Bernard Hemmings, but it was an open secret inside "Five" that the old man was ill and spending less and less time in the office. In his absences, the day-to-day running of the department was passing more and more into the hands of his ambitious deputy, a fact that did not please some of the older veterans of the service.

Sir Bernard was a Five man from way back, and had done his fieldwork once. He could establish empathy with the men who went out on the streets, staked out suspects, tailed hostile couriers, and penetrated subversive organizations. Harcourt-Smith was of the university intake, with a first-class degree, and had been mainly a head-office man, moving smoothly between the departments and steadily up the promotion ladder.

Immaculately dressed, as ever, Harcourt-Smith received Preston warmly in his office. Preston was wary of the warmth. Others had been received just as warmly, so went the stories, and had been out of the service a week later. Harcourt-Smith seated Preston in front of his desk and himself behind it. Preston's report lay on the blotter.

"Now, John, this report of yours. You'll understand, of course, that I take it, along with all your work, extremely seriously."

"Thank you," said Preston.

"So much so," Harcourt-Smith went on, "that I've spent a good part of the festivities break right here in this office to reread and consider it."

Preston thought it wiser to remain silent.

"It is, how shall I put it, pretty radical . . . no holds barred, eh? The question is—and this is the question I have to ask myself before this department proposes any kind of policy based upon it—is it all absolutely true? Can it be verified? This is what *I* should be asked."

"Look, Brian, I've spent two years on that investigation. My people went deep, very deep. The facts, where I've stated them as facts, are true."

"Ah, John. I'd never dispute any facts presented by you. But the conclusions drawn from them—"

"Are based on logic, I think," said Preston.

"A great discipline. I used to study it," resumed Harcourt-Smith. "But not always supported by hard evidence, wouldn't you agree? Let's take this thing here—" He found the place in the report and his finger ran along one line. "The MBR. Pretty extreme, wouldn't you say?"

"Oh, yes, Brian, it's extreme. These are pretty extreme people."

"No doubt about it. But wouldn't it have been helpful to have a copy of the MBR attached to your report?"

"So far as I could discover, it hasn't been written down. It's a series of intentions—albeit very firm intentions—in the minds of certain people."

Harcourt-Smith sucked regretfully at a tooth. "Intentions," he said, as though the word intrigued him, "yes, intentions. But you see, John, there are a lot of intentions in the minds of a lot of people vis-à-vis this country, not all of them friendly. But we can't propose policy, measures, or countermeasures on the basis of these intentions."

Preston was about to speak, but Harcourt-Smith swept on, rising to indicate that the interview was over.

"Look, John, leave this with me awhile longer. I'll have to think on it and perhaps take a few soundings before I decide where I can best place it. By the by, how do you like F1(D)?"

"I like it fine," said Preston, rising also.

"I may have something for you that you'll like even more," said Harcourt-Smith.

When Preston had gone, Harcourt-Smith stared at the door through which he had passed for several minutes. He seemed lost in thought.

Simply to shred the file, which he privately regarded as embarrassing and which might one day prove dangerous, was not possible. It had been formally presented by a section head. It had a file number. He thought long and hard. Then he took his red-ink pen and wrote carefully on the cover of the Preston report. He pressed his buzzer for his secretary.

"Mabel," he said when she entered, "take this down to Registry yourself, please. Right now."

The girl glanced at the cover of the file. Across it were written the letters NFA and Brian Harcourt-Smith's initials. In the service, NFA stands for "no further action." The report was to be buried.

CHAPTER

It was not until Sunday, January 4, that the apartment owner at Fontenoy House was able to get an answer from the number he had been ringing every hour for three days. It was a brief conversation when it took place, but it resulted in his meeting with another man just before the hour of luncheon in a recessed alcove of one of the public rooms in a very discreet West End hotel.

The newcomer was about sixty, with iron-gray hair, soberly dressed, and with the air of a kind of civil servant, which in a way he was. He was the second to arrive, and seated himself with an immediate apology. "I'm terribly sorry I wasn't available these past three days," he said. "Being a single man, I was invited by some kind friends to spend the New Year period with them out of town. Now, what seems to be the problem?"

The apartment owner told him in short, clear sentences. He had had time to think exactly how he would convey the enormity of what had happened and he chose his phrases well. The other man considered the narrative with deepening gravity.

"You're quite right, of course," he said at length. "It could be very serious. When you returned on Thursday night, did you call the police? Or have you, at any time since?"

26

"No, I thought it better to talk to you first."

"Ah, a pity in a way. It's too late now, anyway. Their forensic people would establish the blowing of the safe as three or four days old. Hard to explain that. Unless—"

"Yes?" asked the apartment owner eagerly.

"Unless you could maintain that the mirror was back in its place and everything in such apple-pie order that you could live there for three days and not know you had been burgled?"

"Hardly," said the apartment owner. "The carpet had been taken up all around the edges. The bastard must have walked around the walls to avoid the pressure pads."

"Yes," mused the other. "They'd hardly credit a burglar so neat he even replaced the carpet as well as the mirror. So that won't work. Nor, I fear, could one pretend you had spent the intervening three days somewhere else?"

"But where? I would have been seen. But I haven't. Club? Hotel? I would have had to check in."

"Precisely," said the confidant. "No, it won't work. For better or worse, the die is cast. It's too late to call in the police now."

"Then what the hell do I do?" asked the apartment owner. "They have simply *got* to be recovered."

"How long will your wife remain away from London?" asked the other.

"Who knows? She enjoys it up in Yorkshire. Some weeks, I hope."

"Then we shall have to effect a replacement of the damaged safe with a new and identical model. Also a replica set of the Glen Diamonds. It will take time to arrange."

"But how about what has been stolen?" asked the apartment owner desperately. "They can't just be left somewhere out there on the loose. I've got to have them back."

"True," the other answered, nodding. "Look, as you may imagine, my people have some contacts in the world of diamonds. I'll cause inquiries to be made. The gems will almost certainly be passed to one of the main centers for reshaping. They could not be marketed as they are. Too identifiable. I'll see if the burglar can be traced and the things recovered."

The man rose and prepared to leave. His friend remained seated,

evidently deeply worried. The sober-suited man was equally dis-
mayed but he hid it better.

"Do nothing and say nothing untoward," he advised. "Keep your
wife in the country as long as possible. Behave perfectly normally.
Rest assured, I shall be in touch."

■ The following morning, John Preston was one of those who
joined the great throng of people surging back into central London
after the five-day, too-long New Year break. As he lived in South
Kensington, it suited him to come to work on the Underground. He
disembarked at Goodge Street and made his way the remaining
five hundred yards on foot, an unnoticeable man of medium height
and build, aged forty-six, in a gray raincoat and hatless despite the
chill.

Near the top of Gordon Street he turned into the entrance of
an equally unnoticeable building that could have been an office
block like any other; it was solid, but not modern, and purported to
house an insurance enterprise. Only when one had entered it were
the differences from other office buildings in the neighborhood discernible.

For one thing, there were three men in the lobby—one at the
door, one behind the reception desk, and one by the elevator doors.
All were of a size and a muscularity not normally associated with the
underwriting of insurance policies. Any stray citizen seeking to do
business with this particular company, and declining to be directed
elsewhere, would have learned the hard way that only those pre-
senting identification that could pass the scrutiny of the small computer terminal beneath the reception desk were permitted beyond
the lobby.

The British Security Service, better known as MI5, does not live
in one single place. Discreetly, but inconveniently, it is split up into
four office buildings. The headquarters are on Charles Street (and no
longer at the old HQ, Leconfield House, so habitually mentioned in
the newspapers).

The next-biggest establishment, on Gordon Street, is known simply as "Gordon" and nothing else, just as the head office is known
as "Charles." The other two premises are on Cork Street (known as

"Cork") and a humble annex on Marlborough Street, again known simply by the street name.

The department is divided into six branches, scattered throughout the buildings. Again, discreetly but confusingly, some of the branches have sections in different buildings. In order to avoid an inordinate use of shoe leather, all are linked by extremely secure telephone lines, with a flawless system for identification of the credentials of the caller.

"A" Branch handles in its various sections policy, technical support, property establishment, registry data processing, the office of the legal adviser, and the watcher service. The last-named is the home of that idiosyncratic group of men and (some) women, of all ages and types, streetwise and ingenious, who can mount the finest personal surveillance teams in the world. Even "hostiles" have had to concede that on their own ground MI5's watchers are just about unbeatable.

Unlike the Secret Intelligence Service (MI6), which handles foreign intelligence and has absorbed a number of Americanisms into its in-house jargon, the Security Service (MI5), which covers internal counterintelligence, bases most of its jargon on former police phrases. It avoids terms like "surveillance operative" and still calls its tracker teams simply "the watchers."

"B" Branch handles recruitment, personnel, vetting, promotions, pensions, and finance (meaning salaries and operational expenses).

"C" Branch concerns itself with the security of the civil service (its staffers and its buildings), the security of contractors (mainly those civilian firms handling defense and communications work), military security (in close liaison with the armed forces' own internal-security staffs), and sabotage (in reality or in prospect).

There used to be a "D" Branch, but with the arcane logic known only to its practitioners in the intelligence world, it was long ago renamed "K" Branch. It is one of the biggest, and its largest section, called Soviet, is subdivided into operations, field investigations, and order of battle. Next in K comes Soviet satellites, also divided into the same three subsections, then research, and finally agents.

As may be imagined, K devotes its not inconsiderable labors to keeping track of the huge number of Soviet and satellite agents who operate, or try to, out of the various embassies, consulates, legations, trade missions, banks, news agencies, and commercial enterprises that a lenient British government has allowed to be scattered all over the capital and (in the case of consulates) the provinces.

Also inside K Branch is a modest office inhabited by the officer whose job it is to liaise between MI5 and its sister service, MI6. This officer is in fact a "Six" man, on assignment to Charles Street in order to carry out his liaison duties. The section is known simply as K7.

"E" Branch (the alphabetical sequence resumes with E) covers international Communism and its adherents who may wish to visit Britain for nefarious reasons, or the homegrown variety who may wish to go abroad for the same purposes. Also inside E, the Far East section maintains liaison officers in Hong Kong, New Delhi, Canberra, and Wellington, while the section called All Regions does the same in Washington, Ottawa, the West Indies, and other friendly capitals.

Finally, "F" Branch, to which John Preston belonged, at least until that morning, covers political parties (extreme left and right wings), research, and agents.

F Branch lives at Gordon, on the fourth floor, and it was to his office there that John Preston made his way that January morning. He might not have thought his report of three weeks earlier would establish him as Brian Harcourt-Smith's flavor of the month, but he still believed his report would go to the desk of the Director-General, Sir Bernard Hemmings.

Sir Bernard, Preston was confident, would feel able to impart its information—and, admittedly, partly conjectural findings—to the Chairman of the Joint Intelligence Committee or to the Permanent Under Secretary at the Home Office, the political ministry commanding MI5. A good PUS would probably feel his minister should glance at it, and the Home Secretary could have drawn the attention of the Prime Minister to it.

The memorandum on Preston's desk when he arrived indicated this was not going to happen. After reading the sheet he sat back, lost in thought. He was prepared to stand by that report, and if it had gone higher there would have been questions to answer. He could have answered them—would have answered them, for he was convinced he was right. He could have answered them, that is, as head of F1(D), but not after being transferred to another department.

After his transfer, it would be the new head of F1(D) who would be the one to raise the issue of the Preston report, and Preston was satisfied the man appointed to succeed him, almost certain to be one of Harcourt-Smith's most loyal protégés, would do no such thing.

He made one call to Registry. Yes, the report had been filed. He noted the file number, just for future reference, if any. Then: "What do you mean, NFA?" he asked incredulously. "All right. . . . Sorry. . . . Yes, I know it's not up to you, Charlie. I was just asking. A bit surprised, that's all."

He replaced the receiver and sat back, thinking deeply. Thoughts a man should not think about his superior officer, even if there was no personal empathy between them. But the thoughts would not go away. It was possible, he conceded, that if his report had gone higher, its general burden might eventually have been imparted to Neil Kinnock, leader of the Labour Party opposition in Parliament, who might not have been pleased.

It was also possible that at the next election, due within seventeen months at the outside, Labour could win and that Brian Harcourt-Smith was entertaining the hope that one of the new government's first acts would be to confirm him as Director-General of MI5. His not offending powerful politicians in office, or those who might come to office, was nothing new. For a man of weak and tremulous disposition or of vaulting ambition, refusal to impart bad news could be a powerful motive for inertia.

Everyone in the service recalled the affair of a former Director-General, Sir Roger Hollis. Even to this day, the mystery had never been completely solved, though partisans on both sides had their convinced opinions.

Back in 1962 and 1963, Roger Hollis had known almost from the outset of the business the full details of the Christine Keeler affair, as it came to be known. He had had on his desk, weeks if not months before the scandal blew open, reports of the Cliveden parties, of Stephen Ward, who provided the girls and who was in any case reporting back, of Soviet attaché Ivanov's sharing the favors of the same girl as Britain's own War Minister. Yet he had sat back as the evidence mounted, and never sought, as was his duty, a personal meeting with his own Prime Minister, Harold Macmillan.

Without that warning, Macmillan had walked into the scandal, leading with his jaw. The affair had festered and suppurated through the summer of 1963, hurting Britain at home and abroad, for all the world as if it had been scripted in Moscow.

Years later, the argument still raged: had Roger Hollis been a supine incompetent, or had he been much, much worse . . . ?

"Bollocks," said Preston to himself, and banished his thoughts. He reread the memorandum.

It was from the head of B4 (promotions) personally, and advised him that he was as of that day transferred and promoted to head of C1(A). The tone was of the cozy friendliness that is supposed to soften the blow: "I am advised by the DDG that it would be so helpful if the New Year could begin with all fresh postings occupied . . . most grateful if you could tidy up any outstanding things and hand over to young Maxwell without too much delay, even within a couple of days if possible. . . . My warmest best wishes for your satisfaction with the new post. . . ."

Blah, blah, blah, thought Preston. C1, he knew, was responsible for civil service personnel and buildings, and A Section meant that responsibility within the capital. He was to be in charge of security in all Her Majesty's ministries in London.

"It's a bloody policeman's job," he snorted, and began to call up his team to say good-bye.

■ A mile away across London, Jim Rawlings opened the door of a small but exclusive jewelry shop in a side road, not two hundred yards from the surging traffic of Bond Street. The shop was dark but its discreet lights fell on showcases containing Georgian silver, and in the illuminated counter display cabinets could be seen jewelry of a bygone era. Evidently the emporium specialized in antique pieces rather than their modern counterparts.

Rawlings was wearing a neat dark suit, silk shirt, and muted tie, and carried a dully gleaming attaché case. The girl behind the counter looked up and took him in with a glance of appreciation. At

thirty-six he looked lean and fit, with an aura that was part gentleman, part tough—always a useful combination. She pushed out her
chest and flashed a bright smile.

"Can I help you?"

"I'd like to see Mr. Zablonsky. Personal."

His Cockney accent indicated he was unlikely to be a customer.
Her face fell. "You a rep?" she asked.

"Just say Mr. James would like to speak to him," said Rawlings.

But at that moment the mirrored door at the rear of the shop
opened and Louis Zablonsky came out. He was a short, wizened
man of fifty-six, but looked older.

"Mr. James"—he beamed—"how nice to see you. Please come
into my office. How have you been keeping?" He ushered Rawlings
past the counter and into his inner sanctum, saying, "That's all
right, Sandra, my dear."

Inside his small and cluttered office he closed and locked the mirrored door, through which a view of the outer shop could be had. He
gestured Rawlings to the chair in front of his antique desk and took
the swivel chair behind it. A single spotlight beamed down on the
blotter. He eyed Rawlings keenly. "Well, now, Jim, what have you
been up to?"

"Got something for you, Louis, something you'll like. So don't
tell me it's rubbish."

Rawlings flicked open his attaché case. Zablonsky spread his
hands.

"Jim, would I—" His words were cut off as he saw what Rawlings
was placing on the blotter. When they were all there, he stared at
them in disbelief.

"The Glen Suite," he breathed, "you've gone and nicked the Glen
Diamonds. It's not even been in the papers yet."

"So maybe they're still away from London," said Rawlings.
"There was no alarm raised. I'm good, you know that."

"The best, Jim, the best. But the Glen Suite . . . Why didn't you
tell me?"

Rawlings knew it would have been easier for all if a route for dis-
posing of the Glen Suite had been set up before the robbery. But he
worked in his own way, which was extremely carefully. He trusted
no one, least of all a fence, even a blue-chip, top-of-the-market fence

like Louis Zablonsky. A fence, hit by a police raid and facing a long stretch of porridge, would be quite able to trade information on a coming heist against a let-off for himself. The Serious Crime Squad down at Scotland Yard knew about Zablonsky, even if he had never seen the inside of one of Her Majesty's prisons. That was why Rawlings never preannounced one of his jobs, and always arrived unheralded. So he did not answer.

In any case, Zablonsky was lost in contemplation of the jewels that sparkled on his blotter. He knew their provenance without being told. The ninth Duke of Sheffield, who had inherited the suite in 1936, had had two offspring, a boy and a girl. By 1974, when his son was twenty-five, the saddened Duke had been forced to realize that the exotic young man was what gossip columnists are pleased to call "one of nature's bachelors." There would be no more pretty young countesses of Margate or duchesses of Sheffield to wear the famed Glen Diamonds. So when the ninth Duke died in his turn, in 1980, he bequeathed them not to his son, the heir to the title, but to his daughter, Lady Fiona Glen.

Zablonsky knew that after her father's death Lady Fiona had taken to wearing the diamonds occasionally, with the insurers' grudging permission, usually for charity galas, at which she was a not infrequent presence. The rest of the time they lay where they had spent so many years, in darkness in the vaults of Coutts on Park Lane. He smiled. "The charity gala at Grosvenor House just before the New Year?" he asked. Rawlings shrugged. "Oh, you're a naughty boy, Jim. But such a talented one."

Although he was fluent in Polish, Yiddish, and Hebrew, Louis Zablonsky after forty years in Britain had never quite mastered English, which he spoke with a discernible Polish accent. Also, because he had learned them from books written years earlier, Zablonsky mistakenly used phrases that nowadays could be regarded as "camp." But Rawlings knew there was nothing gay about Louis Zablonsky. In fact, Rawlings knew, because Beryl Zablonsky had told him, that the old man had been neutered in a Nazi concentration camp as a boy.

Zablonsky was still admiring the diamonds, as a true connoisseur will admire any masterpiece. He recalled vaguely having read somewhere that in the mid-1960s Lady Fiona Glen had married a rising

young civil servant who by the mid-1980s had become a senior mandarin in one of the ministries, and that the couple lived somewhere
in the West End at a most elegant and luxurious standard maintained largely by the wife's private fortune.

"So what do you think, Louis?"

"I'm impressed, my dear Jim. Very impressed. But also perplexed. These are not ordinary stones. These are identifiable anywhere in the diamond world. What am I to do with them?"

"You tell me," said Rawlings.

Louis Zablonsky spread his hands wide.

"I will not lie to you, Jim. I will tell you straight. The Glen Diamonds probably have an insured value of seven hundred and fifty
thousand pounds, which is roughly what they would fetch if sold legitimately on the open market by Cartier. But they can't be sold like
that, obviously.

"That leaves two options. One is to find a very rich buyer who
would want to buy the famous Glen Diamonds knowing he could
never display them or admit ownership—a rich miser content to
gloat over them in privacy. There are such people, but very few.
From such a person one could get perhaps half the price I have
named."

"When could you find a buyer like that?"

Zablonsky shrugged. "This year, next year, sometime, never.
You can't just advertise in the personal columns."

"Too long," said Rawlings. "The other way?"

"Prise them out of their settings—that act alone would reduce the
value to six hundred thousand pounds. Repolish them and sell them
separately as four unmatched, individual gems. One might get three
hundred thousand. But the repolisher would want his cut. If I carried those costs personally, I think I could let you have a hundred
thousand—but at the end of the operation. After the sales had been
completed."

"What can you let me have up front? I can't live on fresh air,
Louis."

"Who can?" said the old fence. "Look, for the white-gold setting
I can get maybe two thousand pounds on the scrap market. For the
forty small stones—put through the legitimate market—say, twelve
thousand. That's fourteen thousand pounds, which I can recover

quickly. I can let you have half up front, in cash, now. What do you say?"

They talked for another thirty minutes and clinched their deal. From his safe Louis Zablonsky took £7,000 in cash. Rawlings opened the attaché case and laid the wads of used notes inside.

"Nice," said Zablonsky, admiring the case. "You treated yourself?"

Rawlings shook his head. "Came with the heist," he said.

Zablonsky tut-tutted and wagged a finger under Rawlings's nose. "Get rid of it, Jim. Never keep anything from a job. Not worth the risk."

Rawlings considered, nodded, made his farewells, and left.

■ John Preston had spent the entire day seeking out the various members of his investigative team to say his good-byes. They were gratifyingly sorry to see him go. Then there was the paperwork. Bobby Maxwell, his replacement, had come in to say hello. Preston knew him vaguely. He was an agreeable enough young man, eager to make a career in Five and seeing his best chances of promotion as lying in a policy of hitching his wagon to the rising star of Brian Harcourt-Smith. Preston could not hold that against him.

Preston himself was a late entrant, having been inducted into the service direct from the Army Intelligence Corps in 1981, at the age of forty-one. He knew he would never get to the top. Head of section was about the limit for late entrants.

Just occasionally, always to the dismay of the people who worked in Five, the post of Director-General went to someone from quite outside the service if there was no obviously suitable candidate within. But the Deputy Director-General, all the directors of the six branches, and the heads of most of the departments within the branches were by tradition lifelong staffers.

Preston had agreed with Maxwell that he would spend that day, Monday, finishing off his paperwork and the whole of the next day briefing his successor on every current file and investigation. They had parted on that note with mutual good wishes until the morning.

Preston glanced at his watch. It would be a late night. From his personal office safe he would have to get out every current file, check those that could safely go back to Registry, and spend half the night going through the current "bumpf" page by page, so that he could be ready to brief Maxwell in the morning.

First he needed a decent drink. He took the elevator down to the subbasement, where Gordon has a well-stocked and cozy bar.

■ Louis Zablonsky worked through Tuesday locked in his back room. Only twice did he emerge to see a customer personally. It was a slack day, for which, unusually, he was thankful.

He worked with jacket off and shirtsleeves rolled up over his almost hairless forearms, carefully easing the Glen Diamonds from their white-gold settings. The four principal stones, the two ten-carat gems from the earrings and the matched twenty-carat pair from the tiara and the pendant, came easily and took little time.

When they were out of their beds he could examine them more closely. They were truly beautiful, flaming and sparkling in the light. They were already known to be blue-whites, once also called "top river," but now reclassified under the standardized gradings as "D flawless." These four, when he had finished admiring them, he dropped into a small velvet bag. That done, he began the time-consuming task of easing the forty smaller stones out of the gold. As he worked, the light occasionally caught a faded mark in the form of a five-figure number on the underside of his left forearm. To anyone who knew the significance of such marks, the number meant only one thing. It was the brand of Auschwitz.

Zablonsky had been born in 1930, the third son of a Polish-Jewish jeweler of Warsaw. He was nine when the Germans invaded, and by 1940 the ghetto of Warsaw had been enclosed; incarcerated inside it were close to 400,000 Jews, and rations were fixed at well below starvation level. On April 19, 1943, the 90,000 surviving ghetto inhabitants, led by the few ablebodied men left among them, rose in revolt. Louis Zablonsky had just turned thirteen, but he was so thin and emaciated he could well have been taken for five years younger.

When the ghetto finally fell to the Waffen SS troops of Major-General Juergen Stroop on May 16, Zablonsky was one of the few who lived through the mass shootings. The bulk of the inhabitants, some 60,000, were already dead, from bullet, shot, shell, crushed beneath falling buildings, or executed. The remaining 30,000 were almost exclusively the aged, women, and small children. Into these Zablonsky was herded. Most went off to Treblinka and died.

But in one of those freaks of circumstance that occasionally decide life and death, the engine of the train hauling Zablonsky's cattle car broke down. The car was attached to another engine and ended up at Auschwitz.

Though destined for death, Zablonsky was spared when he gave his profession as jeweler. He was put to work sorting and classifying the trinkets still being found upon the persons of Jews in each fresh intake. Then one day he was summoned to the camp hospital and into the hands of that smiling blond man whom they called "the Angel" and who was still carrying out his manic experiments on the genitalia of pubescent Jewish youths. It was on Josef Mengele's operating table that, without anesthetic, Louis Zablonsky was castrated.

In late 1944 the survivors of Auschwitz were force-marched westward and Zablonsky ended up in Bergen-Belsen, where, more dead than alive, he was finally freed by the British Army. After intensive hospitalization Zablonsky, having been sponsored by a North London rabbi, was brought to Britain, and after further rehabilitation he became a jeweler's apprentice. In the early 1960s he had left his employer for his own shop in the East End. Ten years later, he had opened the present, more prosperous establishment in the West End.

It was in the East End, down in the dockland, that he had first started to handle gems imported by seamen—emeralds from Ceylon, diamonds from Africa, rubies from India, and opals from Australia. By the mid-1980s Zablonsky was a wealthy man from both his enterprises, the legitimate and the illicit. He was one of the top fences in London, a specialist in diamonds, and owned a large detached house in Golders Green, where he was a pillar of his community.

Now he tugged the last of the forty smaller stones from their settings and checked to see that he had missed none. He counted the stones and began to weigh them. Forty in all, averaging half a carat but mostly smaller. Engagement-ring stuff, but worth about £12,000 in all. He could pass them through Hatton Garden and no one the wiser. Cash deals—he knew his contacts. He began to crush the white-gold settings into a shapeless mass.

When the gold was a mangled blob of metal, he dropped the lump into a bag along with other scrap. He saw Sandra off the premises, closed the shop, tidied up his office, and left, taking the four primary stones with him. On the way home he made a phone call from a public box to a number in Belgium, a number situated in a small village, called Nijlen, outside Antwerp. When he got home he rang British Airways and booked a flight for the morrow to Brussels.

■ Along the shore of the River Thames, on its southern bank, where once had stood the rotting wharves of a dying dockland, a huge redevelopment program had been continuing through the early and mid-1980s. The program had left great swaths of demolished rubble between the new buildings, moonscapes where the rank grass tangled with the fallen bricks and dust. One day, it was intended, all would be covered by new apartment buildings, shopping malls, and multistory garages, but when that would be was anybody's guess.

In warm weather the winos camped out in these wastelands and any South London "face" wishing to lose a piece of evidence had but to take the article to the center of these abandoned places and burn it to extinction.

Late on the evening of Tuesday, January 6, Jim Rawlings was walking across an area of several acres, stumbling in the dark as he tripped over unseen chunks of masonry. Had anyone been observing him—and no one was—he would have seen that Rawlings carried in one hand a two-gallon can of gasoline and in the other a beautiful handcrafted calfskin attaché case.

■ Louis Zablonsky passed through Heathrow Airport on Wednesday morning with no trouble. With heavy greatcoat and soft tweed hat, hand luggage and big briar pipe jutting from his jaw, he joined the daily flow of businessmen from London to Brussels.

On the plane, one of the stewardesses leaned over him and whispered, "I'm afraid we can't allow you to light the pipe inside the cabin, sir." Zablonsky apologized profusely and stuffed the briar in his pocket. He did not mind. He did not smoke, and even if he had lit it, it would not have drawn very well. Not with four pear-shaped fifty-eight-facet diamonds crammed into the base below the tamped tobacco.

At Brussels National he rented a car and headed north up the motorway out of Zaventem toward Mechelen, where he pulled right and northeast to Lier and Nijlen.

The bulk of the diamond industry in Belgium is centered upon Antwerp and is specifically located in and around the Pelikaanstraat, where the big enterprises have their showrooms and workshops. But like most industries, the diamond business depends for a part of its functioning upon a mass of small suppliers and outside workers, one-man operations working out of their ateliers, to whom can be subcontracted some of the manufacture of settings, cleaning, and re-polishing.

Some of these outside workers also live in Antwerp, and Jews, many of East European origin, are predominant among them. But east of Antwerp lies an area known as Kempen, a cluster of neat villages in which are also located scores of small shops that undertake work for the Antwerp industry. In the center of Kempen lies Nijlen, astride the main road and rail lines from Lier to Herentals.

Halfway down the Molenstraat lived one Raoul Levy, a Polish Jew who had settled in Belgium after the war and who also happened to be a second cousin of Louis Zablonsky of London. Levy was a diamond polisher, a widower who lived alone in one of the small, neat, red-brick bungalows that line the western side of the Molenstraat. At the back of the house was his workshop. It was here that Zablonsky drove and met his relative a little after lunchtime.

They argued for an hour and struck their deal. Levy would re-polish the four stones, losing as little of their weight as possible, but enough to disguise their identity. They settled on a fee of £50,000, half up front and half upon sale of the last stone. Zablonsky left and returned to London.

The trouble with Raoul Levy was not that he lacked skill; it was that he was lonely. So each week he looked forward to his one expedition. He loved to take the train into Antwerp, go to his favorite café, where all his cronies met in the evenings, and talk shop. Three days later he went there and talked shop once too often.

■ While Louis Zablonsky was in Belgium, John Preston was installing himself in his new office on the second floor. He was glad he did not have to leave Gordon for another building.

His predecessor had retired at the end of the year, and the deputy head of C1(A) had been in charge for a few days, no doubt hoping he would be confirmed in the top man's post. He took his disappointment well and briefed Preston copiously on what the job entailed, which seemed to Preston to be mainly grinding routine.

Left alone that afternoon, Preston cast his eye down the list of ministry buildings that came under A Section. It was longer than might be imagined, but most of the buildings were not security sensitive, save for leakages that might be politically embarrassing. Document leaks concerning, for example, intended social security cuts were always a hazard since the civil service unions had recruited so many staffers with extreme-left political views, but they could usually be handled by the ministry's in-house security people.

The big ones for Preston were the Foreign Office, Cabinet Office, and Defense Ministry, all of which received cosmic-rated papers. But each had pretty tight security, handled by its own internal-security team. Preston sighed. He started to make a series of phone calls, setting up getting-to-know-you meetings with the security chiefs in each of the principal ministries.

Between calls he glanced at the pile of personal stuff he had brought down from his old office, two floors above. Waiting for a call to be returned by some official otherwise engaged, he rose, unlocked his new personal safe, and put the files inside, one by one. The last of them was his report of the previous month, his own copy. Other than the report he knew to have been NFA'ed in Registry, this was the only one in existence. He shrugged and put it at the back of the safe. It would probably never be examined again, but he saw no reason why he should not keep it, for old times' sake. After all, his own copy had taken a hell of a lot of sweat to put together.

The men, when they came to visit Raoul Levy, were four in number; big, heavy men who arrived in two cars. The first car cruised to a halt outside Levy's bungalow on the Molenstraat, while the second halted a hundred yards up the street.

The first car disgorged two of the men, who walked briskly but quietly up the short path to the front door. The two drivers waited, lights doused, engines running. It was a bitter night, just after 7:00 p.m., pitch-dark. No one walked the Molenstraat that evening of January 15.

The men who knocked on the front door were brisk and businesslike, men with little time to waste, a job to do, and the opinion that the sooner it was over, the better. They did not introduce themselves when Levy answered the door. They just stepped inside and pulled the door closed behind them. Levy's protest was hardly out of his mouth when it was cut off by four rigid fingers jabbing into his solar plexus.

The big men pulled Levy's overcoat around his shoulders, clapped his hat on his head, left the front door unlocked, and walked him expertly down the path to the car, whose rear door opened as they approached. When they drove off with Levy sandwiched between them in the rear seat, only twenty seconds had elapsed.

They took him to the Kesselse Heide, a big public park just northwest of Nijlen, whose fifty acres of heather, grass, oaks, and mixed conifers were completely deserted. Well off the road, in the heart of the heath, the two cars stopped. The driver of the second vehicle, who was to be the interrogator, slipped into the front passenger seat.

He turned toward the rear of the car and nodded to his two colleagues. The man on Levy's right swept two arms around the small diamond polisher to hold him still, and the gloved hand of one arm went across Levy's mouth. The other man produced a pair of heavy pliers, took Levy's left hand, and deftly crushed three knuckles, one after the other.

What frightened Levy even more than the shattering pain was that they did not ask him any questions. They seemed uninterested. When his fourth knuckle pulped in the pliers, Levy was screaming to be asked questions.

The interrogator in the front nodded casually and said, "Want to talk?"

Behind the glove Levy nodded furiously. The glove was removed. Levy let out a long, bubbling scream. When he had finished, the interrogator said, "The diamonds. From London. Where are they?" He spoke Flemish but with a marked foreign accent.

Levy told him without delay. No amount of money could compensate him for the loss of his hands and therefore his livelihood.

The interrogator considered the information soberly. "Keys," he said.

They were in Levy's trouser pocket. The interrogator took them and left the car. Seconds later, his sedan crunched away across the crackling grass toward the road. It was gone for fifty minutes.

During that time Levy whimpered and held his ruined hand. The men on either side of him seemed uninterested in him. The driver sat and stared ahead, gloved hands on the wheel.

When the interrogator rejoined them, he made no mention of the four gems that by now were in his pocket. He said only, "One last question. The man who brought them."

Levy shook his head. The interrogator sighed at the waste of time and nodded to the man on Levy's right. The heavy men reversed roles. The one on the right took the pliers and Levy's right hand. After the crushing of two knuckles on that hand, Levy told them. The interrogator had a couple of short supplementary questions and then he seemed satisfied. He left the car and went back to his own vehicle. In convoy the two sedans bumped back toward the road. They drove back to Nijlen.

As they went past his house, Levy saw that it was dark. He hoped they would drop him off there, but they did not. They drove through the center of the town and out to the east. The lights of the cafés, warm and snug against the freezing winter air, went past the car windows, but no one came running out. Levy could even see the blue neon word POLITIE above the police station across from the church, but no one came out.

Two miles to the east of Nijlen the Looy Straat crosses the rail lines at a point where the Lier–Herentals tracks run straight as an arrow, and the big diesel-electric locomotives go through at more than seventy miles an hour. On either side of the level crossing are farm buildings. Both cars stopped short of the level crossing and doused lights and engines.

Without a word the driver opened the glove compartment, produced a bottle, and handed it back to his two colleagues. One held Levy's nose closed and the other poured the white grain spirit of a local brand down the gagging throat. When three quarters of it was gone, they stopped and left him alone. Raoul Levy began to drift away in an alcoholic daze. Even the pain eased a bit. The three men in the car, and the one in the sedan ahead of them, waited.

At 11:15 the interrogator came from the first car and muttered something through the window. Levy was unconscious by then but moving fitfully. The men beside him hauled him out of the car and half carried him toward the tracks. At 11:20 one of them hit him hard on the head with an iron bar, and he died. They laid him on the tracks with his shattered hands on one of the rails and his broken head near it.

Hans Grobbelaar has taken the last express of the night out of Lier at 11:09 exactly, as always. It was a routine run and he would be home in his warm bed in Herentals by 1:00 a.m. It was a nonstop freight and he went through Nijlen on time at 11:19. After the crossings there, he piled on the power and went down the straight toward the Looy Straat crossing at close to seventy miles an hour, the spotlight of the big 6268 lighting up the track for a hundred yards ahead.

Just short of the Looy Straat he saw the huddled figure lying on the track and slammed on his brakes. Sheets of sparks flew out from his wheels. The freight train began to slow, but nowhere near enough. Mouth open, he watched through the windshield as the headlight flew toward the crumpled figure. Two men in the yard had had it happen to them before; whether the victims had been suicides or drunks, no one ever knew. Not afterward. With this kind of rig you don't even feel the thud, they had said. He didn't. The screaming locomotive flashed over the spot at thirty miles an hour.

When he finally stopped he could not even look. He ran to one of the farms and raised the alarm. When the police came with lanterns, the mess under his wheels looked like strawberry jam. Hans Grobbelaar did not reach home until dawn.

■ That same morning, John Preston entered the lobby of the Ministry of Defense in Whitehall, approached the desk, and used his universal pass to identify himself. After the inevitable check call to the man he had come to see, he was escorted into the elevator and down several corridors to the office of the ministry's head of internal security, a room high at the back of the building and overlooking the Thames.

Brigadier Bertie Capstick had changed little since Preston had last seen him, years before, in Ulster. Big, florid, and genial, with apple cheeks that made him look more like a farmer than a soldier, he came forward with a roar of "Johnny, my boy, as I live and breathe. Come in, come in."

Although only ten years older than Preston, Bertie Capstick had a habit of calling almost anyone his junior "my boy," which gave him an avuncular air, matched by his appearance. But he had been a tough soldier once, moving deep into terrorist country during the Malay campaign and later commanding a group of infiltration experts in the jungles of Borneo during what was now called the Indonesian emergency.

Capstick sat Preston down and produced a bottle of single malt from a filing cabinet. "Fancy a snort?"

"Bit early," protested Preston. It was just past eleven o'clock.

"Nonsense. For old times' sake. Anyway, the coffee they bring you here is abysmal."

Capstick sat himself down and pushed the glass toward Preston across his desk. "So, what have they done with you, my boy?"

Preston grimaced. "I told you on the phone what they've given me," he said. "Bloody policeman's job. No disrespect to you, Bertie."

"Well, same with me, Johnny. Out to grass. Of course I'm retired from the Army now, so I'm not too bad. Took my pension at fifty-five and managed to get this slot. Not too bad. Potter up on the train every day, check up on all the security routines, make sure no one's being a bad lad, and go home to the little woman. Could be worse. Anyway, here's to the old days."

"Cheers," said Preston. They drank.

The old days had not been quite so genial as that, thought Preston. When last he had seen Bertie Capstick, then a full colonel, almost six years before, the deceptively extroverted officer had been Deputy Director of Military Intelligence in Northern Ireland, working out of that complex of buildings at Lisburn whose data banks can tell the inquirer which IRA man has scratched his backside recently.

Preston had been one of Capstick's "boys," working in civilian clothes and undercover, moving through hard-line Provo ghettos to talk with informers or pick up packages from dead drops. It was Bertie Capstick who had loyally stuck by him in the face of the wittering civil servants from Holyrood House when Preston was "burned" and nearly killed while on a mission for Capstick.

That was May 28, 1981, and the papers carried a few sparse details the following day. Preston had been in an unmarked car and had entered the Bogside district in Londonderry on his way to a meet with an informer. Whether there had been a leak higher up, whether the car he was driving had been used once too often, or whether his face had been "made" by the Provo intelligence people was never later established. Whatever, there was a foul-up. Just as he entered the Republican stronghold, a car containing four armed Provos had pulled out from a side street and followed him.

He had spotted them quickly in his rearview mirror and called off the rendezvous at once. But the Provos wanted more than that. Deep inside the ghetto they swerved across his front and came tumbling out of their own car, two with Armalites and one with a pistol.

With nowhere to go but heaven or hell, Preston had taken the initiative. Against the odds and to the consternation of his attackers, he came out of his own door in a fast roll, just as the Armalites riddled his vehicle. He had his Browning thirteen-shot nine-millimeter in his hand, set to Automatic. From the cobblestones he let them have it. They had expected him to die decently, and they were too close together.

On rapid fire, he had dropped two dead in their tracks and blown a chunk out of the neck of the third. The Provo driver let in his clutch and disappeared in a plume of burning tires. Preston made his way to a safe house staffed by four SAS troopers, who kept him until Capstick arrived to bring him home.

Of course, there had been the devil to pay—inquiries, interrogations, worried questions from on high. There was no question of Preston's going on. He had been well and truly burned, to use the term-of-art—that is, identified. His usefulness was over. The surviving Provo would know his face again anywhere. They would not even let him go back to his old regiment, the Paras, at Aldershot. Who knew how many Provos hung around Aldershot?

They had offered him Hong Kong or the exit door. Then Bertie Capstick had had a talk with a friend. There was a third choice. Leave the Army as a forty-one-year-old major and become a late entrant into MI5. He had gone for that one.

"Anything particular?" Capstick was asking.

Preston shook his head. "Just a round of getting-to-know-you visits," he said.

"Don't worry, Johnny. Now I know you're on the seat, I'll call if anything crops up here that looks bigger than swiping the Christmas fund. How's Julia, by the way?"

"I'm afraid she's left me. Three years ago."

"Oh, I'm sorry to hear that." Bertie Capstick's face puckered in genuine concern. "Another fella?"

"No. Not then. There's someone now, I think. Just the job . . . you know."

Capstick nodded grimly. "My Betty's always been very good like that," he ruminated. "Been away from home half my life. She always stuck by. Kept the fire burning. Still, no life for a woman. Seen it happen before. Many times. Still, bad luck. See the boy?"

"Now and again," admitted Preston.

Capstick could not have struck a rawer nerve. In his small and lonely South Kensington flat, Preston kept two photographs. One showed him and Julia on their wedding day—he at twenty-six, trim in his Parachute Regiment uniform; she at twenty, beautiful in white. The other was of his son, Tommy, who meant more to him than life itself.

They had lived a normal Army life in a succession of married quarters, and Tommy had been born eight years after their wedding. His arrival had fulfilled John Preston, but not his wife. Soon after, Julia had begun to get bored by the chores of motherhood, compounded by the loneliness of his absences, and had begun to complain of the lack of money. She chivied him to leave the Army and earn more in civilian life, refusing to understand that he loved his job and that the boredom of a desk in commerce or industry would have driven him to distraction.

He transferred to the Intelligence Corps, but that made it worse. They sent him to Ulster, where wives could not follow. Then he went underground and all contact was broken. After the Bogside incident she really made her feelings plain. They gave it one more try, living in the suburbs while he worked at Five. He was able to return almost every evening to Sydenham, and that had solved the separation question, but the marriage had gone sour. Julia wanted more than his salary as a late entrant in Five could provide.

She had taken a job as a receptionist at a fashion house in the West End when Tommy, aged eight, had gone, at her insistence, to a local private school near their small home. That had strained the finances even more. A year later she had left completely, taking Tommy with her. Now, he knew, she was living with her boss, a man old enough to be her father but able to keep her in style and Tommy at a boarding preparatory school at Tonbridge. Now Preston hardly ever saw the twelve-year-old lad.

He had offered her a divorce, but she did not want one. After a three-year separation he could have got the divorce anyway, but she had threatened that, as he could not provide for the boy and pay maintenance, she would settle for Tommy. He was cornered and he knew it. She allowed him to have Tommy for one week in each holiday and for one Sunday each term.

"Well, I must be going, Bertie. You know where I am if anything big blows up."

"Of course, of course." Capstick lumbered to the door to see him out. "Take care of yourself, Johnny. There aren't many of us good guys left anymore."

They parted on a jocular note and Preston went back to Gordon Street.

■ Louis Zablonsky knew the men who arrived in a van and knocked on his front door late on Saturday night. He was alone in the house, as usual on Saturdays; Beryl was out and would not return until the small hours. He supposed they knew that.

He had been watching the late film on television when the knock came, and when he answered the door, they bulled straight into the hallway, closing the door behind them. There were three of them. Unlike the four who had visited Raoul Levy two days earlier (an incident of which Zablonsky knew nothing, since he did not read the Belgian papers), these were hired muscle from London's East End—"slags," in underworld parlance.

Two were brutes, simple steak-faced thugs who would do anything they were told and would obey the orders of the third; he was slight, pocked, mean, with dirty-blond hair. Zablonsky did not know them personally; he just "knew" them; he had seen them in the camps, in uniform. Recognition sapped his will to resist. He understood there was no point. Men like these always did what they wanted to people like him. There was no point in resisting or appealing.

They pushed him back into the sitting room and threw him into his own armchair. One of the big men stood behind the chair, leaned forward, and pinned Zablonsky into it. The other stood by, caressing one fist with the palm of the other hand. The blond man drew up a stool in front of the chair, squatted on it, and stared at the jeweler's face. " 'It 'im," he said.

The slag to Zablonsky's right swung a heavy fist straight into his mouth. The man was wearing brass knuckles. The jeweler's mouth dissolved in a welter of teeth, lips, blood, and gum.

Blondie smiled. "Not there," he chided gently. " 'E's supposed to talk, ain't 'e? Lower down."

The thug slammed two more haymakers into Zablonsky's chest. Several ribs cracked. From Zablonsky's mouth came a high-pitched keening. Blondie smiled. He liked it when they made noise.

Zablonsky struggled feebly but he might as well not have bothered. The muscled arms from behind the chair held him fast, as the other arms had held him down on that stone table so long ago in southern Poland while the blond doctor smiled down at him.

"You been bad, Louis," crooned Blondie. "You upset a friend of mine. 'E reckons you've got something of his and 'e wants it back." He told the jeweler what it was.

Zablonsky choked back some of the blood that filled his mouth. "Not here," he croaked.

Blondie considered. "Search the place," he told his companions. " 'E won't give no trouble. Take it apart."

The two slags searched the house, leaving Blondie with the jeweler in the sitting room. They were thorough and it took an hour. When they had finished, every closet, drawer, nook, and cranny had been turned out. Blondie contented himself with poking the old man in his broken ribs. Just after midnight the slags returned from the attic.

"Nuffink," said one.

"So who's got it, Louis?" asked Blondie. Zablonsky tried not to tell him, so they hit him again and again until he did. When the one behind the chair released him, he fell forward onto the carpet and rolled onto one side. He was going blue around the lips, his eyes starting and his breath coming in short, labored gasps. The three men looked down at him.

" 'E's 'aving a 'eart attack," said one curiously. " 'E's croaking."

" 'It 'im too 'ard, then, dint ya?" said Blondie sarcastically. "Come on, let's go. We've got the name."

"You reckon 'e was telling us straight?" asked one of the slags.

"Yeah, 'e was telling us straight an hour ago," said Blondie.

The three left the house, clambered into their van, and drove off.

On the road south from Golders Green, one of the slags asked Blondie, "So what we going to do now, then?"

"Shut up, I'm thinking," said Blondie. The little sadist liked to think of himself as a commander of criminals. In fact, he was of limited intelligence and now he was in a quandary. On the other hand, the contract had been to visit just one man and recover some stolen property. On the other, they had not recovered it. Near Regent's Park he saw a telephone booth. "Pull over," he said. "I got to make a phone call."

The man who had hired him had given him a telephone number, the location of a phone booth, and three specific hours at which to call. The first of them was only a few minutes ahead.

■ Beryl Zablonsky returned from her Saturday-evening treat just before two in the morning. She parked her Metro across the street and, surprised to see the lights still on, let herself in.

Louis Zablonsky's wife was a nice Jewish girl of working-class origins who had early learned that to expect everything in life is stupid and selfish. Ten years earlier, when she was twenty-five, Zablonsky had plucked her from the second-row chorus line of a no-hope musical and asked her to marry him. He had told her about his disability but she had accepted him nevertheless.

Strangely, it had been a good marriage. Louis had been immeasurably kind and treated her as if he were a too-indulgent father. She doted on him, almost as if she had been his daughter. He had given her everything he could—a fine house, clothes, trinkets, pocket money, security—and she was grateful.

There was one thing he could not give her, of course, but he was understanding and tolerant. All he asked was that he never know who, or be asked to meet any of them. At thirty-five, Beryl was a trifle overripe, a little obvious, earthy and attractive in that kind of way that appeals to younger men, a sentiment she heartily reciprocated. She maintained a small studio flat in the West End for her trysts and unashamedly enjoyed her Saturday-night treats.

Two minutes after entering the house, Beryl Zablonsky was crying and giving her address on the telephone to the ambulance service. They were there six minutes later, put the dying man on a stretcher, and tried to hold him in this life all the way to the Hampstead Free Hospital. Beryl went with him in the ambulance.

On the way he had one brief period of lucidity and beckoned her close to his bleeding mouth. Craning an ear, she caught his few words, and her brow wrinkled in puzzlement. It was all he was able to say. By the time they got to Hampstead, Louis Zablonsky was another of the night's dead-on-arrival cases.

Beryl Zablonsky still retained a soft spot for Jim Rawlings. She had had a brief affair with him seven years earlier, before his marriage. She knew his marriage had now broken up and that he was again living alone in the top-floor apartment in Wandsworth whose telephone number she had called often enough to have memorized it.

When she came on the line she was still crying, and at first Rawlings had some trouble, dazed with sleep as he was, in making out who was calling. She was ringing from a public booth in emergency admissions and the pips kept going as she put in fresh coins. When he understood who it was, Rawlings listened to the message with increasing puzzlement.

"That's all he said? Just that? All right, love. Look, I'm sorry, really very sorry. I'll come up when the fuzz have cleared out. See if there's anything I can do. Oh, and Beryl . . . thanks."

Rawlings replaced the receiver, thought for a moment, and placed two calls, one after the other. Ronnie, from the scrapyard, reached him first, and Syd was there ten minutes later. Both, as instructed, were tooled up, and they were just in time. The visiting party tramped up the eight flights of stairs fifteen minutes later.

Blondie had not wanted to take the second contract, but the extra money the voice on the phone had guaranteed was too much to turn down. He and his mates were East Enders and hated to go south of the river. The animus between the gangs of the East End and the mobs of South London is legendary in the capital's underworld, and for a southerner to go "up East" uninvited, or the reverse, can be a ticket to a lot of trouble. Still, Blondie reckoned that at three-thirty in the morning things should be quiet enough and he could be back in his own manor with the job done before he was spotted.

When Jim Rawlings opened his door, a heavy hand shoved him straight back down the hallway leading to his sitting room. The two slags came in first, with Blondie bringing up the rear. Rawlings backed fast down the hallway to let them all in. When Blondie slammed the door behind him, Ronnie came out of the kitchen and leveled the first slag with a pickax handle. Syd came out of the coat closet in a rush and used a nailbar on the cranium of the second man. Both went down like felled oxen.

Blondie was scrabbling at the doorknob, trying to get back out to the safety of the landing, when Rawlings, stepping over the bodies, caught him by the scruff and slammed him face-first into a glass-fronted portrait of the Madonna, ownership of which was the nearest the little man had ever come to organized religion. The glass broke and Blondie collected several small shards in his cheeks.

Ronnie and Syd tied up the two heavies while Rawlings hauled Blondie into the sitting room. Minutes later, held at the feet by Ronnie and around the waist by Syd, Blondie was protruding several feet out of the window, eight floors above the ground.

"See that parking lot down there?" Rawlings asked him. Even in the blackness of a winter night, the man could just make out the glint of streetlights on cars a long way down. He nodded.

"Well, in twenty minutes that parking lot's going to be full of fuzz. Standing around a plastic sheet. And guess who's going to be under it, all squashed and nasty?"

Blondie, aware that his life expectancy was now measurable in seconds, called from his extremity, "All right, I'll cough."

They brought him in and sat him down. He tried to be ingratiating. "Look, we know the score, squire. I was just 'ired to do a job, right? Recover something what got nicked. . . ."

"That old man in Golders Green," said Rawlings.

"Yeah, well, 'e said you'd got it, so I come 'ere."

"He was a mate of mine. He's dead."

"Well, I'm sorry, squire. I didn't know 'e 'ad an 'eart condition. The boys only tapped 'im a couple of times."

"You crap-eater. His mouth was all over the parish and all his ribs cracked. So what did you come for?"

Blondie told him.

"The what?" asked Rawlings incredulously.

Blondie told him again. "Don't ask me, squire. I was just paid to get it back. Or find out what 'appened to it."

"Well," said Rawlings, "I'm very close to having you and your mates in the Thames before sunup, wearing a nice new line in concrete underpants. Only I don't need the aggro. So I'm letting you go. You tell your punter it was empty. Completely empty. And I burned it . . . to a cinder. There's nothing left of it. You don't really think I'd keep something taken from a job? I'm not a complete fool. Now get out."

At the doorway Rawlings called Ronnie back. "See them back across the river. And give the little rat a present from me, for the old man. Okay?"

Ronnie nodded. Minutes later, down in the parking lot, the more damaged of the East Enders went into the back of his own van, still trussed up. The half-conscious one was put behind the steering wheel with hands untied and told to drive. Blondie was thrown in the front passenger seat, his broken arms in his lap. Ronnie and Syd followed them to Waterloo Bridge, then turned back and went home.

Jim Rawlings was perplexed. He made himself a cup of espresso and thought things over.

He had indeed intended to burn the attaché case amid the rubble. But it was so beautifully hand-tooled; the dull, burnished leather glowed in the light of the flames like metal. He had examined it for any sign of an identification mark. There was none. Against his better judgment and despite Zablonsky's warning, he had decided to risk keeping it.

He went to a closet and brought it down from a high shelf. This time he went over it like a professional cracksman. It took him ten minutes to find the stud on the hinge side of the case that slid sideways when pushed hard with the ball of the thumb. From inside the case he heard a sound. When he reopened the case the base had risen half an inch at one side. With a paper knife he eased up the base and glanced inside the flat compartment between the case's real base and the false one. With tweezers he extracted the ten sheets of paper that lay within.

Rawlings was no expert on government documents, but he could understand the rubric of the Ministry of Defense, and the words TOP SECRET are understandable in any man's language. He sat back and whistled softly.

Rawlings was a burglar and a thief, but like much of the London underworld he would not have anyone "trash" his country. It is a fact that convicted traitors in prison, along with child molesters, have to be kept in seclusion because professional "faces," if left alone with such a man, are likely to rearrange his component parts.

Rawlings knew whose apartment he had burgled, but the robbery had not yet been reported, and he suspected, for reasons he could only now fathom, that it might never be. So he did not need to draw attention to it. On the other hand, with Zablonsky dead, the diamonds were probably gone forever, and his cut of their value with them. He began to hate the man who owned that apartment.

He had already handled the papers without gloves, and he knew his own prints were on file. He dared not identify himself, so he had to wipe the papers clean with a cloth, erasing the traitor's fingerprints as well.

The next afternoon, Sunday, he mailed a plain brown envelope, well sealed and with an excess of stamps, from a post box in the Elephant and Castle. There was no collection until Monday morning and the package did not arrive at its destination until Tuesday.

■ That day, January 20, Brigadier Bertie Capstick called John Preston at Gordon. The bluff geniality was gone from his voice. "Johnny, remember what we were talking about the other day? If anything cropped up . . . ? Well, it has. And it's not the Christmas fund. It's big, Johnny. Someone has mailed me something in the post. . . . No, not a bomb, though it might turn out worse. It looks as if we have a leak here, Johnny. And he has to be very, very high. That means it comes under your department. I think you'd better come down and take a look."

■ That morning also, in the owner's absence, but by appointment and letting themselves in with provided keys, two workmen arrived at an eighth-floor apartment at Fontenoy House. During the day they chipped the damaged Hamber safe out of the masonry of the wall and replaced it with an identical model. By nightfall they had redecorated that wall as it had been before. Then they left.

CHAPTER

Moscow
Wednesday, January 7, 1987

FROM: H. A. R. Philby
TO: The General Secretary of the Communist Party
of the Soviet Union

Permit me to begin, Comrade General Secretary, with the briefest description of the background of the British Labour Party and of its steady penetration and successful eventual domination by the Hard Left over the past fourteen years.

The Party was originally founded by the trade union movement as the political arm of the recently organized British working class. From the outset it espoused the cause of moderate bourgeois social-ism—of reform rather than revolution. The home of the true Marxist-Leninist was then in the Commu-nist Party.

Even though the bedrock of Marxism-Leninism in Britain has always been in the trade union movement, true believers were excluded from the Labour Party itself. From the 1930s onward, a few of our pro-Soviet Hard Left friends in Britain managed to infiltrate the Party by subterfuge, but they had, once inside it, to maintain an extremely low profile. Other friends of Moscow, perceived as they sought to enter the Labour Party, were refused admission or, if spotted inside the Party, were expelled.

The reason our true friends in Britain were for so many years excluded from the mass-support Labour Party can be described in two words: "proscribed list."

This was a list of banned organizations; it prohibited all fraternal contact between the Labour Party and those much-smaller groups inhabited by the true revolutionary socialists—that is, the Marxist-Leninists. Further, no member of a Hard Left group was permitted membership in the Labour Party under the terms of the proscribed list, which were staunchly maintained by successive Labour Party leaders for fifty years.

As the Labour Party was the only mass-support party of the Left with a hope of acceding to government of Britain, infiltration and domination of it by our friends, following the classic Leninist teaching of "entryism," was for all those years an elusive dream. Nevertheless, our friends within the Party, few though they were, worked tirelessly and covertly; in 1973 their efforts were finally crowned with success.

In that year, when the Party was under the weak and vacillating leadership of Harold Wilson, they achieved a wafer-thin majority on the all-important Party National Executive Committee, and used it to pass a resolution abolishing the proscribed list. The outcome was beyond their dreams.

With the floodgates open, shoals of Hard Left young activists of the post-1945 generation swarmed

into the Labour Party and were at once able to offer
themselves for office at every level of the Party organization. The road to entryism, influence, and
eventual takeover was open, and that takeover has
now been achieved.

Since 1973 the absolutely vital National Executive
Committee has seldom been out of the hands of a
Hard Left majority, and it has been through the
skillful use of this tool that the constitution of the
Party and its composition at the higher levels have
been changed out of all recognition.

A brief word of digression, Comrade General Secretary, to explain precisely whom I mean by "our
friends" within the British Labour Party and trade
union movement. They fall into two categories:
the deliberate and the unwilling. With the first category I am referring to people not of the so-called Soft
Left or of the Trotskyite aberration, both of whom
abhor Moscow, albeit for different reasons. I refer to
those of the Hard Left with, at their core, the Ultra-
Hard Left. These are dedicated, dyed-in-the-wool
Marxist-Leninists, who would not appreciate being
called Communists since this implies membership in
the quite useless British Communist Party. They
are, nevertheless, staunch friends of Moscow and in
nine cases out of ten will act in accordance with Moscow's wishes, even though those wishes may remain
unexpressed and even though the person concerned
would stoutly claim he was acting for "conscientious" or "British" reasons.

The second group of friends inside, and now dom-
inating, the British Labour Party can be character-
ized as follows: those persons with a deep political
and emotional commitment to a form of socialism so
far left as to qualify as Marxism-Leninism; persons
who will, in any given set of circumstances or in any
contingency, almost invariably react quite sponta-

neously in a manner completely parallel to, or convergent with, the desires of Soviet foreign policy vis-à-vis Britain and/or the Western Alliance; persons who need no briefing or instructions whatsoever, and who would probably be offended if such were proposed; persons who, wittingly or unwittingly, whether impelled by personal conviction, a warped patriotism, a desire to destroy, a craving for self-advancement, a fear of intimidatory pressure, a sense of their own self-importance, or a desire to move with the herd, will conduct themselves in a manner that suits our Soviet interests perfectly. They all constitute agents of influence to our benefit.

They all, of course, claim to be seekers after democracy. Happily, the overwhelming majority of Britishers today still understand by the word *democracy* a pluralist (multiparty) state, whose governing body shall be chosen at periodic intervals by universal adult suffrage based upon the secret ballot. Obviously, our Hard Left friends over there, being people who eat, drink, breathe, sleep, dream, and work at left-wing politics every waking hour of every day, mean by the word *democracy* a "democracy of the committed," with its controlling roles performed by themselves and like-thinkers. Fortunately, the British press takes few steps to correct this misapprehension.

Thus, from 1973 onward, our Marxist-Leninist friends in the Labour Party were able to devote themselves single-mindedly to the struggle to capture the Party covertly, a program made possible only by the abolition of the proscribed list. This is how it was done.

The Labour Party has always stood like a tripod on three legs: the trade unions, the constituency Labour parties (one each in the constituencies that make up the British electoral pattern), and the Parliamentary Labour Party, the group of Labour MPs who were elected at the previous general election. The Party leader is always drawn from among these.

The trade unions are the most powerful of the three and exercise this power in two ways. One, they are the Party's paymasters, funding the coffers from political levies deducted from millions of workers' pay packets. Two, at Party conferences they dispose of huge "block votes," cast by the Union National Executive on behalf of millions of uncanvassed members. These block votes can ensure the passage of any resolution and elect up to a third of the Party's all-important National Executive Committee.

These vote-casting union executive committees are absolutely vital; they comprise the full-time union activists and officials who decide union policy. They stand at the peak of the pyramid of which the middle ranks are the area officials and the lower ranks are the branch officials. Thus the effective takeover by Hard Left activists of great swaths of trade union officialdom was clearly essential, and has in fact been achieved.

The great ally of our friends in this task has always been the apathy of the largely moderate rank-and-file union members, who cannot be bothered to attend union branch meetings. Thus the activists, who attend everything, have been able to take over thousands of branches, hundreds of areas, and the cream of the executive committees. At present the biggest ten of the eighty unions affiliated to the Labour Party control half the union movement's votes; nine of those ten have Hard Left control at the top, as against two in the early 1970s. All this has been achieved over the heads of millions of British workers by no more than ten thousand dedicated men.

The importance of this Hard Left–dominated union vote will become plain when I describe the electoral college that chooses the new Party leader;

the unions hold forty percent of the votes in this so-called college.

Next, the constituency Labour parties, or CLPs. At the core of these lie the general management committees, which, apart from running the day-to-day business of the Party within the constituency, have one other vital function: they choose the Labour candidate for Parliament. Over the decade 1973 to 1983, hard-line activist young people of the extreme Left began to move into the constituencies, and by assiduous attendance at dull and sparsely filled CLP meetings ousted the old-time officials to gain control of one general management committee after another.

As each successive constituency fell to the new Hard Left activist control, the position of the largely centrist MPs representing those constituencies became tougher and tougher. Still, they could not be easily ousted. For the true triumph of the Hard Left it was necessary to weaken, indeed emasculate, the independence of conscience of a member of Parliament; to transform him from the trustee of all his constituents' interests into a mere legate of his general management committee.

This was brilliantly achieved by the Hard Left at Brighton in 1979 with the passage of the new rule requiring the annual reselection (or deselection) of MPs by their management committees. The rule caused a massive switch of power. A whole group of centrists quit to form the Social Democratic Party; others were deselected and left politics; some of the ablest centrists were harassed into resignation. Still, the Parliamentary Labour Party, though emasculated and humiliated, was left with one vital function: the MPs, and they alone, could elect the Labour Party leader. It was crucial, to complete the three-pronged capture, to take that power away from them. This was achieved, again at the urging of the Hard Left, in 1981 with the creation of the electoral college, in which thirty percent of the votes are held by the Parliamentary Party, thirty percent by the constituency parties, and forty percent by the trade unions. The college will elect each new leader as and when needed, *and reconfirm him annually*. This last function is crucial to the plans now afoot, and which I will explain.

The struggle for control that I have described brings the story to the general election of 1983. The takeover was almost complete, but our friends had made two errors, aberrations from the Leninist doctrine of caution and dissimulation. They had come out too openly, too visibly, to win those titanic struggles, and the premature call for a general election caught them on the hop. The Hard Left needed one extra year to consolidate, mollify, unify. They did not get it. The Party, saddled too early with the most extreme Hard Left manifesto in history, was in complete disarray. Worse, the British public had seen the real face of the Hard Left.

As you will recall, the 1983 election was apparently a disaster for the by now Hard Left–dominated Labour Party. Yet I suggest the outcome was in fact a blessing in disguise. For it led to the gritty and self-denying realism to which our true friends in the Party have agreed to submit themselves over the past forty months.

Briefly, out of 650 constituencies in Britain in 1983, the Labour Party won only 209. But it was not quite so bad as it looked. For one thing, of those 209 sitting Labour MPs, 100 were now firmly of the Left, 40 of them of the Hard Left. It may be small, but today's Parliamentary Labour Party is the farthest left that has ever sat in the House of Commons.

Second, the defeat at the polls gave a jolt to those fools who thought the struggle for total control was already over. They soon realized that after the bitter but necessary struggle by our friends to win control of the Party between 1979 and 1983, the time had come to reestablish unity and to repair the damaged power base in the country, with an eye to the next election. This program began under Hard Left orchestration at the October 1983 Party Conference, and has been unswerving ever since.

Third, they all saw the necessity to return to that clandestinity demanded by Lenin of true believers operating inside a bourgeois society. Thus the leitmotif of the whole span of the Hard Left's conduct these past forty months has been a return to that clandestinity that worked so well through the early and mid-1970s. This has been coupled with a reversion to an apparent and surprising degree of moderation. It has taken a vast effort of self-discipline to achieve this, but again the comrades have not been found wanting in this regard.

Since October 1983, the Hard Left has effectively taken on the clothes of courtesy, tolerance, and moderation; stress is eternally laid upon the primordial importance of Party unity, and a number of hitherto impossible concessions have been made in Hard Left dogma to achieve this. Both the centrist wing, delighted and amicable, and the media appear to have been completely taken by the new, acceptable face of our Marxist-Leninist friends.

More covertly, the takeover of the Party has been finalized. All the lever committees are now either in the hands of the Hard Left or could be taken over during a single emergency meeting. But—and it is an important "but"—they have usually been content to leave the chairmanship of these lever committees in the hands of a Soft Left person, and occasionally, when the voting supremacy is sufficiently overwhelming, even in the hands of a centrist.

The centrist wing, with the exception of about a

dozen skeptics, has been effectively disarmed by the
newfound unity and the absence of harassment of
themselves. Nevertheless, the iron fist is still very
much in the velvet glove.

At constituency level, the takeover of local CLPs
by Hard Left elements has continued quietly and
with very little public or media attention. The same
thing has happened throughout the history of the
trade union movement, as I have already mentioned.
Nine out of the Big Ten and half of the remaining
seventy unions belong now to the Hard Left, and
here again the profile has deliberately been kept
much lower than prior to 1983.

In summation, the entire Labour Party of Britain
now belongs to the Hard Left, whether directly,
through Soft Left surrogates, through intimidated
centrists, or through the holding of a fast emergency
meeting of the appropriate committee; and yet the
rank and file of the Party membership and of the
unions, the media, and the broad masses of the old
Labour voters seem unaware of this fact.

For the rest, the Hard Left has for forty months
approached the next British general election as if
planning a military campaign. To win a simple majority in the British Parliament it would need 325
seats—say, 330. It possesses 210 that are regarded as
in the bag. The other 120, lost in 1979 or 1983, or
both, are regarded as winnable and have been designated as target seats.

It is a fact of political life in Britain that the people, after two full terms of one kind of government,
often seem to think it is time for a change, even if the
incumbent government is not really unpopular. But
the British will change only if they trust what they
are changing to. It has been the aim of the Labour
Party these past forty months to win back that public
trust, albeit by subterfuge on the part of our friends
within it.

To judge by recent public-opinion polls, the campaign has been substantially successful, for the percentage gap between the ruling Conservatives and the Labour Party has closed to a few points. Bearing in mind also that under the British system eighty "marginal" seats actually control the outcome of an election, and that the marginals are swung one way or the other by the fifteen percent "floating vote," the Labour Party has a chance of being returned to government at the next British general election.

The mere election to power of the Labour Party would not alone be enough to destabilize Britain to the revolutionary threshold and beyond it. It would be necessary to topple the newly triumphant Labour leader from office before he could be called to the Palace and sworn in as premier, and for him to be replaced by the preselected Hard Left nominee as Britain's first Marxist-Leninist Prime Minister. It is this plan that is now well advanced.

Permit me to make one second digression to describe the manner of the election of a Labour Party leader. After the inception of the so-called electoral college at the urging of our Hard Left friends, the procedure was thus: following an election, nominations for the post of Party leader closed thirty days after the MPs took their oath. There would then ensue three months during which rival candidates could press their claims before the electoral college met. In the event of a Labour defeat there might well be a change of leader; in the event of a victory it would be unthinkable to topple the Prime Minister, since those three months would permit countrywide canvassing of the masses, who would support him.

Then, last year, at the October conference, our friends who dominated the National Executive Committee managed to secure the passage of a tiny "reform." In the event of a Labour *victory* at the polls, the leader would be confirmed quickly and efficiently by these means: any nominations would have to be in within three days of the declaration of the election result; then an extraordinary meeting of the electoral college would take place within four more days. After the electoral college meeting and the "choice" of the Party leader, no further contest would be held for two years, the intervening year being waived.

Those who wavered in supporting this "reform" were persuaded the whole "confirmation" process would be a formality. No one, obviously, would stand against the newly triumphant leader, still awaiting his call to the Palace. He would simply be reendorsed in an unopposed reelection, would he not?

In fact, the reverse is intended. An alternative candidate *would* propose himself for the leader's post. The shortness of time would prevent any canvassing of the masses; the trade union national executive committees would cast their forty percent on behalf of millions of union members, and those committees are dominated by our friends. Ditto the constituency committees. Together with half the Parliamentary Party, the alliance would cobble together more than fifty percent of the electoral college. It would be the new leader the Queen would have to summon to the Palace.

Now to specifics. Within the heart of the Hard Left of the British Labour Party and the trade union movement there is a group of twenty who, together, may be said to represent the ultra-left wing. They cannot be called a committee because, although in touch with each other, they seldom if ever meet in one place. Each has spent a lifetime working his way slowly upward in the inner apparatus; each has at his fingertips a manipulative influence far, far beyond his apparent office or position. Each is a totally committed, "true believer" Marxist-Leninist. There are twenty in all, nineteen men and one woman. Nine are trade unionists, six (including the woman) are sitting Labour MPs, and the rest comprise two academics, a peer, a lawyer, and a publisher. These are the people who will trigger and stage-manage the takeover.

Once in the Party leadership and holding the office of Prime Minister, the newcomer would have carte blanche, backed by the Hard Left–dominated National Executive Committee of the Party, to reform his Cabinet wholly in his own image and to embark upon the intended legislative program forthwith. In short, the populace would have voted for an apparently Soft Left traditionalist or at least reformist government, but a full Hard Left regime would have taken office *without* the irksome necessity of an intervening election.

As for the legislative program, it constitutes at this stage a plan for twenty desired measures that have not yet, for obvious reasons, been put to paper. All of those measures have long been the sought-after program of the Hard Left, though only a few are included in the official Labour Party manifesto, and then in watered-down form.

The twenty-point plan is known as the Manifesto for the British Revolution—or MBR for short. The first fifteen points concern mass nationalization of private enterprise, property, and wealth; abolition of all private landholding, medical care, and education; subordination of the teaching professions, police force, information media, and law courts to state control; and abolition of the House of Lords, which has the power to veto an act of self-perpetuation by an elected government. (Evidently, the British revolution could not be stopped or put into reverse at the whim of the electorate.)

But the final five points of the MBR vitally concern us here in the Soviet Union, so I will list them.

1. Britain's immediate withdrawal, regardless of any treaty obligations, from the European Economic Community.

2. The downscaling without delay of all Britain's conventional armed forces to one fifth of their present size.

3. The immediate abolition and destruction of all Britain's nuclear weapons and weapon-delivery systems.

4. The expulsion from Britain without delay of all United States forces, nuclear and conventional, along with all their personnel and matériel.

5. Britain's immediate withdrawal from, and repudiation of, the North Atlantic Treaty Organization.

I need hardly underline, Comrade General Secretary, that these last five proposals would wreck the defenses of the Western Alliance beyond any possible hope of repair in our lifetimes, if indeed ever. With Britain gone, the smaller NATO nations would probably follow suit, and NATO would wither on the vine, isolating the United States firmly on the other side of the Atlantic.

Obviously, everything I have outlined and described within this memorandum depends for its full implementation on a Labour Party victory, and for this the next election, expected in the spring of 1988, may well be the last opportunity.

All the above was, in fact, what I meant by my remark at General Kryuchkov's dinner that the political stability of Britain is constantly overestimated in Moscow "and never more so than at the present time."

Yours sincerely,
Harold Adrian Russell Philby

The General Secretary's response to the memorandum was surprisingly and gratifyingly prompt. Barely more than a day after Philby had consigned the memorandum into the hands of Major Pavlov, the inscrutable and cold-eyed young officer from the Ninth Directorate was back. He bore in his hands a single manila envelope, which he handed to Philby without a word before turning away.

It was another handwritten letter from the General Secretary, brief and to the point as usual.

In it the Soviet leader thanked his friend Philby for his efforts. He himself had been able to confirm the contents of the memorandum as perfectly accurate. In consequence of this, he considered the victory of the British Labour Party at the next general election to have become a matter of top priority for the USSR. He was calling into being a small, restricted advisory committee, responsible and answerable only to himself, to counsel him upon possible future courses. He required and requested Harold Philby to act as adviser to that committee.

Preston sat in the office of a very worried Bertie Capstick and examined the ten photocopied sheets spread out on the desk, reading each carefully. "How many people have handled the envelope?" he inquired.

"The postman, obviously. God knows how many people in the sorting office. Inside the building, the front-office people, the messenger who brings the morning mail up to the offices, and myself. I can't see you'll get much joy out of the envelope."

"And the papers inside?"

"Just myself, Johnny. Of course I didn't know what they were until I had pulled them out."

Preston thought for a while. "Apart from the person who mailed them they might, I suppose, contain the prints of someone else who removed them. I'll have to ask Scotland Yard to check them out. Don't have much hope, personally. Now for the contents. It looks like very high-level stuff."

"The tops," said Capstick gloomily. "Nothing short of top secret, the lot. Some of it very sensitive, concerning our NATO allies; contingency plans for NATO to counter a variety of Soviet threats—that sort of stuff."

"All right," said Preston, "let's just run through the possibilities. Bear with me. Supposing this was sent back by a public-spirited citizen who for one reason or another did not want to be identified. It happens; people don't want to get involved. Where could such a person have got these papers? A briefcase left in a cloakroom, a taxi, a club?"

Capstick shook his head. "Not legally, Johnny. This stuff should never under any circumstances have left the building, except possibly in the sealed bag to go across to the Foreign Office or the Cabinet Office. There have been no reports of a Registry bag being tampered with. Besides, they are not marked for a destination outside this building, as they would be if they had been taken legitimately. The people who would even begin to have access to this sort of stuff know the rules. No one—but no one—may carry this sort of stuff home to study. Answer your question?"

"More than somewhat," said Preston. "It came back from outside the ministry. So it had to be taken outside. Illegally. Gross negligence? Or a deliberate attempt to leak?"

"Look at the dates of origin," said Capstick. "These ten sheets cover a full month. There's no chance they all arrived on a single desk in one day. They had to be collected over a period of time."

Preston, using his handkerchief, eased the ten documents back into their envelope of arrival. "I'll have to take them to Charles Street, Bertie. May I use your phone?"

He called Charles Street and asked to be put straight through to the office of Sir Bernard Hemmings. The Director-General was in, and after a delay and some insistence from Preston, took the call himself. Preston simply asked for an appointment within minutes and got it. He put down the phone and turned to Brigadier Capstick.

"Bertie, for the moment don't do or say anything. To anyone. Just carry on as if this were just another routine day," said Preston. "I'll be in touch."

It was out of the question to leave the ministry with these documents but without an escort. Brigadier Capstick loaned him one of the front-hall commissionaires, a burly former guardsman.

Preston left the ministry with the documents in his own briefcase and took a taxi to the Clarges Apartments; he watched the vehicle disappear down Clarges Street before walking the last two hundred yards to Charles and his head office, where he could dismiss his escort. Sir Bernard saw him ten minutes later.

The old spycatcher looked gray, as if he were in pain, which he frequently was. The disease that was growing deep inside him showed little to the observer, but the medical tests left no doubt. A year, they had said, and not operable. He was due to retire on September 1, which with terminal leave meant he could depart in mid-July, six weeks before his sixtieth birthday.

He would probably have gone already but for the personal responsibilities that bore upon him. He had a second wife who had brought to the marriage a stepdaughter on whom the childless man doted. The girl was still at school. Early retirement would severely curtail his pension, leaving his widow and the girl in straitened circumstances. Wisely or not, he sought to carry on until the statutory retirement date in order to leave them his full pension. After a lifetime in the job, he had virtually no other asset.

Preston explained briefly and concisely what had happened at the Ministry of Defense that morning, and the view of Capstick regarding the feasibility of the documents' departure from the ministry's being anything other than a deliberate act.

"Oh, my God, not another," murmured Sir Bernard. The memory of Vassall and Prime still rankled, as did the acid reaction of the Americans when they had been apprised.

"Well, John, where do you want to start?"

"I've told Bertie Capstick to stay silent for the moment," said Preston. "If we have a genuine traitor inside the ministry, there's a second mystery: Who sent the stuff back to us? Passerby? Sneak thief? Wife with feelings of remorse? We don't know. But if we could find that person, we might find where he got the stuff. That would short-circuit a lot of inquiry. I don't hold out much hope for the envelope—standard brown paper sold in thousands of outlets, normal stamps, address in block capitals written with felt-tip pen, and already handled by a score of anonymous people. But the papers inside might have retained prints. I'd like Scotland Yard to test them all—under supervision, of course. After that, we may know where we go next."

"Good thinking. You handle that side of it," said Sir Bernard.

"I'll have to tell Tony Plumb and probably Perry Jones. I'll try to set up a meeting over lunch with them both. It depends on what Perry Jones thinks, of course, but we have to set up the JIC on this one. You get on with your side, John, and stay in touch with me. If the Yard comes up with anything, I shall want to know."

■ Down at Scotland Yard, they were very helpful, putting one of their best lab men at Preston's disposal. Preston stood by the civilian technician as he carefully dusted every sheet. The man could not help reading the TOP SECRET heading on each page.

"Someone been naughty down in Whitehall?" the technician asked archly.

Preston shook his head. "Stupid and lazy," he lied. "That stuff should have been in the shredder, not a wastepaper basket. It'll be a hell of a rap on the knuckles for the clerk responsible if we can identify the knuckles."

The technician lost interest. When he had finished he shook his head. "Nothing," he said. "Clean as a whistle. But I'll tell you one thing. They've been wiped. There's one clear set of prints, of course, probably your own."

Preston nodded. There was no need to reveal that the single set of prints belonged to Brigadier Capstick.

"That's the point," said the technician. "This paper will take prints beautifully, and keep them for weeks, maybe months. There ought to be at least one other set, probably more. The clerk who touched them before you, for example. But nothing. Before they went in the wastepaper basket, they were wiped with a cloth. I can see the fibers. But no prints. Sorry."

Preston had not even offered him the envelope. Whoever had erased the prints from the documents was not going to leave them on the envelope. Moreover, the envelope would give the lie to his cover story about the negligent clerk. He took the ten secret papers and left. Capstick's right, he thought. It's a leak, and a bad one. It was three in the afternoon; he went back to Charles Street and waited for Sir Bernard.

■ Sir Bernard, with some urging, got his lunch with Sir Anthony Plumb, Chairman of the Joint Intelligence Committee, and Sir Peregrine Jones, Permanent Under Secretary at the Defense Ministry. They met in a private room at a St. James's club. Both the other senior civil servants were perturbed by the urgency of the request from the Director-General of Five and ordered their lunch rather pensively. When the waiter had left, Sir Bernard told them what had happened. It ruined both men's appetites.

"I wish Capstick had spoken to me," said Sir Perry Jones with some annoyance. "Damned unsettling to be told like this."

"I think," said Sir Bernard, "my man Preston asked him to stay silent awhile longer because if we have a leak high in the ministry, he mustn't be tipped off we got the documents back."

Sir Peregrine grunted, slightly mollified.

"What do you think, Perry?" asked Sir Anthony Plumb. "Any innocent, or simply negligent, way that stuff could have left the ministry in photocopy form?"

The top civil servant in Defense shook his head. "The leak needn't be all that high," he said. "All the top men have personal staffs. Copies have to be made—sometimes three or four men have to see an original document. But copies are listed as they are made, and later they are destroyed. Three copies taken, three copies shredded after use. Trouble is, a senior man can't shred all his own stuff. He'll give it to one of his staff to be done. They're vetted, of course, but no system is completely perfect. The thing is, those copies, spanning a whole month between them, being taken outside the ministry. That can't be accidental or even negligent. That has to be deliberate. Dammit . . ." He put down his knife and fork on an almost untouched meal. "I'm sorry, Tony, but I think we've got a bad one."

Sir Tony Plumb looked grave. "I think I'm going to have to call into being a restricted subcommittee of the JIC," he said. "At this stage, very restricted. Just Home Office, Foreign Office, Defense, the Cabinet Secretary, heads of Five and Six, and someone from GCHQ. I can't get it smaller."

It was agreed he would set up the subcommittee for a meeting the next morning and Hemmings would inform them if Preston had any luck at Scotland Yard. On that note they parted.

■ The full JIC is a rather large committee. Apart from half a dozen ministries and several agencies, the three armed forces, and the two intelligence services, it would also include the London-based representatives of Canada, Australia, New Zealand, and, of course, America's CIA.

Plenary meetings tend to be rare and rather formal. Restricted subcommittees are more the rule, because those present, concerned with a specific issue, tend to know each other personally and can get through more work in less time.

The subcommittee Sir Anthony Plumb, as Chairman of the JIC and as the Prime Minister's personal coordinator of intelligence, had convened on the morning of January 21 was code-named Paragon. It met at 10:00 a.m. in the Cabinet Office Briefing Room, known as COBRA, two floors below ground level in the Cabinet Office on Whitehall, a conference room that is air-conditioned, soundproof, and swept daily for listening devices.

Technically their host was the Cabinet Secretary, Sir Martin Flannery, but he deferred to Sir Anthony, who took the chair. Sir Perry Jones was there from Defense, Sir Patrick (Paddy) Strickland from the Foreign Office, and Sir Hubert Villiers from the Home Office, which politically commands MI5.

GCHQ, the Government Communications Headquarters, the country's listening service down in Gloucestershire, so important for surveillance in a highly technical age that it is almost an intelligence service in its own right, had sent its Deputy Director-General, the DG being away on vacation.

Sir Bernard Hemmings came from Charles Street, bringing with him Brian Harcourt-Smith. "I thought it would be better if Brian were fully in the picture," Hemmings had explained to Sir Anthony. Everyone understood he meant "in case I cannot attend on a future occasion."

The last man present, sitting impassively at the end of the long table opposite Sir Anthony Plumb, was Sir Nigel Irvine, the Chief of the Secret Intelligence Service, or MI6.

Oddly, although MI5 has a Director-General, MI6 does not. It has a Chief, known throughout the intelligence world and Whitehall simply as "C," whatever his name may be. Nor, even more oddly, does "C" stand for Chief. The first head of MI6 was named

Mansfield-Cummings, and the "C" is the initial of the second half of that name. Ian Fleming, ever tongue-in-cheek, took the other initial, "M," for the Chief in his James Bond novels.

All in all, there were nine men around the table; seven of them were knights of the realm who among them represented more power and influence than any other seven men in the kingdom. They all knew each other well and were on first-name terms. Each could call the two deputy directors-general by their first names, but the DDGs would refer to the senior men as "sir." It was understood.

Sir Anthony Plumb opened the meeting with a brief description of the previous day's discovery, which evoked mutters of consternation, and passed the narrative to Sir Bernard Hemmings. The head of Five filled in more details, including the dead end on the fingerprints from Scotland Yard. Sir Perry Jones concluded with his insistence that there could have been no accidental or merely negligent departure of those photocopies from inside the ministry. It would have been deliberate and clandestine.

When he had finished, there was silence around the table. Two single words hung like a specter above them all: *damage assessment.* How long had it been going on? How many documents had gone missing? To what destination? (Though that seemed fairly obvious.) What kinds of documents had gone? How much damage had been done to Britain and the NATO alliance? And how the devil do we tell our allies?

"Who have you got handling it?" Sir Martin Flannery asked Hemmings.

"His name's John Preston," said Hemmings. "He's C1(A). The ministry's man, Brigadier Capstick, called him when the package arrived in the mail."

"We could . . . er . . . allocate someone more . . . experienced," suggested Brian Harcourt-Smith.

Sir Bernard Hemmings frowned. "John Preston is a late entrant," he explained. "Been with us six years. I've every confidence in him. There is another reason. We have to assume there is a deliberate leak."

Sir Perry Jones nodded glumly.

"We can also assume," continued Hemmings, "that the person responsible—I'll call him 'Chummy'—is aware of the loss of those documents from his possession. We can hope Chummy does *not* know they have been anonymously returned to the ministry. Still, Chummy is likely to be worried and lying low. If I put in a whole team of ferrets, Chummy will know it's over. The last thing we need is a moonlight flit and a starring role at an international press conference in Moscow. I suggest for the moment we try to keep it low-profile and see if we can get an early lead. As newly appointed C1(A), Preston can reasonably make a tour of the ministries and check, in an apparently routine fashion, on procedures. It's as good a cover as we'll get. With a bit of luck, Chummy will think nothing of it."

From his end of the table Sir Nigel Irvine nodded. "Makes sense," he said.

"Any chance of a lead through one of your sources, Nigel?" asked Anthony Plumb.

"I'll put out some feelers," he said noncommittally. Andreyev, he was thinking; he would have to set up a meet with Andreyev. "What about our gallant allies?"

"Informing them, or some of them, will probably come to you," Plumb reminded Irvine, "so what do you think?"

Sir Nigel had been in his office for seven years and was in his last year. Subtle, experienced, and impassive, he was held in high regard by the allied intelligence services of Europe and North America. Still, being the bearer of *these* tidings was going to be no joke. Not a good note on which to leave the game. He was thinking of Alan Fox, the CIA's acerbic and occasionally sarcastic senior liaison man in London. Alan was going to make a five-course dinner out of this. Sir Nigel shrugged and smiled. "I agree with Bernard. Chummy must be a worried man. I think we can assume he will not rush to purloin another bunch of top-secret material in the next few days. It would be nice to be able to go to our allies with some sort of progress, some kind of damage assessment. I'd like to wait and see what this man Preston can do. At least for a few days."

Sir Anthony nodded. "Damage assessment is of the essence. And that seems almost impossible until we can find Chummy and persuade him to answer a few questions. So for the moment we seem to depend on Preston's progress."

"Sounds like the title of a book," muttered one of the group as they broke up, the permanent under secretaries heading to brief

their ministers in closest confidence, and Sir Martin Flannery knowing he was going to have an uncomfortable few moments with the
redoubtable Mrs. Margaret Thatcher.

■ The next day, in Moscow, another committee had its inaugural
meeting.

Major Pavlov had called Philby just after lunch to say that he
would collect the Comrade Colonel at six; the Comrade General Secretary of the CPSU wished to see him. Philby supposed (rightly) that
the five-hour warning was so that he could be sober and properly
dressed.

The roads at that hour, in driving snow, had been clogged with
crawling traffic, but the Chaika with the MOC license plates had
sped down the center lane reserved for the *vlasti*, the elite, the fat
cats in what Marx had dreamed would be a classless society—it had
become a society rigidly structured, layered, and class-ridden as
only a vast bureaucratic hierarchy can be.

When they passed the Ukraina Hotel, Philby had thought they
might be going all the way to the dacha at Usovo, but after half a mile
they swung toward the barred entrance to the huge eight-story
building at Kutuzovsky Prospekt 26. Philby was amazed; to enter
the private living quarters of the Politburo was a rare honor.

There were plainclothes Ninth Directorate men up and down the
pavement, but at the steel entrance gate they were in uniform, thick
gray coats, fur *shapkas* with the earflaps down, and the blue insignia
of the Kremlin Guards. Major Pavlov identified himself and the steel
gates swung open. The Chaika crept into the courtyard of the hollow
square and parked.

Without a word the major led Philby into the building, through
two more identity checks, a hidden metal-detector and X-ray scan-
ner, and into the elevator. At the third floor they stepped out; this
entire floor belonged to the General Secretary. Major Pavlov
knocked on a door; it opened to reveal a majordomo in white, who
gestured Philby inside. The silent major stepped back and the door
closed behind Philby. Stewards took his coat and hat and he was
ushered into a large sitting room, very warm since old men feel the
cold, but surprisingly simply furnished.

Unlike Leonid Brezhnev, who had loved the ornate, the rococo, and the luxurious, the General Secretary was known to be an ascetic man in his private tastes. The furniture was Swedish or Finnish whitewood, spare, clean cut, and functional. Apart from two no-doubt-priceless Bokhara rugs, there was nothing antique. There was a low coffee table and four chairs arranged around it, the grouping being open at one end to permit a fifth absent chair. Still standing—no one was about to sit without permission—were three men. Philby knew them all, and they nodded greetings.

One was Vladimir Ilich Krilov. He was a professor of modern history at Moscow University. His real importance was as a walking encyclopedia on the subject of the Socialist and Communist parties of Western Europe; he specialized in Britain. More important, he was a member of the Supreme Soviet, the USSR's rubber-stamp, one-party parliament; a member of the Academy of Sciences; and a frequent consultant for the International Department of the Central Committee, of which the General Secretary had once been the head.

The man in civilian clothes but with a soldierly bearing was General Pyotr Sergeivitch Marchenko. Philby knew him only vaguely, but was aware that he was a senior officer in the GRU, the Soviet armed forces' own military intelligence arm. Marchenko was an expert on the techniques of internal security and of its counterpart, destabilization, and his particular area of interest had always been the democracies of Western Europe, whose police and internal-security forces he had studied half his life.

The third man was Dr. Josef Viktorovitch Rogov, also an academician, a physicist by discipline. But his fame lay in another title—chess grand master. He was known to be one of the General Secretary's few personal friends, a man on whom the Soviet leader had called several times in the past when he felt he needed to use that remarkable brain in the planning stages of certain operations.

The four men had been there two minutes when the double doors at the end of the room opened and the undisputed master of Soviet Russia, her dominions, satellites, and colonies, entered.

He was in a wheelchair, pushed by a tall steward in a white jacket. The chair was propelled to the vacant space left for it.

"Please be seated," said the General Secretary.

Philby was surprised by the changes in the man. He was seventy-five, and his face and the backs of his hands were blotched and mottled in the manner of very old men. The open-heart surgery of 1985 seemed to have worked, and the pacemaker appeared to be doing the job. And yet he looked frail. The white hair, thick and lustrous in the May Day portraits, making him look like every family's favorite doctor, had almost vanished. There were brown smudges around both eyes.

A mile up the Kutuzovsky Prospekt, near the old village of Kuntsevo, set in a huge territory inside a two-meter timber palisade fence in the heart of a birch forest, stood the hyperexclusive Central Committee Hospital. It was a modernization and extension of the old Kuntsevo Clinic. In the grounds of the hospital stood Stalin's old dacha, the surprisingly modest bungalow in which the tyrant had spent so much of his time and where he had finally died. The whole of this dacha had been converted into the country's most modern intensive-care medical unit for the benefit of this man who now sat in his wheelchair studying them one by one. Six top specialists were on permanent call at the dacha at Kuntsevo, and to them each week went the General Secretary for treatment. It was evident they were keeping him alive—just. But the brain was still there, behind the chilly eyes that looked through the gold-rimmed glasses. He blinked rarely, and then slowly, like a bird of prey.

He wasted no time with preamble. Philby knew he never did. Nodding to the other three, he said, "You Comrades have read the memorandum of our friend, Comrade Colonel Philby."

It was not a question, but the other three nodded their assent.

"Then you will experience no surprise to learn that I regard the victory of Britain's Labour Party, and thence of the ultra-left wing of that Party, as a priority of Soviet interest. I wish you four to form a very discreet committee to advise me on any method that might occur to you that would enable us to assist—completely covertly, of course—in that victory.

"You will discuss this with no one. Documents, if any, will be prepared by you alone. Notes will be burned. Meetings will be held in personal residences. You will not associate in public. You will consult no one else. And you will report to me by telephoning here and speaking to Major Pavlov. I will then arrange a meeting at which you can report your proposals."

It was clear to Philby that the Soviet leader was taking the issue of confidentiality extremely seriously. He could have held this meeting at his suite of offices in the Central Committee building, the big gray block on Novaya Ploshed where all Soviet leaders have worked since Stalin's time. But other Politburo members might have seen them arriving or leaving, or heard about their meeting. The General Secretary was evidently establishing a committee that was so totally private that no one else was to be allowed to know of it.

There was another odd thing. Apart from the General Secretary himself—and he was no longer its head—there was no one from the KGB present; yet the First Chief Directorate had massive files on Britain and experts to match. For reasons of his own, the wily leader had chosen to keep the matter outside the service of which he had once been Chairman.

"Are there any points of query?"

Philby raised a tentative hand. The General Secretary nodded.

"Comrade General Secretary, I used to drive myself around in my own Volga. Since my stroke last year, the doctors have prohibited this. Now my wife drives me. But in this instance, for the sake of confidentiality . . ."

"I will assign a KGB driver to you for the duration," said the General Secretary softly. They all knew the other three men already had drivers, as of right.

There were no other points. At the General Secretary's nod, the steward propelled the wheelchair and its occupant back through the double doors. The four advisers rose and prepared to leave.

Two days later, in the country dacha of one of the two academics, the Albion Committee went into intensive session.

■ Book title or not, Preston *was* making some progress. Even while the inaugural session of Paragon was going on, he was ensconced in the Registry, deep under the Ministry of Defense.

"Bertie," he had told Brigadier Capstick, "so far as the staff here are concerned, I'm a new broom making a bloody nuisance of myself. Put it about that I'm only trying to make a mark with my own superiors. Routine checking of procedures, nothing to worry about, just a pain in the arse."

Capstick had done his bit, trumpeting that the new head of C1(A) was going through all the ministries showing what an eager beaver he was. The Registry clerks rolled their eyes to heaven and cooperated with thinly veiled exasperation. But Preston was given access to the files—the withdrawals and the returns, who had seen the documents and, most important, over what dates.

He had one early break. All the papers but one would have been available at the Foreign Office or the Cabinet Office, since they all touched upon Britain's NATO allies and the areas of joint NATO response to a variety of possible Soviet initiatives.

But one document had not gone outside the Defense Ministry. The Permanent Under Secretary, Sir Peregrine Jones, had recently returned from talks in Washington at the Pentagon; the subject had been joint patrolling by British and American nuclear submarines in the Mediterranean, Central and South Atlantic, and Indian Ocean. He had prepared a draft paper on his talks and circulated it to a score of senior mandarins inside the ministry. The fact that it was among the stolen papers, in photocopy form, meant at least that the leak was inside the one ministry.

Preston began an analysis, going back for months, of the distribution of top-secret documents. It became clear the papers in the returned package covered a period, first to last, of four weeks. It was also plain that every mandarin who had had all those documents on his desk had also had more than these. So the thief was being selective.

There were twenty-four men who could have had access to *all* ten, Preston established at the end of his second day. Then he began checking absences from offices, trips abroad, incidences of flu— eliminating those who could not have had access within the period of theft.

He was hampered by two things: He had to pretend to examine a host of other withdrawals in order not to draw attention to those particular ten documents. Even Registry clerks gossip, and the source of the leak could have been a low-level staffer, a secretary or typist, capable of exchanging coffee-break gossip with a clerk. Second, he could not penetrate to the floors above to check on the number of photocopies made of originals. He knew it was common for one man to have a top-secret document officially out to him by name, but that man might wish to take the advice of a colleague. So a photocopy would be run off, numbered, and given to the colleague. On its return it would be shredded—or, in this case, not. The master document would then go back to Registry. But several pairs of eyes could have seen the photocopy.

To solve the second problem Preston returned to the ministry with Capstick after dark and spent two nights on the upper floors—empty apart from the incurious cleaning ladies—checking the number of copies run off. More eliminations were made possible where a document had gone to a senior civil servant who made no copies at all before returning it to Registry. On January 27 Preston reported back to Charles Street with an interim progress sheet.

■ It was Brian Harcourt-Smith who received him. Sir Bernard was away from the office again.

"Glad you've got something for us, John," said Harcourt-Smith. "I've had two calls from Sir Anthony Plumb. It seems the Paragon people are pressing. Shoot."

"First," said Preston, "the documents. They were carefully selected, as if our thief were taking the sort of stuff he had been asked for. That requires expertise. I think that counts out really low-level staffers. They would operate according to the magpie syndrome, grabbing what came by. It's tentative but it cuts down the numbers. I think it's somebody of experience and with an awareness of content. Which counts out clerks and messengers. In any case, the leak isn't in Registry. No broken bag seals, no illicit withdrawals or unauthorized copying."

Harcourt-Smith nodded. "So you think it's upstairs?"

"Yes, Brian, I do. Here's the second reason why. I spent two nights checking every single copy made. There are no discrepancies. So that leaves only one thing. The shredding of copies. Someone has had three copies to shred and destroyed only two, smuggling the third out of the building. Now to numbers of senior men who could have done that.

"There were twenty-four who could have had access to all ten documents. I think I can count out twelve because they got only copies—one each—on a give-me-your-advice basis. The rules are quite clear. A man receiving a photocopy on that basis must return it to the man who sent it to him. To retain one would be irregular and arouse suspicion. To retain ten would be unheard of. So we come to the twelve men who had the originals out from Registry.

"Of these, three were away for varying reasons on the days shown as the withdrawal dates on the photocopies returned by the anonymous sender. Those men made their withdrawals on other days and must be counted out. That leaves nine.

"Of these nine, four never had any copies made for advisory purposes at all, and of course unauthorized copying without logging is not possible.

"And then there were five," murmured Harcourt-Smith.

"Right. Now, it's only tentative, but it's the best I can do for the moment. Three of those five, during the period, had other documents on their desks that fall well within the type of the stolen papers, and which were much more interesting, but which were not stolen. By rights they ought to have been stolen. So I come down to two men. Nothing certain, just prime suspects."

He pushed two files across the desk to Harcourt-Smith, who looked at them with curiosity.

"Sir Richard Peters and Mr. George Berenson," Harcourt-Smith read. "The first being the Assistant Under Secretary responsible for International and Industrial Policy, and the second the Deputy Chief of Defense Procurement. Both men would have personal staffs, of course."

"Yes."

"But you are not listing their staffers as suspects? May I ask why?"

"They *are* suspects," said Preston. "Those two men would probably rely on their assistants to make the copies and later shred them. But that widens the net to a dozen people. If one could clear the two top men, trapping the underling with the department head's cooperation would be child's play. I'd like to start with the top two."

"What are you asking for?" said Harcourt-Smith.

"Total covert surveillance on both men for a limited period, with postal intercept and telephone tap," said Preston.

"I'll ask the Paragon Committee," said Harcourt-Smith. "But these are senior men. You'd better be right."

■ The second meeting of Paragon took place in the COBRA late that afternoon. Harcourt-Smith deputized for Sir Bernard Hemmings. He had a transcript of Preston's report for everyone present. The senior men read the report in silence. When all had finished, Sir Anthony Plumb asked, "Well?"

"Seems logical," said Sir Hubert Villiers.

"I think Mr. Preston has done well in the time," said Sir Nigel Irvine.

Harcourt-Smith smiled thinly. "Of course, it could be neither of these two very senior men," he said. "A clerk, given the copies to shred, could just as easily have taken ten documents."

Brian Harcourt-Smith was the product of a very minor private school and carried on his shoulder a sizable and quite unnecessary chip. Beneath his polished veneer he had a considerable capacity for ill will. All his life he had resented the seemingly effortless ease that the men around him could bring to the business of life. He resented their endless and interwoven network of contacts and friendships, often forged long ago in schools, universities, or fighting regiments, on which they could draw when they wished. It was called the "old boy network," or the "magic circle," and he was annoyed most of all that he was not a member of it. One day, he had told himself many times, when he had the director-generalship and his knighthood, he would sit among these men as an equal, and they would listen, really listen to him.

Down the table, Sir Nigel Irvine, a perceptive man, caught the look in Harcourt-Smith's eyes and was troubled. There was a capacity for anger in that man, he mused. Irvine was a contemporary of Sir Bernard Hemmings and they went back a long way. He wondered about the DG's successor in the autumn. He wondered about the anger in Harcourt-Smith, the hidden ambition, and where they might both lead or, perhaps, already had led.

"Well, we've heard what Mr. Preston wants," said Sir Anthony Plumb. "Total surveillance. Does he get it?"

The hands went up.

■ Every Friday in MI5 is held what they call the "bidding" conference. The director of K Branch, he of the joint sections, is in the chair. At the bidding conference the other directors put in their requests for what they think they need—finance, technical services, and surveillance of their pet suspects. The pressure is always on the director of A Branch, who controls the watchers. That week the conference was preempted as far as the watchers were concerned. Those attending on Friday, January 30, found the cupboard was bare. Two days earlier Harcourt-Smith, at the requirement of Paragon, had allocated to Preston the watchers he wanted. At six watchers to a team (four forming the "box" and two in parked cars) and four teams in every twenty-four hours, and with two men to survey, he had taken forty-eight watchers off other duties. There was some outrage, but nobody could do anything about it.

"There are two targets," the briefing officers in Cork told the teams. "One is married but his wife is away in the country. They live in a West End apartment and he usually walks to the ministry every morning, about a mile and a half. The other is a bachelor and lives outside Edenbridge, in Kent. He commutes by train every day. We start tomorrow."

Technical Support took care of the telephone tap and the mail intercept, and both Sir Richard Peters and Mr. George Berenson went under the microscope.

■ The A team was just too late to observe the delivery by hand of a package at Fontenoy House. It was collected from the hall porter by the addressee on his return from work. It contained a replica, using zirconium stones, of the Glen Suite, which was deposited with Coutts Bank the following day.

CHAPTER

Friday the thirteenth is supposed to be an unlucky day, but for John Preston it was the opposite. It brought him his first break in the wearisome tailing of the two senior civil servants.

The surveillance had gone on for sixteen days without result. Both men were creatures of habit and neither was surveillance-conscious—that is, they did not look for a tail and therefore made the watchers' task easy. But boring.

The Londoner left his Belgravia apartment every day at the same hour, walked to Hyde Park Corner, turned down Constitution Hill and across St. James's Park. That brought him to Horse Guards Parade. He went across this, traversed Whitehall, and went straight into the ministry. He sometimes lunched out, sometimes inside. He spent most evenings at home or in his club.

The commuter, who lived alone in a picturesque cottage outside Edenbridge, caught the same train to London each day, strolled from Charing Cross Station to the ministry, and disappeared inside. The watchers "housed" him each night and kept chilly vigil until relieved at dawn by the first day-team. Neither man did anything suspicious. Mail intercepts and phone taps on both men showed up only the usual bills, personal mail, banal phone calls, and a modest and respectable social life. Until the thirteenth of February.

Preston, as operations controller, was in the radio-link room in the basement at Cork Street when a call came through from the B team following Sir Richard Peters.

"Joe is hailing a cab. We're behind him in the cars."

In watcher parlance, the target is always "Joe," "Chummy," or "our friend." When the B team came off shift, Preston had a session with its leader, Harry Burkinshaw. He was a small, rotund man, middle-aged, a veteran of his job-for-life profession, who could spend hours blended into the background of a London street and then move with remarkable speed if the target tried to slip him.

He was wearing a plaid jacket and porkpie hat, carried a raincoat, and wore a camera around his neck, like an ordinary American tourist. As with all watchers, the hat, jacket, and raincoat were soft and reversible, providing six combinations. Watchers treasure their props and the various roles into which they can slip in a matter of seconds.

"So what happened, Harry?" Preston asked.

"He came out of the ministry at the usual time. We picked him up, got him in the middle of the box. But instead of walking in the usual direction, he went as far as Trafalgar Square and hailed a cab. We were at the end of the shift. We alerted our mates on the swing shift to hold station and set off after the cab.

"He dismissed it by Panzer's Delicatessen on the Bayswater Road and ducked down Clanricarde Gardens. Halfway down, he shot into a front forecourt and went down the steps to the basement. One of my lads got close enough to see there was nothing down the steps but the door of the basement flat. He had shot in there. Then my boy had to move on—Joe was coming back out again and up the steps. He went back to the Bayswater Road, took another cab, and headed for the West End again. After that, he resumed his normal routine. We passed him to the swing shift at the bottom of Park Lane."

"How long was he down the basement steps?"

"Thirty, forty seconds," said Burkinshaw. "Either he was let in damn fast or he had his own key. No lights showing inside. Looked like he'd stopped by to pick up mail or check for it."

"What kind of house?"

"Dirty-looking house, dirty-looking basement. It'll all be in the log in the morning. Mind if I go now? My feet are killing me."

Preston spent the evening wondering about the incident. Why on earth would Sir Richard Peters want to visit a seedy flat in Bayswater? For forty seconds. He couldn't see someone inside. Not enough time. Pick up mail? Or *leave* a message? Preston arranged for the house to be put under surveillance as well, and a car with a man and a camera was there within an hour.

Weekends are weekends. Preston could have rousted the civilian authorities to start investigating the apartment through Saturday and Sunday, but that would have caused waves. This was an ultra-covert surveillance. He decided to wait until Monday.

■ The Albion Committee had agreed upon Professor Krilov as its chairman and spokesman, and it was he who alerted Major Pavlov that the committee was ready to report its considerations to the General Secretary. That was on Saturday morning. Within hours, each of the four on the committee had been told to report to the Comrade General Secretary's weekend dacha at Usovo.

The other three came in their own cars. Major Pavlov drove Philby, who was therefore able to dispense with Gregoriev, the KGB pool chauffeur who had been driving him about for the past three weeks.

West of Moscow, across the Uspenskoye Bridge and lying close to the banks of the Moskva River, is a complex of artificial villages around which are grouped the weekend retreats of the high and mighty in Soviet society. Even here the gradings are inflexible. At Peredelkino are the cottages of artists, academics, and military men; at Zhukovka are the dachas of the Central Committee and others just below the Politburo; but the last-named, the men at the supreme pinnacle, have their homes grouped around Usovo, the most exclusive area of all. The original Russian dacha was a country cottage, but these are veritable mansions of luxury, set in hundreds of acres of pine and birch forest, the territories patrolled around the clock by cohorts of Ninth Directorate bodyguards to ensure the utter privacy and security of the *vlasti*.

Philby knew that every member of the Politburo, on elevation to that office, secured the right to four residences. There is the family apartment on Kutuzovsky Prospekt that, unless the hierarch falls into disgrace, will remain in the family forever. Then there is the official villa in the Lenin Hills, always maintained with staff and comforts, inevitably bugged, and hardly ever used, save for the entertaining of foreign dignitaries. Third comes the dacha in the forests west of Moscow, which the newly promoted bigshot may design and build to his own tastes. Last, there is the summer retreat, often in the Crimea, on the Black Sea. The General Secretary, however, had long ago had his summer home built at Kislovodsk, a mineral-water spa in the Caucasus specializing in the treatment of abdominal ailments.

Philby had never seen the General Secretary's dacha at Usovo. As the Chaika arrived that freezing evening, he observed it was long and low, of cut stone, with shingled roof, and, like the furniture at Kutuzovsky Prospekt, owed much to Scandinavian simplicity. Inside, the temperature was very high and the General Secretary received them all in a spacious sitting room where a roaring log fire added to the heat. After the minimal formalities the General Secretary gestured to Professor Krilov to reveal to him the Albion Committee's thinking.

"You will understand, Comrade General Secretary, that what we have sought is a means of swinging a portion of the British electorate of not less than ten percent across the nation to two cardinal viewpoints: one is a massive loss of their popular confidence in the existing Conservative government, the second a conviction that in the election of a Labour government lies their best chance for contentment and security.

"In order to simplify that search, we asked ourselves if there were not perhaps one single issue that could dominate, or be brought to dominate, the entire election. After profound consideration we have all come to the view that no economic aspect—not job losses, factory closures, increasing automation in industry, even public-service cuts—would constitute this single issue we have been seeking.

"We believe there is but one: the greatest and most emotional noneconomic political issue in Britain and all Western Europe at the present time. This is the question of nuclear disarmament. This has become huge in the West, involving millions of ordinary people. It is basically a matter of mass fear, and it is this which we feel should become the main thrust, the issue we should covertly exploit."

"And your specific proposals?" asked the General Secretary silkily.

"You will know, Comrade General Secretary, of our efforts so far in this field. Not millions but billions of rubles have been spent encouraging the various antinuclear lobbies, in proposing to the West European people that unilateral nuclear disarmament really is synonymous with their best chance for peace. Our covert efforts and their results have been huge, but nothing compared to what we believe should now be sought and achieved.

"The British Labour Party is the only one of four contesting the next election that is committed to unilateral nuclear disarmament. Our view is that all the stops should now be pulled out, using funds, disinformation, propaganda, to persuade that minimum wavering ten percent of the British electorate to switch their vote, convinced at last that the Labour vote is the peace vote."

The silence as they waited for the General Secretary's reaction was almost tangible. He spoke at last. "Those efforts that we have made and of which you spoke—have they worked?"

Professor Krilov looked as if he had been hit by an air-to-air missile. Philby caught the Soviet leader's mood and shook his head. The General Secretary noted the gesture and went on speaking.

"For eight years we have put a huge effort into destabilizing the confidence of the Western European electorates in their governments on this issue. Today, true, all the unilateralist movements are so left wing that by one means or another they have come under the control of our friends and work to our ends. The campaign has brought a rich harvest in agents of sympathy and influence. But—"

The General Secretary suddenly smacked both palms onto the arms of his wheelchair. The violent gesture in a man normally so ice-cold shook his four listeners badly.

"Nothing has changed," shouted the General Secretary. His voice then resumed its even tenor. "Five years ago, and four years ago, all our experts on the Central Committee and in the universities and the KGB analytical study groups told us in the Politburo that the unilateralist movements were so powerful that they could stop the deployment of Cruise and Pershing missiles. We believed that. We were misled. At Geneva we dug in our toes, persuaded by our own propaganda that if we held on long enough the governments of Western Europe would give in to the huge peace demonstrations we were covertly supporting and refuse to deploy Pershing and Cruise. But they *did* deploy, and we had to walk out."

Philby nodded, looking suitably modest. Back in 1983 he had stuck his neck out with a paper suggesting that the peacenik movement in the West, despite noisy popular demonstrations, would not swing any major election or change any government's mind. He had been proved right. Things, he suspected, were moving his way.

"It rankles, Comrades, it still rankles," said the General Secretary. "Now you are proposing more of the same. Comrade Colonel Philby, what are the results of the latest British public-opinion polls on this issue?"

"Not good, I'm afraid," said Philby. "The last suggests that twenty percent of the British now support unilateral nuclear disarmament. But even that is confusing. Among the working class, Labour's traditional voters, the figure is lower. It is a dismal fact, Comrade General Secretary, that the British working class is one of the most conservative groups in the world. Polls also show they are among the most patriotic, in a traditionalist way. During the Falklands affair, die-hard trade unionists threw the rule book away and worked around the clock to get the warships ready for sea. I'm afraid if one is going to face harsh reality, one must admit that the British workingman has steadily refused to see that his best interests lie with us, or at least in a weakening of Britain's defenses. And there is no reason to think he will change his mind now."

"Harsh reality—that is what I asked this committee to face," said the General Secretary. He paused again for several more minutes. Then: "Go away, Comrades. Go back to your deliberations. And bring me a plan—an active measure—that will exploit as never before that mass fear of which you spoke; a plan that will persuade even levelheaded men and women to vote to get rid of nuclear weapons from their soil, and thus to vote Labour."

When they had gone the old Russian rose and with the aid of a cane walked slowly to the window. He gazed out at the crackling birch forest beneath the snow. When he had swept to power with his predecessor still unburied, he had been personally committed to the achievement of five tasks in the time left to him. He wanted to be remembered as the man who had increased food production and its efficient distribution; who had doubled consumer goods in number and quality by a huge overhaul of a chronically inefficient industry; who had tightened Party discipline at all levels; who had extirpated the scourge of corruption that gnawed at the country's vitals; and who had secured the final supremacy in men and arms over his country's serried ranks of enemies. Now he knew he had failed in them all.

He was an old man, and sick, and time was running out. He had always prided himself on being a pragmatic man, a realistic man, within the framework of strict Marxist orthodoxy. But even pragmatic men have their dreams, and old men have their vanities. His dream was simple: he wanted one gigantic triumph, one great monument that was his and his alone. Just how much he wanted it, that bitter winter night, he alone knew.

■ On Sunday, Preston took a stroll past the house in Clanricarde Gardens, a street running due north from the Bayswater Road. Burkinshaw had been right; it was one of those once-prosperous Victorian five-story houses that had gone badly to seed, the sort now let out in bedsitters. Its small front area was weed-infested; five steps ran up to a peeling front door above the street. From the front patch, a set of steps led down to a tiny basement area, with the top of a door just in view—the basement flat. Preston puzzled again as to why a senior civil servant and knight of the realm should wish to visit such a dingy place.

Somewhere in view, he knew, would be the watcher, probably in a parked vehicle with a long-lens camera at the ready. He made no attempt to spot the man, but knew he himself would have been seen. (On Monday he showed up in the log as "an undistinguished character who walked by at 11:21 and showed some interest in the house." Thanks for nothing, Preston thought.)

On Monday morning he visited the local town hall and had a look at the list of householders for that street. The owner of the house in question was a Mr. Michael Z. Mifsud. Preston was grateful for the "Z"; there could not be many of that name around.) Called up on the radio, the watcher at Clanricarde Gardens slipped across the street and checked the bell-push buttons. M. Mifsud lived on the ground floor. Owner-occupier, thought Preston, letting out the rest of the house as furnished accommodation; tenants of unfurnished property would pay their own local assessments.

In the late morning he ran Michael Z. Mifsud through the immigration computer down at Croydon. He was from Malta and had been in the country thirty years. Nothing known, but a question mark fifteen years back. Not followed up, and no explanation. Scotland Yard's Criminal Records Office computer explained the question mark: the man had nearly been deported. Instead, he had served two years for living off immoral earnings.

After lunch Preston went to see Armstrong in Finance at Charles Street. "Can I be an Inland Revenue inspector tomorrow?" he asked.

Armstrong sighed. "I'll try to fix it. Call back before closing time."

Then Preston went along to Five's legal adviser. "Would you ask Special Branch to fix me a search warrant for this address? Also I want a sergeant on call in case I want to make an arrest." MI5 has no powers of arrest. Only a police officer can take a suspect into custody, save in emergencies, when a citizen's arrest is possible. When MI5 wants to pick someone up, Special Branch usually obliges.

"You're not going to do a break-in?" asked the lawyer suspiciously.

"Certainly not," said Preston. "I want to wait until the tenant of this flat turns up, then move in and search. An arrest may be necessary, depending on what I find."

"All right," sighed the lawyer. "I'll get on to our tame magistrate. You'll have them both tomorrow morning."

Just before five that afternoon, Preston picked up his Inland Revenue identification from Finance. Armstrong gave him another card, with a telephone number.

"If there's a query, have the suspect phone that number. It's the Inland Revenue in Willesden Green. Ask for Mr. Charnley. He'll vouch for you. Your name is Brent, by the way."

"So I see," said Preston.

■ Mr. Michael Z. Mifsud, interviewed the next morning, was not a nice man. Unshaven, in an undershirt, surly, and uncooperative. But he let Preston into his grubby sitting room.

"What you tell me?" protested Mifsud. "What income? All I make, I declare."

"Mr. Mifsud, I assure you it's a routine spot check. Happens all the time. You declare all the rents, you've got nothing to hide."

"I got nothing to hide. So you take it up with my accountants," said Mifsud defiantly.

"I can if you wish," said Preston. "But I assure you that if I do, your accountant's fees will eventually come to an awful lot of money. Let me be frank: if the rent roll is in order, I just go away and do another spot check on someone else. But if, God forbid, any of these flats are let out for immoral purposes, that's different. Me, I'm concerned with income taxes. But I'd be duty bound to pass my findings on to the police. You know what living off immoral earnings means?"

"What you mean?" protested Mifsud. "Is no immoral earnings here. Is all good tenants. They pay rents, I pay taxes. Everything."

But he had gone a shade paler, and grudgingly produced the rent books. Preston pretended to be interested in them all. He noted that the basement was let to a Mr. Dickie at £40 per week. It took an hour to get all the details. Mifsud had never met the basement tenant. He paid by cash, regular as clockwork. But there was a typed letter that had originated the tenancy. It was signed by Mr. Dickie. Preston took the letter with him when he left, over Mifsud's protests. By lunchtime he had handed it to Scotland Yard's graphology people, along with copies of Sir Richard Peters's handwriting and signature. By close of play the Yard had rung him back. Same handwriting but disguised.

So, thought Preston, Peters himself maintains his own pied-à-terre. For cozy meetings with his controller? Most probably. Preston gave his orders: if Peters started heading toward the flat again, he, Preston, was to be alerted at once, wherever he was. The watch on the basement flat was to be maintained in case anyone else showed up.

Wednesday dragged by, and Thursday. Then, as he left the ministry on Thursday evening, Sir Richard Peters hailed a cab again and directed it toward Bayswater. The watchers contacted Preston in the bar at Gordon Street, whence he called Scotland Yard and hauled the designated Special Branch sergeant out of the canteen. He gave the man on the telephone the address. "Meet me across the street, as fast as you can, but no noise," he said.

They all congregated in the cold darkness of the pavement opposite the suspect house. Preston had dismissed his taxi two hundred yards up the street. The Special Branch man had come in an unmarked car, which, with its driver, was parked around a corner with no lights. Detective Sergeant Lander turned out to be young and a bit green; it was his first bust with the MI5 people and he seemed impressed. Harry Burkinshaw materialized out of the shadows.

"How long's he been in there, Harry?"

"Fifty-five minutes," said Burkinshaw.

"Any visitors?"

"Nope."

Preston took out his search warrant and showed it to Lander. "Okay, let's go in," he said.

"Is he likely to be violent, sir?" asked Lander.

"Oh, I hope not," said Preston. "He's a middle-aged civil servant. He might get hurt."

They crossed the street and quietly entered the front yard. A dim light was burning behind the curtains of the basement flat. They descended the steps in silence and Preston rang the bell. There was the clack of heels inside, and the door opened. Framed in the light was a woman.

When she saw the two men, the smile of welcome dropped from her heavily carmined lips. She tried to shut the door but Lander pushed it open, elbowed her aside, and ran past her.

She was no spring chicken, but she had done her best. Wavy dark hair falling to her shoulders framed her heavily made-up face. There had been extravagant use of mascara and shadow around the eyes, rouge on the cheeks, and a smear of bright lipstick across the mouth. Before she had time to close the front of her housecoat, Preston caught a glimpse of black stockings and garter belt, and a tight-waisted bodice picked out in red ribbon.

He guided her by the elbow down the hall to the sitting room and sat her down. She stared at the carpet. They sat in silence while Lander searched the flat. The sergeant knew that fugitives sometimes hid under beds and in closets and he did a good job. After ten minutes he emerged, slightly flushed, from the rear area.

"Not a sign of him, sir. He must have done a bunk through the back and over the garden fence to the next street."

Just then there was a ring at the front door.

"Your people, sir?"

Preston shook his head. "Not with a single ring," he replied.

Lander went to open the front door. Preston heard an oath and the sound of running footsteps. Later it transpired that a man had come to the door and, on seeing the detective opening it, had tried to flee. Burkinshaw's people had closed in at the top of the steps and held the man until the pursuing Lander had got the cuffs on him. After that, the man went quietly and was led away to the police car.

Preston sat with the woman and listened to the tumult die away. "It's not an arrest," he said quietly, "but I think we should go to head office, don't you?"

The woman nodded miserably. "Do you mind if I get changed first?"

"I think that would be a good idea, Sir Richard," said Preston.

An hour later, a burly but very gay truck driver was released from Paddington Green police station, having been seriously advised on the unwisdom of answering blind-date advertisements in adult contact magazines.

■ John Preston escorted Sir Richard Peters to the country, stayed with him, listening to what he had to say, until midnight, drove back to London, and spent the rest of the night writing his report. This document was in front of each member of the Paragon Committee when they met at eleven in the morning of Friday, February 20. The expressions of bewilderment and distaste were general.

Good grief, thought Sir Martin Flannery, the Cabinet Secretary, to himself. First Hayman, then Trestrail, then Dunnett, and now this. Can't these wretches ever keep their flies zipped?

The last man to finish the report looked up. "Quite appalling," remarked Sir Hubert Villiers of the Home Office.

"Don't think we'll be wanting the chap back at the ministry," said Sir Perry Jones of Defense.

"Where is he now?" asked Sir Anthony Plumb of MI5's Director-General, who sat next to Brian Harcourt-Smith.

"In one of our houses in the country," said Sir Bernard Hemmings. "He has already telephoned the ministry, purporting to phone from his cottage at Edenbridge, to say he slipped on a patch of ice yesterday evening and cracked a bone in his ankle. He said he's in a cast and will be off for a fortnight. Doctor's orders. That should hold things for a while."

"Aren't we overlooking one question?" murmured Sir Nigel Irvine of MI6. "Regardless of his unusual tastes, is he our man? Is he the source of the leak?"

Brian Harcourt-Smith cleared his throat. "Interrogation, gentlemen, is in its early stages," he said, "but it does seem likely that he is. Certainly he would be a prime candidate for recruitment by blackmail."

"Time is becoming of the very essence," interposed Sir Patrick Strickland of the Foreign Office. "We still have the matter of damage assessment hanging over us, and at my end the question of when and what we tell our allies."

"We could . . . er . . . intensify the interrogation," suggested Harcourt-Smith. "I believe that way we would have our answer within twenty-four hours."

There was an uncomfortable silence. The thought of one of their colleagues, whatever he had done, being worked over by the "hard" team was a disquieting one. Sir Martin Flannery felt his stomach turn. He had a deep personal aversion to violence. "Surely that is not necessary at this stage?" he asked.

Sir Nigel Irvine raised his head from the report. "Bernard, this man Preston, the investigating officer—he seems a pretty good man."

"He is," affirmed Sir Bernard Hemmings.

"I was wondering . . . " continued Sir Nigel with deceptive diffidence. "He seems to have spent some hours with Peters in the immediate aftermath of the events in Bayswater. I wonder if it might be helpful for this committee to have the opportunity of listening to him."

"I debriefed him myself this morning," interjected Harcourt-Smith rapidly. "I am sure I can answer any questions as to what happened."

The Chief of Six was consumed with apology. "My dear Brian, there is no doubt in my mind about that," he said. "It is just that . . . well . . . sometimes one can get an impression from interrogating a suspect that ill conveys itself to paper. I don't know what the committee thinks, but we are going to have to make a decision as to what happens next. I just thought it might be helpful to listen to the one man who has talked to Peters."

There was a succession of nods around the table. Hemmings dispatched an evidently irritated Harcourt-Smith to the telephone to summon Preston. While the mandarins waited, coffee was served.

Preston was shown in thirty minutes later. The senior men examined him with some curiosity. He was given a chair at the center of the table, opposite his own Director-General and DDG.

Sir Anthony Plumb explained the committee's dilemma and asked, "Just what happened between you?"

Preston thought for a moment. "In the car, on the way down to the country, he broke down. Up till then he had maintained a form of composure, although under great strain. I took him down alone, driving myself. He started to cry, and to talk."

"Yes?" prompted Sir Anthony. "What did he say?"

"He admitted his taste for transvestite fetishism, but seemed stunned by the accusation of treason. He denied it hotly, and continued to do so until I left him with the 'minders.' "

"Well, he would," said Brian Harcourt-Smith. "He could still be our man."

"Yes, indeed, he could," agreed Preston.

"But your impression, your gut feeling?" murmured Sir Nigel Irvine.

Preston took a deep breath. "Gentlemen, I don't think he is."

"May we ask why?" said Sir Anthony.

"As Sir Nigel implies, it's just a gut feeling," said Preston. "I've seen two men whose world had shattered about them and who believed they had not much left to live for. When men in that mood talk, they tend to spill the lot. A rare man of great composure, like Philby or Blunt, can hold out. But these were ideological traitors, convinced Marxists. If Sir Richard Peters was blackmailed into treachery, I think he would either have admitted it when the house of cards came tumbling down, or at least shown no surprise at the accusation of treason. He did show complete surprise; he could have been acting, but I think he was beyond it by then. Either that, or he ought to have an Oscar."

It was a long speech from such a junior man in the presence of the Paragon Committee, and there was silence for a while. Harcourt-Smith was looking daggers at Preston. Sir Nigel was studying Preston with interest. In view of his office, he knew about the Londonderry incident that had blown Preston's cover as an Army undercover man. He also noted Harcourt-Smith's gaze and wondered why the DDG at Five seemed to dislike Preston. His own opinion of the man was favorable.

"What do you think, Nigel?" asked Anthony Plumb.

Irvine nodded. "I, too, have seen the mood of utter collapse that overtakes a traitor when he is exposed. Vassall, Prime—both weak and inadequate men, and they both spilled the lot when the house came tumbling down. So, if not Peters, that seems to leave George Berenson."

"It's been a month," complained Sir Patrick Strickland. "We really have got to nail the culprit one way or the other."

"The culprit could still be a personal assistant or secretary on the staff of either of these two men," pointed out Sir Perry Jones. "Isn't that so, Mr. Preston?"

"Quite true, sir," said Preston.

"Then we are going to have to clear George Berenson or prove he's our man," said Sir Patrick in some exasperation. "Even if he's cleared, that leaves us Peters. And if *he* won't cough, we're back to square one."

"May I make a suggestion?" asked Preston quietly.

There was some surprise. He had not been asked here to make suggestions. But Sir Anthony Plumb was a courteous man. "Please do," he said.

"The ten documents returned by the anonymous sender all fell within a pattern," said Preston.

The men around the table nodded.

"Seven of them," Preston continued, "contained material affecting Britain's and NATO's naval dispositions in the Atlantic, North or South. That seems to be an area of NATO planning of particular interest to our man or his controllers. Would it be possible to cause to pass across Mr. Berenson's desk a document of such irresistible tastiness that, if he is the guilty party, he would be sorely tempted to abstract a copy and make a move to pass it on?"

A number of heads around the table nodded thoughtfully.

"Smoke him out, you mean?" mused Sir Bernard Hemmings. "What do you think, Nigel?"

"You know, I think I like it. It might just work. Could it be done, Perry?"

Sir Peregrine Jones pursed his lips. "Actually, more realistically than you think," he said. "When I was in America, the idea was mooted—although I haven't passed it further yet—that we might one day need to increase to refueling and revictualing level our installations on Ascension Island, to include facilities for our nuclear submarines. The Americans were very interested, and suggested they might help with the costs if they, too, could have access to them. It would save our subs going back to Faslane and those endless demonstrations up there, and save the Yankees having to go back to Norfolk, Virginia. I suppose I could prepare a very confidential personal paper, beefing that idea up to agreed-policy level, and slip it across four or five desks, including Berenson's."

"Would Berenson normally see that kind of paper?" asked Sir Paddy Strickland.

"Certainly," said Jones. "As Deputy Chief of Defense Procurement he is responsible for the nuclear side of things. He would have to get it, along with three or four others. Some copies would be run off for close colleagues' eyes only. Then they would be returned and shredded. Originals back to me, by hand."

It was agreed. The Ascension Island paper would land on George Berenson's desk on Tuesday.

As they left the Cabinet Office, Sir Nigel Irvine invited Sir Bernard Hemmings to join him for lunch.

"Good man, that Preston," suggested Irvine, "like the cut of his jib. Is he loyal to you?"

"I've every reason to think so," said Sir Bernard, puzzled.

Ah, that might explain things, thought C enigmatically.

■ That Sunday, the twenty-second, the British Prime Minister spent at her official country residence, Chequers, in the county of Buckinghamshire. In conditions of complete secrecy she asked three of her closest advisers in the Cabinet and the chairman of the Conservative Party to drive over privately to see her.

What she had to say caused them all deep thought. That coming June she would have been in power for four years of her second term. She was determined to go for a third successive election victory. The economic indicators suggested a downturn in the autumn, accompanied by a wave of wage demands. There could be strikes. She wished to have no repeat of the "winter of discontent" of 1978, when a wave of work stoppages crippled the credibility of the Labour government and led to its fall in May 1979.

Furthermore, with the Social Democrat/Liberal alliance stuck in the public-opinion polls at twenty percent, Labour, with its new-found veneer of unity and moderation, had increased its popular rating to thirty-seven percent of the electorate, just six points behind the Conservatives. And the gap was closing. In short, she wanted to go for a snap June election, but without the damaging speculation that preceded and hastened her decision in 1983. A sudden, out-of-the-blue declaration and a three-week election campaign was what she wanted, not in 1988, or even in the autumn of 1987, but that very summer.

She bound her colleagues to silence, but the date she favored was the penultimate Thursday in June, the eighteenth.

■ On Monday, Sir Nigel Irvine had his meeting with Andreyev. It was very covert, on Hampstead Heath. A screen of Irvine's own people was scattered over the heath to ensure Andreyev was himself not under surveillance by the Soviet Embassy's own KR (counterintelligence) goons. But he was clean. Britain's own cover of the Soviet diplomat's movements had been called off.

Sir Nigel Irvine handled Andreyev as a "director's case." It is unusual for men as high in the service (any service) as the Chief to run an agent personally. However, it may happen because of the exceptional importance of the agent, or because the original recruiting was done before the controller became his service's director and the agent refuses to be handled by anyone else. Such was the situation with Andreyev.

Back in February 1972, the Chief, then plain Mr. Irvine, had been head of station in Tokyo. In that month the Japanese counterterrorist people had decided to take out the headquarters of the fanatical Ultra-Left Red Army Faction, which had been located in a villa in the snow on the slopes of Mount Otakine, at a place called Asamaso. The National Police Agency actually did the job, but under the command of the redoubtable counterterrorist chief, Sassa, who was a friend of Irvine's.

Providing some of the experience gleaned by Britain's crack SAS units, Irvine was able to be of some advisory help to Sassa, and some of his suggestions saved a number of Japanese lives. In view of his country's strict neutrality, Sassa could not thank Irvine in any practical way. But at a diplomatic cocktail party a month later, the brilliant and subtle Japanese had caught Irvine's eye and nodded in the direction of a Russian diplomat across the room. Then he had smiled and moved away. Irvine closed in on the Russian and discovered that he was newly arrived in Tokyo and his name was Andreyev.

Irvine had had the man tailed and discovered he was foolishly having a clandestine affair with a Japanese girl, an offense that would immediately break him with his own people. Of course the Japanese already knew this because every Soviet diplomat in Tokyo is quietly followed whenever he leaves the embassy.

Irvine had set up a honey trap, acquired the appropriate photographs and tape recordings, and finally burst in on Andreyev, using the crash-bang-gotcha technique. The Russian had nearly collapsed, thinking he was being raided by his own people. As he pulled his trousers on, he agreed to talk to Irvine. He was something of a catch. For one thing, he was from the KGB's Illegals Directorate, a Line N man.

The First Chief Directorate of the KGB, responsible for all overseas activities, is itself divided into directorates, special departments, and ordinary departments. Ordinary Soviet KGB agents under diplomatic cover come from one of the territorial departments (the Seventh Department happens to cover Japan). These staffers are called PR Line when on posting abroad, and they do the run-of-the-mill trawling for information, making of useful contacts, reading of technical publications, and so on.

But at the most secret heart of the First Chief Directorate lies the Illegals, or S, Directorate, which knows no territorial boundaries. This department trains and runs "illegal" agents—those not under diplomatic immunity, those who go in on the ground, under deep cover, with false papers and on secret missions. The illegals operate outside the embassy. Nevertheless, inside every KGB rezidentura in every Soviet embassy, there is usually one S Directorate man, known on overseas posting as a Line N man. Line N men handle special assignments only, often running spies indigenous to the country against which they are spying, or assisting, with backup and technical support, a deep-cover illegal coming in from the Soviet bloc.

Andreyev was from the S Directorate. Oddly, he was not a Japan expert, as all his Seventh Department colleagues in the embassy would have to be. He was an English-language expert, and the reason he was in Japan was to pursue a contact with a United States Air Force master sergeant who had been talent-spotted in San Diego before he was transferred to the joint USAF-Japanese base at Tashikawa. With no hope of explaining himself to his own superiors back in Moscow, Andreyev had agreed to work for Irvine.

The cozy arrangement had come to an end when the American sergeant, pushed beyond endurance, dispatched himself rather untidily with his service revolver in the commissary latrine and Andreyev was sent back to Moscow in a hurry. Irvine thought of "burning" the man there and then, but he desisted.

And then Andreyev had shown up in London. A batch of new photographs had drifted across Sir Nigel Irvine's desk six months earlier, and there he was. Transferred out of the S Directorate and back onto PR Line work, Andreyev was accredited as a second secretary in the Soviet Embassy. Sir Nigel had put the hooks in again. Andreyev had had little choice but to cooperate, but he had refused to be handled by anyone else, so Sir Nigel had taken him on as a director's case.

On the matter of the leak in the British Defense Ministry, Andreyev had little to offer. He knew of no such thing. If there was such a leak, then the man in the ministry might be controlled directly by some illegal Soviet agent resident in Britain, who would contact Moscow direct, or he might be run by one of the three Line N people inside the embassy. But such people would not discuss a case of that importance over coffee in the canteen. He personally had heard nothing, but he would keep his eyes and ears open. On that note, the two men on Hampstead Heath parted.

■ The Ascension Island paper was distributed on Tuesday, February 24, by Sir Peregrine Jones, who had spent Monday preparing it. It went to four men. Bertie Capstick had agreed to enter the ministry each night and check on legitimate photocopies made. Preston had told his watchers he wanted to know if George Berenson scratched his neck, immediately. He told his mail-intercept people the same, and put his phone-tap team on full alert. Then they settled down to wait.

On the first day, nothing happened. That night, Brigadier Capstick went into the Ministry of Defense with John Preston while the staff were sleeping and checked the number of photocopies run off. There were seven: three by George Berenson, two each by two of the other mandarins who had had the Ascension Island paper circulated to them, and none by the fourth man.

On the evening of the second day, Berenson did something strange. The watchers reported that in the middle of the evening he left his Belgravia apartment and walked to a nearby call-box. They could not tell the number he dialed, but he spoke only a few words, replaced the receiver, and walked home. Why, Preston wondered, should a man do that who had a perfectly serviceable telephone in his flat—something Preston could vouch for, since he was tapping it?

On the third day, Thursday, February 26, George Berenson left the ministry at the usual time, hailed a cab, and went to St. John's Wood. In the High Street of this parish, with its villagelike atmosphere, was an ice-cream parlor and coffee shop. The Defense official went in, sat down, and ordered a sundae, one of the specialties of the house.

John Preston sat in the basement radio room on Cork Street and listened to the watcher team leader reporting in. It was Len Stewart, heading the A team. "I've got two people in there," he said, "and two more out here on the street. Plus my cars."

"What's he doing in there?" asked Preston.

"Can't see," said Stewart over the radio. "Have to wait until the people with him get a chance to tell me."

In fact, Berenson, ensconced in an alcove, was eating his ice-cream sundae and filling in the last squares of the crossword in the *Daily Telegraph* that he had produced from his briefcase. He took no notice of the two jeans-clad students canoodling in the corner.

After thirty minutes the official called for his bill, took it to the cash desk, paid, and left.

"He's back on the street," called Len Stewart. "My two have stayed inside. He's walking up the High Street. Looking for a taxi, I think. I can see my people inside now. They are paying at the desk."

"Can you ask them just what he did in there?" asked Preston. There was something odd, he thought, about the whole episode. It might be a special ice-cream parlor, but there were others in Mayfair and the West End, in a straight line from the ministry to Belgravia. Why go north of Regent's Park to St. John's Wood for an ice cream?

Stewart's voice came over the air again. "There's a taxi coming. He's hailing it. Hold on, here are my people from inside." There was a pause in transmission. Then: "It seems he ate his ice cream and completed the *Daily Telegraph* crossword. Then he paid up and left."

"Where's the newspaper?" asked Preston.

"He left it when he finished. . . . Hold on. . . . Then the proprietor came over and cleared the table, taking the dirty bowl and paper back into the kitchen area. . . . He's inside the taxi and cruising. What do we do . . . stay with him?"

Preston thought furiously. Harry Burkinshaw and the B team had been taken off Sir Richard Peters and allowed a few days' rest. They had been out in rain, cold, and fog for weeks. There was only one team on the job now. If he split them up and lost Berenson, who then went on to make his contact somewhere else, Harcourt-Smith would have his hide nailed to a barn door. He made his decision.

"Len, leave one car and driver to tail the taxi. I know it's not enough if he slips away on foot. But switch the rest of your people to the ice-cream parlor."

"Will do," said Len Stewart, and went off the air.

Preston was in luck. The taxi went straight to Berenson's West End club and dropped him off. He went inside. But then, thought Preston, the contact could be in there.

Len Stewart entered the ice-cream shop and sat until closing time with a coffee and the *Evening Standard*. Nothing happened. He was asked to leave at closing time and did so. From up and down the street the four-man team saw the staff of the shop leave, the proprietor close up, the lights go out.

From Cork Street, Preston was trying to get a phone tap on the ice-cream shop and a make on the proprietor. He turned out to be a Signor Benotti, a legal immigrant, originally from Naples, who had led a blameless life for twenty years. By midnight Preston had a tap on the ice-cream parlor and on Signor Benotti's home in Swiss Cottage. They produced nothing.

Preston spent a sleepless night at Cork Street. Stewart's relief shift had moved in at 8:00 p.m. and watched the ice-cream shop and Benotti's house through the night. At 9:00 on Friday morning, Benotti walked back to his shop, and at 10:00 it opened for business. Len Stewart and the day shift took over at the same hour. At 11:00, Stewart called in.

"There's a small delivery van at the front door," he told Preston. "The driver seems to be loading gallon tubs of ice cream. It seems they do a customer-delivery service."

Preston stirred his twentieth cup of awful coffee. His mind was fogging with lack of sleep. "I know," he said, "there've been references to it on the telephone already. Detach a car and two people to stay with the van. Note every recipient of ice-cream deliveries."

"That only leaves me a car and two people here, including myself," said Stewart. "It's damn thin on the ground."

"There's a bidding conference going on up at Charles. I'll try to get an extra team," said Preston.

The ice-cream van made twelve calls that morning, all in the St. John's Wood/Swiss Cottage area, with two as far south as Marylebone.

Some of the deliveries were in apartment buildings, where it was hard for the watchers to appear inconspicuous, but they noted every address. Then the van drove back to the shop. It made no afternoon deliveries.

"Will you drop that list at Cork on your way home?" Preston asked Stewart.

That evening, the phone-tap people reported that Berenson had had four telephone calls while he was at home, including one in which the caller turned out to have a wrong number. He had made no outgoing calls. Everything was on tape. Did Preston want to play it? There was nothing remotely suspicious on it. He thought he might as well.

On Saturday morning, Preston played the longest shot of his life. Using a tape recorder set up by the Technical Support people, and a variety of excuses to the householders, he called up each one of the recipients of the ice cream, asking whenever a woman answered if he might speak to her husband. Since it was Saturday, he got all but one.

One voice seemed slightly familiar. What was it—a hint of accent? And where could he have heard it before? He checked the name of the householder. It meant nothing.

He ate a moody lunch in a café near Cork Street. The connection came to him over the coffee. He hurried back to Cork Street and played the tapes again. Possible—not conclusive, but possible.

Scotland Yard, among the copious facilities of its Forensic Science Department, has a section devoted to voice analysis, which is useful whenever a target criminal, having had his phone tapped, denies it was his voice on the tape. MI5, having no forensic facilities, has to rely on Scotland Yard for this sort of thing, an arrangement usually secured via the Special Branch.

Preston called Detective Sergeant Lander at home, and it was Lander who fixed a priority meeting in Scotland Yard's voice-analysis section that same afternoon. There was only one technician available, and he was loath to leave his televised football game to come to work, but he did. A thin young man with thick-lensed glasses, he played Preston's tapes half a dozen times, watching the illuminated line on the oscilloscope screen rise and fall to record the tiniest shades of tone and timbre in the voices.

"Same voice," he said at last, "no question about it."

On Sunday, Preston identified the owner of the accented voice by using the Diplomatic List. He also called a friend in the Physics Department of London University, spoiled his day off by asking for a considerable favor, and finally telephoned Sir Bernard Hemmings at his Surrey home.

"I think there is something that we should report to the Paragon Committee, sir," he said, "tomorrow morning."

■ The Paragon Committee met at 11:00 a.m. on Monday, March 2, and Sir Anthony Plumb asked Preston to make his report. There was an air of expectancy, although Sir Bernard Hemmings looked grave.

Preston detailed the events of the first two days following the distribution of the Ascension Island paper as briefly as he could. There was a stir of interest at the news of Berenson's odd and very brief call from a public phone box on the previous Wednesday evening.

"Did you tape-record that call?" asked Sir Peregrine Jones.

"No, sir, we couldn't get near enough," replied Preston.

"Then what do you think it was for?"

"I believe Mr. Berenson was alerting his controller to a pending 'drop,' probably using a code to indicate the time and place."

"Have you any proof of that?" asked Sir Hubert Villiers of the Home Office.

"No, sir."

Preston went on to describe the visit to the ice-cream parlor, the abandonment of the *Daily Telegraph*, and the fact that it was cleared away by the proprietor himself.

"Did you manage to recover the paper?" asked Sir Paddy Strickland.

"No, sir. To have raided the ice-cream shop then might have caused the arrest of Mr. Benotti, and perhaps of Mr. Berenson, but Benotti could have pleaded complete innocence that there was anything inside the newspaper, and Berenson could have pleaded that he had made a terribly careless mistake."

"But you believe that visit to the ice-cream shop was the drop?" asked Sir Anthony Plumb.

"I'm sure of it," said Preston. He went on to describe the delivery of one-gallon tubs of ice cream to a dozen customers the next morning, how he had obtained voice samples of eleven of them, and Berenson's receipt of a wrong-number call that same evening. "The voice that dialed him that evening and established that the caller had obtained a wrong number, apologized, and rang off was the voice of one of the recipients of the ice cream."

There was silence around the table.

"Could it have been a coincidence?" asked Sir Hubert Villiers doubtfully. "There are an awful lot of perfectly innocent wrong numbers dialed in this city. Get 'em myself, all the time."

"I checked with a friend yesterday who has access to a computer," said Preston levelly. "The chances of a man in a city of twelve million going into an ice-cream parlor for a sundae, of that ice-cream parlor's delivering to twelve customers the next morning, and of one of those customers speaking through a wrong number to the ice-cream eater by midnight are more than a million to one. The telephone call on Friday evening was an acknowledgment of safe receipt."

"Let me see if I understand," said Sir Perry Jones. "Berenson recovered from his colleagues their photocopies of my fictitious paper and pretended to shred them all. In fact, he retained one. He folded it inside his newspaper and left it in the ice-cream shop. The proprietor collected the paper, plastic-wrapped the classified document, and delivered it next morning to the controller in a tub of ice cream. The controller then alerted Berenson that he had got it."

"That is what I believe happened," said Preston.

"Chances of a million to one," mused Sir Anthony Plumb. "Nigel, what do you think?"

The Chief of the SIS shook his head. "I don't believe in chances of a million to one," he said. "Not in our work—eh, Bernard? No, it was a drop, all right, from the source to the controller via a cutout, Signor Benotti. John Preston has got it right. My congratulations. Berenson's our man."

"What has happened since you made this connection, Mr. Preston?" asked Sir Anthony.

"I have switched the surveillance from Berenson to the controller," said Preston. "I've identified him. In fact, this morning I joined the watchers and followed him from his Marylebone flat, where he lives alone as a bachelor, to his office. He is a foreign diplomat. His name is Jan Marais."

"Jan? Sounds Czech," said Sir Perry Jones.

"Not quite," said Preston somberly. "Jan Marais is an accredited diplomat on the staff of the embassy of the Republic of South Africa."

There was a stunned, disbelieving silence. Sir Paddy Strickland, in language not habitually favored by diplomats, muttered, "Bloody hell." All eyes turned on Sir Nigel Irvine.

He sat at the end of the table, badly shaken. If it's true, he thought privately, I'll have his balls for cocktail olives. He was thinking of General Henry Pienaar, head of South Africa's National Intelligence Service, successor to the late, unlamented Bureau of State Security. For the South Africans to hire a few London crooks to burgle the archives of the African National Congress was one thing; to run a spy ring inside the British Defense Ministry was, between services, a declaration of war.

"I think, gentlemen, with your indulgence I am going to have to ask for a few days to investigate this matter a little further," said Sir Nigel.

■ Two days later, on March 4, one of the senior Cabinet ministers in whom Mrs. Thatcher had confided her desire to go for an early general election was having breakfast with his wife in their handsome town house in Holland Park, London. The wife was browsing through a sheaf of holiday brochures.

"Corfu is nice," she said, "or Crete." There was no response, so she pressed her point. "Darling, we should try to get away for a fortnight of complete rest this summer. It's been nearly two years, after all. What about June? Before the crush but when the weather is at its best."

"Not June," said the minister, without looking up.

"But June's beautiful," she protested.

"Not June," he repeated, "anything but June."

Her eyes widened. "What's so important about June?"

"Never mind."

"You cunning old fox," she said breathlessly. "It's Margaret, isn't it? That cozy little chat at Chequers last Sunday week. She's going to the country. Well, I'll be damned."

"Shush," said her husband, but after twenty-five years she knew when she had got it right. She looked up to see Emma, their daughter, standing in the doorway.

"Are you off, darling?"

"Yeah," said the girl, "see you."

Emma Lockwood was nineteen, a student at art college who subscribed with all her youthful enthusiasm to the cult called "radical politics." She abominated her father's political views and sought to protest against them by her own life-style. To her parents' tolerant exasperation she was never missing from antinuclear demonstrations or the noisier manifestations of left-wing protest. One of her means of personal protest was to sleep with Simon Devine, a lecturer at a polytechnic college whom she had met at a demonstration.

He was no great lover, but he impressed her with his firebrand Trotskyism and pathological hatred of the "bourgeoisie," which appeared to include anyone who did not agree with him. Those able to disagree more effectively than the bourgeois were termed fascists. To Devine that evening, in his bedsitter, she vouchsafed the tip she had overheard while standing in the doorway of her parents' breakfast room.

Devine was a member of a number of revolutionary study groups and contributed articles to Hard Left publications of great passion and small circulation. Two days later, he mentioned the nugget he had obtained from Emma Lockwood while he was in conference with one of the editors of a small broadsheet for which he had prepared an article calling on all freedom-loving automobile workers at Cowley to destroy the production line over the issue of one of their number who had been fired for theft.

The editor advised Devine there was not enough in the rumor to make an article for the publication but that he would discuss the information with his colleagues, and he advised Devine to keep it to himself. When Devine had gone, the editor did indeed discuss it with one of his colleagues—his conduit—and the conduit passed it on to the controller in the rezidentura inside the Soviet Embassy. On March 10, the news reached Moscow. Devine would have been ap-

palled. As an ardent follower of Trotsky's call for instant global revolution, he hated Moscow and all it stood for.

■ Sir Nigel Irvine, shaken by the revelation that the controller of a
major spy within the British establishment was a South African diplomat, took up the only option left to him—a direct approach to the
South African National Intelligence Service to ask for an explanation.

The relationship between the British SIS and the South African
NIS (and its predecessor, the BOSS) would be described by a poli-
tician of either country as nonexistent. "Arm's-length" would be
more realistic. A relationship exists, but for political reasons it is a
difficult one.

Under successive British governments, because of the widespread
distaste for the apartheid doctrine, the connection has always been
frowned on, more under Labour than under Conservative governments. During the Labour years between 1964 and 1979 it was allowed to continue—oddly, because of the Rhodesian imbroglio.
Labour Prime Minister Harold Wilson accepted that he needed all
the information he could get on Ian Smith's Rhodesia to implement
his sanctions, and the South Africans had most of it.

The Conservatives were back in power in May 1979, by the time
that affair was over, and the relationship continued, this time due to
concern over Namibia and Angola, where, it had to be admitted, the
South Africans had good networks. Nor was the relationship one-
sided. It was the British who received a tip from the West Germans
about the East German links of the wife of South African Navy Com-
modore Dieter Gerhardt—he was later arrested as a Sovbloc spy.
The British, using the SIS's encyclopedic files on such gentlemen,
also tipped the South Africans about a couple of Soviet illegals entering southern Africa.

There was one unpleasant hiccup in 1967, when an agent of the
BOSS, one Norman Blackburn, working as a barman at the Zambezi
Club, bestowed his charms upon one of the "Garden Girls." These
are secretaries at 10 Downing Street, so called because they work in
a room facing the garden.

The infatuated Helen (this name will suffice because she has long since settled down to raise a family) passed several classified documents to Blackburn before the affair was discovered. It caused a stink and led to Harold Wilson's conviction ever afterward that whatever went wrong, from corked wine to crop failure, was due to the BOSS.

After that, the relationship steadied onto a more civilized course. The British maintain, therefore, a head of station, of whom the NIS is informed, and who is normally resident in Johannesburg. No "active measures" are conducted by the British on South African territory. The South Africans maintain several staffers at their embassy in London, of whom SIS is aware, and a few outside the embassy, on whom MI5 keeps a watchful eye. The task of the latter is to monitor the London-end activities of various southern African revolutionary organizations, such as ANC, SWAPO, and so forth. So long as the South Africans confine themselves to this, they are left alone.

It was the British head of station in Johannesburg who sought and got a personal interview with General Henry Pienaar and reported back to his Chief in London what the head of the NIS had to say. Sir Nigel convened a meeting of the Paragon Committee on March 10.

"The great and good General Pienaar swears by all that he holds to be holy that he has no knowledge of Jan Marais. He claims Marais does not work for him and never has," said Sir Nigel.

"Is he telling the truth?" asked Sir Paddy Strickland.

"In this game, one should never count on it. But it could be he is. For one thing, he would have known for three days now that we have uncovered Marais. If Marais is his, he would know we would take terrible revenge. He has not moved any of his people out, which I think he would if he knew he were guilty."

"Then what the hell *is* Marais?" asked Sir Perry Jones.

"Pienaar claims he would like to know as much as we would," answered C. "In fact, he has agreed to my request to receive our investigator to carry out a joint hunt with his own people. I want to send a man down there."

"What is the position on Berenson and Marais now?" asked Sir Anthony Plumb of Harcourt-Smith, who was representing Five.

"Both men are under discreet surveillance, but no moves have been made to close in. No break-in to either man's apartment. Just mail intercept, phone tap, and the watchers around the clock," replied Harcourt-Smith.

"How long do you want, Nigel?" asked Plumb.

"Ten days."

"All right, but that's the limit. In ten days we have to move against Berenson with whatever we have got and start into damage assessment, with his willing or unwilling cooperation."

■ The next day, Sir Nigel Irvine called Sir Bernard Hemmings at his home outside Farnham, where the ailing man was confined.

"Bernard, that man of yours, Preston. I know it's unusual—could send one of my own people, and all that—but I like his style. Could I borrow him for the South African trip?"

Sir Bernard agreed. Preston flew to Johannesburg on the overnight flight of March 12–13. It was not until he was airborne that the information reached the desk of Brian Harcourt-Smith. He was icily angry, but knew he had been outranked.

■ The Albion Committee reported to the General Secretary on the evening of the twelfth, and was received in his apartment on Kutuzovsky Prospekt.

"And what, pray, have you got for me?" the Soviet leader asked quietly.

Professor Krilov, as chairman of the committee, gestured toward Grand Master Rogov, who opened the file in front of him and began to read.

As always in the presence of the General Secretary, Philby was impressed, even awed, by the sheer untrammeled power of the man. During the committee's researches the mere mention of his name as the overriding authority could have secured them anything they wanted in the USSR and no questions asked. As a student of power and its application, Philby admired the ruthless and cunning way in which the General Secretary had secured absolute control over every tendril of life in the Soviet Union.

Years earlier, when he had been given the powerful chairmanship of the KGB, it had not been as an appointee of Brezhnev, but of the unpublicized kingmaker of the Politburo, the Party ideologue Mikhail Suslov. With this residual independence from Brezhnev and his personal "Mafia," he had ensured that the KGB never became Brezhnev's unquestioning poodle. When, in May 1982, with Suslov dead and Brezhnev dying, he had quit the KGB to return to the Central Committee, he had not made the same mistake.

Behind him as Chairman of the KGB he had left his own man, General Fedorchuk. From inside the Party, the present General Secretary had consolidated his position with the Central Committee and then bided his time through the brief Andropov and Chernenko eras until his eventual succession. Within months of that accession, he had sewn up the power sources: Party, armed forces, KGB, Interior Ministry, MVD. With all the aces in his hands, no one dared oppose or conspire against him.

"We have devised a plan, Comrade General Secretary," said Dr. Rogov, using, as they were among others, the formal term of address. "It is a concrete plan, an active measure, a proposal to cause a destabilization among the British people that would make the Sarajevo affair and the Berlin Reichstag fire pale into insignificance. We have called it Plan Aurora."

It took him an hour to read the full details. He glanced up occasionally to see if there was any reaction, but the General Secretary was a grand master in a much bigger game of chess and his face remained blank. At last Dr. Rogov had finished. There was silence while they waited.

"It has risks," said the General Secretary quietly. "What guarantees are there that it will not backfire like certain . . . other operations?"

They all knew what he meant. He had been badly shaken by the dismal failure of the Wojtyla Affair. It had taken three years for the rumbles and accusations to die away, and it had caused the sort of global publicity the USSR definitely did not need.

In the early spring of 1981, the Bulgarian Secret Service had reported that their people among the Turkish community in West Germany had trawled a strange fish. For ethnic, cultural, and historical reasons, the Bulgars, most loyal and subservient of Russia's satellites, were deeply involved in Turkey and the Turks. The man they had picked up was a dedicated terrorist killer who had been trained by the Ultra Left in Lebanon, had killed for the Ultra-Right Gray Wolves in Turkey, escaped from prison, and fled to West Germany.

The odd thing about him was that he had expressed a personal obsession to kill the Pope. Should they throw Mehmet Ali Agca back to the ocean or give him funds and false papers, along with a gun, and let him run?

In normal circumstances the KGB response would have been the cautious one: Kill him. But circumstances were not normal. Karol Wojtyla, the world's first Polish Pope, was a major menace. Poland was in an uproar; Communist rule there could soon be blown apart by the dissident Solidarity movement.

The dissident Wojtyla had already visited Poland once, with disastrous results from the Soviet point of view. He had to be stopped or discredited. The KGB replied to the Bulgars: Go ahead, but we don't want to know. In May 1981, with money, false papers, and a gun, Agca was escorted to Rome, pointed in the right direction, and given his head. As a result, a lot of people had lost theirs.

"With respect, I do not believe the two can be compared," said Dr. Rogov, who had been the principal architect of Plan Aurora and was prepared to defend it. "The Wojtyla Affair was a disaster for three reasons: the target did not die; the assassin was caught alive; and, worst of all, there was no highly developed, in-place disinformation conspiracy to blame—for example, the Italian or American Extreme Right. There should have been a tidal wave of believable evidence available for release, proving to the world it was the Right that put Agca up to it."

The General Secretary nodded like an old lizard.

"Here," proceeded Rogov, "the situation is different. There are fallbacks and cutouts at every stage. The executant would be a top professional who would end his own life before capture. The physical artifacts are mostly harmless to look at, and none can be traced back to the USSR. The executant officer cannot survive the execution of the plan. And there are subsequent subplans to place the blame firmly and convincingly on the Americans."

The General Secretary turned to General Marchenko. "Would it work?" he asked.

The three committee members were uncomfortable. It would be easier if they could grasp the General Secretary's reaction, then simply agree with it. But he had given nothing away.

Marchenko took a deep breath and nodded. "It is feasible," he agreed. "I believe it would take from ten to sixteen months to put into operation."

"Comrade Colonel?" asked the General Secretary of Philby.

Philby's stutter increased as he spoke. It always did when he was under stress. "As to the risks, I am not best able to judge them. Nor the question of technical feasibility. As to effect—it would, beyond any doubt, swing over ten percent of the British 'floating' vote into a hasty decision to vote Labour."

"Comrade Professor Krilov?"

"I have to oppose it, Comrade General Secretary. I regard it as extremely hazardous, in execution and in its possible consequences. It is completely contrary to the terms of the Fourth Protocol. If that is ever breached, we may all suffer."

The General Secretary seemed lost in meditation, which no one was about to disturb. The hooded eyes brooded behind the glittering glasses for five minutes. At length he raised his head.

"There are no notes, no tape recordings, no shreds of this plan outside this room?"

"None," agreed the four committeemen.

"Gather up the files and folders and pass them to me," said the General Secretary. When this was done, he went on, in his habitual monotone.

"It is reckless, crazy, adventurist, and dangerous beyond belief," he intoned. "The committee is disbanded. You are to return to your professions and never mention either the Albion Committee or Plan Aurora again."

He was still sitting there, staring at the table, when the four subdued and humbled men trooped out. They put on their coats and hats in silence, hardly meeting one another's eyes, and were led downstairs to their cars.

In the courtyard, each climbed into his own car. In his Volga, Philby waited for Gregoriev to start the engine, but the man just sat there. The three other limousines swept out of the square, under the arch, and into the boulevard. There was a tap on Philby's window. He wound it down to see the face of Major Pavlov.

"Would you come with me, please, Comrade Colonel?"

Philby's heart sank. He understood now that he knew too much; he was the one foreigner in the group. The General Secretary had a reputation for tying up loose ends rather permanently. He followed Major Pavlov back into the building. Two minutes later he was shown into the General Secretary's sitting room. The old man was still in his wheelchair at the low coffee table. He gestured Philby to a seat. In trepidation the British traitor took it.

"What did you really think of it?" asked the General Secretary softly.

Philby swallowed hard. "Ingenious, audacious, hazardous, but, if it worked, effective," he said.

"It's brilliant," murmured the General Secretary. "And it is going ahead. But under my personal auspices. This is to be no one else's operation, just mine. And you will be closely involved in it."

"May I ask one thing?" Philby ventured. "Why me? I am a foreigner. Even though I have served the Soviet Union all my life and have lived here for a third of it, I am still a foreigner."

"Precisely," replied the General Secretary, "and you have no patronage except mine. You could not begin to conspire against me.

"You will take leave of your wife and family and dismiss your driver. You will take up residence in the guest suite at my dacha at Usovo. There you will put together the team that will undertake Plan Aurora. You will have any authority you need—it will come from my office at the Central Committee. You, personally, will not show yourself." He pressed a buzzer under the table. "You will work at all times under the eye of this man. I believe you already know him."

The door had opened. In it stood the impassive, cold Major Pavlov.

"He is highly intelligent and extremely suspicious," said the General Secretary with approval. "He is also totally loyal. He happens to be my nephew."

As Philby rose to accompany the major, the General Secretary held out a slip of paper to him. It was a flimsy from the First Chief Directorate marked for the personal attention of the General Secretary of the CPSU. Philby read it with disbelief.

"Yes," said the General Secretary, "it reached me yesterday. You will not have General Marchenko's ten to sixteen months. It appears that Mrs. Thatcher is going to make her move in June. We must make ours one week before that."

Philby let out his breath slowly. In 1917 it had taken ten days to complete the Russian Revolution. Britain's greatest turncoat of them all was being given just ninety days to guarantee the British one.

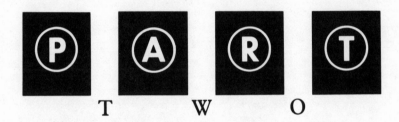

PART

TWO

CHAPTER

When John Preston landed at Jan Smuts Airport on the morning of March 13, the local head of station, a tall, thin, blond man named Dennis Grey, was there to meet him. From the observation terrace two South African NIS men watched his arrival but made no move to come closer.

Customs and immigration were a formality, and within thirty minutes of touchdown the two Englishmen were speeding north to Pretoria. Preston looked at the landscape of the highveld with curiosity; it did not look much like his impression of Africa—just a modern six-lane blacktop highway running across a bare plain and flanked by modern, European-style farms and factories.

"I've booked you into the Burgerspark," said Grey. "In central Pretoria. I was told you wanted to stay in a hotel rather than at the residency."

"Yes," said Preston. "Thank you."

"We'll go and check in first. We have an appointment to meet 'the Beast' at eleven." The not-too-affectionate title had originally been bestowed upon General Van Den Berg, a police general and head of the former Bureau of State Security, or BOSS. After the so-called Muldergate scandal of 1979, the unhappy marriage of the South Af-

125

rican state's intelligence arm and its security police had been dissolved, to the great relief of the professional intelligence officers and the foreign service, some of whom had been consistently embarrassed by the BOSS's brass-knuckle tactics.

The intelligence arm had been reconstituted under the title National Intelligence Service (NIS), and General Henry Pienaar had moved across from his post as head of Military Intelligence. He was not a police general, but a military one, and while he was not a lifelong intelligence officer like Sir Nigel Irvine, his years garnering military intelligence had taught him there were more ways to kill a cat than by thumping it with blunt objects. General Van Den Berg had passed into retirement, still prepared to tell anyone who would listen that "the hand of God" was upon him. Unkindly, the British had passed his nickname onto the shoulders of General Pienaar.

Preston registered at the hotel on Van Der Walt Street, dumped his bags, had a quick wash and shave, and joined Grey in the lobby at half past ten. From there they drove to Union Building.

The seat of most of the South African government is a huge, long, ocher-brown sandstone block, three stories high, its four-hundred-yard frontage studded by four colonnaded projections. It stands in central Pretoria on a hill gazing south across a valley along whose bed runs Kerk Straat, and the esplanade at the front of the building commands a panoramic view across the valley to the brown hills of the highveld to the south, topped by the squat, square mass of the Voortrekker Monument.

Dennis Grey presented his identification at the reception desk and mentioned his appointment with the chief of Intelligence. In minutes a young official had appeared, to lead them to the office of General Pienaar. The headquarters of the NIS chief is on the top floor at the western end of the building. Grey and Preston were led down interminable corridors decorated in what appeared to be a standard South African civil service brown-and-cream motif with a heavy accent on dark wood paneling. The general's office, at the end of the last corridor on the third floor, is flanked on the right by an office containing two secretaries and on the left by another containing two staff officers.

The official knocked on the last door, waited for the gruff command to enter, and showed the British visitors in. It was a fairly somber, formal office, containing a large and obviously cleared desk facing the door and with four leather club chairs grouped around a low table near the windows, which looked down toward Kerk Straat and across the valley to the hills. There were a number of apparently operational maps coyly covered by green curtains around the walls.

General Pienaar was a big, heavy man who rose as they entered, and walked forward to shake hands. Grey made the introductions and the general gestured them to the club chairs. Coffee was served, but the conversation remained at the level of small talk. Grey took the hint, made his farewells, and left. General Pienaar stared at Preston for some time.

"So, Mr. Preston," he said in almost unaccented English, "the subject of our diplomat Jan Marais. I have already told Sir Nigel, and now I tell you: he does not work for me or my government, at least not as a controller of agents in Britain. You are here to try to find out who he *does* work for?"

"That's my job, General, if I can."

General Pienaar nodded several times. "I have given Sir Nigel my word that you will have our complete cooperation here. And I will abide by my word."

"Thank you, General."

"I am going to attach to you one of my two personal staff officers. He will help you in anything you need: obtain files that you may wish to examine, interpret if necessary. You speak any Afrikaans?"

"No, General, not a word."

"Then there will be some translating to be done. Perhaps some interpreting."

He pressed a buzzer on the table and in seconds the door opened to admit a man of the same physical size as the general but much younger. Preston put him in his early thirties. He had ginger hair and sandy eyebrows.

"Let me introduce Captain Andries Viljoen. Andy, this is Mr. John Preston from London, the man you will be working with."

Preston rose to shake hands. He sensed a thinly veiled hostility in the young Afrikaner, perhaps a mirror of his superior's better-masked feelings.

"I have put at your disposal a room down the corridor," said General Pienaar. "Well, let's waste no more time, gentlemen. Please get on with it."

When they were alone in the office set aside for them, Viljoen asked, "What would you like to start with, Mr. Preston?"

Preston sighed inwardly. The casual first-name informality back at Charles and Gordon was a lot easier to get along with. "The file on Jan Marais, if you please, Captain Viljoen."

The captain's triumph was evident as he produced it from a desk drawer. "We have, of course, been through it already," he said. "I took it out of Foreign Ministry Personnel Registry myself some days ago." He placed a fat file in a buff cover in front of Preston. "Let me summarize what we have been able to glean from it, if this will help you. Marais entered the South African foreign service in Cape Town in the spring of 1946. He has been in the service for forty years—a bit more—and is due to retire in December. He comes from a perfect Afrikaner background and has never come under the slightest suspicion. That is why his behavior in London appears such a mystery."

Preston nodded. He did not need it spelled out any more clearly. The view here was that London had made a mistake. He opened the file. Among the top documents was a sheaf of papers handwritten in English.

"That," said Viljoen, "is his autobiography, a requirement of candidates for the foreign service. In those days, when the United Party under Jan Smuts was in power, there was a much greater use of English than today. Now such a document would be written in Afrikaans. Of course, candidates must be fluent in both languages."

"Then I suppose we had better start with it," said Preston. "While I read it, could you please make a synopsis of his career while in the service? Especially foreign postings—where, when, and for how long."

"All right"—Viljoen nodded—"*if* he did go rotten, *if* he was turned, it probably happened somewhere abroad." Viljoen's stress on the word *if* was just enough to imply his doubt, and the corrosive effect of foreigners upon good Afrikaners came out in the word *abroad*. Preston began to read.

I was born in August 1925 in the small farming town of
Duiwelskloof in the northern Transvaal, the only son of a
farmer in the Mootseki Valley just outside the town. My
father, Laurens Marais, was a pure Afrikaner, but my
mother, Mary, was an Anglo. It was an unusual marriage in
those days, but because of it I was brought up fluent in
both English and Afrikaans.

My father was considerably older than my mother, who
was of frail disposition and died when I was ten in one of
the typhoid epidemics that in those days swept that region
from time to time. My father was forty-six when I was
born, and my mother only twenty-five. He farmed potatoes
and tobacco mainly, and also some chickens, geese,
turkeys, cattle, sheep, and wheat. All his life he was a
strong supporter of the United Party, and I was named
after Marshal Jan Smuts.

Preston broke off. "I suppose all this would not have done his can-
didature any harm," he suggested.

"No harm at all," said Viljoen, looking over the passages. "The
United Party was still in power then. The National Party won the
country only in 1948." Preston read on.

When I was seven I went to the local farm school in
Duiwelskloof, and at the age of twelve went on to
Merensky High, which had been founded five years earlier.
After the outbreak of war in 1939, my father, who was a
keen admirer of Britain and the empire, followed every
item of news about the war in Europe on his wireless set,
sitting on the stoep in the evenings after work. After my
mother died we had become even closer, and I, too, soon
began to yearn to take part in the war.

Two days after my eighteenth birthday, in August 1943,
I said good-bye to my father and took the train to
Pietersburg and then changed for the line south to Pretoria.
My father came as far as Pietersburg, and my last sight of

him was standing on the platform there, waving me off to
the war. The next day I walked into Defense Headquarters
in Pretoria, signed on, and was sent to Roberts Heights
camp for basic training, kitting out, drilling, and small-
arms instruction. There I also volunteered to be red-
tabbed.

"What does 'red-tabbed' mean?" asked Preston.

Viljoen looked up from his writing. "In those days only volunteers
could be sent to fight outside the borders of South Africa," he said.
"They could not be compelled. Those volunteering for combat overseas were given a red tab to wear."

From Roberts Heights I was posted to the Witwatersrand
Rifles/De La Rey Regiment, which had been amalgamated
after the losses at Tobruk to form the Wits/De La Rey. We
were sent by train to a transit camp at Hay Paddock, near
Pietermaritzburg, and attached to reinforcements for the
South African Sixth Division, awaiting transport to Italy.
Finally, at Durban, we were all shipped out on the *Duchess
of Richmond*, up through the Suez Canal, and disembarked
in late January at Taranto.

Most of that Italian spring we were moving up toward
Rome, and it was with the Sixth Division, then composed
of the Twelfth Motorized Brigade and the Eleventh
Armored Brigade, that we in the Wits/De La Rey went
through Rome and began the move on Florence. On July
13 I was forward of Monte Benichi in the Chianti
Mountains with a scouting patrol from C Company. In
thickly wooded country I became separated from the rest of
the patrol after dark and minutes later found myself
surrounded by German troops of the Hermann Goering
Division. I was, as they say, "put in the bag."

I was lucky to stay alive, but they put me in a truck with
some other Allied prisoners and took us to a "cage" or
temporary camp, at a place called La Tarina, north of
Florence. The senior South African NCO, I recall, was

Warrant Officer Snyman. It was not to be for long. As the
Allies advanced through Florence we were suddenly
subjected to a brutal night evacuation. It was chaos. Some
prisoners tried to escape and were shot. They were left
lying in the road as the trucks rolled over them. From the
trucks we were put into railcars built for cattle and went
north for days through the Alps and finally to a POW camp
at Moosberg, twenty-five miles north of Munich.

Even this was not for long. After only fourteen days
about half of us were marched out of Moosberg and back to
the railhead, where we were entrained in cattle cars again.
With hardly any food or drink we rolled across Germany
for six days and nights, and in late August 1944 we were
finally disembarked again and marched to another and
much bigger camp. It was, we discovered, called Stalag
344, and was at Lamsdorf, near Breslau, in what was then
German Silesia. I think Stalag 344 must have been the
worst stalag of them all. There were 11,000 Allied POWs
there, on virtual starvation rations, kept alive mainly by
Red Cross parcels.

As I was then a corporal I was required to join working
parties, and was sent every day with many others by truck
to work at a synthetic-petrol factory twelve miles away.
That winter in the Silesian plain was bitter. One day, just
before Christmas, our truck broke down. Two POWs tried
to fix it while the German guards kept them covered. Some
of us were allowed to jump down near the tailboard. A
young South African soldier near me stared at the pine
forest only thirty yards away, looked at me, and raised an
eyebrow. I will never know why I did it, but the next
moment we were both running through the thigh-deep
snow while our comrades jostled the German guards to
upset their aim. We made the forest line alive and ran on
into the heart of the woods.

"Do you want to go out for lunch?" asked Viljoen. "We have a
canteen here."

"Could we have sandwiches and coffee here, do you think?" asked Preston.

"Sure. I'll ring for it."

Preston resumed the tale of Jan Marais.

We soon discovered that we had in effect jumped from the frying pan into the fire, except that it was not a fire but a freezing hell where the night temperatures sank to thirty below zero. We had our feet wrapped in paper inside our boots, but neither this nor our greatcoats could keep out the cold. After two days we were weak and at the point of giving ourselves up.

On the second night we were trying to sleep in a tumbledown barn when we were roughly jerked awake. We thought it must be the Germans, but with Afrikaans I could understand some German words and these voices were not German. They were Polish; we had been discovered by a band of Polish partisans. They came within an inch of shooting us as German deserters, but I screamed that we were English and one of them seemed to understand.

It appeared that while most of the urban dwellers of Breslau and Lamsdorf were ethnic Germans, the peasants were of Polish stock, and as the Russian Army advanced, numbers of them had taken to the woods to harass the retreating Germans. There were two kinds of partisans: the Communist and the Catholic. We were lucky—it was a group of Catholic resistance fighters who had taken us in. They kept us through that bitter winter as the Russian guns rumbled in the east and the advance came closer. Then, in January, my comrade caught pneumonia; I tried to nurse him through it, but without antibiotics he died and we buried him in the forest.

Preston munched his sandwiches moodily and sipped his coffee. There were only a few pages left, he noted.

In March 1945 the Russian Army was suddenly upon us.
In the woods we could hear their armor rumbling westward
down the roads. The Poles elected to stay in the forests, but
I could take no more of it. They showed me the way to go,
and one morning, with my hands above my head, I
stumbled out of the forest and gave myself up to a group of
Russian soldiers.

At first they thought I was a German and nearly shot me.
But the Poles had told me to shout "*Angleeski*," which I did
repeatedly. They put up their rifles and called an officer.
He spoke no English but after examining my dog tag said
something to his soldiers, and they were all smiles. But if I
had hoped for an early repatriation, I was wrong again.
They handed me over to the NKVD.

For five months, in a series of damp and icy cells, I was
accorded brutal treatment, all of it in solitary confinement.
I was subjected to repeated third-degree interrogations in
an attempt to make me confess I was a spy. I refused, and
was sent naked back to my cell. By the late spring (the war
was ending in Europe but I did not know this) my health
had broken completely and I was given a pallet bed to sleep
on, and better food, though still uneatable by our South
African standards.

Then some word must have come from the top. In
August 1945, more dead than alive, I was taken many miles
in a truck and finally at Potsdam in Germany handed over
to the British Army. They were more kind than I can say,
and after a period in a military hospital outside Bielefeld I
was sent to England. I spent a further three months at
Killearn EMS Hospital, north of Glasgow, and finally in
December 1945 I sailed on the *Ile de France* from
Southampton for Cape Town, arriving in late January this
year.

It was in Cape Town that I heard of the death of my dear
father, my only relative left in the world. It caused me such
distress that my health suffered a relapse and I entered the
Wynberg Military Hospital here at Cape Town, where I
stayed for a further two months.

I am now discharged, given a clean bill of health, and
hereby apply to join the South African foreign service.

Preston closed the file, and Viljoen looked up.

"Well," said the South African, "he has had a steady and blameless, if unspectacular, career since then, rising to the rank of first secretary. He has had eight foreign postings, all the countries firmly
pro-Western. That's quite a lot, but then he's a bachelor and that
can make life easier in the service, except at the level of ambassador
or minister, where a wife is more or less expected. You still think he
went rotten somewhere along the line?" Preston shrugged. Viljoen
leaned over and tapped the folder. "You see what those Russian bastards did to him? That's why I think you are wrong, Mr. Preston.
So he likes ice cream, and he made a wrong-number phone call. A
coincidence."

"Maybe," mused Preston. "This life story . . . There's something odd about it."

Captain Viljoen shook his head. "We've had this file in our hands
ever since your Sir Nigel Irvine contacted the general. We have been
over and over it. It's absolutely accurate. Every name, date, place,
Army camp, military unit, campaign, and tiny detail. Even to the
crops they used to grow before the war in the Mootseki Valley. The
agriculture people confirmed that. Now they grow tomatoes and
avocados up there, but in those days potatoes and tobacco. Nobody
could have invented that story. No, if he went wrong at all, which I
doubt, it was somewhere abroad."

Preston looked glum. Outside the windows, dusk was falling.

"All right," said Viljoen, "I am here to help you. Where do you
want to go next?"

"I'd like to start at the beginning," said Preston. "This place Duiwelskloof, is it far?"

"About a four-hour drive. You want to go there?"

"Yes, please. Could we start early? Say at six tomorrow morning?"

"I'll get a car from the pool and be at your hotel at six," said Viljoen.

■ It's a long haul on the road north to Zimbabwe, but the motorway is modern and Viljoen had drawn a Chevair without insignia, the car usually driven by the NIS. It ate up the miles through Nylstroom and Potgietersrus to Pietersburg, which they reached in three hours. The drive gave Preston a chance to see the great limitless horizons of Africa that impress the European visitor accustomed to smaller dimensions.

At Pietersburg they turned east and ran for fifty kilometers over flat middle veld, with more endless horizons under a robin's-egg blue vault of sky, until they reached the bluff called Buffalo Hill, or Buffelberg, where the middle veld drops to the Mootseki Valley. As they started down the twisting gradient Preston drew in his breath in amazement.

Far below lay the valley, rich and lush, its open floor strewn with a thousand beehive-shaped African huts, the rondavels, surrounded by kraals, cattle pens, and mealie gardens. Some of the rondavels were perched on the side of the Buffelberg but most were scattered across the floor of the Mootseki. Timber smoke eddied from their central smokeholes, and even from that height and distance Preston could make out the African boys tending small groups of humped cattle, and women bent over their garden patches.

This, he thought, was African Africa, at last. It must have looked much the same when the impis of Mzilikazi, founder of the Matabele nation, marched north to escape the wrath of Chaka Zulu, to cross the Limpopo and found the kingdom of the people of the long shields. The road bucked and twisted down the bluff and into the Mootseki. Across the valley was another range of hills, and in their center a deep cleft, through which the road ran. This was the Devil's Gap, the Duiwelskloof.

Ten minutes later they were into the gap and cruising slowly past the new primary school and down Botha Avenue, the principal street of the small township.

"Where do you want to go?" asked Viljoen.

"When old farmer Marais died, he must have left a will," mused Preston. "And that would have to be executed, and that means a lawyer. Can we find out if there is a lawyer in Duiwelskloof, and if he is available on a Saturday morning?"

Viljoen drew up to Kirstens Garage and pointed across the road at the Imp Inn. "Go and have a coffee and order one for me. I'll fill the tank and ask around."

He rejoined Preston in the hotel lounge five minutes later.

"There's one lawyer," he said as he sipped his coffee. "He's an Anglo, name of Benson. His office is right there across the street, two doors from the garage, and he'll probably be in this morning. Let's go."

Mr. Benson was in, and when Viljoen flashed a card in a plastic wallet at Benson's secretary, the effect was immediate. She spoke in Afrikaans into an intercom and they were shown without delay into the office of Benson, a friendly and rubicund man in a tan suit. He greeted them both in Afrikaans. Viljoen replied in his heavily accented English.

"This is Mr. John Preston. He has come from London, England. He wishes to ask you some questions."

Benson bade them be seated and resumed his chair behind the desk. "Please," he said, "anything I can do."

"Can you tell me how old you are?" asked Preston.

Benson gazed at him in amazement. "All the way from London to ask how old I am? As a matter of fact, I'm fifty-three."

"So in 1946 you would have been twelve?"

"Yes."

"Can you tell me, please, who was the lawyer here in Duiwelskloof in that year?"

"Certainly. My father, Cedric Benson."

"Is he alive?"

"Yes. He's over eighty and he handed the business over to me fifteen years ago. But he's pretty spry."

"Would it be possible to talk to him?"

For answer Benson reached for a telephone and dialed a number. His father must have answered, for the son explained there were visitors, one from London, who would like to talk to him. He replaced the receiver.

"He lives about six miles away, but he still drives, to the terror of all other road users. He says he'll be here directly."

"In the interim," asked Preston, "could you consult your files for the year 1946 and see if you, or rather your father, executed the will of a local farmer, one Laurens Marais, who died in January of that year?"

"I'll try," said Benson Junior. "Of course, this Mr. Marais may have been with a lawyer from Pietersburg. But local people tended to stay local in those days. The 1946 box must be around somewhere. Excuse me."

He left the office. The secretary served coffee. Ten minutes later there were voices in the outer office. The two Bensons entered together, the son carrying a dusty cardboard box. The old man had a fuzz of white hair and looked as alert as a young kestrel. After the introductions Preston explained his problem.

Without a word the older Benson took the chair behind the desk, forcing his son to draw up another one. Old Benson placed glasses on his nose and gazed at the visitors over them. "I remember Laurens Marais," he said. "And yes, we did handle his will when he died. I did so myself."

The son passed him a dusty and faded document tied in pink ribbon. The old man blew the dust off it, untied the ribbon, and spread it out. He began to read it silently.

"Ah yes, I remember it now. He was a widower. Lived alone. Had one son, Jan. A tragic case. The boy had just come back from the Second World War. Laurens Marais was going down to Cape Town to visit him when he died. Tragic."

"Can you tell me about the bequests?" asked Preston.

"Everything to the son," said Benson simply. "Farm, house, equipment, contents of house. Oh, the usual small bequests in money to the native farmworkers, the foreman—that sort of thing."

"Any other bequests—anything of a personal nature?" persisted Preston.

"Humph. One here. 'And to my old and good friend Joop Van Rensberg my ivory chess set in memory of the many contented evenings we spent playing together at the farm.' That's all."

"Was the son back home in South Africa when the father died?" asked Preston.

"Must have been. Old Laurens was going down to see him. A long trip in those days. No airliners then. One went by train."

"Did you handle the sale of the farm and the other property, Mr. Benson?"

"The auctioneers did the sale, right out at the farm. It went to the Van Zyls. They bought the lot. All that land belongs to Bertie Van Zyl now. But I was there as chief executor of the will."

"Were there any personal memorabilia that did not sell?" asked Preston.

The old man furrowed his brow. "Not much. It all went. Oh, I recall there was a photograph album. It had no commercial value. I believe I gave it to Mr. Van Rensberg."

"Who was he?"

"The schoolmaster," cut in the son. "He taught me until I went to Merensky High. He ran the old farm school until they built the primary school. Then he retired and stayed here in Duiwelskloof."

"Is he still alive?"

"No, he died about ten years ago," said the older Benson. "I went to the funeral."

"But there was a daughter," said his son helpfully. "Cissy. She was at Merensky with me. Must be the same age."

"Do you know what happened to her?"

"Certainly. She married, years ago. A sawmill owner out on the Tzaneen road."

"One last question"—Preston addressed himself to the old man—"why did you sell the property? Didn't the son want it?"

"Apparently not," said the old man. "He was in the Wynberg Military Hospital at the time. He sent me a cable. I got his address from the military authorities and they vouched for his identity. His cable asked me to dispose of the entire estate and cable the money to him."

"He did not come for the funeral?"

"No time. January is our summer in South Africa. In those days there were few morgue facilities. Bodies had to be buried without delay. In fact I don't think he ever returned at all. Understandable. With his father gone, there was nothing to come back for."

"Where is Laurens Marais buried?"

"In the graveyard up on the hill," said Benson Senior. "Is that all? Then I'll be off to my lunch."

The climate east and west of the mountains at Duiwelskloof varies dramatically. West of the range the rainfall in the Mootseki is about twenty inches a year. East of the range the great clouds beat up from the Indian Ocean, drift across Mozambique and the Kruger Park, and butt into the mountains, whose eastern slopes are drenched with eighty inches of rain a year. On this side the industry comes from the forests of blue gum trees. Six miles up the Tzaneen road Viljoen and Preston found the sawmill of Mr. du Plessis. It was his wife, the schoolmaster's daughter, who opened the door; she was a plump, apple-cheeked woman of about fifty with flour on her hands and apron. She was in the throes of baking.

She listened to their problem intently, then shook her head. "I remember as a small girl going out to the farm, and my father playing chess with farmer Marais," she said. "That would have been about 1944 or 1945. I recall the ivory chess set, but not the album."

"When your father died, did you not inherit his effects?" asked Preston.

"No," said Mrs. du Plessis. "You see, my mother died in 1955, leaving Daddy a widower. I looked after him myself until I married in 1958, when I was twenty-three. After that, he couldn't cope. His house was always a mess. I tried to keep going to cook and clean for him. But when the children came, it was too much.

"Then in 1960 his sister, my aunt, was widowed in her turn. She had lived at Pietersburg. It made sense for her to come and stay with my father and look after him. So she did. When he died I had already asked him to leave it all to her—the house, furniture, and so forth."

"What happened to your aunt?" asked Preston.

"Oh, she still lives there. It's a modest bungalow just behind the Imp Inn back in Duiwelskloof."

She agreed to accompany them. Her aunt, Mrs. Winter, a bright, sparrowlike lady with blue-rinsed hair, was at home. When she had heard what they had to say, she went to a closet and pulled out a flat box. "Poor Joop used to love playing with this," she said. It was the ivory chess set. "Is this what you want?"

"Not quite, it's more the photograph album," said Preston.

She looked puzzled. "There *is* a box of old junk up in the loft," she said. "It went up there after he died. Just papers and things from his schoolmastering days."

Andries Viljoen went up to the attic and brought it down. At the bottom of the yellowed school reports was the Marais family album. Preston leafed through it slowly. It was all there: the frail, pretty bride of 1920, the shyly smiling mother of 1930, the frowning boy astride his first pony, the father with pipe clamped in his teeth, trying not to look too proud, with his son by his side and the row of rabbits on the grass in front of them. At the end was a monochrome photo of a boy in cricket flannels, a handsome lad of seventeen, coming up to the wicket to bowl. The caption read *Janni, captain of cricket, Merensky High, 1943.*

"May I keep this?" asked Preston.

"Certainly," said Mrs. Winter.

"Did your late brother ever talk to you about Mr. Marais?"

"Sometimes," she said. "They were very good friends for many years."

"Did your brother ever say what he died of?"

She frowned. "Didn't they tell you at the lawyer's office? Tut. Old Cedric must be losing his wits. It was a hit-and-run accident, Joop told me. It seems old Marais had stopped to repair a puncture and he was hit by a passing truck. At the time it was thought to be some drunken kaffirs—oops"—her hand flew to her mouth and she looked at Viljoen with embarrassment—"I'm not supposed to say that anymore. Well, anyway, they never found out who was driving the truck."

On the way back down the hill to the main road, they passed the graveyard. Preston asked Viljoen to stop. It was a pleasant, quiet plot, high above the town, fringed by pine and fir, dominated in its center by an old *mwataba* tree with a cleft trunk, and enclosed by a hedge of poinsettia. In one corner they found a moss-covered stone. Scraping away the moss, Preston found the epitaph carved in the granite: *Laurens Marais 1879–1946. Beloved husband of Mary and father of Jan. Always with God. RIP.*

Preston strolled across to the hedge, plucked a sprig of flaming poinsettia, and laid it by the stone. Viljoen looked at him oddly.

"Pretoria next, I think," said Preston.

As they were climbing the Buffelberg on the road out of the Mootseki, Preston turned to look back across the valley. Dark gray storm-clouds had built up behind the Devil's Gap. As he watched they closed in, blotting out the little town and its macabre secret, known only to a middle-aged Englishman in a retreating car. Then he put his head back and fell asleep.

■ That evening, Harold Philby was escorted from the dacha's guest suite to the sitting room of the General Secretary, where the Soviet leader awaited him. Philby laid several documents in front of the old man. The General Secretary read them and laid them down.

"There are not many people involved," he said.

"Permit me to make two important points, Comrade General Secretary. First, because of the extreme confidentiality of Plan Aurora I have thought it wise to keep the number of participants to an absolute minimum. On a need-to-know basis, even fewer would know what is really intended. Second, because of the extreme shortness of time there will have to be some cutting of corners. The weeks, even months, of briefing habitually required for an important 'active measure' will have to be telescoped into days."

The General Secretary nodded slowly. "Explain why you need these men."

"The key to the whole operation," Philby continued, "is the executive officer, the man who will actually go into Britain and live there for weeks as a Britisher, and who will finally carry out Aurora.

"Supplying him with what he needs will be twelve couriers, or 'mules.' They will have to smuggle the items in, either through a customs point or, on occasion, through an unchecked entry point. Each will know nothing of what he is carrying, or why. Each will have memorized a rendezvous, and another as fallback in case of a nonconnect. Each will hand over the package to the executive officer and then return to our territory, to pass immediately into total quarantine. There will be one other man, apart from the executive officer, who will never return. But neither of these men should know this.

"Commanding the couriers will be the dispatching officer, with responsibility to ensure that the consignments reach the executive officer in Britain. He will be supported by a procurement/supply officer charged with securing the packages for delivery. This man will have four subordinates, each with one specialty.

"One of the subordinates will furnish the couriers' documentation and transportation; another will concern himself with obtaining the high technology materials required; the third will provide the milled and engineered artifacts; and the fourth will assure communications. It is vital that the executive officer be able to inform us of progress, problems, and, above all, of the moment he is operationally ready; and we must be able to inform him of any change of plan, and, of course, give him the order to execute the plan.

"In the matter of communications there is one more thing to say. Because of the time element, it will not be possible to proceed through normal channels of mailed letters or personal meetings. We will communicate with the executive officer by coded Morse signals sent on Radio Moscow's commercial wavebands, using one-time pads. But for him to reach us urgently, he is going to need a transmitter somewhere in Britain. It's an old-fashioned and risky system, mainly intended for use in time of war. But it will have to be. You will see I have made mention of it."

The General Secretary studied the documents again, identifying the operatives that the plan would need. Finally he looked up.

"You will get your men," he said. "I will have them traced one by one, the very best we have, and transferred to special duties. One last thing. I do not wish anyone connected with Aurora to make contact in any form with the KGB people inside our rezidentura at the embassy in London. One never knows who is under surveillance, or—"

Whatever his other fear, he left it unsaid.

"That is all."

CHAPTER

Preston and Viljoen convened in their office on the third floor of Union Building the next morning, at the Englishman's request. As it was a Sunday, they had the building almost to themselves.

"Well, what next?" asked Captain Viljoen.

"I lay awake last night, thinking," said Preston, "and there's something that doesn't fit."

"You slept all the way back from the north," said Viljoen grimly. "I had to drive."

"Ah, but you're so much fitter," said Preston. That pleased Viljoen, who was proud of his physique, which he exercised regularly. He unbent somewhat. "I want to trace the other soldier," Preston went on.

"What other soldier?"

"The one Marais escaped with. He never mentions his name. Just calls him 'the other soldier' or 'my comrade.' Why doesn't he give him a name?"

Viljoen shrugged. "He didn't think it necessary. He must have told the authorities at Wynberg Hospital so that the man's next of kin could be informed."

143

"That was verbal," mused Preston. "The officers who heard him would soon have scattered into civilian life. Only the written record remains, and it mentions no name. I want to trace that other soldier."

"But he's dead," protested Viljoen. "He's been in a grave in a Polish forest for forty-two years."

"Then I want to find out who he was."

"Where the hell do we start?"

"Marais says they were kept alive in the POW camp mainly by Red Cross food parcels," Preston said, as if thinking aloud. "He also says they escaped just before Christmas. That would have upset the Germans a bit. It was usual for the whole block to be punished with loss of privileges, including food parcels. Anyone in the block would be likely to remember that Christmas for the rest of his life. Can we find someone who was there?"

There is no formal organization of former prisoners-of-war in South Africa, but there is a brotherhood of war veterans, confined to those who have actually been in combat. It is called the "Order of Tin Hats," and its members are known as "MOTHs." MOTH branch meeting rooms are called "shell holes," and the commanding officer is the "Old Bull." Using a telephone each, Preston and Viljoen began to call every shell hole in South Africa, trying to find anyone who had been in Stalag 344.

It was a wearying task. Of the 11,000 Allied prisoners in that camp, the great bulk had come from Britain, Canada, Australia, New Zealand, and America. The South Africans had been a minority.

Moreover, in the intervening years many had died. Of the MOTHs, some were out on the golf links, others away from home. They got regretful disclaimers and a host of helpful suggestions that turned out to be blind alleys. They stopped for the day at sundown and started again on Monday morning. Viljoen got his break just before noon; it came in the form of a retired meat packer in Cape Town. Viljoen, who was speaking in Afrikaans, put his hand over the receiver. "Guy here says he was in Stalag 344."

Preston took over. "Mr. Anderson? My name is Preston. I am doing some research about Stalag 344. . . . Thank you, very kind. . . . Yes, I believe you were there. Do you remember Christ-mas 1944? Two young South African soldiers escaped from an out-side work party. . . . Ah, you do recall it. . . . Yes, I'm sure it was pretty awful. Do you remember their names? . . . Ah, not in their hut? No, of course, Well, do you remember the name of the senior South African NCO? . . . Good. Warrant Officer Roberts. Any first name? Please try to remember. . . . What? . . . Wally. You're sure of that? . . . Many thanks indeed."

Preston put the phone down. "Warrant Officer Wally Roberts. Probably Walter Roberts. Can we go to the Military Archive?"

The South African Military Archive is found, for some reason, under the Department of Education and is situated beneath 20 Vis-agie Street, Pretoria. There were more than a hundred Robertses listed, nineteen of them with the initial *W*, and seven named Walter. None fitted. They went through the rest of the W. Robertses. Noth-ing. Preston started with the A. Roberts files and was lucky one hour later. James Walter Roberts had been a warrant officer in the Second World War; he had been captured at Tobruk and imprisoned in North Africa, Italy, and finally eastern Germany. He had stayed on in the Army after the war and risen to the rank of colonel. He had retired in 1972.

"You'd better pray he's still alive," said Viljoen.

"If he is, he'll be drawing a pension," said Preston. "The Pen-sions people might have him."

They did. Colonel (Rt.) Wally Roberts was spending the autumn of his life at Orangeville, a small town set amid lakes and forests a hundred miles south of Johannesburg. It was dark out on Visagie Street when they emerged. They decided to drive down the next morning.

It was Mrs. Roberts who opened the door of the neat bungalow the following day and examined Captain Viljoen's identity card with flustered alarm.

"He's down by the lake, feeding the birds," she told them, and pointed out the path. They found the old warrior distributing mor-sels of bread to a grateful flock of water birds. He straightened up when they approached, and examined Viljoen's card. Then he nod-ded as if to say "Carry on."

He was in his seventies, ramrod-erect, a bristle of white across his upper lip. He was dressed in tweeds and highly polished brown shoes. He listened gravely to Preston's question.

"Certainly I remember. I was hauled up before the German commandant, who was in the devil of a rage. The whole hut lost their Red Cross parcels for that episode. Damn young fools; we were evacuated westward on January 22, 1945, and liberated in late April."

"Do you remember their names?" asked Preston.

"Certainly. Never forget a name. Both were young—late teens, I should think. Both were corporals. One was called Marais; the other was Brandt. Frikki Brandt. Both Afrikaners. Can't recall their units, though. We were all so muffled up, wearing whatever we could. Hardly ever saw regimental flashes."

They thanked him profusely and drove back to Pretoria, for another session at Visagie Street. Unfortunately, Brandt is a very common Dutch name, with its variation Brand, which lacks the terminal *t* but is pronounced the same. There were hundreds of them.

By nightfall, with the aid of the archive staff, they had culled six corporal Frederik Brandts, all deceased. Two had died in action in North Africa, two in Italy, and one in a capsized landing craft. They opened the sixth file.

Captain Viljoen stared wide-eyed at the open folder. "I don't believe it," he said softly. "Who could have done it?"

"Who knows?" Preston replied. "But it was done a long time ago."

The file was completely empty.

"I'm sorry about that," said Viljoen as he drove Preston back to the Burgerspark. "But it looks like the end of the trail."

Late that evening, from his hotel room, Preston called Colonel Roberts. "Sorry to trouble you again, Colonel. Do you recall at all whether Corporal Brandt had any special mate in that hut? My own experience in the Army is that there is usually one close friend."

"Quite right, there usually is. I can't recall offhand. Let me sleep on it. If I think of anything, I'll call you in the morning."

The helpful colonel called Preston during breakfast. The clipped voice came down the line as if he were making a battle report to headquarters. "Remembered something," he said. "Those huts were built for about a hundred men. But we were jammed in there at the end like sardines. More than two hundred chaps to a hut. Some slept on the floor, others had to share a bunk. Nothing poofy, you know, just had to be done."

"I understand," said Preston. "And Brandt?"

"Shared a bunk with another corporal. Name of Levinson. RDLI."

"I beg your pardon?"

"Royal Durban Light Infantry, Levinson was."

Visagie Street came up with the information faster this time. Levinson was not nearly so common a name, and they had a regiment. The file was out in fifteen minutes. His name was Max Levinson and he had been born in Durban. He had quit the Army at the end of the war, so there was no pension and no address. But they knew he was sixty-five years old.

Preston tried the Durban telephone directory while Viljoen had the Durban police run the name through their files. Viljoen got the first lead. There were two parking tickets and an address. Max Levinson ran a small hotel on the seafront. Viljoen called and got Mrs. Levinson. She confirmed that her husband had been in Stalag 344. At the moment he was out fishing.

They twiddled their thumbs until nightfall, when Preston reached him by phone. The cheerful hotelier boomed down the line from the east coast.

"Sure I remember Frikki. Silly bastard did a runner into the woods. Never did hear of him again. What about him?"

"Where did he come from?" asked Preston.

"East London," said Levinson without hesitation.

"What was his background?"

"He never said much about it," replied Levinson. "Afrikaner, of course. Fluent Afrikaans, poor English. Working class. Oh, I remember, he said his dad was a shunter in the railway yards there."

Preston made his good-byes and turned to Viljoen. "East London," he said. "Can we drive there?"

Viljoen sighed. "I wouldn't advise it," he said, "it's hundreds of miles. We're a very big country, you know, Mr. Preston. If you really want, we'll go by plane tomorrow. I'll arrange a police car and driver to meet us."

"Unmarked car, please," said Preston. "And the driver in plain-clothes."

■ Although the headquarters of the KGB is at the "Center," 2 Dzerzhinsky Square, in central Moscow, and though the building is not small, it would be far too cramped to contain even a portion of one of the chief directorates, directorates, and departments that make up this huge organization. So the subheadquarters are scattered all over.

The First Chief Directorate is based out at Yasyenevo, on the outer ring road that circles Moscow, almost due south of the city. Almost all the FCD is housed in a modern aluminum-and-glass seven-story edifice shaped in the form of a three-pointed star, rather like the logo of Mercedes cars.

It was built by the Finns on contract, and was intended for the International Department of the Central Committee. But when it was finished, the ID people did not like it; they wanted to stay close to central Moscow; so it was given to the First Chief Directorate. It suits the FCD admirably, being well out of town and away from prying eyes.

Staffers of the FCD are officially undercover, even in their own country. Since many of them will have to go abroad (or already have been) posing as diplomats, the last thing they need is to be seen coming out of FCD headquarters by a nosy tourist who might put them on candid camera.

But there is one directorate within the FCD that is so secret it is not even based with the rest at Yasyenevo. If the FCD is secret, the S, or Illegals, Directorate is top secret. Not only do its agents not meet their FCD colleagues; they do not even meet each other. Their training and briefing is on a one-to-one basis—just the instructor and one pupil. They do not check in each morning to any office, since that way they might see each other.

The reason is simple in Soviet psychology: Russians are paranoid about secrecy and betrayal—there is nothing particularly Communist about this, it goes back to Tsarist days. The illegals are men (and occasionally women) who are rigorously trained to go into foreign countries and live under deep cover. Unfortunately, some illegals have been caught and have cooperated with their captors; others have defected and spilled all they know. Therefore, the less they know, the better. It is axiomatic in espionage that one cannot betray what or whom one does not know.

The illegals, therefore, are scattered among scores of small flats in central Moscow and report singly for training and briefing. In order to be close to his "lads," the head of the S Directorate still keeps his office at the Center on Dzerzhinsky Square. It is on the sixth floor, three stories above that of KGB Chairman Chebrikov and two above those of the first deputy chairmen, Generals Tsinev and Kryuchkov.

It was to this unpretentious sanctum that two men came on the afternoon of Wednesday, March 18, while Preston was talking to Max Levinson, to confront the director, a seamy old veteran who had been in clandestine espionage all his adult life. What they presented to him did not please him.

"There is only one man who fits this bill," he grudgingly admitted. "He is outstanding."

One of the men from the Central Committee offered a small card. "Then, Comrade Major General, you will detach him from his duties forthwith and require him to report to this address."

The director nodded glumly. He knew the address. When the men had gone he recalled their authorization again. It was from the Central Committee, all right, and though it did not say so in as many words, he had no doubt from whom it came with that kind of authority rating. He sighed resignedly. It was hard to lose one of the best men he had ever trained, a really exceptional agent, but there was no arguing with that particular order. He was a serving officer; it was not for him to question orders. He depressed a switch on his intercom. "Tell Major Valeri Petrofsky to report to me."

■ The first plane out of Johannesburg for East London arrived on time at Ben Schoeman, the small, neat, blue-and-white airport that serves South Africa's fourth commercial port and city. The police driver was waiting in the concourse and led them to a plain Ford sedan in the parking lot.

"Where to, Captain?" he asked. Viljoen raised an eyebrow at Preston.

"The railway headquarters," said Preston. "More particularly, the administration building."

The driver nodded and set off. East London's modern railway station is on Fleet Street, and directly opposite stands a rather shabby old complex of single-story buildings in green and cream, the administration offices. Viljoen's open-sesame identity card brought them quickly to the director of the finance department. He listened to Preston's query.

"Yes, we do pay pensions to all retired railway staff still living in this area," he said. "What was the name?"

"Brandt," said Preston. "I'm afraid I don't have a first name. But he was a shunter, many years ago."

The director summoned an assistant and they all trooped down dingy corridors to the records office. The assistant burrowed for a while and came up with a pension slip.

"Here he is," he said. "The only one we have. Retired three years ago. Koos Brandt."

"How old would he be?" asked Preston.

"Sixty-three," said the assistant after a glance at the card.

Preston shook his head. If Frikki Brandt had been the same age as Jan Marais, and his father about thirty years older, the old man would be over ninety by now. The director and his assistant were adamant. There were no other retired Brandts.

"Then can you find me," asked Preston, "the three oldest pensioners still alive and in receipt of their weekly check?"

"They're not listed by age," protested the assistant, "they're listed alphabetically."

Viljoen drew the director aside and spoke urgently in his ear in Afrikaans. Whatever he said had its effect. The director looked impressed. "Go ahead," he told his assistant. "One by one. Anyone born before 1910. We'll be in my office."

It took an hour. The assistant produced three pension slips. "There's one who's ninety," he said, "but he was a porter at the passenger terminal. One of eighty, a former cleaner. This one is eighty-one. He's a former shunter from the marshaling yards." The man was called Fourie and his address was given as somewhere up in the Quigney.

Ten minutes later they were driving through the Quigney, the old quarter of East London, dating back fifty years and more. Some of its humble bungalows had been well kept up; others were shabby and run-down, the homes of the poorer white working class. From behind Moore Street they could hear the clang of the railway workshops and the shunting yards, where the big trains are assembled to haul freight from the docks of East London up to the landlocked Transvaal via Pietermaritzburg. They found the house one block off Moore Street.

An old Colored woman answered the door, her face like a pickled walnut and her white hair drawn back in a bun. Viljoen spoke to her in Afrikaans. The old woman pointed toward the horizon and muttered something before firmly closing the door. Viljoen escorted Preston back to the car.

"She says he's up at the institute," Viljoen told the driver. "Know what she means?"

"Yes, sir. The old Railway Institute. Now they call it Turnbull Park. Up Paterson Street. It's the social and recreation club for railway workers."

It turned out to be a large, one-story building adjacent to three bowling greens. Beyond the doors, they passed an array of snooker tables and TV rooms before arriving at a flourishing bar.

"Papa Fourie?" said the barman. "Sure. He's out there watching the bowling."

They found the old man by one of the greens, sitting in the warm autumn sunshine nursing a pint of beer. Preston put his question.

The old man stared at him for a while before nodding. "Yes, I remember Joe Brandt. He's been dead these many years."

"He had a son. Frederik—Frikki."

"That's right. Good heavens, young man, you're taking me back quite a bit. Nice kid. Used to come down to the yards sometimes after school. Joe used to let him ride the engines with him. Quite a treat for a lad in those days."

"That would be the mid- to late 1930s?" asked Preston.

The old man nodded. "About then. Just after Joe and his family came here."

"Around 1943 the boy Frikki went away to the war," Preston suggested.

Papa Fourie stared at him for a while from rheumy eyes that were trying to look backward through more than fifty years of an uneventful life. "That's right," he said. "The boy never came back. They told Joe he had died somewhere in Germany. It broke Joe's heart. He doted on that boy, had great plans for him. He was never the same, not after that telegram arrived at the end of the war. He died in 1950—I always reckoned of a broken heart. His wife wasn't long after him—couple of years, perhaps."

"Awhile ago you said, 'Just after Joe and his family came here,' " Viljoen reminded him. "Which part of South Africa did they come from?"

Papa Fourie looked puzzled. "They didn't come from South Africa."

"But they were an Afrikaner family," Viljoen protested.

"Who told you that?"

"The Army," said Viljoen.

The old man smiled. "I suppose young Frikki would have passed himself off as an Afrikaner in the Army. No, they came from Germany. Immigrants. About the middle of the 1930s. Joe never spoke good Afrikaans to the day he died. Of course, the boy did. Learned it at school."

When they were back in the parked car, Viljoen turned to Preston and asked, "Well?"

"Where are the immigration records kept?"

"In the basement of the Union Building in Pretoria, along with the rest of the state archives," said Viljoen.

"Could the archivists up there run a check while we wait here?" asked Preston.

"Sure. Let's go to the police station. We can phone better from there."

The police station is also on Fleet Street; it is a three-story yellow-brick fortress with opaque windows, right next to the drill hall of the Kaffrarian Rifles. Preston and Viljoen put in their request and lunched in the canteen, while up in Pretoria an archivist lost his lunch hour while he went through the files. Happily they had all been computerized by 1987 and the file number came up quickly. The archivist withdrew the file, typed up a résumé, and put it on the telex.

In East London the telex was brought to Preston and Viljoen over coffee. Viljoen translated it, word for word.

"Good God," he said when he had finished. "Who would ever have thought it?"

Preston seemed pensive. He rose and crossed the canteen to speak to their driver, who was at a separate table. "Is there a synagogue in East London?"

"Yes, sir. On Park Avenue. Two minutes from here."

The white-painted, black-domed synagogue, surmounted by the star of David, was empty this Thursday afternoon save for a Colored caretaker in an old Army greatcoat and wool cap. He gave them the address of Rabbi Blum in the suburb of Salbourne. They knocked on his door just after three o'clock. He opened it himself, a stalwart bearded man with iron-gray hair who appeared to be in his mid-fifties. One glance was enough; he was too young. Preston introduced himself and asked, "Can you tell me, please, who was the rabbi here before yourself?"

"Certainly. Rabbi Shapiro."

"Have you any idea if he is still alive and where I might find him?"

"You'd better come in," said Rabbi Blum. He led the way into his house, down a corridor, and opened a door at the end. The room was a bedsitter, in which a very old man sat before a gas fire sipping a cup of black tea. "Uncle Solomon, there's someone here to see you," he said.

Preston left the house an hour later and joined Viljoen, who had returned to the car. "The airport," Preston told the driver, and to Viljoen, "Could you arrange a meeting with General Pienaar for tomorrow morning?"

■ That Thursday afternoon, two more men were transferred from their posts in the Soviet armed forces to special assignment.

About a hundred miles west of Moscow, just off the road to Minsk and set in a large forest is a complex of radio dish aerials and supporting buildings. It is one of the USSR's listening posts for radio signals coming in from Warsaw Pact military units and from abroad, but it can also intercept messages between other parties far outside the Soviet borders. One section of the complex is screened off and is solely for KGB use. One of the men detached for special duty was a warrant officer radio operator from this section.

"He's the best man I've got," complained the commanding colonel to his deputy when the men from the Central Committee had left. "Good? I'll say he's good. Given the right equipment, he can pick up a cockroach scratching its arse in California."

The other posted man was a colonel in the Soviet Army, and if he had been in uniform, which he seldom was, his flashes would have indicated that he was with the artillery. In fact he was more scientist than soldier, and worked in the Directorate of Ordnance, Research Division.

■ "So," said General Pienaar when they were seated in the leather club chairs around the coffee table, "our diplomat, Jan Marais. Is he guilty or not?"

"Guilty," said Preston, "as hell."

"I think I'd like to hear you prove that, Mr. Preston. Where did he go wrong? Where was he turned?"

"He didn't and he wasn't," answered Preston. "He never put a foot wrong. You have read his handwritten autobiography?"

"Yes, and as Captain Viljoen may have pointed out, we, too, have checked everything in that man's career from his birth to the present day. We can find not one discrepancy."

"There aren't any," said Preston. "The story of his boyhood is absolutely accurate to the last detail. I believe he could even today describe that boyhood for five hours without repeating himself once and without being wrong in a single detail."

"Then it's true. Everything that is checkable is true," said the general.

"Everything that is checkable, yes. It is all true up to the point when those two young soldiers dropped from the tailboard of a German truck in Silesia and started running. After that, it's all lies. Let me explain by starting at the other end, with the story of Frikki Brandt, the man who jumped with Jan Marais.

"In 1933 Adolf Hitler came to power in Germany. In 1935 a German railway worker named Josef Brandt went to the South African legation in Berlin and pleaded for an emigration visa on compassionate grounds—he was in danger of persecution because he was a Jew. His appeal was heard and he was granted a visa to enter South Africa with his young family. Your own archives confirm the application and the issuance of the visa."

"That's right." General Pienaar nodded. "There were many Jewish immigrants to South Africa during the Hitler period. South Africa has a good record on that issue—better than some."

"In September 1935," continued Preston, "Josef Brandt, with his wife, Ilse, and his ten-year-old son, Friedrich, boarded ship at Bremerhaven, and six weeks later they disembarked at East London. There was then a large German community and a small Jewish one there. Brandt elected to stay in East London, and sought a job on the railways. A kindly immigration official informed the local rabbi of the arrival of the new family.

"The rabbi, an energetic young man named Solomon Shapiro, visited the newcomers and tried to help by encouraging them to join the Jewish community life. They refused, and he assumed they wished to try to assimilate into the Gentile community. He was disappointed but not suspicious.

"Then, in 1938, the boy, whose name was now Afrikanerized into Frederik, or Frikki, turned thirteen. It was time for his bar mitzvah, the coming-of-age for a Jewish boy. However much the Brandts might wish to assimilate, that is an important ceremony for a man with an only son. Although none of them had ever been to shul, Rabbi Shapiro visited the family to ask if they would like him to officiate. They gave him a flea in his ear, and his suspicions hardened into certainty."

"What certainty?" asked the general, perplexed.

"The certainty that they were not Jewish," said Preston. "He told me so last night. At a bar mitzvah, the boy is blessed by the rabbi. First the rabbi must be convinced of the boy's Jewishness. In the Jewish faith, that is inherited through the mother, not the father. The mother must produce a document, called a ketubah, confirming that she is Jewish. Ilse Brandt had no ketubah. There could be no bar mitzvah."

"So they entered South Africa under false pretenses," said General Pienaar. "It was a hell of a long time ago."

"More than that," said Preston. "I can't prove it, but I think I'm right. Josef Brandt was correct when he told your legation all those years ago that he was under threat from the Gestapo. But not as a Jew. As a militant, activist German Communist. He knew if he told your legation that, he'd never get a visa."

"Go on," said the general grimly.

"By the time he was eighteen, Frikki was completely imbued with his father's secret ideals; he was a dedicated Communist prepared to work for the Comintern.

"In 1943 two young men joined the South African Army and went to war: Jan Marais, from Duiwelskloof, to fight for South Africa and the British Commonwealth, and Frikki Brandt to fight for his ideological motherland, the Soviet Union.

"They never met in basic training, or on the troop convoy, or in Italy, or at Moosberg. But they met at Stalag 344. I don't know whether Brandt had worked out his escape plans by then, but he picked for his companion a young man tall and blond like himself. It was Brandt who initiated that run into the forest when the truck broke down."

"But what about the pneumonia?" asked Viljoen.

"There was no pneumonia," said Preston, "nor did they fall into the hands of Catholic Polish partisans. More likely they fell in with Communist partisans, to whom Brandt could talk in fluent German. They would have led Brandt to the Red Army, and thence to the NKVD, with the trusting Marais tailing along.

"It was between March and August 1945 when the switch took place. All that talk about freezing cells was rubbish. Marais would have been squeezed for every last detail of his childhood and education, and Brandt would have memorized it until, despite his poor written English, he could write that curriculum vitae with his eyes closed.

"The NKVD probably gave Brandt a crash course in English as well, changed his appearance a bit, put Marais's dog tags around his neck, and then they were ready. With his usefulness ended, Jan Marais was probably liquidated.

"The Soviets roughed Brandt up a bit, gave him a few chemicals to make him realistically ill, and handed him to the British at Potsdam. He spent time in a hospital at Bielefeld, and more outside Glasgow. By the winter of 1945 all South African soldiers would have gone home; he was unlikely to run across anyone from the Wits/De La Rey Regiment in Britain. In December he sailed for Cape Town, arriving in January 1946.

"There was one problem. Someone at Defense HQ had sent old farmer Marais a cable to say his son was home at last, having been posted 'missing, presumed dead.' To Brandt's horror a cable arrived—I admit I am guessing here, but it makes sense—urging him to return home. Of course, he could not show himself in Duiwelskloof. He made himself ill again and went into Wynberg Military Hospital.

"The old father would not be put off. He cabled again, to say he was coming all the way to Cape Town. In desperation Brandt appealed to his friends in the Comintern, and the matter was arranged. They ran the old man down on a lonely road in the Mootseki Valley, making it look like a hit-and-run accident while Marais was changing a flat tire. After that it was plain sailing for Brandt. The young man could not get home for the funeral—everyone at Duiwelskloof understood that—and lawyer Benson had no suspicion when he was asked to sell the estate and mail the proceeds to Cape Town."

The silence in the office was disturbed only by the buzzing of a fly on the windowpane. The general nodded. "It makes sense," he conceded. "But there's no proof. We cannot prove the Brandts were not Jewish, let alone that they were Communists. Can you give me anything that puts it beyond doubt?"

Preston reached into his pocket and produced the photograph, which he laid on General Pienaar's desk. "That is a picture—the last picture—of the real Jan Marais. As you see, he was a useful cricketer in his boyhood. He was a bowler. If you look, you will see that his fingers are gripping the ball in the manner of a spin bowler. You will also notice that he is left-handed. I have spent more than a week studying the Jan Marais in London—at close range, through binoculars. When driving, smoking, eating, drinking, he is right-handed. General, you can do many things to a man to change him; you can change his hair, his speech, his face, his mannerisms. But you cannot turn a left-handed spin bowler into a right-handed man."

General Pienaar, who had played cricket for half his life, stared down at the photograph. "So what have we got up there in London, Mr. Preston?"

"General, you have got a dedicated, dyed-in-the-wool Communist agent who has worked inside the South African foreign service more than forty years for the Soviet Union."

General Pienaar lifted his eyes from the desk and gazed out across the valley to the Voortrekker Monument. "I'll break him," he whispered, "I'll break him into tiny pieces and stamp them into the bushveld."

Preston coughed. "Bearing in mind that we British also have a problem because of this man, could I ask you to restrain your hand until you have talked personally to Sir Nigel Irvine?"

"Very well, Mr. Preston," General Pienaar answered, nodding. "I will talk to Sir Nigel first. Now, what are your plans?"

"There is a flight back to London this evening, sir. I would like to be on it."

General Pienaar rose and held out his hand. "Good day, Mr. Preston. Captain Viljoen will see you onto the plane. And thank you for your assistance."

From the hotel, as he packed, Preston made a call to Dennis Grey, who drove up from Johannesburg and took a message for coded transmission to London. Preston had his answer two hours later. Sir Bernard Hemmings would come into the office the next day, Saturday, to meet him.

Preston and Viljoen stood in the departure lounge at just before 8:00 p.m. as the last calls for passengers on the South African Airways flight for London were made. Preston showed his boarding pass and Viljoen his all-purpose ID card. They went through to the cooler darkness of the tarmac.

"I'll say this for you, *Engelsman,* you're a damned good *jagdhond.*"

"Thank you," said Preston.

"Do you know what a *jagdhond* is?"

"I believe," said Preston carefully, "that the Cape hunting dog is slow, ungainly, but very tenacious."

It was the first time that week that Captain Viljoen threw back his head and laughed. Then he grew serious. "May I ask you some-thing?"

"Yes."

"Why did you put a flower on the old man's grave?"

Preston stared across at the waiting airliner, its cabin lights blaz-ing in the semidarkness twenty yards away. The last passengers were climbing the steps.

"They had taken away his son," he said, "and then they killed him to stop him from finding out. It seemed the thing to do."

Viljoen held out his hand. "Good-bye, John, and good luck."

"Good-bye, Andries."

Ten minutes later, the flying springbok on the fin of the jetliner tilted its straining nose toward the sky and lifted off for the north and Europe.

CHAPTER

Sir Bernard Hemmings, with Brian Harcourt-Smith at his side, sat in silence and listened to Preston's report until he had finished.

"Good God," he said heavily, when Preston was silent, "so it *was* Moscow after all. There'll be the devil to pay. The damage must have been huge. Brian, are both men still under surveillance?"

"Yes, sir."

"Keep it that way through the weekend. Make no move to close in until the Paragon Committee have had a chance to hear what we have. John, I know you must be tired, but can you have your report written up by tomorrow night?"

"Yes, sir."

"Have it on my desk first thing Monday morning. I'll reach the various committee members at their homes and ask for an urgent meeting for Monday morning."

■ When Major Valeri Petrofsky was shown into the sitting room of the elegant dacha at Usovo, he was in a spirit of extreme trepidation.

160

He had never met the General Secretary of the Communist Party of the Soviet Union and never had imagined he would do so.

He had had a confusing, even terrifying, four days. Since being detached for special duties by his director, he had been sequestered in a flat in central Moscow, guarded night and day by two men from the Ninth Directorate, the Kremlin Guards. Not unnaturally, he had feared the worst, without having the faintest idea what he was supposed to have done.

Then the abrupt order that Sunday evening to dress in his best suit of civilian clothes and follow the guards downstairs to a waiting Chaika, followed by the silent drive to Usovo. He had not recognized the dacha to which he was brought.

It was only when Major Pavlov had told him, "The Comrade General Secretary will see you now," that he had realized where he was. His throat was dry as he stepped through the door into the sitting room. He tried to compose himself, telling himself he would answer respectfully and truthfully any accusations leveled at him.

Inside the room he stood rigidly at attention. The old man in the wheelchair observed him silently for several minutes, then raised a hand and beckoned him forward. Petrofsky took four smart steps and stopped again, still at attention. But when the Soviet leader spoke, the whiplash of accusation in his voice was missing. He spoke quite softly.

"Major Petrofsky, you are not a tailor's dummy. Come forward into the light, where I can see you. And sit down."

Petrofsky was stunned. To be seated in the presence of the General Secretary was, for a young major, unheard of. He did as he was told, perching on the edge of the indicated chair, back stiff, knees together.

"Have you any idea why I have sent for you?"

"No, Comrade General Secretary."

"No, I suppose not. It was necessary that no one know. I will tell you.

"There is a mission that has to be performed. Its outcome will be of quite incalculable importance to the Soviet Union and the victory of the Revolution. If it succeeds, the benefits to our country will be inestimable; if it fails, the damage to us will be catastrophic. I have chosen you, Valeri Alexeivitch, to carry out that mission."

Petrofsky's mind whirled. His original fear that he was destined for disgrace and exile was replaced by an almost uncontrollable jubilation. As a brilliant scholar at Moscow University, he had been plucked from an intended career in the Foreign Ministry to become one of the First Chief Directorate's bright young men; ever since he had volunteered for and been accepted by the elite Illegals Directorate, he had dreamed of an important mission. But his wildest fantasies had not encompassed anything like this. He allowed himself at last to look the General Secretary straight in the eye. "Thank you, Comrade General Secretary."

"Others will brief you as to the details," the General Secretary continued. "Time will be short, but you have already been trained to the peak of our abilities, and you will have all for the mission that you need.

"I have asked to see you for one reason. There is something that must be put to you, and I have chosen to ask it myself. If the operation succeeds—and I have no doubt it will—you will return here to promotion and honors beyond your imaginings. I will see to it.

"But if anything should go wrong, if the police and troops of the country to which you will be sent are seen to be closing in, you will have to take steps without hesitation to ensure that you are not taken alive. Do you understand, Valeri Alexeivitch?"

"Yes, I do, Comrade General Secretary."

"To be taken alive, to be rigorously interrogated, to be broken—oh, yes, it is possible nowadays, there are no reserves of courage that can resist the chemicals—to be paraded before an international press conference—all this would be a living hell, anyway. But the damage of such a spectacle to the Soviet Union, to this your country, would be beyond estimation and beyond repair."

Major Petrofsky took a deep breath. "I will not fail," he said. "But if it comes to it, I will never be taken alive."

The General Secretary pressed a buzzer beneath the table and the door opened. Major Pavlov stood there.

"Now go, young man. You will be told here in this house, by a man whom you may have seen before, what the mission involves. Then you will go to another place for intensive briefing. We will not meet again—until you return."

When the door closed upon the two majors of the KGB, the General Secretary stared for a while into the flickering flames of the log fire. Such a fine young man, he thought. Such a pity.

As Petrofsky followed Major Pavlov down two long corridors to the guest wing, he felt as if his ribcage could scarcely contain the emotions of expectation and pride within it.

Major Valeri Alexeivitch Petrofsky was a Russian soldier and a patriot. Steeped in the English language, he had heard the phrase "to die for God, King, and country" and he understood its meaning. He had no God, but he had been entrusted with a mission by the leader of his country, and he was determined, as he walked down that corridor at Usovo, that if the moment should ever come he would not shrink from what had to be done.

Major Pavlov stopped at a door, knocked, and pushed it open. He stood aside to let Petrofsky enter. Then he closed the door and withdrew.

A white-haired man rose from a chair beside a table covered by notes and maps, and came forward. He smiled, holding out his hand. "So you are Major Petrofsky."

Petrofsky was surprised by the stutter. He knew the face, though they had never met. In the folklore of the FCD this man was one who younger entrants were taught was one of the "Five Stars," a man to be respected, a man who represented one of the great triumphs of Soviet ideology over capitalism. "Yes, Comrade Colonel," he said.

Philby had read the file until he knew it perfectly. Petrofsky was only thirty-six and had been trained for a decade to pass for an Englishman. He had twice been in Britain on familiarization trips, each time living under deep cover, each time going nowhere near the Soviet Embassy, and each time undertaking no mission at all. Such familiarization trips were intended simply to enable illegals, before they went operational, to acclimatize themselves to everything they would one day see again; simple things, opening a bank account, having a scrape with another car driver and knowing what to do, using the London Underground, and always improving the use of modern slang phrases.

Philby knew that the young man in front of him not only spoke perfect English but was tone-perfect in four regional accents and had faultless command of Welsh and Irish. He dropped into English himself.

"Sit down," he said. "Now, I am simply going to describe to you the broad outlines of the mission. Others will give you all the details. Time will be short, desperately short, so you will have to absorb everything faster than ever before in your life."

As they talked, Philby realized that after thirty years away from his native land, and despite reading every newspaper and magazine from Britain that he could lay hands on, it was he who was out of practice, he whose phraseology was stilted and old-fashioned. The young Russian spoke like a modern Englishman of his age.

It took two hours for Philby to outline the plan called Aurora and what it involved. Petrofsky drank in the details. He was excited and amazed by the audacity of it.

"You will spend the next few days with a team of four men only. They will brief you on a whole range of names, places, dates, transmission times, rendezvous, and backup rendezvous. You will memorize them all. The only thing you will have to take in with you will be a block of one-time pads. Well, that's it."

Petrofsky sat nodding at what he had been told. "I have promised the Comrade General Secretary that I will not fail," he said. "It will be done, as required and on time. If the components arrive, it will be done."

Philby rose. "Good, then I will have you driven back to Moscow to the place where you will spend the time remaining until your departure."

As Philby crossed the room to the house phone, Petrofsky was startled by a loud *coo* from the corner. He turned to see a large cage from which a handsome pigeon with a splint on one leg was regarding them. Philby grinned apologetically. "I call him Hopalong," he said as he dialed for Major Pavlov to return. "Found him in the street last winter with a broken wing and leg. The wing has mended but the leg keeps giving trouble."

Petrofsky crossed to the cage and scratched the bars with a fingernail. But the pigeon waddled away to the far side. The door opened to admit Major Pavlov. As usual he said nothing, but gestured Petrofsky to follow him.

"Until we meet again, good luck," said Philby.

■ On Monday, March 23, the members of the Paragon Committee assembled to read Preston's report.

"So," said Sir Anthony Plumb, opening the discussion, "now at least we know what, where, when, and who. We still don't know why."

"Nor how much," interposed Sir Patrick Strickland. "The damage assessment is still unattempted and we simply have got to inform our allies. Even though nothing sensitive—save for one fictitious paper—has gone on its way to Moscow since January."

"Agreed," said Sir Anthony. "All right, gentlemen, I think we must concur that the time for further investigation is over. How do we handle this man? Any ideas? Brian?"

Brian Harcourt-Smith was without his Director-General, and represented MI5 alone. He chose his words carefully. "We take the view that with Berenson, Marais, and the cutout Benotti the ring is complete. It seems to the Security Service that it is unlikely there were more agents being run by this one ring. Berenson would have been so important, it seems to us likely the entire ring was set up to handle him alone."

There were nods of agreement around the table.

"And your recommendation?" asked Sir Anthony.

"That we pick them all up, roll up the whole ring," said Harcourt-Smith.

"There's a foreign diplomat involved," objected Sir Hubert Villiers of the Home Office.

"I think Pretoria may be prepared to waive immunity in this case," said Sir Patrick Strickland. "General Pienaar must have reported all this to Mr. Botha by now. They'll no doubt want Marais when we have had a chat with him."

"Well, that seems decisive enough," said Sir Anthony. "How about you, Nigel?"

Sir Nigel Irvine had been staring at the ceiling as if lost in thought. At the question he seemed to wake up. "I was just wondering," he said quietly. "We pick them up. Then what?"

"Interrogation," said Harcourt-Smith crisply. "We can begin damage assessment and inform our allies of the roundup of the entire ring to sweeten the pill a bit."

"Yes," said Sir Nigel, "it's good. But what after that?" He began to address the secretaries of the three ministries and the Cabinet. "It seems to me we have four choices. We can pick up Berenson and formally charge him under the Official Secrets Act, which we'll have to do if we arrest him. But do we actually have a case that will stand up in court? We know we are right, but can we prove it against a first-class legal defense? Apart from anything else, a formal arrest and charge would cause a major scandal, which would be certain to rebound against the government."

Sir Martin Flannery, the Cabinet Secretary, took the point. Unlike anyone else in the room, he knew of the intention to hold a snap summer election, because the Prime Minister had told him in strictest confidence. A lifelong civil servant of the old school, Sir Martin had offered his total loyalty to the present government, as he had to three previous governments, two of them Labour. He would offer that same loyalty to any democratically elected successor government. He pursed his lips.

"Then," resumed Sir Nigel, "we could leave Berenson and Marais in place, but seek to feed Berenson doctored documents to pass on to Moscow. But that wouldn't work for long. Berenson is too highly placed and knowledgeable to be fooled by that."

Sir Peregrine Jones nodded. He knew that on that point Sir Nigel was right.

"Or we could pick Berenson up and try to get his complete cooperation in damage assessment by offering him immunity from prosecution. Personally, I hate immunity for traitors. You never know whether they have told you the whole truth or have tricked you, as Blunt did. And it always gets out eventually, with an even worse scandal."

Sir Hubert Villiers, whose ministry contained the law officers to the crown, frowned in agreement. He, too, hated immunity deals, and they all knew the Prime Minister felt the same.

"That seems to leave," continued the Chief of the SIS smoothly, "the question of detention without trial, and rigorous interrogation. In a word, third degree. I suppose I'm just old-fashioned, but I've never had much confidence in it. He might admit to fifty documents, but we'd none of us know to the day we died if there weren't another fifty."

There was silence for a while.

"They're all pretty unpleasant," agreed Sir Anthony Plumb, "but it looks as if we'll have to go with Brian's suggestion if there aren't any others."

"There might just be one," said Sir Nigel gently. "It could be, you know, that Berenson's recruitment was a genuine false-flag approach."

Most of those present knew what a false-flag recruitment was, but Sir Hubert Villiers of the Home Office and Sir Martin Flannery of the Cabinet frowned in puzzlement. Sir Nigel explained.

"It involves the recruitment of a source by men who pretend to be working for one country, with whom the subject is sympathetic, while in reality they are working for another. The Israeli Mossad are particular experts at this technique. Being able to produce agents who can pass for just about any nationality under the sun, the Israelis have worked some remarkable 'stings' with false flags.

"For example: A loyal West German working in the Middle East is approached while on furlough at home by two fellow Germans who, with impeccable supporting evidence, prove to him that they represent the BND, the West German intelligence arm. They spin him a tale to the effect that a Frenchman working on the same project as he is passing technology secrets that are patently forbidden by NATO. Would the German help his own country by reporting back on what is going on? As a loyal German he agrees, and spends years working for Mossad. Such things have happened many times.

"It makes sense, you know," pursued Sir Nigel. "We've all been through Berenson's file until we are no doubt sick of it. But with what we now know, the false-flag technique could be the answer."

There were several nods as they recalled the contents of Berenson's file. He had started his career, straight out of the university, in the Foreign Office. He had progressed quite well, serving abroad on three occasions and rising steadily, if not spectacularly, in the diplomatic corps.

In the mid-1960s he had married Lady Fiona Glen and shortly afterward had been posted to Pretoria, where he was accompanied by his new wife. It was probably there, confronted by the traditional and almost limitless South African hospitality, that he had developed his deep sympathy and admiration for that country. With a Labour government in power in Britain and Rhodesia in rebellion,

Berenson's increasingly outspoken admiration of Pretoria had not gone down very well at home.

On his return to Britain in 1969, word had apparently reached him that his next posting was likely to be somewhere less controversial—say, to Bolivia. The men around the table could only surmise, but it was perfectly likely that Lady Fiona, while prepared to take Pretoria in her stride, had put her foot down flatly at the idea of leaving her beloved horses and social life to spend three years halfway up the Andes.

Whatever had been the reason, George Berenson had applied for a transfer to the Ministry of Defense, which was regarded in the Foreign Office as going down-market. But with his wife's fortune, he didn't care. With the constraints of the diplomatic service removed from his life, he had become a member of several pro–South African friendship societies, usually the preserve of those politically of the right wing.

Sir Peregrine Jones, at least, knew that Berenson's known and too-overt right-wing sympathies had made it impossible for him, Jones, to recommend Berenson for a knighthood, something he now realized might well have fueled Berenson's resentment.

When reading the report an hour earlier, the senior civil servants had assumed Berenson's pro–South African sympathies to be the cover of a secret Soviet sympathizer. Now Sir Nigel Irvine's suggestion had put a different cast on things.

"A false flag?" mused Sir Paddy Strickland. "You mean he really thought he was passing secrets to South Africa?"

"I am seized by this enigma," said the Chief of the SIS. "If he was a secret Soviet sympathizer or closet Communist all along, why didn't the Center run him with a Soviet controller? I can think of five in their embassy who could have done the job equally well."

"Well, I confess I don't know," said Sir Anthony Plumb. At that moment he glanced up and looked down the table, catching Sir Nigel's eye. Irvine dropped one eyelid quickly down and then back up again. Sir Anthony forced his gaze back to the Berenson file in front of him. You cunning bastard, Nigel, he thought, you're not speculating at all. You actually know.

In fact, two days earlier, Andreyev had reported something interesting. It was not much, just canteen scuttlebutt from inside the Soviet Embassy. Andreyev had been drinking with the Line N man and discussing tradecraft in general. He had mentioned the usefulness, on occasion, of false-flag recruitment; the Illegals Directorate representative had laughed, winked, and tapped the side of his nose with a forefinger. Andreyev took the gesture to mean that there *was* a false-flag operation going on in London at that moment of which the Line N man knew something. Sir Nigel, when he heard, had taken the same view.

Another thought occurred to Sir Anthony. If you really do know, Nigel, it must be because you have a source right inside their rezidentura. You old fox. Then another thought, which was less pleasant: Why not say so outright? They were all completely reliable around that table, were they not? A cold worm of unease stirred inside him. He looked up. "Well, I think we should seriously consider Nigel's suggestion. It does make sense. What have you in mind, Nigel?"

"The man's a traitor, no doubt about that. If he's presented with the documents that were anonymously returned to us, I've no doubt he'll be pretty shaken. But if he's then given John Preston's South Africa file to read, and he *did* think he was working for Pretoria, I don't think he'll be able to mask his collapse. However, if he *was* a secret Communist all along, he'll have known the truth about Marais, so it won't come as a surprise to him. I think a trained observer should be able to tell the difference."

"And if it *was* a false-flag approach?" asked Sir Perry Jones.

"Then I think we'll get his complete and unstinted cooperation in damage assessment. More, I think he could be persuaded to 'turn' voluntarily, enabling us to mount a major disinformation operation against Moscow. Now *that* we could take to our allies as a big plus."

Sir Paddy Strickland of the Foreign Office was won over. It was agreed to pursue Sir Nigel's tactic.

"One last thing: who goes to see him?" asked Sir Anthony.

Sir Nigel coughed delicately. "Well, of course, it's really up to Five," he said, "But a disinformation operation against the Center would be for Six to handle. Then again, I happen to know the man. Actually, we were at school together."

"Good Lord," exclaimed Plumb. "He's a bit younger than you, isn't he?"

"Five years, actually. He used to clean my boots."

"All right. Are we agreed? Anyone against? You've got it, Nigel. You take him, he's yours. Tell us how you get on."

■ On Tuesday, March 24, a South African tourist from Johannesburg arrived at London's Heathrow Airport, where he passed through the formalities without difficulty. As he emerged from the customs hall carrying his suitcase, a young man moved forward and murmured a question in his ear. The burly South African nodded in confirmation. The younger man took his bag and led him outside to a waiting car.

Instead of heading toward London, the driver took the M25 ring road and then the M3 toward Hampshire. An hour later they drew up in front of a handsome country house outside Basingstoke. The South African, relieved of his coat, was ushered into the library. From a seat by the fire an Englishman in country tweeds and of the same age rose to greet him.

"Henry Pienaar, how good to see you again. It's been too long. Welcome to England."

"Nigel, how have you been keeping?"

The heads of the two intelligence services had an hour before lunch was called, so after the usual preliminaries they settled down to discuss the problem that had brought General Pienaar to the country house maintained by the SIS for the hospitality of notable but clandestine guests.

By evening Sir Nigel Irvine had secured the agreement he sought. The South Africans would agree to leave Jan Marais in place to give Irvine a chance to mount a major disinformation exercise through George Berenson, assuming he would play ball.

The British would keep Marais under total surveillance; it was their responsibility to ensure that Marais would have no chance to do a moonlight flit to Moscow, since the South Africans now had their own damage assessment to face—forty years' worth of it.

It was further agreed that when the disinformation exercise had run its course, Irvine would inform Pienaar that Marais was no longer needed. The South African would be called home, the British would "house" him aboard the South African jet, and Pienaar's men would make the arrest when the jet was airborne—that is, on South African sovereign territory.

After dinner, Sir Nigel excused himself; his car was waiting. Pienaar would spend the night, do some shopping in London's West End the next day, and take the evening flight home.

"Just don't let him go," said General Pienaar as he saw Sir Nigel off at the door. "I want that bastard back home by the end of the year."

"You'll have him," promised Sir Nigel. "Just don't spook him in the meantime."

■ While the head of the NIS was trying to find something on Bond Street for Mrs. Pienaar, John Preston was at Charles Street for a meeting with Brian Harcourt-Smith. The Deputy Director-General was in his most eager-to-please mood.

"Well, John, I gather congratulations are in order. The committee was most impressed by your revelations from South Africa."

"Thanks, Brian."

"Yes, indeed. It'll all be handled by the committee from now on. Can't say exactly what's to be done, but Tony Plumb asked me to pass on his personal sentiments. Now"—he spread his hands flat and placed them on his blotter—"to the future."

"The future?"

"You see, I'm in a bit of a dilemma. You've been on this case for eight weeks, some of the time out on the streets with the watchers, most of it in the basement at Cork, and then South Africa. During all this time young March, your number two, has been running C1(A), and doing very well into the bargain.

"Now, I ask myself, what am I supposed to do with him? I don't think it would be quite fair to bang him back to the two slot—after all, he's been around to all the ministries, made some extremely useful suggestions and a couple of very positive changes."

He would, thought Preston. March was a young eager beaver, very much one of Harcourt-Smith's protégés.

"Anyway, I know you've only been at C1(A) for eleven weeks, and that's pretty short, but seeing as you've covered yourself with glory, it might be a well-judged moment to move on. I've had a word with Personnel, and as luck would have it, Cranley at C5(C) is taking early retirement at the end of the week. His wife, you know, has not been well for a long time and he wants to take her off to the Lake District. So he's taking his pension and leaving. I thought it would suit you."

Preston pondered. "C5(C)? Ports and airports?" he queried.

It was another liaison job. Immigration, Customs, Special Branch, Serious Crimes Squad, Narcotics Squad—all monitored ports and airports, checking on various kinds of unsavory characters seeking to bring themselves or their illicit cargoes into the country. Preston suspected that C5(C) would have to try to pick up whatever did not fall into anyone else's category.

Harcourt-Smith raised an admonitory finger. "It's important, John. The special responsibility, of course, is to keep a weather eye open for Sovbloc illegals and couriers—and so forth. It gets one out and about—the sort of thing you like."

And away from the head office while the struggle for the succession to the director-generalship of Five goes on, thought Preston. Preston was a Hemmings man down the line, and he was aware that Harcourt-Smith knew it. He thought of protesting, of demanding a meeting with Sir Bernard to put his case for staying where he was.

"Anyway, I want you to give it a try," said Harcourt-Smith. "It's still in Gordon, so you won't have to move."

Preston knew he was outmaneuvered. Harcourt-Smith had spent half a lifetime working the head-office system. At least, Preston thought, he could be a field man again, even if it was what he termed another "policeman's job."

"I'll expect you to start on the first of the month, then," concluded Harcourt-Smith.

■ That Friday, March 27, Major Valeri Petrofsky slipped quietly into Britain.

He had flown from Moscow to Zurich with Swedish identity papers, dropped them into a sealed envelope addressed to a KGB safe house in that city, and adopted the papers identifying him as a Swiss engineer that were waiting for him in another envelope deposited

with the post office in the airport concourse. From Zurich he had
flown to Dublin.

On the same flight was his escort, who neither knew nor cared
what his charge was doing. The escort was simply carrying out his
orders. In a room at Dublin's International Airport Hotel, the two
men came together. Petrofsky stripped to the skin and handed back
his European-style clothes. He put on what the escort had brought
in his own suitcase—British clothes from top to toe, plus an overnight case filled with the usual medley of pajamas, toilet articles,
half-read novel, and change of clothes.

The escort had already plucked an envelope from the airport's
messages board that had been prepared by the Line N man at the
Dublin embassy and pinned to the notice board four hours earlier.
It contained a ticket stub for the previous evening's performance at
the Eblana Theatre, a receipt for an overnight stay at the New Jury's
Hotel for the previous evening in the appropriate name, and the return half of a London–Dublin round-trip ticket on Aer Lingus.

Finally, Petrofsky was handed his new passport. When he went
back to the airport concourse and checked in, not an eyebrow was
raised. He was an Englishman returning home from a one-day business trip to Dublin. There are no passport checks between Dublin
and London; at the London end, arriving passengers must produce
their boarding pass or ticket stub as identification. They are also
scrutinized by two blank-eyed Special Branch men who affect to see
nothing but miss very, very little. Neither had ever seen Petrofsky's
face because he had never before entered Britain through Heathrow
Airport. Had they asked, he could have produced a perfect British
passport in the name of James Duncan Ross. It was a document that
could not have been faulted by the Passport Office itself, for the
good and simple reason that the Passport Office itself had issued it.

Having passed through customs without a check, the Russian
took a taxi to King's Cross Station. There he went to a luggage locker
for which he already had the key. The locker was one of several
around the British capital maintained permanently by the Line N
man in the embassy. From the locker the Russian withdrew a package, sealed exactly as when it had arrived in the diplomatic bag at the
embassy two days earlier. The Line N man had not seen its contents,
nor had he wanted to. He had not asked why the package had to be

left in a locker in a train station either. It was not his job to question orders.

Petrofsky slipped the package unopened into his bag. He could open it later, at leisure. He already knew what it contained. From King's Cross he took another taxi across London to Liverpool Street Station, and there boarded an early-evening train for Ipswich, in the county of Suffolk, where, just in time for dinner, he checked into the Great White Horse hotel.

Had any curious policeman insisted on looking inside the package stowed in the hand luggage of the young Englishman on the Ipswich train, he would have been amazed. In part, it contained a Finnish Sako automatic pistol with a full magazine and the nose cone of each round carefully cut in the form of an X. The cuts had been filled with a mixture of gelatin and potassium cyanide concentrate. Not only would the rounds expand on impact with the human body, but recovery from the venom would be out of the question.

The other part of the contents consisted of the rest of the legend of James Duncan Ross. A "legend," in term-of-art parlance, is the fictitious life story of a nonexistent man, supported by a host of perfectly real documents of every kind and description. Usually, the person on whom the legend is built did exist once, but died under circumstances that left no trace and caused no stir. The identity is then taken over and fleshed out, as the skeleton of the dead man can never be, by supportive documentation going backward and forward over the life span.

The real James Duncan Ross, or what little was left of him, had been rotting for years in the deep bush bordering the Zambezi River. He had been born in 1950, the son of Angus and Kirstie Ross of Kilbride, Scotland. In 1951 Angus Ross, tired of the cheerless rationing of postwar Britain, had emigrated with his wife and baby son to Southern Rhodesia. An engineer, he had got a job designing agricultural implements and machinery and by 1960 was able to found his own business.

He prospered, being able to send the young James to a good preparatory school and then on to Michaelhouse. By 1971 the boy, with his national service behind him, was able to join his father in the company. But this was Ian Smith's Rhodesia now, and the war against the guerrillas of Joshua Nkomo's ZIPRA and Robert Mugabe's ZANLA was getting more vicious.

Every ablebodied male was in the reserve, and periods spent in the Army became longer and longer. In 1976, serving with the Rhodesian Light Infantry, James Ross was caught in a ZIPRA ambush on the southern bank of the Zambezi and was killed. The ZIPRA guerrillas closed in, stripped the body, and vanished back to their bases in Zambia.

Ross should not have been carrying any identification at all, but just before his patrol set off he had received a letter from his girlfriend and had stuffed it into his combat jacket pocket. It came back to Zambia and fell into the hands of the KGB.

A very senior KGB officer, Vassili Solodovnikov, was then ambassador to Lusaka, and he ran various networks across all southern Africa. One of them picked up the letter addressed to James Ross, care of his parents' home. The first checks into the deceased young officer produced a bonus: British-born, Angus Ross and his son, James, had never abandoned their British passports. So the KGB caused James Duncan Ross to live again.

When, after Rhodesian independence as Zimbabwe, Angus and Kirstie Ross left for South Africa, James apparently decided to return to Britain. Unseen hands withdrew a copy of his birth certificate from Somerset House, in London; other hands filled out and sent in the postal application for a new passport. Checks were made, and it was granted.

In the making of a good legend, scores of people and thousands of hours are expended. The KGB has never lacked the staff or the patience. Bank accounts are opened and closed; driver's licenses are carefully renewed before expiration; cars are bought and sold, so that the name shows up on the Vehicle Licensing Center computer. Jobs are taken and promotions earned; references are prepared, company pension funds added to. One of the chores of junior intelligence staff is to keep this mass of documentation up to date.

Other teams go back into the past. What was the child's nickname? Where did he go to school? What did the boys call the science teacher behind his back? What was the family dog's name?

By the time the legend is complete—and it can take years—and by the time it has been memorized by its new bearer, it would need weeks of investigation to crack it, if it could be done at all. This was what Petrofsky carried in his head and suitcase. He was—and could prove he was—James Duncan Ross, who was moving from the West Country to take over the East Anglian representation of a Swiss-based corporation marketing computer software. He had a handsome bank balance at Barclays Bank, Dorchester, Dorset, which he was about to transfer to nearby Colchester. He had mastered the scrawled Ross signature to perfection.

Britain is a very private country. Almost alone in the world, the British do not have to carry any identification on their persons. If one is asked, the production of a letter addressed to oneself will usually do, as if that proved anything. A driver's license, even though British licenses bear no photograph, is proof positive. A man is expected to be who he says he is.

As he dined that night in Ipswich, Valeri Alexeivitch Petrofsky was perfectly confident, and rightly so, that no one would doubt he was James Duncan Ross. After dinner, he sought from the reception desk the Yellow Pages commercial directory and turned to the section listing real-estate agents.

CHAPTER

While Major Petrofsky was dining at the Great White Horse in Ipswich, the doorbell rang at an apartment on the eighth floor of Fontenoy House in Belgravia. It was opened by the owner, George Berenson. For a second he stared in surprise at the figure in the corridor. "Good Lord. Nigel. . . ."

They knew each other vaguely, not so much from shared school-days many years before as from having seen each other occasionally around the Whitehall circuit.

The Chief of the SIS nodded politely but formally. " 'Evening, Berenson. Mind if I come in?"

"Of course, of course, by all means. . . ."

George Berenson was flustered, though he had no idea of the purpose of the visit. The use by Sir Nigel Irvine of his surname without prefix indicated that the tone of the visit was to be courteous but by no means chatty. There would be no "George" and "Nigel" informality.

"Is Lady Fiona in?"

"No, she's gone off to one of her committee meetings. We have the place to ourselves."

Sir Nigel knew that, anyway. He had sat in his car and watched Berenson's wife leave before making his approach.

Relieved of his coat but retaining his briefcase, Sir Nigel was shown to a chair in the sitting room, not ten feet from the by-now-repaired wall safe behind the mirror. Berenson seated himself opposite.

"Well, now, what can I do for you?"

Sir Nigel opened his case and carefully laid ten photocopies on the glass-topped coffee table. "I think you might, with advantage, have a look at these."

Berenson silently studied the top copy, lifted it to look at the one underneath, and then the third. At the third sheet he stopped and put them down. He had gone very pale but was still in control of himself. He kept his eyes on the papers. "I don't suppose there is anything I can say. . . ."

"Not much," said Sir Nigel calmly. "They were returned to us some time ago. We know how you came to lose them—rather bad luck from your point of view. After they were returned, we kept you under surveillance for some weeks, watched the abstraction of the Ascension Island paper, the passing of it to Benotti and thence to Marais. It's pretty well tied up, you know."

A little of what he said was provable, but most was pure bluff; he had no wish to let Berenson know just how weak the legal case against him was. The Deputy Chief of Defense Procurement straightened his back and raised his eyes. Now comes the defiance, thought Irvine, the attempt at self-justification. Funny how they all run to pattern. Berenson met his gaze. The defiance was there.

"Well, since you know it all, what are you going to do?"

"Ask a few questions," replied Sir Nigel. "For example, how long has it been going on, and why did you start?"

Despite his effort at self-control and defiance, Berenson was still confused enough not to have wondered at one very simple point: it was not the duty of the Chief of the SIS to have this sort of confrontation. Spies for foreign powers were picked up by counterintelligence. But his desire to justify himself overcame his capacity for analysis.

"As to the first, just over two years."

Could be worse, thought Sir Nigel. He knew Marais had been in

Britain for almost three years, but Berenson might have been run by another South African pro-Soviet "sleeper" even before that. Apparently not.

"As to the second, I would have thought it was obvious."

"Let's assume I'm a bit slow," suggested Sir Nigel. "Enlighten me. Why?"

Berenson drew a deep breath. Perhaps, like so many before him, he had prepared his defense inside his own head often enough, arguing before the courtroom of his own conscience—or what passed for it.

"I take the view, and have done for years, that the only struggle on this planet worth a light is the one against Communism and Soviet imperialism," he began.

"In that struggle, South Africa forms one of the bastions. Probably the principal bastion, if not the only one, south of the Sahara. For a long time I have thought it futile and self-defeating for the Western powers, on dubious moral grounds, to treat South Africa as if she were a leper, to deprive her of any share in our joint planning to respond to the Soviet threat on a global scale.

"I have believed for years that South Africa has been shabbily treated by the Western powers, that it was both wrong and stupid to exclude her from access to NATO's contingency planning."

Sir Nigel nodded, as if the thought had never occurred to him. "And you thought it right and proper to redress the balance?"

"Yes, I did. And, the Official Secrets Act notwithstanding, I still do."

The vanity, thought Sir Nigel, always the vanity, the monumental self-esteem of inadequate men. Nunn May, Pontecorvo, Fuchs, Prime—the thread ran through them all: the self-arrogated right to play God, the conviction that the traitor alone is right and all his colleagues fools, coupled with the druglike love of power derived from what he sees as the manipulation of policy, through the transfer of secrets, to the ends in which he believes and to the confusion of his supposed opponents in his own government, those who have passed him over for promotion or honors.

"Mmmm. Tell me, did you begin at your own suggestion, or at Marais's?"

Berenson thought for a while. "Jan Marais is a diplomat, so he is

beyond your power," he said. "There's no harm in my answering.
It was at his suggestion. We never met when I was stationed in Pre-
toria. We met here, just after he had arrived. We found we had a lot
in common. He persuaded me that if a time of conflict with the
USSR ever came, South Africa would have to stand alone in the
Southern Hemisphere, astride the vital routes from the Indian
Ocean to the South Atlantic, and probably with Soviet bases strung
throughout black Africa. It seemed to us both that without some in-
dication of how NATO would operate in these two spheres, South
Africa would be hamstrung, even though she was our staunchest ally
in those parts."

"Powerful argument." Sir Nigel nodded regretfully. "You know,
when we traced Marais as your controller, I took a risk and put the
name straight to General Pienaar. He denied Marais had ever
worked for him."

"Well, he would."

"Yes, he would. But we sent a man down there to check out
Pienaar's claim. Perhaps you ought to look at this." He produced
from his briefcase the report Preston had written on his return from
Pretoria, with the photograph of the boy Marais clipped to the top.

With a shrug Berenson began to read the seven foolscap pages. At
one point he sucked in his breath sharply, pushed his knuckles into
his mouth, and gnawed at one. When he had turned the last page,
he put both open hands up to cover his face and rocked slowly back
and forth. "Oh, my God," he breathed, "what have I done?"

"A hell of a lot of damage, actually," said Sir Nigel. He let Berenson absorb the full measure of his misery without interruption. He
sat back and gazed without pity at the destroyed mandarin. For Sir
Nigel, Berenson was just another grubby little traitor who could take
a solemn oath to his Queen and country, and for his own conceit betray them all. A man of the same degree, if not the scale, of Donald
Maclean.

Berenson was no longer pale, he was ashen gray. When he took his
hands from his face, he had aged by many years. "Is there anything,
anything at all, that I can do?"

Sir Nigel shrugged as if there was little enough that anyone could
do. He decided to turn the knife a few more twists. "There's a fac-

tion, of course, who want you and Marais arrested immediately. Pretoria has waived his immunity. You'd get a middle-class, middle-aged jury—the crown counsel would see to that. Honest people, but not devious. They'd probably never believe in the false-flag recruitment at all. We're talking about life—and at your age that would mean *life*—in Parkhurst or Dartmoor."

He let that sink in for several minutes, then continued: "As it happens, I've managed to keep the hard-line faction at bay for a while. There is another way. . . ."

"Sir Nigel, I will do anything, I mean it. Anything."

How true, thought the Chief, how very true. If only you knew. "Three things, actually," he said out loud. "One: You continue going to the ministry as if nothing had happened, maintain the usual facade, the usual routines, let not a ripple disturb the surface of the water.

"Two: Here in this apartment, after dark and if necessary through the night, you help us with the damage assessment. The only possible way to mitigate the harm already done is for us to know everything, every single thing, that went to Moscow. You withhold one dot or comma, and it'll be porridge and mailbags until you croak."

"Yes, yes, of course. That I can do. I recall every single document that was passed. Everything. . . . Er, you said three things."

"Yes," said Sir Nigel, studying his fingernails. "The third is tricky. You maintain relations with Marais—"

"I . . . what?"

"You don't have to see him. I'd prefer you didn't. I don't think you're enough of an actor to keep up the pretense in his presence. Just the usual contact through coded phone calls when you want to make a delivery."

Berenson was genuinely bewildered. "A delivery of what?"

"Material that my people, in collaboration with others, will prepare for you. Disinformation, if you like. Apart from your work with the Defense people on damage assessment, I want you to collaborate with me. Do some real damage to the Soviets."

Berenson grasped, as a drowning man at a straw. Five minutes later, Sir Nigel rose. The damage-assessment people would be around after the weekend. He let himself out. As he walked down

the corridor to the elevator, he was quietly satisfied. He thought of
the broken and terrified man he had left behind. "From now on, you
bastard, you work for me," he muttered.

■ The young girl in the front office at Oxborrows looked up as the
stranger entered. She took in his appearance with appreciation. Medium height, compact and fit-looking, with a ready smile, nut-
brown hair, and hazel eyes. She liked the hazel eyes.

"Can I help you?"

"I hope so. I'm new to the district, but I've been told you have
houses for rent."

"Oh, yes. You'll want to speak to Mr. Knights. He handles the
rentals. What name shall I say?"

He smiled again. "Ross," he said, "James Ross."

She depressed a switch and spoke into the intercom. "There's a
Mr. Ross in the office, Mr. Knights. About a house. Can you see
him?"

Two minutes later, James Ross was seated in the office of Mr.
Knights. "I've just moved up from Dorset to take over East Anglia
for my company," he began easily. "Ideally I'd like my wife and kids
to come up and join me as soon as possible."

"Perhaps you're looking to buy a house, then?"

"Not just yet. For one thing, one wants to look around for the
right house. Then, the details tend to take a bit of time. Second, I
may only be here for a limited period. Depends on the head office.
You know."

"Of course, of course." Mr. Knights understood completely. "A
short lease on a house would help you to get settled while waiting to
see if you would be staying longer?"

"Exactly," said Ross. "In a nutshell."

"Furnished or unfurnished?"

"Furnished, if you have such a thing."

"Quite right," said Mr. Knights, reaching for a selection of folders. "Unfurnished houses are almost impossible to come by. You
can't always get the people out at the end of the lease. Now, we've
got four that might suit you on the books at the moment."

He offered Mr. Ross the brochures. Two were evidently too large to be plausible for a commercial representative and needed a lot of upkeep. The other two were possibles. Mr. Knights had an hour and drove his client to see both. One was perfect, a small, neat brick house on a small, neat brick road in a small, neat brick housing development off the Belstead Road.

"It belongs to a Mr. Johnson," said Mr. Knights as they came downstairs, "an engineer working on contract in Saudi Arabia for a year. But there's only a six-month lease left to run."

"That should do very well," said Mr. Ross.

The address was 12 Cherryhayes Close. All the surrounding streets had names ending in "hayes," so that the whole complex was known simply as "The Hayes." Brackenhayes, Gorsehayes, Almondhayes, and Heatherhayes were all around. Number 12 Cherryhayes was separated from the sidewalk by a six-foot strip of grass and there was no fence. A garage was attached to one side—Petrofsky knew he would need a garage. The back garden was small and fenced, reached through a door from the tiny kitchen. The downstairs contained the glass-paneled front door, which led into a narrow hall. Straight in line with the front door was the staircase to the upper landing. Under the stairs was a broom closet.

For the rest there was the single sitting room at the front and the kitchen down the hall between the stairs and the sitting-room door. Upstairs were two bedrooms, one front and one back, and the bathroom. The house was inconspicuous and blended with all the other identical brick boxes down the street, themselves occupied mostly by young couples, he in commerce or industry, she coping with the house and one or two toddlers. The place a man waiting for his wife and children to join him from Dorset at the end of the school term would choose and not be noticed very much.

"I'll take it," he said.

"If we can just go back to the office and sort out the details . . ." said Mr. Knights.

The details were easy. A two-sheet formal lease to be signed and witnessed, a deposit, and a month's rent in advance. Mr. Ross produced a reference from his employers in Geneva and asked Mr. Knights to call his bank in Dorchester on Monday morning to clear the check that he wrote out there and then. Mr. Knights felt he could have the paperwork sorted to everyone's satisfaction by Monday evening if the check and the references were in order. Mr. Ross smiled. They would be, he knew.

■ Alan Fox was also in his office that Saturday morning, at the special request of his friend Sir Nigel Irvine, who had called to say he needed a meeting. The English knight was ushered up the stairs at the American Embassy shortly after ten o'clock.

Alan Fox was the local head of station for the CIA and he went back a long way. He had known Nigel Irvine for twenty years.

"I'm afraid we seem to have come across a small problem," said Sir Nigel when he was seated. "One of our civil servants in the Defense Ministry turns out to have been a bad egg."

"Oh, for Christ's sake, Nigel, not another leak," expostulated Fox.

Irvine looked apologetic. "I'm afraid that's what it has to be," he admitted. "Something rather like your Harper affair."

Fox winced. The blow had struck home. Back in 1983 the Americans had been badly hurt on discovering that an engineer working in California's Silicon Valley had blown to the Poles (and thence to the Russians) a vast tract of secret information about the Minuteman missile systems.

Sir Nigel felt that, along with the earlier Boyce spying case, the Harper affair had evened the score somewhat. The British had long tolerated rib-tickling references from the Americans about Philby, Burgess, and Maclean, not to mention Blake, Vassall, Blunt, and Prime, and even after all these years, the stigma remained. It had almost made the British feel a bit better when the Americans had had two bad ones over Boyce and Harper. At least other people had traitors as well.

"Ouch," said Fox. "That's what I've always liked about you, Nigel. You can't see a belt without wanting to hit below it."

Fox was known in London for his acerbic wit. He had early made his mark at a meeting of the Joint Intelligence Committee, when Sir Anthony Plumb had been complaining that unlike all the others he had no nice little acronym to describe his job. He was just the Chairman of the JIC, or the coordinator of intelligence. Why could he not have a group of initials that made up a short word in themselves?

"How about," drawled Fox from his end of the table, "Supreme Head of Intelligence Targeting?"

Sir Anthony preferred not to be known as the SHIT of Whitehall and dropped the matter of the missing acronym.

"Okay, how bad is it?" Fox now asked.

"Not as bad as it might be," said Sir Nigel, and told Fox the story from beginning to end.

The American leaned forward with interest. "You mean he's really been turned right around? He's going to pass over just what he's told?"

"It's either that or spending the rest of his life eating prison porridge. He'll be under surveillance all the time. Of course, he may have a warning code for Marais that he can slip into a phone call, but I think not. He really is of the extreme Right, and it *was* a false-flag recruitment."

Fox pondered for a while. "How high do you reckon the Center rates this Berenson, Nigel?"

"We start damage assessment on Monday," said Irvine, "but I think in view of his eminence in the ministry, he must be rated very high in Moscow. Maybe even as a director's case."

"Could we pass some of our disinformation down the same line?" asked Fox. His mind could already see some useful ploys that Langley would love to pass to Moscow.

"I don't want to overload the circuits," said Sir Nigel. "The rhythm of the stuff passed over must be maintained, as well as the type of material. But yes, we *could* cut you in on this one."

"And you want me to persuade my people to go easy on London?"

Sir Nigel shrugged. "The damage is done. It's very good for the ego to make a hell of a fuss. But nonproductive. I'd like us to rectify the damage and inflict some of our own."

"Okay, Nigel, you've got it. I'll tell our people to back off. We get the damage assessment right off the presses, and we'll prepare a couple of pieces about our nuclear subs in the Atlantic and Indian Ocean that will make the Center look the wrong way. I'll stay in touch."

■ On Monday morning, March 30, Petrofsky rented a small and modest family sedan from an agency in Colchester. He explained that he was from Dorchester and was house-hunting in Essex and Suffolk. His own car was with his wife and family in Dorset, which was why he did not wish to buy a car for such a short spell. His driver's license was in perfect order and gave a Dorchester address. Auto insurance came with the rental, of course. He wished for a long-term lease, possibly for up to three months, and opted for the budget plan. He paid a week's rental in cash, and left a check to cover April as well.

The next problem was going to be harder and would need the services of an insurance broker. He located and visited such a man in the same town and explained his position. He had worked abroad for some years, and prior to that had always driven a company car, so he had no regular insurance company in Britain. Now he had decided to return home and start his own business. He would need to purchase a vehicle and therefore would need insurance coverage. Could the broker assist him?

The broker would be delighted. He ascertained that the new client had a spotless driving record, an international driver's license, a solid and respectable appearance, and a bank account which that very morning he had transferred from Dorchester to Colchester.

What sort of vehicle did he intend to buy? A motorcycle. Yes, indeed. So much easier in dense traffic. Of course, in the hands of teenagers these were difficult to insure. But for a mature professional man there would be no problem. Comprehensive insurance would be a bit difficult perhaps . . . ah, the client would settle for a "third-party" policy? And the address? House-hunting at the moment. Quite understandable. But staying at the Great White Horse in Ipswich? Perfectly acceptable. Then if Mr. Ross would inform him of the registration number of his motorcycle when he made the purchase, and any change of address, he was sure he could secure third-party insurance coverage in one or two days.

Petrofsky returned in his rented car to Ipswich. It had been a busy day but he was satisfied he had raised no suspicions and yet left behind no pursuable trail. The car rental agency and the Great White Horse hotel had been given an address in Dorchester that did not exist. Oxborrows, the real-estate agency, and the insurance broker had the hotel as a temporary address, and Oxborrows knew about

12 Cherryhayes Close. Barclays Bank in Colchester also had the hotel as his address while he was "house-hunting."

He would retain the room at the hotel until he had secured his insurance coverage from the broker, then leave. The possibility that any of the parties would ever be able to get in touch with each other was remote in the extreme. Apart from Oxborrows, the trail stopped at the hotel or at a nonexistent address in Dorchester. So long as payments were kept up on the house and the car, so long as the broker got a valid check for one year's insurance premium on the motorcycle, none of them would think anything of him. Barclays at Colchester had been told to send him statements once a quarter, but by the end of June he would be long gone.

He returned to the real-estate agency to sign the lease and complete the formalities.

■ That evening, the spearhead of the damage-assessment team arrived at George Berenson's apartment in Belgravia to begin their work.

It was a small group of MI5 experts and Defense Ministry analysts. The first task was the identification of every single document that had been passed to Moscow. The team had with them copies of the Registry files—withdrawals and returns—in case Berenson's memory failed him.

Later, other analysts, basing their studies on the list of documents passed, would try to assess and mitigate the harm done, proposing what could still be changed, what plans would have to be canceled, what tactical and strategic dispositions would have to be annulled, and which could stay in place.

The team worked through the night and were later able to report that Berenson had been cooperation itself. What they thought of him privately did not form part of their report, since it was unprintable.

Another group of experts, working deep inside the ministry, bean to prepare the next batch of classified documents that Berenson would pass to Jan Marais and his controllers somewhere inside the First Chief Directorate at Yasyenevo.

■ John Preston moved into his new office as head of C5(C) on Wednesday, bringing his personal files with him. Fortunately he was moving up only one floor, to the third at Gordon. As he sat at his desk his eye caught sight of the calendar on the wall. It was April 1, April Fools' Day. How very appropriate, he thought bitterly.

The only ray on his horizon was the knowledge that in a week his son, Tommy, would be home for the spring vacation. They would have a full week together before Julia, back from skiing with her boyfriend at Verbier, would claim him for the rest of the holiday.

For a whole week his small South Kensington flat would reverberate to the sound of twelve-year-old enthusiasms, to tales of prowess on the rugby field, jokes played on the French master, and the need for further supplies of jam and cake for illegal consumption after lights-out in the dormitory. Preston smiled at the prospect and resolved to take at least four days off. He had planned a few good father-and-son expeditions and hoped they would meet with Tommy's approval. He was interrupted by Jeff Bright, his deputy head of section.

Bright, Preston knew, would have had his job except that his youth simply did not make it possible. Bright was another of Harcourt-Smith's protégés, happy and flattered to be invited regularly for a quiet drink by the Deputy Director-General and to report everything that went on in the section. He would go far under the forthcoming director-generalship of Harcourt-Smith.

"I thought you might like to see the list of ports and airports we have to keep an eye on, John," said Bright.

Preston studied the information put before him. Were there really that number of airports with flights originating or terminating outside the British Isles? And the list of ports able to receive commercial cargo vessels arriving from foreign ports went on for pages. He sighed and started to read.

■ The following day, Petrofsky found what he was looking for. Operating on a policy of making different purchases in different towns in the Suffolk/Essex area, he had gone to Stowmarket. The motorcycle was a BMW shaft-drive K100, not new but in excellent condition, a big, powerful machine, three years old but with only 22,000 miles on the clock. The same shop also stocked the accessories—black leather trousers and jacket, gauntlets, zip-sided jackboots, and crash helmet with dark, slide-down visor. He bought a complete outfit.

A twenty-percent deposit secured him the motorcycle, but not to take away. He asked for saddlebags to be fitted outside the rear wheel, with a lockable fiberglass box on top of them, and was told he could collect the machine with its fittings in two days.

From a phone booth he called the insurance broker in Colchester and gave him the registration number of the BMW. The broker was confident he could have temporary thirty-day insurance coverage by the next day. He would mail the policy to the Great White Horse hotel in Ipswich.

From Stowmarket, Petrofsky motored north to Thetford, just over the county border in Norfolk. There was nothing particular about Thetford; it just lay approximately in the line he needed. He found what he wanted just after lunch. On Magdalen Street, between No. 13A and the Salvation Army hall, is a recessed rectangular yard containing thirty garages. One had a To LET notice stuck on its door.

He traced the owner, who lived locally, and rented the garage for three months, paying in cash, and was given the key. The garage was small and musty, but would serve his purpose admirably. The owner had been happy to take tax-free cash and had asked for no form of identification. Petrofsky had therefore given him a fictitious name and address.

He stored his motorcycle leathers, helmet, and boots in the garage, and during what remained of the afternoon bought two ten-gallon plastic drums from two different shops, filled them with gasoline at two different stations, and locked them in the garage as well. At sundown he motored back to Ipswich and told the hotel receptionist that he would be checking out the following morning.

■ Preston realized he was becoming bored to the point of distraction. He had been in the job only two days, and they had been spent reading files.

He sat over lunch in the canteen and thought seriously of taking early retirement. That presented two problems. First, it would not be easy for a man in his mid-forties to get good employment, the more so since his arcane qualifications were hardly the type that the big corporations would find of irresistible interest.

The second concern was his loyalty to Sir Bernard Hemmings. Preston had been in the service only six years, but the Old Man had been very good to him. He liked Sir Bernard and he knew the knives were out for the ailing Director-General.

The ultimate decision on who will be head of MI5 or Chief of MI6 in Britain lies with a committee of so-called Wise Men. In the case of MI5, these would normally be the Permanent Under Secretary at the Home Office (the ministry that controls Five), plus the PUS at Defense, the Cabinet Secretary, and the Chairman of the Joint Intelligence Committee.

These would "recommend" a favored candidate to the Home Secretary and Prime Minister, the two senior politicians involved. It would be unusual for the politicians to decline the recommendation of the Wise Men.

But before they made a decision the mandarins would take soundings in their own inimitable way. There would be discreet lunches in clubs, drinks at bars, murmured discussions over coffee. In the case of the proposed Director-General of MI5, the Chief of the SIS would be consulted, but since Sir Nigel Irvine was himself moving close to retirement, he would need a very good reason for advising against a leading candidate for the other intelligence service. After all, *he* would not have to work with the man.

Among the most influential of the sources sounded out by the Wise Men would be the outgoing DG of Five himself. Preston knew that an honorable man like Sir Bernard Hemmings would feel bound to take a straw poll of his own heads of section throughout the six branches of the service. That straw poll would weigh heavily with him, whatever his personal feelings might be. Not for nothing had Brian Harcourt-Smith used his increasing dominance in the day-to-day running of the service to place one after another of his protégés at the head of the numerous sections.

Preston was in no doubt that Harcourt-Smith would like him to leave before the autumn, to follow two or three others who had gone into civilian life over the past twelve months.

"Sod him," he remarked to no one in particular in a largely empty canteen. "I'll stay."

■ While Preston was at lunch, Petrofsky left the hotel, his luggage by now augmented by a large suitcase full of clothes that he had bought locally. He told the receptionist that he would be moving to the Norfolk area and that any mail arriving for him should be held pending collection.

He rang the insurance broker in Colchester and learned that the temporary coverage for the motorcycle had been issued. The Russian asked the broker not to mail it; he would collect it himself. This he did immediately, and late that afternoon moved into 12 Cherryhayes Close. He spent part of the night working carefully with his one-time pads, preparing a coded message that no computer would break. Code-breaking, he knew, was based on patterns and repetitions, however sophisticated the computer used to crack the code. Using a one-time pad for each word of a short message left no patterns and no repetitions.

The next morning, Saturday, he drove to Thetford, garaged his car, and took a local taxi to Stowmarket. Here, with a certified check, he paid the balance of the price of the BMW, borrowed the toilet to change into his leathers and crash helmet, which he had brought in a canvas bag, stuffed the bag and his ordinary jacket, trousers, and shoes into the saddlebags, and rode away.

It was a long ride and took him many hours. It was not until late evening that he arrived back at Thetford, changed clothes, exchanged motorcycle for family sedan, and motored sedately back to Cherryhayes Close, Ipswich, where he arrived at midnight. He was not observed, but if he had been, it would have been as "that nice young Mr. Ross who moved into Number Twelve yesterday."

■ On a Saturday evening, Master Sergeant Averell Cook of the U.S. Army would have preferred to be dating his girlfriend in nearby Bedford. Or even playing pool with friends in the commissary. Instead he was taking the swing shift at the joint British-American listening station at Chicksands.

The "head office" of the British electronic monitoring and code-breaking complex is at the Government Communications Head-quarters at Cheltenham, Gloucestershire, in the south of England. But GCHQ has outstations in various parts of the country, and one of them, Chicksands, in Bedfordshire, is run jointly by GCHQ and the American National Security Agency.

The days when attentive men sat hunched into earphones trying to pick up and record the manual tapping of a Morse key operated by some German agent in Britain are long gone. In the business of listening, analyzing, filtering the innocent from the not-so-innocent, recording the latter, and decoding, computers have taken over.

Sergeant Cook was confident, and rightly so, that if any of the forest of aerials above him picked up an electronic whisper, it would pass that whisper to the banks of computers below. The scanning of the bands was automatic and the recording of any whisper in the ether that should not be there equally automatic. If such a whisper occurred, the eternally watchful computer would trigger its own hit button deep inside its own multicolored entrails, record the transmission, take an immediate bearing on its source, instruct other, brother computers across the country to take a crossbearing, and alert Sergeant Cook.

At 11:43 p.m., something caused the master computer to operate its own hit button. Something or someone had transmitted what was not expected, and out of the whirling kaleidoscope of electronic signals that fill the air of this planet twenty-four hours in every day, the computer had noticed and traced it. Sergeant Cook noted the warning signal and reached for a telephone.

What the computer had picked up was a "squirt," a brief shriek of sound that lasted only a few seconds and would make no sense to the human ear. A squirt is the end product of quite a laborious procedure in the sending of clandestine messages. First the message is written out in clear and made as brief as possible. Then it is encoded, but it still remains a list of letters or figures. The encoded message is tapped out on a Morse key, not to a listening world but to a tape machine. The tape is then speeded up to an extreme degree, so that the dots and dashes that make up the transmission are telescoped, to emerge as a single screech lasting only a few seconds. When the transmitter is ready to go, the operator simply sends that single screech, then packs up his set and moves sharply somewhere else.

Within ten minutes that Saturday night, the triangulators had pinpointed the spot from which the screech had come. Other computers, at Menwith Hill in Yorkshire and Brawdy in Wales, had also caught the brief squirt transmission and taken a bearing. When the local police got there, the spot turned out to be the shoulder of a lonely road high in the Derbyshire Peak District. There was no one there.

In due course the message went to Cheltenham and was slowed down to a pace at which the dots and dashes could be transcribed into letters. But after twenty-four hours of going through the electronic brains called the code-breakers, the answer was still a big zero.

"It's a sleeper transmitter, probably somewhere in the Midlands, and he's gone to 'active,' " the chief analyst reported to the Director-General of GCHQ. "But our man seems to be using a fresh one-time pad for every word. Unless we can have a lot more of it, we won't break it."

It was decided to keep a close watch on the channel the secret sender had used, though if he broadcast again he would almost certainly use a different channel.

A brief flimsy recording the incident went to the desks, among others, of Sir Bernard Hemmings and Sir Nigel Irvine.

The message had been received elsewhere, notably in Moscow. Decoded with a replica of the one-time pad used in a quiet backwater of Ipswich, the message told those interested that the man on the ground had completed all his preliminary tasks ahead of schedule and was ready to receive his first courier.

CHAPTER

The spring thaw would not be long in coming, but for the moment crusted snow hung on the branches of the birch and fir trees far below. From the spectacular double-glazed window on the seventh and top floor of the First Chief Directorate building at Yasyenevo, the man gazing at the landscape could make out, across the sea of winter trees, the tip of the western end of the lake where, in summer, the foreign diplomats from Moscow liked to come and disport themselves.

That Sunday morning, Lieutenant General Yevgeni Sergeivitch Karpov would have preferred to be with his wife and teenage children at their dacha at Peredelkino, but even when one has risen as high in the service as Karpov, there are some things that have to be taken care of personally. The arrival of the bagman due home from Copenhagen was such a matter. He glanced at his watch. It was nearly noon and the man was late. Turning from the window, he sighed and threw himself into the swivel chair behind his desk.

At fifty-seven, Yevgeni Karpov was at the pinnacle of promotion and power achievable by a professional intelligence officer within the KGB, or at least within the First Chief Directorate. Fedorchuk had gone higher, right up to the chairmanship itself, and on to the MVD, but that had been on the General Secretary's coattails. Moreover, Fedorchuk had not been FCD; he rarely left the Soviet Union; he had made his bones crushing internal dissident and nationalist movements.

But for a man who had spent years serving his country abroad—always a minus in terms of promotion to the highest offices in the USSR—Karpov had done well. A lean, fit-looking man in a beautifully cut suit (one of the perks of being FCD), he was a lieutenant general and First Deputy Head of the First Chief Directorate. As such, he was the Soviet Union's highest-ranking professional officer in foreign intelligence, on the same level as the deputy directors of operations and intelligence at the CIA and Sir Nigel Irvine at the SIS.

Years earlier, on his accession to power, the General Secretary had plucked General Fedorchuk out of the chairmanship of the KGB to overlord the Interior Ministry, and General Chebrikov had gone up to replace him. A slot had been left vacant—Chebrikov had been one of the two first deputy chairmen of the KGB.

The vacant post of First Deputy Chairman had been offered to Colonel-General Kryuchkov, who had jumped at it. The trouble was, Kryuchkov was then head of the First Chief Directorate and he did not want to relinquish that powerful post. He wanted to hold both jobs together. Even Kryuchkov had realized—and Karpov privately thought the man as thick as two short planks—that he could not be in two places simultaneously; he could not at the same time be in his First Deputy Chairman's office at the Center on Dzerzhinsky Square and in the office of the head of the FCD out at Yasyenevo.

What had happened was that the post of First Deputy Head of the First Chief Directorate, which had existed for years, had increased substantially in importance. It had already been a job for an officer of considerable operational experience, indeed the highest in the FCD to which a career officer could aspire. With Kryuchkov no longer resident at "the Village"—KGB house jargon for Yasyenevo—the job of his first deputy had become even more important.

When the incumbent, General B. S. Ivanov, had retired, there had been two possible candidates in line to succeed: Karpov, then a bit young but heading up the important Third Department in Room 6013, the section that covered Britain, Australia, New Zealand, and Scandinavia; and Vadim Vassilyevitch Kirpichenko, rather older, a bit senior, who headed the S, or Illegals, Directorate. Kirpichenko had got the job. As a sort of consolation prize, Karpov had been promoted to be head of the Illegals Directorate, a post he had held for two fascinating years.

Then, in the early spring of 1985, Kirpichenko had done the decent thing: speeding down the Sadovaya Spasskaya ring road at close to a hundred miles an hour, his car had clipped a pool of oil left by a leaking truck and had gone completely out of control. A week later there had been a quiet private ceremony at Novodevichii Cemetery, and a week after that, Karpov had got the job, rising in rank from major general to lieutenant general.

He had been happy to hand the Illegals Directorate over to old Borisov, who had been number two there for so long few cared to remember just how many years it had been, and who deserved the job, anyway.

The phone on his desk rang and he snatched it up.

"Comrade Major General Borisov on the line for you."

Speak of the devil, Karpov thought. Then he frowned. He had a private line that did not pass through the switchboard, but his old colleague had not used it. Must be phoning from outside. Telling his secretary to bring the bagman from Copenhagen to him the moment he arrived, Karpov depressed the outside-line switch and took Borisov's call. "Pavel Petrovitch, how are you this fine day?"

"I tried you at home, then at the dacha. Ludmilla said you were at work."

"So I am. It's all right for some." Karpov was gently pulling the older man's leg. Borisov was a widower who lived alone and put in more working weekends than almost anyone else.

"Yevgeni Sergeivitch, I need to see you."

"Of course. You don't have to ask. You want to come over here tomorrow, or shall I come into town?"

"Could you make it today?"

Even odder, thought Karpov. Something must have really got into the old boy. He sounded as though he might have been drinking. "Have you been on the bottle, Pavel Petrovitch?"

"Maybe I have," said the truculent voice on the line. "Maybe a man needs a few drams now and again. Especially when he has problems."

Karpov realized that, whatever it was, the problem was serious. He dropped the bantering tone. "All right, *Starets*," he said soothingly, "where are you?"

"You know my cottage?"

"Of course. You want me to come out there?"

"Yes, I'd be grateful," said Borisov. "When can you make it?"

"Say about six," proposed Karpov.

"I'll have a bottle of pepper vodka ready," said the voice, and Borisov hung up.

"Not on my account," muttered Karpov. Unlike most Russians, Karpov hardly drank at all, and when he did, he preferred a decent Armenian brandy or the Scotch single malt that came to him in the bag from London. Vodka he regarded as an abomination, and pepper vodka even worse.

Bang goes my Sunday afternoon at Peredelkino, he thought, and rang to tell Ludmilla he could not make it. He made no mention of Borisov; just told her he could not get away and that he would see her at their central Moscow apartment at about midnight.

Still, he was perturbed by Borisov's unusual truculence; they went back a long way together, too long for him to take offense, but Borisov's mood was odd in a man habitually so genial and phlegmatic.

■ That Sunday afternoon, the regular Aeroflot service from Moscow came into London's Heathrow Airport at just after five.

As with all Aeroflot crews there was one member who worked for two masters, the Soviet state airline and the KGB. First Officer Romanov was not a KGB staffer, only *agyent*—meaning an informer upon his colleagues and from time to time a runner of messages and errands.

The whole crew closed the aircraft down and left it in the hands of the ground staff for the night. They would fly it back to Moscow the next day. As usual, they went through the flight-crew entry procedures, and customs made a cursory check of their shoulder bags and hand luggage. Several were carrying portable transistor radios, and no one took any notice of Romanov's Sony model on its shoulder strap. Western luxury items were part of the perks of foreign travel for Soviet citizens—everyone knew that—and although they had an extremely tight foreign-currency allowance, cassettes and players, along with radios and perfume for the wife back in Moscow, were among the top priorities.

After clearing immigration and customs formalities the whole crew boarded their minibus for the Green Park Hotel, where Aeroflot crews often stay. Whoever had given Romanov that transistor radio in Moscow just three hours before takeoff must have known that Aeroflot crews are hardly ever shadowed at Heathrow. The British counterintelligence people seem to accept that though they may constitute a risk, it must be a tolerable one compared to the mounting of a pretty major surveillance operation.

When he got to his bedroom, Romanov could not help looking at the radio with curiosity. Then he shrugged, locked it in his suitcase, and went down to the bar to join the other officers in a drink. He knew exactly what to do with it after breakfast the next day. He would do it, then forget all about it. He did not know then that on his return to Moscow he would be going straight into quarantine.

■ Karpov's car crunched up the snow-clogged track just before six o'clock, and he cursed Borisov's insistence on having his weekend cottage in such a forsaken place.

Everyone in the service knew Borisov was one of a kind. In a society that regards all individualism or deviation from the norm, not to mention eccentricity, as extremely suspect, Borisov got away with it because he was unusually good at his job. He had been in clandestine intelligence since he was a boy, and some of the coups he had mounted against the West were legendary in the training schools and the canteens where the junior men took their lunch.

After half a mile down the track, Karpov could make out the lights of the *izba*, or log cabin, that Borisov favored for his retreat. Others were content, even eager, to site their weekend places in the approved zones according to their station in the pecking order, and those areas were all west of Moscow, along the curve of the river across the Uspenskoye Bridge. Not Borisov. He liked to retire on the weekends—or on those when he could get away from his desk—to play rustic peasant in a traditional *izba* deep in the forest well east of the capital. The Chaika came to a halt in front of the timber door.

"Wait here," Karpov told Misha, his driver.

"I'd better turn around and get some of those logs under the wheels or we'll stick solid," grumbled Misha.

Karpov nodded his agreement and climbed out. He had not brought galoshes because he had not envisaged wading through snow up to the knees. He stumbled to the door and hammered on it. The door opened to reveal an oblong of yellow light, thrown apparently by paraffin lamps, and in the glow stood Major General Pavel Petrovitch Borisov, dressed in a Siberian shirt, corduroy trousers, and felt boots.

"You look like something out of a Tolstoy novel," remarked Karpov as he was shown into the main sitting room, where a brick stove full of logs gave the cottage a womblike warmth.

"Better than something out of a Bond Street window," grumbled Borisov as he took Karpov's coat and hung it on a wooden peg. He uncorked a bottle of vodka so strong it poured like syrup, and filled two shot glasses. The men seated themselves, a table between them.

"Bottoms up," Karpov offered, raising his glass, Russian style, between forefinger and thumb, pinkie extended.

"Up yours," Borisov replied testily, and they drained the first slug.

An old peasant woman shaped like a tea cozy, looking like an incarnation of Mother Russia with her blank face and gray hair in a tight bun, came in from the back, banged down a collation of black bread, onions, gherkins, and cheese cubes, and left without a word.

"So what's the problem, *Starets*?" asked Karpov.

Borisov was five years older than himself, and not for the first time Karpov was struck by the man's close resemblance to the late Dwight Eisenhower. Borisov, unlike many in the service, was much liked by his colleagues and adored by his young agents. They had long ago given him the affectionate nickname *Starets*, a word that originally meant village headman but now had the connotations of the English "Old Man" and the French *patron*.

Borisov stared moodily across the table. "Yevgeni Sergeivitch, how long have we known each other?"

"More years than I care to remember," said Karpov.

"And in that time, have I ever lied to you?"

"Not that I know of." Karpov was pensive.

"And are you now going to lie to me?"

"Not if I can help it," said Karpov carefully. What on earth had got into the old boy?

"Then what the hell are you doing to my department?" demanded Borisov loudly.

Karpov considered the question carefully. "Why don't you tell me what is happening to your department?" he countered.

"It's being stripped, that's what," snarled Borisov. "You have to be behind it. Or aware of it. How the hell am I supposed to run the S operation when my best men, my best documents, and my best facilities are being stripped from me? Bloody years of hard work—all confiscated within a matter of days."

He had had his explosion, the thing that he had bottled up until now. Karpov sat back, lost in thought, while Borisov filled the glasses. Karpov had not risen as high as he had within the labyrinthine corridors of the KGB without developing a sixth sense for danger. Borisov was no alarmist; there had to be something behind what he said, but Karpov quite genuinely did not know what it was. He leaned forward.

"Pal Petrovitch," he said, dropping into the very familiar diminutive of Pavel, "as you say, we have been around for a good many years. Believe me, I don't know what you're talking about. Will you please stop shouting and tell me?"

Borisov was mollified, although puzzled by Karpov's assertion of ignorance. "All right," he said, as if explaining the obvious to a child. "First, two goons arrive from the Central Committee and demand that I hand over to them my best illegal, a man I've spent years training and of whom I had the greatest hopes. They say he has to be detached for 'special duties,' whatever that may mean. Okay, I give them my best man. I don't like it, but I do it. Two days later they are back. They want my best legend, a story that took more than ten years to put together. Not since that damned Iranian affair have I been treated like that. You remember the Iranian business? I still haven't recovered from that."

Karpov nodded. He had not been with the Illegals Directorate then, but Borisov had told him all about it later when they worked together during Karpov's tenure as its head. In the last days of the Shah of Iran, the International Department of the Central Committee had decided it would be a nice idea to spirit the entire Politburo of the Iranian Tudeh (Communist) Party out of Iran covertly. They had raided Borisov's magpie-hoarded files and confiscated twenty-two perfect Iranian legends, cover stories Borisov had been saving to send people *into* Iran, not get them out. "Stripped to the bone!" he had screamed at the time. "Just to get those flea-bitten wogs to safety." Later he had complained to Karpov, "It didn't do them much good, either. The Ayatollah's in charge, the Tudeh is still banned, and we can't even mount an operation in there anymore."

Karpov knew that the affair still rankled, but the new business was odder. For one thing, any request for personnel or legend should have come to him. "Whom did you give them?" he asked.

"Petrofsky," said Borisov resignedly. "I had to. They asked for the best, and he was way ahead of the others. Remember Petrofsky?"

Karpov nodded. He had headed the Illegals Directorate for two years only, but he recalled all their best names and ongoing operations. In his present post he had total access, anyway. "Whose authorization was on these requisitions?"

"Well, technically the Central Committee's. But from the authority rating . . ." Borisov pointed a rigid finger at the ceiling and, by inference, the sky.

"God?" queried Karpov.

"Almost. Our beloved General Secretary. At least, that's my guess."

"Anything else?"

"Yes. Just after they got the legend, the same clowns came back again. This time they took the receiver crystal for one of the covert transmitters you planted in England four years ago. That was why I thought you were behind it."

Karpov's eyes narrowed. During the time he was head of the Illegals Directorate the NATO countries had been deploying Pershing II and Cruise missiles. Washington had been running around the world trying to reenact the last reel of every John Wayne movie ever written, and the Politburo had been worried sick. Karpov had received orders to upgrade the Illegals' contingency planning for massive behind-the-lines sabotage operations in Western Europe, for use in the event of any actual outbreak of hostilities.

To fulfill this order he had had a number of clandestine radio transmitters placed in Western Europe, including three in Britain. The men guarding the sets and trained to operate them were all "sleepers," ordered to lie low until activated by an agent with the proper identification codes. The sets were ultramodern, scrambling their messages as they were transmitted; to unscramble a message the receiving set would need a programmed crystal. The crystals were stored in a safe in the Illegals Directorate.

"Which transmitter?" Karpov inquired.

"The one you called 'Poplar.' "

Karpov nodded. All operations, agents, and assets had official code names. But Karpov had been a specialist on Britain for so long and knew London so well that he had private code names for his own operations, and they were based on London suburbs whose names contained two syllables. The three transmitters he had caused to be placed in Britain were, for him, "Hackney," "Shoreditch," and "Poplar."

"Any more, Pal Petrovitch?"

"Sure. These guys are never satisfied. The last one they took was Igor Volkov."

Karpov knew of this Major Volkov, formerly of the Executive Action Department. (When the Politburo had decided that straight hit-jobs—"executive actions"—were becoming too embarrassing and that the Bulgars and East Germans should be told to do the dirty work, the department had begun to concentrate on sabotage.) "What's his specialty?" he asked.

"Bringing clandestine packages across state borders, particularly in Western Europe."

"Smuggling."

"All right, smuggling. He's good. He knows more about the borders in that part of the world, the customs and immigration procedures and how to get around them, than anyone else we've got. Well . . . *had*, I should say. They took him, too."

Karpov rose and leaned forward, placing both hands on the older man's shoulders. "Look, *Starets*, I give you my word, this is not my operation. I didn't even know about it. But we both know it has to be very big, and that means dangerous to start poking into. Stay cool, bite the bullet, absorb your losses. I'll try to find out quietly what is going on and when you will get your assets back. For your part, stay buttoned up tighter than a Georgian's purse, okay?"

Borisov raised both his hands, palms forward, in a gesture of innocence. "You know me, Yevgeni Sergeivitch, I'm going to die the oldest man in Russia."

Karpov laughed. "I think you will, too." He pulled on his coat and made for the door. Borisov followed to see him out.

When he reached his car, Karpov tapped on his driver's window. "I want to walk for a bit. Follow me until I want to get in," he said. He started down the snowy track, oblivious of the ice that clung to his town shoes and worsted trousers. The freezing night air was refreshing on his face, driving away some of the vodka fumes, and he needed a clear head to think. What he had learned had made him very angry indeed. Someone—and he had few doubts who it might be—was mounting a private operation in Britain. Apart from the massive snub to him as First Deputy Head of the First Chief Directorate, he, Karpov, had spent so many years in Britain, or running agents there, that he regarded it as his private preserve.

■ As General Karpov walked down the track lost in thought, a phone rang in a small flat in Highgate, London, not five hundred yards from the tomb of Karl Marx.

"Are you there, Barry?" a woman's voice called from the kitchen.

From the sitting room a male voice replied, "Yes, I'll get it."

The man walked to the hall and took the phone while his wife continued preparing their Sunday dinner.

"Barry?"

"Speaking."

"Ah, sorry to disturb you on a Sunday evening. It's C."

"Oh, good evening, sir."

Barry Banks was surprised. It was not unheard of, but not often, that the Master called one of his people at home.

"Look, Barry, what time do you normally get to Charles Street in the morning?"

"About ten, sir."

"Could you leave an hour earlier tomorrow and drop by Sentinel to have a word with me?"

"Yes. Of course."

"Good. Then I'll see you about nine."

Barry Banks was K7 at the Charles Street headquarters of MI5, but he was actually an MI6 man whose job was to act as Sir Nigel Irvine's link with the Security Service. He wondered idly, as he ate the supper his wife had prepared, what Sir Nigel Irvine could want and why it had to be asked out of hours.

■ Yevgeni Karpov had not a shred of doubt that a secret operation had been mounted and was being carried out, and that it concerned Britain. Petrofsky, he knew, was an expert at passing for a Britisher right in the heart of that country; the legend that had been abstracted from Borisov's files fitted Petrofsky to a *T*; the Poplar transmitter was hidden away in the north Midlands of England. If Volkov had been transferred because of his expertise at smuggling packages, there must have been transfers of other specialists, but from different directorates outside Borisov's orbit.

All of which pointed unswervingly to the likelihood that Petrofsky would be going to Britain under deep cover, or that he had already gone. Nothing strange in that, it was what he had been trained for. What *was* strange was that the First Chief Directorate in the form of Karpov himself had been kept rigorously out of the operation. It made little sense, bearing in mind his own personal expertise concerning Britain and British affairs.

He went back twenty years in his connection with Britain, since that evening in September 1967 when he had been trawling in the bars of West Berlin frequented by off-duty British service personnel. As a keen and rising illegal, this was his assignment at the time.

His eye had fallen on a morose, sour-looking young man farther down the bar who was in civilian clothes but whose haircut had shouted "British armed forces." Karpov had moved in on the lonely drinker and discovered he was a twenty-nine-year-old radio operator with a signals/intelligence (monitoring) unit, serving with the Royal Air Force at Gatow. The young man was thoroughly discontented with his lot in life.

Between that September and January 1968, Karpov had worked on the RAF man, first pretending to be a German, as was his cover, and then admitting he was a Russian. It was an easy "pull," so simple as almost to be suspect. But it was genuine, all right; the Englishman was flattered to be the subject of KGB attention, had the inadequate man's hatred of his own service and country, and had agreed to work for Moscow. During the summer of 1968 Karpov trained him in East Berlin, getting to know and to despise him more. The man's tour in Berlin and his contract in the RAF was coming to a close, and he was due that September to return to Britain and demobilization. It was suggested that on leaving the Air Force, he apply for a job at Government Communications Headquarters at Cheltenham. He agreed, and in September 1968 he did precisely that. The young man's name was Geoffrey Prime.

Karpov, to be able to continue to run Prime, was transferred under diplomatic cover to the Soviet Embassy in London. There he controlled Prime for three years until 1971, when he came back to Moscow and handed the job over to a successor. But the case had done his career a power of good, and he was promoted to major, with a transfer back to the Third Department. From there he handled Prime's source material throughout the mid-1970s. It is axiomatic in any intelligence service that an operation producing excellent material will be noted and praised, and the officer controlling that operation is inseparable from the praise.

In 1977 Prime resigned from GCHQ; the British knew there was a leak there somewhere and the hounds were sniffing. In 1978 Karpov went back to London, this time as head of the entire rezidentura and with the rank of colonel. Although out of GCHQ, Prime was still an agent, and Karpov sought to warn him to keep a very low profile indeed. There was, Karpov pointed out, not a shred of proof as to his pre-1977 activities.

He'd be a free man today if he'd only been able to keep his dirty hands off little girls, thought Karpov savagely. For he had long known of Prime's inadequacy, and it was eventually a grubby indecent-assault charge that brought the police to his door and led to his confession. He'd got thirty-five years on seven charges of spying.

But London brought two bonuses to offset the reverse of the Prime affair. At a cocktail party in 1980 Karpov had been introduced to a civil servant from the British Defense Ministry. At first the man had not heard Karpov's name correctly, and there were several minutes of polite conversation before the man realized Karpov was a Russian. When he did so, his attitude changed. Behind his abrupt and icy attitude Karpov discerned a visceral loathing of himself, both as a Russian and as a Communist.

Karpov was not upset, merely intrigued. He learned that the man's name was George Berenson, and further inquiries over the succeeding weeks revealed that the man was a dedicated anti-Communist and a passionate admirer of South Africa. Karpov privately tagged Berenson as a possible for a false-flag approach.

In May 1981, when Karpov returned to Moscow to head the Third Department, he asked around for a possible South African pro-Soviet sleeper. The Illegals Directorate mentioned that they had two men, one an officer in the South African Navy named Gerhardt, the other a diplomat named Marais. But Marais had just returned to Pretoria after three years in Bonn.

It was in the spring of 1983 that Karpov rose to major general and became head of the Illegals Directorate, which controlled Marais. He ordered the South African to ask for a London posting to terminate his long career, and in 1984 Marais got it. Karpov personally flew to Paris under deep cover and briefed Marais himself: Marais was to cultivate George Berenson and try to recruit him for South Africa.

In February 1985, after the death of Kirpichenko, Karpov succeeded to his present post, and a month later Marais reported that Berenson was on the hook. That month, the first batch of Berenson material came through, and it was solid twenty-four-karat gold, the mother lode. Since then Karpov had personally run the Berenson/Marais operation as a director's case, twice in two years meeting Marais in European cities to congratulate and debrief him. That very lunch hour, the bagman had brought the latest batch of

Berenson material, mailed by Marais to a KGB address in Copenhagen.

The London spell from 1978 to 1981 had brought a second benefit. As was his wont, Karpov had given Prime and Berenson his personal code names: Prime had been "Knightsbridge" and Berenson was "Hampstead." And then there was "Chelsea". . .

Karpov respected Chelsea, as he despised Prime and Berenson. Unlike the other two, Chelsea was not an agent but a contact, a man high in his own country's establishment and a man who, like Karpov, was a pragmatist, a man wedded to the realities of his job, his country, and the surrounding world. Karpov never ceased to be amazed at journalistic references in the West to intelligence officers living in a world of fantasy; for Karpov, it was the politicians who lived in a dream world, seduced and bemused by their own propaganda.

Intelligence officers, Karpov believed, might walk on shadowed streets, lie and deceive to carry out their missions, but if they ever wandered into the realm of fantasy, as the CIA's covert-action people had done so often, that was when they came badly unstuck.

Chelsea had twice dropped hints that if the USSR continued on a certain course there would soon be a fearsome mess for them all to clear up; twice he had been right. Karpov, able to warn his own people of impending danger, had scored a mountain of credits when he turned out to be correct.

He stopped and forced his mind back to the present problem. Borisov was right; the General Secretary was mounting some kind of personal and private operation right under his nose, and inside Britain, but excluding the KGB from any part of it. Karpov sensed danger; despite his years as Chairman of the KGB, the General Secretary was not a professional intelligence officer. Karpov's own career might hang in the balance, but it was vital to find out what on earth was going on. But carefully, very carefully.

He checked his watch. Half past eleven. He beckoned his driver forward, climbed into the Chaika, and was driven home to Moscow.

■ Barry Banks arrived at the headquarters of the SIS at ten to nine that Monday morning. Sentinel House is a large, square, and surprisingly tawdry-looking building on the south bank of the Thames and is leased to a certain government ministry by the Greater London Council. Its elevators are erratic and around its lower floors a mosaic mural is forever shedding its tiles like ceramic dandruff.

Banks identified himself at the front desk and went straight up. The Master, bluff and genial as he always was toward aspiring underlings, received him at once.

"Do you know a chap at Five named John Preston, by any chance?" asked C.

"Yes, sir. Not well, but I've met him several times. Usually in the bar at Gordon, when I've been over there."

"He heads C1(A), doesn't he, Barry?"

"Not anymore. He's been transferred to C5(C). He started there last week."

"Oh, really? That was rather sudden. I heard he'd done rather well at C1(A)."

Sir Nigel felt no need to inform Banks that he had met Preston at the JIC meetings or that he had used him as his personal ferret in South Africa. Banks knew nothing of the Berenson affair, nor did he need to know. For his part, Banks wondered what the Master had in mind. So far as he knew, Preston had nothing to do with Six.

"Very sudden," Banks replied. "In fact, he was only at C1(A) for a few weeks. Up till the New Year he was head of F1(D). Then he must have done something that upset Sir Bernard—or, more likely, Brian Harcourt-Smith. He was booted out of there and into C1(A). Then last month he was given the heave-ho again."

Ah, thought Sir Nigel. Upset Harcourt-Smith, did he? Suspected as much. Wonder why. Aloud, he said, "Any idea what he could have done to annoy Harcourt-Smith?"

"I did hear something, sir. From Preston. He wasn't talking to me, but I was close enough to hear. He was in the bar at Gordon at the time, about two weeks back. He seemed a bit upset himself. Apparently he spent years preparing a report, and submitted it last Christmas. He thought it was worth attention, but Harcourt-Smith NFA'ed it."

"Mmmmmm. F1(D) . . . that's Extreme Left activities, isn't it? Look, Barry, I want you to do something for me. No need to make a song and dance about it. Just quietly. Find out the file number on that report and draw it from Registry, will you? Put it in the bag and send it over here, marked for me personally."

Banks found himself back on the street and heading north toward Charles at just before ten.

■ The Aeroflot crew had a leisurely breakfast and at nine-twenty-nine First Officer Romanov checked his watch and went to the men's room. He had been there before and ascertained the cubicle he was to take. It was the second from the end. The one at the end already had its door closed and locked. He went into the adjacent one and locked the door.

At nine-thirty he placed a small card, on which he had written the prescribed six figures, on the floor next to the partition. A hand came under the partition, withdrew the card, wrote something on it, and placed it back on the floor. Romanov picked it up. On the reverse side were the six figures he had been expecting.

With identification established, he placed the transistor on the floor and the same hand drew it silently into the next cubicle. Outside, someone was using the urinal. Romanov flushed the toilet, unlocked the door, washed his hands until the urinal user had left, then followed him out. The minibus for Heathrow was at the door. Courier One had delivered.

■ Barry Banks phoned Sir Nigel just before the hour of noon. It was an internal line and very secure.

"It's rather odd, sir," he said. "I secured the file number of that report you wanted and went to Registry for it. I know the file clerk pretty well. He confirmed it's in the NFA section. But it's out."

"Out?"

"Out. Withdrawn."

"By whom?"

"A man named Swanton. I know him. The odd thing is, he's in Finance. So I asked him if I could borrow it. That's the second odd thing. He refused, said he wasn't finished with it yet. According to Registry, he's had it three weeks. Before that, it was out to someone else."

"The lavatory attendant?" asked Sir Nigel wryly.

"Almost. Someone in Administration."

Sir Nigel thought for a while. The best way to keep a file permanently out of circulation was to keep it on permanent withdrawal to oneself or to one's protégés. He had little doubt Swanton and the other man were Harcourt-Smith's own men. "Barry, I want you to find out Preston's home address. Then meet me here at five o'clock."

■ General Karpov sat at his desk that afternoon at Yasyenevo and rubbed his stiff neck. It had not been a restful night. He had lain awake most of it, with Ludmilla sleeping by his side. By dawn he had come to a conclusion, and further thought in the moments he could snatch from his daily work had not altered it.

It was the General Secretary who was behind the mysterious operation being mounted in Britain, but despite his pretensions to read and speak English, he had no knowledge of the country. He would have relied on the advice of someone who did. There were many such—in the Foreign Ministry, the International Department of the Central Committee, the GRU, and the KGB. But if he was avoiding the KGB, why not avoid the others as well?

So, a personal adviser. And the more Karpov thought, the more the name of his own bête noire kept cropping up. Years ago, as a young man making his way in the service, he had admired Philby. They all had. But with the passing years he had risen while Philby had fallen. He had also watched the English renegade deteriorate into a drunken wreck. The fact was, Philby had not been near a British classified document (except those shown to him by the KGB) since 1951. He had quit Britain in 1955 for Beirut and had not even been in the West since his final defection in 1963. Twenty-four years. Karpov reckoned that by now *he* knew Britain better than Philby did.

There was more. Karpov knew that during the time the General Secretary had been at the KGB he had in some way become impressed by Philby, by his Old World mannerisms and tastes, his affectation of the English gentleman, his dislike of the modern world with all its pop music, motorcycles, and blue jeans—tastes that mirrored the General Secretary's own. Several times, to Karpov's certain knowledge, the General Secretary had had recourse to Philby's advice as a sort of backup to the counsel he received from the First Chief Directorate. Why not now?

Finally, in Karpov's catalogue, there was the tip that once—just once—Philby had let something slip, something extremely interesting. He wanted to return home. For that, if for nothing else, Karpov did not trust him. Not one inch. He recalled the lined, smiling face across the table from him at Kryuchkov's dinner party before the New Year. What had he said about Britain then? Something about her political stability's being overestimated here in Moscow?

There were pieces, and they were beginning to fit together. Karpov decided to check out Mr. Harold Adrian Russell Philby. But he knew that even at his level things were noted: withdrawals from Registry, official requests for information, phone calls, memoranda. His investigation had to be unofficial, personal, and, above all, verbal. The General Secretary was a very dangerous man to antagonize.

■ John Preston had arrived on his own street and was a hundred yards from the entrance to his apartment house when he heard the hail. He turned to see Barry Banks crossing the street toward him.

"Hello, Barry, small world. What are you doing here?" He knew that the man from K7 lived up north, in the Highgate area. Perhaps he was going to a concert at the nearby Albert Hall.

"Waiting for you, actually," said Banks with a friendly grin. "Look, a colleague of mine wants to meet you. Would you mind?"

Preston was intrigued but not suspicious. He knew Banks was from Six, but not who might want to meet him. He allowed Banks to guide him across the street and a hundred yards down. Banks stopped at a parked Ford Granada, opened the back door, and gestured to Preston to look inside. He did so.

"Good evening, John. Do you mind if we have a couple of words?"

In surprise Preston climbed in beside the seated figure in the greatcoat. Banks closed the door and wandered away.

"Look, I know it's an odd way to meet. But there we are. Don't want to cause any waves, do we? I just felt I had not had a decent opportunity to thank you for the work you did down in South Africa. It was a first-class job. Henry Pienaar was most impressed. So was I."

"Thank you, Sir Nigel." Now, what on earth did the wily old fox want? It certainly wasn't merely to compliment him. But C seemed lost in thought.

"There *is* another matter," he said at length, as if thinking aloud. "Young Barry tells me it has come to his notice that last Christmas you put in a most interesting report about the Extreme Left in this country. I could well be wrong, but there might have been a foreign dimension to some of the funding going on, if you see what I mean. The thing is, your report was not circulated to us in the Firm. Pity, that."

"It was NFA'ed," said Preston quickly.

"Yes, yes, so Barry tells me. Pity, really. I'd have liked to have a glance at it. No chance of getting hold of a copy?"

"It's in the Registry," said Preston, puzzled. "It may be NFA'ed, but it's on file. Barry has only got to withdraw it and send it over in the bag."

"Actually, no," said Sir Nigel. "It's already been withdrawn. By Swanton. And he hasn't finished with it. Won't pass it over."

"But he's in Finance," protested Preston.

"Yes," murmured Sir Nigel regretfully, "and before that it was out to someone in Administration. One might almost think it was being kept out of sight."

Preston sat there, stunned. Through the windshield he could see Banks dawdling up the street. "There is another copy," he suggested. "My own. It's in my office safe."

Banks drove them. In the evening traffic it was a crawl from Kensington to Gordon Street. An hour later Preston leaned through the window of the Granada and handed his report to Sir Nigel.

CHAPTER

General Yevgeni Karpov climbed the last of the stairs to the third floor of the apartment building on Mira Prospekt and rang the buzzer. After several minutes the door opened. Philby's wife stood in the frame. Karpov could hear the sound of small boys at their tea inside. He had chosen 6:00 p.m. on the hunch that they would be home from school by then.

"Hello, Erita."

She tilted her head back in a small gesture of defiance. A very protective lady, he thought. Perhaps she knew Karpov was no admirer of her husband.

"Comrade General."

"Is Kim at home?"

"No. He's away."

Not "he's out," but "he's away," thought Karpov. He affected surprise. "Oh, I had hoped to catch him. Do you know when he'll be back?"

"No. He'll be back when he'll be back."

"Any idea where I might contact him?"

"No."

Karpov frowned. Something Philby had said at the Kryuchkov

213

dinner . . . about not being allowed to drive since his stroke. Karpov had already checked the basement parking area. Philby's Volga was there.

"I thought you drove him around these days, Erita."

She was half smiling. Not the expression of a woman whose husband has walked out on her. More the smile of a woman whose husband has obtained a promotion. "Not anymore. He has a driver."

"I'm impressed. Well, sorry to have missed him. I'll try to catch him when he gets back."

He descended the stairs deep in thought. Retired colonels did not rate personal drivers. Back in his own flat, two blocks behind the Ukraina Hotel, Karpov called the KGB motor pool and insisted on speaking to the chief clerk. When he identified himself, the clerk's reaction was suitably deferential. Karpov was bluff and jovial. "I'm not in the habit of handing out bouquets of carnations, but I see no reason not to when good work has been done."

"Thank you, Comrade General."

"That chauffeur who has been driving for my friend Comrade Colonel Philby. He speaks extremely highly of him. A very fine driver, so he says. If my own man is ever sick, I must ask for him personally."

"Thank you again, Comrade General. I'll tell Gregoriev myself."

Karpov hung up. Gregoriev. Never heard of him. But a quiet talk with the man might be useful.

■ The next morning, April 8, the *Akademik Komarov* moved quietly past Greenock and into the Clyde, bound upriver for the port of Glasgow. She stopped briefly at Greenock to pick up the pilot and two customs officers. They had the usual glass in the captain's cabin and ascertained that the ship was out of Leningrad and in ballast to pick up a cargo of heavy-duty pump accessories from Weir of Cathcart Limited. The customs men checked the crew list but did not memorize any particular name. Later it would be established that deckhand Konstantin Semyonov was on the list.

The habitual practice when Soviet illegals enter a country by ship is that their names do *not* appear on the crew list. The illegal arrives crouched in a tiny cubbyhole, or oubliette, that has been skillfully cut into the ship's structure and so well hidden that the most thorough search would not uncover it. Then, if the man for operational or accidental reasons fails to go out on the same ship, there is no discrepancy in the crew list. But this had been a hurried operation. There had been no time for structural changes.

The extra crewman had arrived with the men from Moscow only hours before the *Komarov* was due to leave Leningrad for Glasgow on a long-scheduled freight run, and the captain and his resident political officer had had no choice but to put him on the crew list. His seaman's paybook was in order, and he would be returning, they were told.

Nevertheless, the man had taken a cabin to himself, spent the whole voyage in it, and the two genuine deckhands whose cabin it was had become fed up with their sleeping bags on the wardroom floor. These bags were cleared away by the time the Scottish pilot came on board. Down in his cabin, tense, for evident reasons, Courier Two was waiting for midnight.

■ While the Clyde pilot stood on the bridge of the *Komarov* and the fields of Strathclyde slid by as he munched his breakfast sandwiches, it was already noon in Moscow. Karpov called the KGB motor pool again. There was a new chief clerk on duty, as he knew there would be.

"My driver looks as if he's coming down with the flu," he said. "He'll see the day out, but I'm giving him tomorrow off."

"I'll ensure that you get a replacement, Comrade General."

"I'd prefer Gregoriev. Is he available? I've heard the best reports of him."

There was a rustle of paper as the clerk checked his files. "Yes, indeed. He's been on temporary assignment but he's back in the pool."

"Good. Have him report to my Moscow flat at eight tomorrow morning. I'll have the keys, and the Chaika will be in the basement."

Stranger and stranger, Karpov thought as he put the phone down. Gregoriev had been ordered to drive Philby around for a while. Why? Because there was a great deal of driving to do, too much for Erita to cope with? Or so that Erita should not know where he was going? And now the man was back in the pool again. Meaning? Probably that Philby was now somewhere else and did not need a driver anymore, at least not until the end of whatever operation he was involved in.

That evening, Karpov told his grateful regular driver he could have the following day off to take his family out.

■ The same Wednesday evening, Sir Nigel Irvine had a dinner date with a friend in Oxford.

One of the charming things about Saint Antony's College, Oxford, is that, like so many highly influential British institutions, so far as the general public is concerned it does not exist.

In fact it does exist but is so small and so discreet that if anyone surveying the groves of academe in the British Isles were to blink, he would probably miss it. Its Hall is small, elegant, and tucked away out of sight; it offers no degree courses, educates no students, has no undergraduates and therefore no graduates, and awards no degrees. It has a few resident professors and fellows, who sometimes dine together in Hall but live in rooms scattered around the city, and others who live elsewhere and simply visit. It occasionally invites outsiders to address the fellows—an extraordinary honor—and the professors and fellows occasionally submit papers to the higher echelons of the British establishment, where they are taken very seriously. Its funding is as private as the profile it maintains.

In fact it is a think tank where assembled intellects, often with estensive nonacademic experience, pursue the study of one single discipline: current affairs.

That evening, Sir Nigel dined in Hall with his host, Professor Jeremy Sweeting, and after an excellent repast the professor took the Master back to his rooms in an agreeable house on the outskirts of Oxford for port and coffee.

"Now, Nigel," said Professor Sweeting when they had broached a vintage Taylor and were at ease before the fire in the study, "what can I do for you?"

"Have you by any chance, Jeremy, heard of a thing called the MBR?"

Professor Sweeting held his port in midair. He stared at it for a long while. "You know, Nigel, you really do have a way of spoiling a chap's evening when you have a mind to. Where did you hear those letters?"

For answer, Sir Nigel Irvine passed over the Preston report. Professor Sweeting read it carefully, and it took him an hour. Irvine knew that the professor, unlike John Preston, was no legman. He did not get out on the ground. But he had an encyclopedic knowledge of Marxian theory and practice, of dialectical materialism, and of the teachings of Lenin on the applicability of theory to the practice of the achievement of power. His pursuit and his absorption was to read, study, collate, and analyze.

"Remarkable," said Sweeting as he handed back the report. "A different approach, a different attitude, of course, and a completely different methodology. But we've come up with the same answers."

"Care to tell me what those answers are?" asked Sir Nigel gently.

"It's only theory, of course," apologized Professor Sweeting. "A thousand straws in the wind that may—or may not—make up a bale of hay. Anyway, this is what *I've* been on since June 1983. . . ."

He talked for two hours, and when, much later, Sir Nigel left to be driven back to London, he was a very pensive man.

■ The *Akademik Komarov* was tied up at the Finnieston Quay in the heart of Glasgow, so that the giant crane there could hoist the pumps aboard in the morning. There are no customs or immigration checks there; foreign seamen can simply walk off their ships, across the quay, and into the streets of Glasgow.

At midnight, while Professor Sweeting was still talking, deckhand Semyonov walked down the gangplank, followed the quay for a hundred yards, avoided Betty's Bar, outside whose door a few drunken sailors were still protesting their right to just one more drink, and turned up Finnieston Street.

He was unremarkable in appearance, being dressed in a turtleneck sweater, corduroy trousers, and an anorak; his shoes were scuffed. Under one arm he clutched a canvas gunnysack held closed by a drawstring. Passing under the Clydeside Expressway, he reached Argyle Street, turned left, and followed it to Partick Cross. He consulted no map but headed on into Hyndland Road. A mile farther on, he reached another major artery, the Great Western Road. He had memorized his route days before.

Here he checked his watch; it told him he still had half an hour. The rendezvous could not be more than ten minutes' walk ahead. He turned left and proceeded in the direction of the Pond Hotel, next to the boating lake and a hundred yards past the BP service station whose lights he could see blazing in the distance. He was almost at the bus stop at the junction of the Great Western and Hughenden roads when he saw them. They were lounging about in the passenger shelter of the bus stop. It was half past one in the morning, and there were five of them.

In some parts of Britain they call them "skinheads" or "punks," but in Glasgow they call them "Neds." Semyonov thought of crossing the street but he was too late. One of them called out to him, and they spilled out of the bus shelter. He could speak some English, but their broad, drink-slurred Glaswegian dialect defeated him. They blocked the sidewalk, so he stepped into the street. One of them grabbed his arm and shouted at him. What the lout actually said was "Wha' ha' ya got in ya wee sack, then?"

But Semyonov could not understand, so he shook his head and tried to walk past. Then they were on him and he went down under a rain of blows. When he was in the gutter the kicking started. He dimly felt hands tearing at his gunnysack, so he clutched it to his belly with both hands and rolled over, taking the blows around the head and kidneys.

Devonshire Terrace overlooks that road junction; it is a row of solid, four-story, middle-class houses of buff and gray sandstone blocks. On the top floor of one, Mrs. Sylvester, old, widowed, alone, and riddled with arthritis, was unable to sleep. She heard the shouts from the street below and hobbled from her bed to the window. What she saw caused her to limp across the room to the telephone, where she dialed 999 and asked for the police. She told the police operator where to send the patrol car but hung up when asked for her name and address. Respectable people—and those of Devonshire Terrace are very respectable—do not like to get involved.

Police Constables Alistair Craig and Hugh McBain were in their patrol car a mile down the Great Western at the Hillhead end when

the call came through. Traffic was nearly nonexistent and they
reached the bus stop in ninety seconds. When the Neds saw the
headlights and heard the siren, they ceased trying to rip away the
gunnysack and chose to race away across the grass verge that sepa-
rates Hughenden Road from the Great Western, so the patrol car
could not follow them. By the time Police Constable Craig could leap
out of the car they were disappearing shadows and pursuit was useless. In any case, the priority was the victim.

Craig bent over the man. He was unconscious and huddled in the
fetal position. "Ambulance, Hughie," Craig called across to Mc-
Bain, who was already on the radio. The ambulance from the Western Infirmary came six minutes later. Meanwhile, the two officers
left the injured man strictly alone, as per procedure, save that they
covered him with a blanket.

The ambulance men eased the limp form onto a gurney and into
the back of the vehicle. As they were tucking the blanket around the
victim, Craig lifted the gunnysack and placed it in the rear of the ambulance. "You go with him, I'll follow," shouted McBain, so Craig
climbed into the ambulance as well.

They all arrived at the hospital in less than five minutes. The ambulance men quickly wheeled the injured man through the swinging
doors, down the corridor, around two corners, and into the rear of
the casualty ward. As this was an emergency admission, there was
no need for them to pass through the public waiting room, where the
usual collection of small-hours-of-the-morning drunks nursed the
cuts and bruises collected while in earlier contact with a number of
unyielding objects.

Craig waited at the entrance while McBain parked the patrol car.
When his partner joined him, he said, "You handle the admission
forms, Hughie. I'll go along and see if I can get you a name and address." McBain sighed. Admission forms went on forever.

Craig collected the gunnysack and followed the gurney down the
corridor to Emergency. This department at the Western Infirmary
consists of a passage with swinging doors at each end and twelve cur-
tained examination rooms, six at either side of the central corridor.
Eleven of the rooms are used for examinations; the twelfth is the
nurse's office, and it is located nearest the rear entrance through

which the gurneys come. The doors at the other end have one-way mirrors in their panels and give onto the public waiting room where the walking wounded are made to sit and wait their turn.

Leaving McBain with a sheaf of admission forms to fill in, Craig went through the mirrored doors to see the unconscious man on his gurney, parked at the other end. The nurse gave the injured man the usual once-over—he was alive, at any rate—and asked the orderlies to put him on a table in one of the examination rooms so that the gurney could be returned to the ambulance. The cubicle they chose was the one opposite the nurse's office.

The house physician on duty that night, an Indian named Mehta, was summoned. He had the orderlies strip the injured man to the waist—he could see no signs of blood leaking through the trousers—and made a lengthier examination before ordering an X-ray. Then he left to attend to another emergency admission from a car crash.

The nurse telephoned X-Ray but it was occupied. They would let her know when they were free. She put on her kettle to make a cup of tea.

Police Constable Craig, having ascertained that his anonymous charge was still unconscious on his back across the corridor, took the man's anorak, entered the nurse's office, and placed both anorak and gunnysack on her desk. "Have you a spare cup of that brew?" he asked in the jocular familiarity used by people of the night who spend their duty hours cleaning up the mess of a major city.

"I might," she said, "but I don't see why I should waste it on the likes of you."

Craig grinned. He felt through the pockets of the anorak and extracted a seaman's paybook. It bore the photograph of the man in the examination room across the way, and was in two languages, Russian and French. He understood neither. He could not read Cyrillic script, but the name was in Roman letters also, in the French-language section.

"Who's the patient?" asked the nurse, preparing two cups of tea.

"Looks like a seaman, and a Russian at that," said Craig, perturbed. A citizen of Glasgow roughed up by a gang of Neds was one thing; a foreigner—and a Russian, at that—could spell problems. To try to discover what ship the man could be from, Craig emptied the gunnysack. It contained simply a rolled-up, thick-knit sweater, which was wrapped around a circular, screw-top tobacco tin. Inside the tin was not tobacco but a wad of cotton that shrouded two disks of aluminum with, between them, another two-inch-diameter disk of a dull gray metal. Craig examined the three disks without interest, replaced them in their bed of cotton, screwed the tin shut again, and laid it on the table beside the paybook. What he did not know was that across the corridor the victim of the mugging attack had come to and was peering through the curtains at him. What he did know was that it was time to tell Division that he had an injured Russian on his hands.

"Use your phone, pet?" he asked the nurse, and reached out for it.

"Don't you 'pet' me," called back the nurse, who was somewhat older than the twenty-four-year-old Craig. "God, they get younger every day."

Craig began to dial. Just what went through Konstantin Semyonov's mind will never be known. Dazed and confused, probably suffering a concussion from the kicks to his head, he could see the unmistakable black uniform of a British policeman with his back to him across the corridor. He could see his own paybook and the consignment he had been told to bring to Britain and deliver to the agent at the boating lake sitting on the table by the policeman's hand. He had watched the officer examine the consignment—Semyonov himself had never dared open the tobacco tin—and now the man was phoning. Perhaps the seaman had visions of an endless third-degree examination in some reeking cellar beneath Strathclyde police headquarters. . . .

The first thing Craig knew, he was roughly elbowed aside, caught completely unawares. A bare arm pushed past him, reached for the tin, and grabbed it. Craig responded quickly, dropping the telephone and grasping the outstretched arm. "What the hell!" he shouted; then, assuming the poor fellow was hallucinating, he grabbed the man and tried to restrain him. The tin was shaken from the Russian's hand and fell to the floor. For a moment Semyonov stared at the Scottish policeman, then panicked and ran. Still calling, "Hey, come back here!" Craig thundered down the corridor after him.

Shortie Patterson was a drunk. A lifetime dedicated to sampling

the produce of Scotland had made him unemployed and unemploy-
able. He was no ordinary drunk; he had elevated intoxication to an
art form. The previous day he had drawn his welfare allowance and
gone to the nearest boozer; by midnight he had been paralyzed. In
the small hours he had taken exception to the offensive attitude of a
lamppost that refused to respond to his entreaties for the price of a
dram, so he had hit the creature.

He had been in X-Ray with his broken hand and was going back
down the corridor to his cubicle when a man with a bare and battered
torso and bruised and bloody face came running out of an adjacent
room pursued by a policeman. Shortie knew his duty to a fellow suf-
ferer. He had no love for policemen, who seemed to have nothing
better to do than pluck him out of perfectly comfortable gutters and
hand him over to people who made him bathe. He let the running
man pass him, then stuck out a foot.

"You stupid wee bugger!" shouted Craig as he crashed down. By
the time he was up, he had lost ten yards on the Russian.

Semyonov came through the mirrored doors into the public waiting room, missed seeing the narrow door to the outside that lay to
his left, and ran through the larger double doors to his right. This
led him back into the corridor down which he had been wheeled
thirty minutes earlier. He turned right again, to find approaching
him a gurney surrounded by a doctor and two nurses holding up
plasma bottles—Dr. Mehta's accident victim. The gurney blocked
the whole corridor; behind him Semyonov heard running boots.

To his left was a lobby containing two elevators. The door to one
was just closing, and Semyonov managed to hurl himself through
the gap. As the elevator rose, he heard the policeman banging im-
potently on the closed door. Semyonov leaned back and closed his
eyes in misery.

Craig made for the stairwell and ran up. At every level he checked
the lights above the elevator doors. It was still climbing. At the top
and tenth floor he was hot, angry, and puffing.

Semyonov had got out at the tenth floor. He looked into one door
available to him, but it opened onto a ward of sleeping patients.
There was one other door, open and leading to a staircase. He ran up
the stairs, only to find himself in another corridor, with shower
rooms, a pantry, and storerooms along the sides. At the far end was

the last door, and in the warm, humid night it stood open. It led to the flat roof of the building.

Craig had lost ground, but he made the final doorway eventually and stepped out into the night air. His eyes adjusting to the darkness, he made out the figure of a man by the north parapet. His annoyance died away. I'd probably panic if I woke up in a Moscow hospital, he thought. He started to walk toward the figure, hands held up to show they were empty.

"C'mon, Ivan, or whatever your name is. You're all right. You got a bang on the heed, tha's all. Come on away down wi' me."

Craig was accustomed to the darkness now. He could see the Russian's face quite clearly in the glow from the city below. The man watched him approach until he was twenty feet away. Then he looked down, took a deep breath, closed his eyes, and jumped.

Craig could not believe it for several seconds, even after he heard the soggy smack of the body crashing a hundred feet down into the staff parking lot.

"Oh, Christ," he breathed, "I'm in trouble." With fumbling fingers he reached for his radio and called Division.

■ A hundred yards beyond the BP service station and half a mile from the bus stop lies a boating pond, in the shadow of the Pond Hotel. From the sidewalk a set of stone steps leads down to the walkway around the water, and close to the bottom of the steps are two wooden benches.

The silent figure in black motorcycle leathers checked his watch. Three o'clock. The rendezvous had been for two. One hour's delay was all that was allowed. There was a second, backup rendezvous in a different place, twenty-four hours later. He would be there. If the contact failed to show up, he would have to use the radio again. He rose and left.

■ Police Constable McBain had missed the entire chase. He had been at his car checking exact times for the mugging attack and the logged appeal calls. The first thing he knew about it was when his "neighbor" (Glasgow slang for partner) came down into the waiting room looking pale and shaken.

"Alistair, have you got that name and address yet?" he asked.

"He is . . . he was . . . a Russian seaman," said Craig.

"Oh, hell, that's all we needed. How do you spell it?"

"Hughie, he's just . . . thrown himself off the roof."

McBain put down his pen and stared in disbelief at his neighbor. Then the training took over. Any policeman knows that when things go wrong you cover yourself—you follow the procedures right down the line, no cowboy tactics, no clever-clever initiatives. "Have you called Division?" he asked.

"Aye, someone's on the way over."

"Let's get the doctor," said McBain.

They found Dr. Mehta, who was already worked to fatigue by the night's admissions. He followed them to the parking lot, spent no more than two minutes examining the gross and burst cadaver, pronounced it dead and no longer his concern, and returned to his duties. Two orderlies brought a blanket to cover it, and thirty minutes later an ambulance took the thing to the city mortuary on Jocelyn Square by the Salt Market. There other hands would strip off the rest of the clothing—shoes, socks, trousers, underpants, belt, and wristwatch—each item to be bagged and tagged for collection by investigating officers.

Inside the hospital there were more forms to fill out—the admission forms were kept as evidence, although now useless for practical purposes—and the two police constables bagged and tagged the rest of the dead man's possessions. They were listed as: anorak, 1; turtleneck pullover, 1; canvas gunnysack, 1; thick-knit sweater (rolled), 1; and round tobacco tin, 1.

Before they were finished, about fifteen minutes after Craig's call, an inspector and a sergeant, both uniformed, had arrived from Division. They were loaned an empty administrator's office and began to take statements from the two constables. After ten minutes the inspector sent the sergeant to his car to call in the duty chief superintendent. It was then four in the morning of Thursday, April 9, but in Moscow it was eight o'clock.

■ General Yevgeni Karpov waited until they were out of the main traffic of southern Moscow and on the open road to Yasyenevo before he started to converse with Gregoriev. Apparently the thirty-year-old driver knew he had been singled out by the general and was eager to please him.

"How do you like driving for us?"

"Very much, sir."

"Well, it gets you out and about, I suppose. Better than a stuffy desk job."

"Yes, sir."

"Been driving for my friend Colonel Philby recently, I hear."

A slight pause. Damn, he's been told not to mention it, thought Karpov.

"Er . . . yes, sir."

"Used to drive himself until he had his stroke."

"So he told me, sir."

Better get on with it. "Whereabouts did you drive him?"

A longer pause. Karpov could see the driver's face in the mirror. He was disturbed, in a quandary.

"Oh, just around Moscow, sir."

"Anywhere specific around Moscow, Gregoriev?"

"No, sir. Just around."

"Pull over, Gregoriev."

The Chaika pulled out of the privileged center lane, through the southbound traffic, and onto a shoulder.

Karpov leaned forward. "You know who I am, Gregoriev?"

"Yes, sir."

"And you know my rank in the KGB?"

"Yes, sir. Lieutenant general."

"Then don't play games with me, young man. Where, exactly, did you drive him?"

Gregoriev swallowed. Karpov could see he was wrestling with himself. The question was: Who had told him to stay silent as to where he had driven Philby? If it was Philby himself, Karpov outranked him. But if it was someone higher . . . In fact, it had been Major Pavlov, and he had frightened Gregoriev badly. He was only a major, but to a Russian the people from the First Chief Directorate

are an unknown quantity, whereas a major of the Kremlin Guards
. . . Still, a general was a general.

"Mostly to a series of conferences, Comrade General. Some at
central Moscow apartments, but I never went inside, so I never saw
which exact apartment he went to."

"Some in central Moscow . . . And the others?"

"Mainly—no sir, always, I think—at a dacha out at Zhukovka."

Central Committee country, thought Karpov. Or Supreme Soviet. "Do you know whose?"

"No, sir. Honestly. He just gave me directions to it. Then I used
to wait in the car."

"Who else turned up at these conferences?"

"There was one occasion, sir, when two cars arrived together. I
saw the man from the other car get out and enter the dacha. . . ."

"And you recognized him?"

"Yes, sir. Before I joined the KGB motor pool, I was a driver in
the Army. In 1985 I used to drive for a colonel of the GRU. We were
based at Kandahar, in Afghanistan. Once this officer was in the rear
seat with my colonel. It was General Marchenko."

Well, well, well, thought Karpov, my old friend Pyotr Marchenko, specialist in destabilization. "Anyone else at these conferences?"

"Just one other car, sir. We drivers chatted a bit, what with the
hours of waiting and that. But he was a surly devil. All I learned was
that he drove for a member of the Academy of Sciences. Honestly,
sir, that's all I know."

"Drive on, Gregoriev."

Karpov leaned back and watched the passing landscape of trees.
So, there were four of them, meeting to prepare something for the
General Secretary. The host was a member of the Central Commit-
tee, or maybe the Supreme Soviet, and the other three were Philby,
Marchenko, and an unnamed academician.

Tomorrow, Friday, the *vlasti* finished work as early as they could
and went to their dachas. Karpov knew that Marchenko had a villa
close to Peredelkino, not far from his own. He also knew Marchenko's weakness, and sighed. He had better take a lot of brandy with
him. It would be a heavy session.

■ Chief Superintendent Charlie Forbes listened carefully and quietly to Constables Craig and McBain, and now and again interjected a soft-spoken question. Forbes had no doubt they were telling the truth, but he had been on the force long enough to know the truth does not always save your neck.

It was a bad business. Technically, the Russian had been in police custody, even though under treatment at a hospital. There had been no one else on that roof but Police Constable Craig. There was no evident reason why the man should have jumped. Forbes did not even care why, assuming, like everyone else, that the man had been severely concussed and in a state of panic due to temporary hallucination. His whole attention was on the possible perspectives for the Strathclyde police.

There would be the ship to trace, the captain to interview, formal identification of the body, the Soviet consul to be informed, and of course the press, the bloody press, some elements of whom would hint darkly at their usual hobbyhorse, police brutality. The darn thing was, when they asked their pointed questions, he did not have any answers. Why should the silly man have jumped?

At half past four there was nothing more to do at the hospital. The investigative machinery would roll into action by dawn. Forbes ordered them all back to divisional headquarters. By six o'clock the two constables had finished their lengthy statements and Charlie Forbes was in his office coping with the demands of the procedural machinery. A search—probably futile—was on for the lady who had dialed 999. Statements had been taken from the two ambulance men who had answered McBain's call via the divisional switchboard. At least there would be no doubt about the beating the Neds had given the man.

The emergency ward nurse had told her version; the harassed Dr. Mehta had made a statement; the front desk attendant had testified to seeing the bare-chested man, pursued by Craig, run through the waiting room. After that, during the chase up to the roof, no one had seen either of them.

Forbes had identified the only Soviet ship in port as the *Akademik Komarov* and dispatched a police car to ask the captain to identify the body; he had woken the Soviet consul, who would be at his office at nine—protesting, no doubt. He had alerted his own chief constable, and the procurator fiscal, whose office, in Scotland, includes the duties of coroner.

The dead man's personal effects—the "productions"—had all been bagged and were being taken to Partick police station (the mugging had occurred in Partick) to be retained under lock and key on the direction of the procurator fiscal, who had promised to authorize the postmortem for ten that morning. Charlie Forbes stretched and called the canteen for coffee and rolls.

■ While Chief Superintendent Forbes at the Strathclyde HQ on Pitt Street did the paperwork, Constables Craig and McBain signed their statements at Division and repaired to their canteen for breakfast. Both were worried men, and they shared their concerns with a grizzled detective sergeant from the plainclothes branch who sat at their table. After breakfast they sought and received permission to go home to sleep.

Something they said caused the detective to go to the pay phone in the hall outside the canteen and make a call. The man he disturbed—at that moment with a faceful of shaving cream—was Detective Inspector Carmichael, who listened carefully, hung up, and finished his shaving in a pensive mood. Carmichael was from Special Branch.

At half past seven, Carmichael traced the chief inspector in the uniformed branch who would be attending the postmortem and asked if he might tag along. "Be my guest," said the chief inspector. "City morgue at ten."

At that same morgue, at eight o'clock, the captain of the *Akademik Komarov*, accompanied by his inseparable political officer, stared at a videoscreen on which the battered face of deckhand Semyonov soon appeared. He nodded slowly and muttered in Russian.

"That is him," said the political officer. "We wish to see our consul."

"He'll be at Pitt Street at nine o'clock," said the uniformed sergeant who was accompanying them. Both Russians appeared shaken and subdued. It must be bad to lose a close shipmate, thought the sergeant.

At nine the Soviet consul was ushered into the Pitt Street office of Chief Superintendent Forbes. He spoke fluent English. Forbes asked him to be seated and launched into a narration of the night's events. Before he finished, the consul was coming back at him.

"This is outrage," the Russian began. "I must contact Soviet Embassy in London without delay. . . ."

There was a knock on the door and the *Komarov*'s captain and his political officer were shown in. The uniformed sergeant was their escort, but another man was with them. He nodded to Forbes. "Morning, sir. Mind if I sit in?"

"Help yourself, Carmichael. I think it's going to be a rough one."

But no. The political officer had been in the room barely ten seconds before he drew the consul aside and whispered furiously in his ear. The consul made his excuses and the two men withdrew to the corridor. Three minutes later they were back. The consul was formal and correct. He would, of course, have to communicate with his embassy. He was sure the Strathclyde police would do all in their power to apprehend the hooligans. Would it be possible for the body of the seaman and all his effects to depart for Leningrad on the *Akademik Komarov*, which was due to sail this day?

Forbes was polite but adamant. Police inquiries and efforts to arrest the muggers would continue. During that period the body would have to remain at the morgue and all the dead man's effects would be retained under lock and key at Partick police station. The consul nodded. He, too, understood procedures. And with that, the Russians left.

At ten o'clock, Carmichael entered the postmortem room, where Professor Harland was scrubbing. The chatter, as usual, was about the weather, the golf prospects, the norms of everyday life. A few feet away on a slab above the drains lay the battered and pulped body of Semyonov.

"Mind if I have a look?" asked Carmichael. The police pathologist nodded.

Carmichael spent ten minutes examining what remained of Semyonov. When he left, just as the professor was starting to cut, he went to his office at Pitt Street and made a call to Edinburgh—more precisely, to the Scottish Home and Health Department, known as the Scottish Office, at Saint Andrew's House. There he spoke to a retired assistant commissioner who was on the staff of the Scottish Office for one reason: as liaison with MI5 in London.

At noon the phone rang in the office of C5(C) in Gordon. Bright took it, listened for a moment, and held it out to Preston. "It's for you. They won't talk to anyone else."

"Who is it?"

"The Scottish Office, Edinburgh."

Preston took the phone. "John Preston . . . Yes, good morning to you. . . ." He listened for several minutes, his brow furrowed. He noted the name *Carmichael* on a scratch pad. "Yes, I think I'd better come up. Would you tell Inspector Carmichael I'll be on the three o'clock shuttle, and could he meet me at Glasgow Airport? Thank you."

"Glasgow?" asked Bright. "What have they been up to?"

"Oh, some Russian seaman who took a tumble off a roof, and who may not have been all he should have been. I'll be back tomorrow. It's probably nothing. Still, anything to get out of the office. . . ."

Glasgow Airport lies eight miles southwest of the city and is linked to it by the M8 motorway. Preston's flight landed at just after half past four, and with only hand luggage to carry he was in the concourse ten minutes later. He went to Airport Information and they paged "Mr. Carmichael." The detective inspector from Special Branch appeared and introduced himself. Five minutes later, they were in the inspector's car and pulling onto the motorway leading to the darkening city.

"Let's talk as we drive," suggested Preston. "Start from the beginning and tell me what happened."

Carmichael was succinct and accurate. There were a lot of gaps he could not fill, but he had had time to read the statements of the two police constables, especially that of PC Craig, so he could recount most of it. Preston heard him out in silence.

"What caused you to phone the Scottish Office and ask for someone to come up from London?" he asked at length.

"I could be wrong, but there seems to me a possibility the man was not a merchant seaman," said Carmichael.

"Go on."

"It was something Craig said in the canteen at Division this morning," said Carmichael. "I wasn't there, but the remark was over-heard by a CID man, who called me up. What Craig said, McBain agreed with. But neither of them mentioned it in their official statements. As you know, statements are about the facts; this was the police officers' speculation. Still, it seemed worth checking out."

"I'm listening."

"They said that when they found the seaman he was huddled in the fetal position, his hands clasped around the gunnysack, which was pressed into his own belly. The phrase Craig used was that 'he seemed to be protecting it like a baby.' "

Preston could see the oddity. If a man is being kicked half to death, the instinct is to roll into a ball, as Semyonov had done, but to use the hands to protect the head. Why would a man take the force of the kicks on his unprotected head in order to guard a worthless canvas bag?

"Then," resumed Carmichael, "I began to wonder about the time and place. Seamen in the port of Glasgow go to Betty's or the Stable Bar. This man was four miles from the docks, walking up a road toward nowhere, long after closing hours, without a bar in sight. What the hell was he doing there at that hour?"

"Good question," said Preston. "What next?"

"At ten this morning I went to the postmortem. The body was pretty badly smashed by the fall, but the front of the face was all right except for a couple of bruises. Most of the blows from the Neds were to the back of the head and the body. I've seen the faces of merchant navy deckhands before. They are weatherbeaten, wind-burned, brown, and lined. This man had a bland, pale face—the face of a man not accustomed to life on the foredeck.

"Then, his hands. They should have been brown on the backs, callused on the palms. They were soft and white, like those of a desk worker. Lastly, the teeth. I'd expect a deckhand out of Leningrad to have basic dentistry, the fillings of amalgam and any false teeth of steel, Russian-style. This man had gold fillings and two gold caps."

Preston nodded approvingly. Carmichael was sharp. They had arrived in the parking lot of the hotel where Carmichael had booked Preston for the night.

"One last thing. Small, but it may mean something," said Carmichael. "Before the postmortem the Soviet consul went to see our chief superintendent at Pitt Street. It seems he was on the verge of lodging a protest when the captain of the ship arrived with his political officer. I was with them. The political officer pulled the consul into the hall and they had a whispered conversation. When the consul returned, he was all civility and understanding. It was as if the political officer had told him something about the dead man. I got the impression they didn't want to make any waves at all until they had checked with the embassy in London."

"Have you told anyone in the uniformed branch that I'm coming?" asked Preston.

"Not yet," replied Carmichael. "Do you want me to?"

Preston shook his head. "Wait till the morning. We'll decide then. It may be nothing."

"Anything else you want?"

"Copies of the various statements—the lot, if you can get them. And the list of the man's effects. By the way, where are they?"

"Locked up at Partick police station. I'll get you the copies and drop them off here later."

■ General Karpov called a friend in the GRU and spun a story to the effect that one of his bagmen had brought him a couple of bottles of French brandy from Paris. He personally never touched the stuff, but he owed Pyotr Marchenko a favor. He would drop the brandy at Marchenko's dacha during the weekend. He just needed to know there would be someone to take it in. Did the colleague have Marchenko's country number at Peredelkino? The GRU man did indeed. He gave it to Karpov and thought no more about it.

In most of the dachas of the Soviet elite there is a housekeeper or manservant in residence during the winter months to keep the fires alight so that the owner's weekends do not start freezing cold. It was Marchenko's housekeeper who answered Karpov's phone call. Yes, the general *was* expected the following day, Friday; he usually arrived at about six in the evening. Karpov thanked her and hung up. He decided he would dismiss his chauffeur, drive himself, and surprise the GRU general at seven o'clock.

■ Preston lay awake in his bed, thinking. Carmichael had brought him all the statements taken at the Western Infirmary and at Division. Like all police-recorded depositions, they were stilted and formal, quite unlike the way people actually narrate what they have seen and heard. The facts were there, of course, but not the impressions.

What Preston could not know, because Craig had not mentioned it and the nurse had not seen it, was that before running off down the corridor between the examination rooms, Semyonov had grabbed for the round tobacco tin. Craig had simply said the injured man "pushed past me."

Nor was the list of personal effects—the "productions"—much more helpful. It mentioned a round tobacco tin and "contents"—which could have been two ounces of shag tobacco.

Preston ran over the possibilities in his mind. First: Semyonov was an illegal being landed in Britain. Conclusion: Very unlikely. He was on the crew list of the ship and would be conspicuous by his absence when the vessel departed for Leningrad.

All right. Second: He was to come into Glasgow with the ship, and leave with it that Thursday night. What was he doing in the small hours halfway up the Great Western Road? Making a drop or keeping a rendezvous? Good. Or even *collecting* a package to bring back to Leningrad? Even better. But after that, Preston's options ran out.

If Semyonov had delivered what he had come to deliver, why had he tried to protect his gunnysack as if his life depended on it? It would have been empty of its cargo.

If he had come to pick something up, but had not yet done that, the same reasoning applied. If he had already made the pickup, why had not something of considerable interest, such as a packet of papers, been found on his person?

If what he had come to deliver or collect could be concealed about a human form, why had he brought a gunnysack at all? If there was something sewn into his anorak or pants or concealed in the heel of his shoe, why not let the Neds take the sack, which was what they were after? He could have saved himself a beating, and got to his rendezvous or back to his ship (whichever direction he was heading) with no more than a couple of bruises.

Preston threw a few more possibilities into the food-mixer.

Semyonov had come as a courier for a face-to-face rendezvous with a Soviet illegal already resident in Britain. To pass a verbal message? Unlikely; there were a score of better ways of passing coded information. To receive a verbal report? Same applied. To change places with a resident illegal, to replace the man? No, the photograph in his paybook was identifiably Semyonov. If he had been changing places with an illegal, Moscow would have given him a duplicate paybook with the appropriate photograph, so the man he was replacing could go out on the *Komarov* as deckhand Semyonov. The second paybook would have been on his person. Unless it were sewn into the lining . . . of what? The lining of his jacket? Then why take a beating to protect the sack? Would it have been concealed in the canvas base of the sack itself? Much more likely.

It all seemed to come back to that damned sack. Just before midnight, Preston called Carmichael at his home.

"Can you pick me up at eight tomorrow morning?" he asked. "I want to go to Partick and have a look at the productions."

■ Over breakfast that Friday morning, Yevgeni Karpov asked his wife, Ludmilla, "Can you take the kids out to the dacha in the Volga this afternoon?"

"Of course. You'll join us straight from the office?"

He nodded absently. "I'll be late. I've got to see someone from the GRU."

Ludmilla Karpova sighed inwardly. She knew he kept a partridge-plump little secretary in a small apartment in the Arbat district. She knew because wives will talk, and in a society as stratified as theirs, most of her friends were the wives of officers of similar rank. She also knew he did not know she knew.

She was fifty and they had been married twenty-eight years. It had been a good marriage, considering the job he did, and she had been a good wife. Like others who had married officers of the FCD, she had long since lost count of the evenings she had waited up for him while he had been buried in the cipher room of an embassy on foreign soil. She had stuck it through the endless tedium of countless diplomatic cocktail parties, although she spoke no foreign language, while her husband made the rounds, elegant, affable, fluent in English, French, and German, doing his job under embassy cover.

She had lost count of the weeks she had spent alone when the children were small and he was a junior officer, their home a tiny and cramped apartment without any daily help, and he away on a course, or an assignment, or standing in the shadows by the Berlin Wall waiting for a bagman to come home to the East.

She had known the panic and nameless fear that even the innocent feel when, at a certain foreign station, one of Karpov's colleagues had gone over to the West, and the KR (counterintelligence) people had grilled her for hours about anything the man or his wife might have said in her hearing. She had watched in pity as the defector's wife, a woman she had known well but now dared not approach, was escorted out to the waiting Aeroflot plane. It went with the job, Karpov had said, as he comforted her.

That had been years before. Now her Zhenia was a general; the Moscow apartment was airy and spacious; she had made the dacha lovely in the way she knew he liked, with pine and rugs, comfortable but rustic. The two boys were a credit to them; both at the university, one to be a doctor, the other a physicist. There would be no more horrid embassy apartments, and in three years he could retire with honors and a good pension. So, if he had to have a bit of skirt one evening a week, he was no different from most of his contemporaries. It was better, perhaps, this way than if he had been a drunken brute, like some, or a passed-over major going nowhere but to one of the godforsaken Asian republics to end his career. Still, she sighed inwardly.

■ Partick police station is not the most glamorous edifice in the fine city of Glasgow, but Carmichael and Preston were not on an architectural tour. They were interested in the "productions" from the previous night's mugging/suicide, which had entered the station's routine. The duty sergeant handed the desk to a constable and led them to the rear, where he unlocked the door to a room stacked with filing cabinets. With no expression of surprise, he accepted Carmichael's card and his explanation that he and his colleague had to check the productions in order to complete their own reports, the dead man being a foreign seaman and all that. The sergeant knew about reports; he spent half his life filling them in. But he declined to leave the room while they opened the bags and looked over the contents.

Preston started with the shoes, checking for false heels, detachable soles, or cavities in the toecaps. Nothing. The socks took less time, as did the underpants. He had the back off the shattered wristwatch, but it was just a wristwatch. The trousers took longer; he felt all the seams and hems, looking for new stitching or a thickness that could not be accounted for by a double layer of the fabric. Nothing.

The turtleneck sweater the man had been wearing was easy; there were no seams and no hidden papers or hard lumps. He spent much longer on the anorak, but it yielded no fruit, either. By the time he got to the gunnysack he was more convinced than before that if the mysterious Comrade Semyonov had had something with him, the answer lay here.

He started with the rolled-up sweater that had been in it, more for elimination purposes than anything. It was clean. Then he began on the sack itself. It took half an hour before he was satisfied that the base was just a double-stitched disk of canvas, the sides were of single canvas, and the eyelets at the top were not miniature transmitters or the drawstring a secret aerial.

That left the tobacco tin. It was of Russian origin, an ordinary screw-top tin that still smelled faintly of pungent tobacco. The cotton was cotton, and that left three metal disks: two shiny, like aluminum, and light in weight; the other dull and heavy, like lead. He sat staring at them for a while as they lay on the table; Carmichael looked at him, and the sergeant looked at the floor.

It was not what they were that puzzled him; it was what they were not. They were not anything. The aluminum disks had been above and below the heavy disk; the heavy one was two inches in diameter, and the lighter ones, three inches. He tried to imagine what purpose they could possibly serve, in radio communications, in coding and decoding, in photography. And the answer was—none. They were just metal disks. Still, he was more than ever convinced that a man had died rather than let them fall into the hands of the Neds—who would have thrown them into the gutter, anyway—and rather than let himself be interrogated about them.

Preston rose and suggested lunch. The sergeant, who felt he had wasted a morning, put the productions back into their bags and locked them in a filing cabinet. Then he showed them out.

During lunch at the Pond Hotel—Preston had suggested they drive past the spot of the mugging—he excused himself to make a telephone call. "It may take a while," he told Carmichael. "Have a brandy on the Sassenachs."

Carmichael grinned. "I'll do that, and I'll toast Bannockburn."

Out of sight of the dining room, Preston left the hotel and walked over to the BP filling station, where he made several small purchases from the rack of parts in the adjacent shop. Then he went back to the hotel and made his call to London. He gave his assistant, Bright, the Partick police station's number and told him exactly when he wanted to be called back.

Half an hour later, Preston and Carmichael were back in the police station, where a plainly disgruntled sergeant led them once again to the room where the productions were stored. Preston seated himself behind the table facing the wall phone across the room. In front of him on the table he built up a rampart of clothing from the various bags. At three o'clock the phone rang; the switchboard was putting the London call on the extension. The sergeant took it.

"It's for you, sir. London on the line," he said to Preston.

"Would you mind taking it?" Preston asked Carmichael. "Find out if it's urgent."

Carmichael rose and crossed the room to where the sergeant held the phone. For a second both Scottish officers were facing the wall.

Ten minutes later Preston was finished for the last time. Carmichael drove him back to the airport.

"I'll file a report, of course," said Preston. "But I can't see what the hell the Russian was so fussed about. How long will those productions be locked up in Partick?"

"Oh, weeks yet. The Soviet consul's been told that. The search for the Neds is still on, but it's a long shot. We might pick up one of them on another charge and get a squeal. But I doubt it."

Preston checked in for his flight. Boarding was immediate.

"You know, the stupid thing is," said Carmichael as he saw him off, "if that Russian had stayed cool, we'd have driven him back to his ship with our apologies, him and his wee toy with him."

When the plane was airborne, Preston went to the toilet for a bit of privacy and examined the three disks that he had wrapped in his handkerchief. They still meant nothing to him.

The three washers he had obtained from the garage shop and switched for the Russian's "wee toys" would suffice for a while. In the meantime there was a man he wanted to look at the Russian disks. He worked outside London, and Bright should have asked him to stay on that Friday evening until Preston arrived.

■ Karpov arrived at General Marchenko's dacha in darkness, at just after seven. The door was answered by the general's batman, who showed him into the sitting room. Marchenko was already on his feet and seemed both surprised and pleased to see his friend from the other, and bigger, intelligence service. "Yevgeni Sergeivitch," he boomed. "What brings you to my humble cottage?"

Karpov had a shopping bag in his hand. He held it up and delved inside. "One of my boys just got back from Turkey, via Armenia," he said. "A bright lad, he knows not to come empty-handed. Since there's nothing to buy in Anatolia, he stopped at Erevan and put these in his suitcase." He produced one of the four bottles the bag contained, the finest of all the Armenian brandies.

Marchenko's eyes lit up. "Akhtamar!" he shouted. "Nothing but the best for the FCD."

"Well," continued Karpov easily, "I was driving to my own place up the road, and I thought: Who will take a glass of Akhtamar to help me through it? And back came the answer: Old Pyotr Marchenko. So I made a short detour. Shall we see what it tastes like?"

Marchenko roared with laughter. "Sasha! Glasses!" he shouted.

■ Preston landed just before five o'clock, collected his car from the short-term parking lot, and headed for the M4 motorway. Instead of turning east for London, he took the west lane, toward Berkshire. Thirty minutes brought him to his destination, an institution on the outskirts of the village of Aldermaston.

Known simply as "Aldermaston," the Atomic Weapons Research Establishment so beloved of peace marchers looking for a target is in fact a multidiscipline unit. Its workers do, indeed, design and build nuclear devices, but it also houses researchers into chemistry, phys-ics, conventional explosives, engineering, pure and applied mathe-matics, radiobiology, medicine, health and safety standards, and electronics. By the by, it has a very fine metallurgy department.

Years earlier, one of the scientists based at Aldermaston had given a lecture to a group of intelligence officers in Ulster on the kinds of metals the IRA bombmakers favored for their devices. Preston had been one of those in the audience and had remembered the scien-tist's name.

Dr. Dafydd Wynne-Evans was waiting for him in the hallway. Preston introduced himself and reminded Dr. Wynne-Evans of his lecture many years before.

"Well, well, what a memory you've got," the scientist said in his lilting Welsh accent. "All right, Mr. Preston, what can I do for you?"

Preston dug into his pocket, produced the handkerchief, and held it out to show the three disks it contained. "These were taken off somebody in Glasgow," he said. "They defeat me. I'd like to know what they are and what they could be used for."

The doctor looked at them closely. "Nefarious purposes, you think?"

"Could be."

"Difficult to say without tests," said the metallurgist. "Look, I've got a dinner tonight and my daughter's wedding tomorrow. Can I run them through some tests on Monday and call you?"

"Monday will do fine," said Preston. "I'm taking a few days off, actually. I'll be at home. Can I give you my number in Kensington?"

Dr. Wynne-Evans hurried upstairs, locked the disks in his safe for the night, bade good-bye to Preston, and hurried to his dinner. Pres-ton drove back to London.

■ While Preston was on the road, the listening station at Menwith Hill in Yorkshire picked up a single squirt from a clandestine trans-mitter. Menwith got it first, but Brawdy in Wales and Chicksands in Bedfordshire also got a trace and computed the crossbearings. The source was somewhere in the hills north of Sheffield.

When the Sheffield police got there, the spot turned out to be the shoulder of a lonely road between Barnsley and Pontefract. There was no one there.

Later that evening, one of the duty officers at GCHQ Cheltenham accepted a drink in the office of the duty director.

"It's the same bugger," the officer said. "He's carborne and he's got a good set. He only spent five seconds on the air, and it looks indecipherable. First the Derbyshire Peak District, now the Yorkshire hills. It looks as if he's somewhere in the north Midlands."

"Keep after him," said the director. "We haven't had a sleeper transmitter go suddenly active in ages. I wonder what he's saying."

What Major Valeri Petrofsky had been saying, although transmitted by his operator when he was long gone, was: *Courier Two never showed. Inform soonest re arrival substitute.*

■ The first bottle of Akhtamar stood empty on the table, and the second was well broached. Marchenko was flushed, but he could be a two-bottle-a-day man when the mood took him, so he was still well in control.

Karpov, though he seldom drank for pleasure, and even more rarely drank alone, had seasoned his stomach for years on the diplomatic circuit. He had a good head when he needed it. Apart from that, he had forced half a pound of white butter down his throat before leaving Yasyenevo, and though he had nearly gagged on it, the fat had lined his stomach and was now retarding the onset of the alcohol's effect.

"What are you up to these days, Petya?" he asked, dropping into the diminutive and familiar form of the name.

Marchenko's eyes narrowed. "Why do you ask?"

"Come on, Petya, we go back a long way. Remember when I saved your ass in Afghanistan three years back? You owe me a favor. What's going on?"

Marchenko remembered. He nodded solemnly. In 1984 he had been heading a big GRU operation against the Muslim rebels up near the Khyber Pass. There was one particularly outstanding guerrilla leader who ran raids into Afghanistan, using as his bases the refugee camps inside Pakistan. Marchenko had rashly sent a snatch-squad over the border to get him. They had run into bad trouble. The pro-Soviet Afghans had been unmasked by the Pathans and had died horribly. The single Russian accompanying them was lucky to survive; the Pathans had handed him to the Pakistani authorities of the North-West Frontier District, hoping for some arms in exchange.

Marchenko had been out on a limb. He had appealed to Karpov, then head of the Illegals Directorate, and Karpov had endangered one of his best undercover Pakistani officers in Islamabad to get the Russian sprung and back over the border. A big international incident then could have broken Marchenko, and he would have joined the long list of Soviet officers whose careers had crashed in that miserable country.

"Yes, all right, I know I owe you, Zhenia, but don't ask what I've been on for the past few weeks. Special assignment, very close to the chest. Top secret—know what I mean?" He tapped the side of his nose with a sausagelike forefinger and nodded solemnly.

Karpov leaned forward and refilled the GRU general's glass from the third bottle. "Sure, I know, sorry I asked," he said reassuringly. "Won't mention it again. Won't mention the operation again."

Marchenko waved an admonitory finger. His eyes were bloodshot. He reminded Karpov of a wounded boar in a thicket, his brain dimmed by alcohol instead of pain and blood loss, but dangerous nevertheless. "Not operation . . . no operation . . . canceled. Sworn to secrecy . . . all of us. Very high up . . . higher than you could imagine. Don't mention it again, okay?"

"Wouldn't dream of it," said Karpov, filling the glasses again. He was taking advantage of Marchenko's drunkenness to put more brandy in the GRU man's glass than in his own, but he was still finding it difficult to focus.

Two hours later, the last of the Akhtamar was a third gone. Marchenko was slumped, chin on chest. Karpov raised his glass in yet another of the endless toasts. "Here's to oblivion."

"Oblivion?" Marchenko shook his head in bewilderment. "I'm all right. Drink you FCD bastards under the table anytime. Not oblivious . . ."

"No," corrected Karpov. "Oblivion of the plan. We just forget it, right?"

"Aurora? Right, forget it. Bloody good idea, though."

They drank. Karpov filled the glasses again. "Damn them all," he proposed. "Screw Philby . . . and the academician."

Marchenko nodded in agreement, the brandy that had missed his mouth dripping off his jowls.

"Krilov? Asshole. Forget 'em all."

It was midnight when Karpov staggered to his car. He leaned against a tree, stuck two fingers down his throat, and threw up what he could into the snow. Sucking in gulps of the freezing night air helped, but the drive to his dacha was murder. He made it with a scraped fender and two nasty scares. Ludmilla was still up, in a housecoat, and she put him to bed, terrified that he had actually driven out from Moscow in that condition.

■ On Saturday morning, John Preston drove down to Tonbridge to pick up his son, Tommy. As usual when his dad collected him from school, the boy was a torrent of words, memories of the term just past, projects for the term yet to come, plans for the holiday about to begin, praise for his best friends and their virtues, scorn for the infamies of those he disliked.

For Preston, the drive back to London was bliss. He mentioned the several things he had planned for their week together and was happy they seemed to meet with Tommy's approval. The lad's face fell only when he recalled he would be returned after a week to the smart, brittle, and pricelessly expensive Mayfair apartment where Julia lived with her boyfriend, a dress manufacturer. The man was old enough to be Tommy's grandfather, and Preston suspected that any breakages in the flat would lead to a severe frost in the atmosphere.

"Dad," said Tommy as they drove over Vauxhall Bridge, "why can't I come and stay with you all the time?"

Preston sighed. It was not easy to explain the breakup of a marriage, or the cost of it, to a twelve-year-old. "Because," he said carefully, "your mummy and Archie aren't actually married. If I insisted on a formal divorce, Mummy could ask for and get an allowance from me called maintenance. Which, incidentally, I couldn't afford, not on my salary. At least, not enough to keep myself, you at school, and her. It just wouldn't go that far. And if I couldn't pay that allowance, the court might decide your best chances in life were with Mummy. So we wouldn't get to see each other even as often as we do now."

"I didn't know it came down to money," said the boy sadly.

"In the end, most things come down to money. Sad but true. Years ago, if I had been able to afford a better kind of life for all three of us, Mummy and I might not have broken up. I was just an Army officer, and even when I quit the Army to join the Home Office, the salary still wasn't enough."

"Just what *do* you do in the Home Office?" asked the boy. He was dropping the subject of his parents' estrangement, the way the young will try to blank out something that hurts them.

"Oh, I'm a sort of minor civil servant," said Preston.

"Gosh, that must be jolly dull."

"Yes," Preston conceded, "I suppose it is, really."

■ Yevgeni Karpov woke at noon with an imperial hangover that half a dozen aspirins were only just able to contain. After lunch he felt somewhat better and decided to go for a stroll.

There was something at the back of his mind—a memory, a half-recollection, that he had heard the name Krilov somewhere in the not-too-distant past. It bothered him. One of the restricted-list reference books he kept at the dacha had given him the details of Krilov, Vladimir Ilich: historian, professor at Moscow University, lifelong member of the Party, member of the Academy of Sciences, member of the Supreme Soviet, etc., etc. All that he knew; but there was something else. He plowed through the snow, his head bowed, deep in thought.

The boys had gone off on their skis to take advantage of the last of the good powder snow before the coming thaw spoiled it all. Ludmilla Karpova trailed along behind her husband. She knew his mood and refrained from interrupting. The previous evening she had been surprised but quite happy at the state he had been in. She knew he hardly ever drank—and never that heavily—which meant he had not been visiting his girlfriend. Perhaps he really had been with a colleague from the GRU, one of the so-called neighbors. Whatever, something had got on top of him, but it was not a partridge in the Arbat.

At just after three, whatever he had been racking his brains for came to him. He stopped several yards ahead of her, said, "Damn! Of course," and perked up at once. All smiles, he took her arm, and they walked back to the dacha.

General Karpov knew he had some quiet research to do in his office the next morning, and that he would visit Professor Krilov in his Moscow apartment on Monday evening.

CHAPTER

The phone call on Monday morning caught John Preston just as he was about to go out with his son.

"Mr. Preston? Dafydd Wynne-Evans here."

For a moment the name meant nothing; then Preston recalled his request of Friday evening.

"I've had a look at your little piece of metal. Very interesting. Can you come out here and have a chat with me?"

"Well, actually, I'm taking a few days off," said Preston. "Would the end of the week suit?"

There was a pause from the Aldermaston end. "I think it might be better before then, if you could spare the time."

"Er . . . oh . . . well, could you give me the gist of it on the phone?"

"Much better if we talk about it face-to-face," said Dr. Wynne-Evans.

Preston thought for a moment. He was taking Tommy to the Windsor Safari Park for the day. But that was also in Berkshire. "Could I come by this afternoon—say, about five?" he asked.

"Five it is," said the scientist. "Ask for me at the desk. I'll have you shown up."

■ Professor Krilov lived on the top floor of an apartment building on Komsomolski Prospekt that provided commanding views of the Moskva River and was handy for the university on the southern bank. General Karpov pressed the buzzer at just after six o'clock, and it was the academic himself who answered it. He surveyed his visitor without recognition.

"Comrade Professor Krilov?"

"Yes."

"My name is Yevgeni Karpov. I wonder if we might have a word or two?"

He held out his identification. Professor Krilov studied it, taking in Karpov's rank and the fact that the visitor came from the First Chief Directorate of the KGB. Then he handed it back and gestured Karpov to enter. He led the way to a well-furnished sitting room, took his guest's coat, and bade him be seated.

"To what do I owe this honor?" he asked when he had seated himself opposite Karpov. He was a man of distinction in his own right, not in any way awed by a general of the KGB.

Karpov realized the professor was different. Erita Philby could be tricked into revealing the existence of the chauffeur; Gregoriev could be browbeaten by his intimidating rank; Marchenko was an old colleague and a too-heavy drinker. But Krilov was high in the Party, the Supreme Soviet, the Academy of Sciences, and the elite of the state. Karpov decided to waste no time, but to play his cards fast and without mercy. It was the only way.

"Professor Krilov, in the interests of the state, I wish you to tell me something. I wish you to tell me what you know about Plan Aurora."

Krilov sat as if he had been slapped. Then he flushed angrily. "General Karpov, you exceed yourself," he snapped. "I do not know what you are talking about."

"I believe you do," said Karpov evenly, "and I believe you should tell me what this plan entails."

For answer, Krilov held out a peremptory hand. "Your authorization, please."

"My authorization is my rank and my service," said Karpov.

"If you have no signed authorization from the Comrade General Secretary, you have none at all," said Krilov icily. He rose and made for the telephone. "Indeed, I think it high time your line of questioning came to the attention of someone far higher in rank than yourself."

He picked up the receiver and prepared to dial.

"That might not be a very good idea," said Karpov. "Did you know that one of your fellow consultants, Philby, a retired colonel of the KGB, is missing?"

Krilov stopped dialing. "What do you mean, missing?" he asked. The first edge of hesitation had entered his hitherto completely assured bearing.

"Please sit down and hear me out," said Karpov. The academic did so. In another room of the apartment, a door opened. A blare of Western jazz could be heard, which muted when the door closed.

"I mean missing," continued Karpov, "gone from his apartment, driver dismissed, wife no idea where he is or when, if at all, he'll be back."

It was a gamble, and a damnably high one. But an air of worry entered the professor's gaze. Then he reasserted himself. "There can be no question of my discussing affairs of state with you, Comrade General. I think I must ask you to leave."

"It's not quite that easy," said Karpov. "Tell me, Professor, you have a son, Leonid, do you not?"

The sudden switch of topic genuinely dumbfounded the professor. "Yes," he conceded. "I do. So what?"

"Let me explain," suggested Karpov.

■ On the other side of Europe, John Preston and his son were driving out of the Windsor Safari Park at the close of a warm spring day.

"I've just got one call to make before we go home," said Preston. "It's not far and it shouldn't take long. Have you ever been to Aldermaston."

The boy's eyes opened wide. "The bomb factory?" he asked.

"It's not quite a bomb factory," Preston corrected, "it's a research establishment."

"Gosh, no. Are we going there? Will they let us in?"

"Well, they'll let me in. You'll have to wait in the car. But it won't take long." He turned north to cut into the M4 motorway.

■ "Your son returned nine weeks ago from a visit to Canada, where he acted as one of the interpreters for a trade delegation," Karpov began quietly.

Krilov nodded. "So?"

"While he was there, my own KR people noted that an attractive young person was spending a good deal of time—too much time, it was judged—trying to get into conversation with the members of our delegation, notably the younger members—secretaries, interpreters, and so forth. The person concerned was photographed and finally identified as an entrapment agent—American, not Canadian, and almost certainly employed by the CIA. As a result, that young agent was put under surveillance and was observed to set up a rendezvous with your son, Leonid, in a hotel room. Not to put too fine a point on it, the pair had a brief but torrid affair."

Professor Krilov's face was mottled with rage. He seemed to have trouble enunciating his words. "How dare you. How dare you have the impertinence to come here and seek to subject me, a member of the Academy of Sciences and the Supreme Soviet, to crude blackmail. The Party will hear of this. You know the rule: only the Party can discipline the Party. You may be a general of the KGB, but you have overstepped your authority by a hundred miles, General Karpov."

Yevgeni Karpov sat as if humbled, staring at the table, as the professor went on.

"So, my son screwed a foreign girl while in Canada. That the girl turned out to be an American was certainly something of which he was completely unaware. He was indiscreet, perhaps, but no more. Was he recruited by this CIA girl?"

"No," admitted Karpov.

"Did he betray any state secrets?"

"No."

"Then you have nothing, Comrade General, but a brief youthful indiscretion. He'll be rebuked. But the rebuke for your counterintelligence people will be the greater. They should have warned him. As to the bedroom business, we are not so unworldly in the Soviet Union as you seem to think. Strong young men have been screwing girls since time began. . . ."

Karpov had opened his attaché case and produced a large photograph, one of a sheaf that lay inside the case, and placed it on the table. Professor Krilov stared at it, and his words died. The flush went out of his cheeks, draining away until his elderly face appeared gray in the lamplight. He shook his head several times.

"I am sorry," said Karpov very gently, "truly sorry. The surveillance was on the American boy, not on your son. It was not intended that it should come to this."

"I don't believe it," croaked the professor.

"I have sons of my own," murmured Karpov. "I believe I can understand, or try to understand, how you feel."

The academic sucked in his breath, rose, muttered, "Excuse me," and left the room. Karpov sighed and replaced the photograph in his case. From down the corridor he heard the blare of jazz as a door opened, the sudden ending of the music, and voices, two voices, raised in anger. One was the roar of the father, the other a higher-pitched voice, as of a young man. The altercation ended with the sound of a slap. Seconds later, Professor Krilov reentered the room. He seated himself, eyes dull, shoulders sloping. "What are you going to do?" he whispered.

Karpov sighed. "My duty is very clear. As you said, only the Party may discipline the Party. I should by rights hand over the report and the photographs to the Central Committee. You know the law. You know what they do to 'golden boys.' It's five years without remission, and 'severe regime.' I'm afraid that word gets around in the camps. After that, the young man becomes—how shall I put it?—anybody's property. A lad from a sheltered background would be hard put to survive that sort of thing."

"But—" prompted the professor.

"But I can decide that there is a chance the CIA will seek to pursue the matter. I have that right. I can decide the Americans could become impatient and send their agent into the Soviet Union to resume contact with Leonid. I have the right to decide that the entrapment of your son could possibly be turned into an operation to trap a CIA agent. While waiting, I would be able to keep the file in my safe, and the waiting could take a very long time. I have that authority; in operational matters, yes, I have that authority."

"And the price?"

"I think you know that."

"What do you want to know about Plan Aurora?"

"Just start from the beginning."

■ Preston swung into the main gate at Aldermaston, found a slot in the visitors' parking area, and got out of the car.

"Sorry, Tommy, no farther for you. Just wait for me here. I hope I won't be long."

He crossed in the dusk to the swinging doors and presented himself to the two men at the desk. They examined his ID card and rang Dr. Wynne-Evans, who sanctioned the visit to his office. It was three floors up. Preston was shown in and gestured to a seat facing Wynne-Evans's desk.

The scientist regarded him over his glasses. "May I ask where you got this little exhibit?" he inquired, pointing to the heavy, leadlike disk of metal, which now sat in a sealed glass jar.

"It was taken from someone in Glasgow during the small hours of Thursday morning. What about the other two disks?"

"Oh, they're just ordinary aluminum, boyo. Nothing strange about them. Just used to keep this one safe and sound. This is the one that interests me."

"Do you know what it is?" asked Preston.

Dr. Wynne-Evans seemed startled by the naiveté of the question. "Of course I know what it is," he said. "It's my job to know. It's a disk of pure polonium."

Preston frowned. He had never heard of such a metal.

■ "Well, it all started in early January with a memorandum submitted by Philby to the General Secretary, in which Philby maintained there existed within the British Labour Party a Hard Left wing that had grown so strong it was in a position to take over complete control of the Party machine more or less when it wished. That corresponds to my own view."

"And mine," murmured Karpov.

"Philby went further. He claimed that within the Hard Left wing there was a group, an inner kernel, of dedicated Marxist-Leninists who had framed an intention to do just that—not in the period before Britain's next general election, but afterward, in the very wake of a Labour electoral victory. In short, to await the victory at the polls of Mr. Neil Kinnock and then to topple him from the Party leadership. His replacement would be Britain's first Marxist-Leninist premier, who would institute a series of policies wholly in line with Soviet foreign and defense interests, most notably in the area of unilateral nuclear disarmament and the expulsion of all American forces."

"Feasible," remarked Karpov, nodding. "So a committee of four of you were called together to advise on how this electoral victory could best be achieved?"

Krilov looked up, surprised. "Yes. There were Philby, General Marchenko, myself, and Dr. Rogov."

"The chess grand master?"

"And physicist," added Krilov. "What we came up with was Plan Aurora, which would have been an act of massive destabilization of the British electorate by pushing millions toward a mood of determined unilateralism."

"You say . . . *would* have?"

"Yes. The plan was principally Rogov's idea. He supported it strongly. Marchenko went along, with reservations. Philby—well, no one could tell what Philby was really thinking. Just kept nodding and smiling, waiting to see which way the wind blew."

"That's Philby," agreed Karpov. "And then you presented it?"

"Yes. On March twelfth. I opposed the plan. The General Secretary agreed with me. He denounced it roundly, ordered all notes and files destroyed, and made all four of us swear never to mention the matter again under any circumstances."

"Tell me, why did you oppose it?"

"It seemed to me reckless and dangerous. Apart from anything, it was in complete contravention of the Fourth Protocol. If that protocol is ever breached, God knows where the world will end up."

"The Fourth Protocol?"

"Yes. To the international Nuclear Nonproliferation Treaty. You remember that, of course."

"One has to remember so much," said Karpov gently. "Please remind me."

■ "I've never heard of polonium," said Preston.

"No, well, you probably wouldn't have," said Wynne-Evans. "I mean, you don't find it hanging about on your workbench. It's very rare."

"And what are its uses, Doctor?"

"Well, it is occasionally—only very occasionally, mind—used in curative medicine. Was your man in Glasgow on his way to a medical conference or exhibition?"

"No," said Preston firmly, "he was in no way heading for a medical conference."

"Well, that would have accounted for a ten-percent possibility of what it was intended for—before you relieved him of his burden. Since he wasn't going to a medical conference, I'm afraid that leaves the ninety-percent likelihood. Apart from these two functions, polonium has no known use on this planet."

"And the other use?"

"Well, a disk of polonium this size will do nothing on its own. But if it is placed in close juxtaposition with a disk of another metal called lithium, the two combine to form an initiator."

"A what?"

"An initiator."

"And what the hell, pray, is that?"

■ "On July first, 1968," said Professor Krilov, "the Nuclear Non-proliferation Treaty was signed by the three (then) nuclear powers of the world, the United States, Great Britain, and the Soviet Union.

"By that treaty the three signatory nations pledged themselves not to impart the technology or the matériel capable of enabling the construction of a nuclear weapon to any nation not then in possession of such technology or matériel. Do you recall that?"

"Yes," said Karpov, "I remember that much."

"Well, the signing ceremonies in Washington, London, and Moscow were attended by huge and worldwide publicity. A complete absence of publicity surrounded the later signing of four secret protocols to that treaty.

"Each of the protocols foresaw the development of a possible future hazard, which was not then technically possible but which, it was then estimated, might one day become technically possible.

"Over the years, the first three protocols passed into history, either because the hazard was established to be quite impossible or because an antidote was discovered as fast as the threat became reality. But by the early 1980s the Fourth Protocol, the most secret of them all, had become a living nightmare."

"What, exactly, did the Fourth Protocol envisage?" asked Karpov.

Krilov sighed. "We relied on Dr. Rogov for this information. As you know, he is a nuclear physicist; that is his branch of science. The Fourth Protocol foresaw technological advances in the manufacture of nuclear bombs, mainly in the areas of miniaturization and simplification. This, apparently, is what has happened. In one area, the weapons have become infinitely more powerful, but more complex to construct and larger in size. Another branch of the science has gone the other way. The basic atomic bomb, which required a huge bomber for its delivery to Japan in 1945, can now be made small enough to go in a suitcase and simple enough to be assembled from a dozen prefabricated, milled and threaded components, like a child's construction kit."

"And that is what the Fourth Protocol banned?"

Krilov shook his head. "It went further. It forbade any of the signatory nations to introduce onto the territory of any nation a device in assembled or unassembled form by covert means, for detonation in, say, a rented house or flat in the heart of a city."

"No four-minute warning," mused Karpov, "no radar detection of an incoming missile, no counterstrike, no identification of the perpetrator. Just a megaton explosion from a basement bedsitter."

The professor nodded. "That's right. That's why I called it a living nightmare. The open societies of the West are more vulnerable, but we are none of us immune from smuggled artifacts. If the Fourth Protocol is ever breached, all those ranks of rockets and electronic countermeasures, indeed most of the military-industrial complex, become irrelevant."

"And that was what Plan Aurora had in mind."

Krilov nodded again. He seemed to clam up.

"But since," pursued Karpov, "it was all stopped and prohibited, the whole plan has become what, in the service, we call 'archival.' "

Krilov seemed to grasp at the word. "That's right. It's just archival now."

"But tell me what it *would* have meant," Karpov pressed.

"Well, the plan was to infiltrate into Britain a top-class Soviet agent who would act as the executive officer of Aurora. To him, using a variety of couriers, would have been smuggled the ten or so component parts of a small atomic bomb of about one-and-a-half-kilotons power."

"So small? The Hiroshima bomb was ten kilotons."

"It was not intended to cause huge damage. That would have canceled the general election. It was intended to create a supposed nuclear accident and panic the ten-percent 'floating vote' into supporting unilateral nuclear disarmament and voting at the polls for the only party pledged to unilateralism, the Labour Party."

"I'm sorry," said Karpov. "Please go on."

"The device would have been detonated six days before polling day," said the professor. "The place was vitally important. The one selected was the United States Air Force base at Bentwaters in Suffolk. Apparently, F-5 strike planes are based there and they carry small tactical nuclear devices for use against our massed tank divisions in the event of our invading Western Europe."

Karpov nodded. He knew Bentwaters, and the information was correct.

"The executive officer," Professor Krilov went on, "would have been ordered to take the assembled device by car to the very perimeter wire of the base in the small hours of the morning. The whole base, it seems, is in the heart of Rendlesham Forest. He would have set off the explosion just before dawn.

"Because of the smallness of the device, damage would have been limited to the airbase itself, which would have been vaporized, along with Rendlesham Forest, three hamlets, a village, the foreshore, and a bird sanctuary. Since the base is right next to the Suffolk coast, the cloud of radioactive dust thrown up would have drifted on the prevailing west wind out over the North Sea. By the time it had reached the coast of Holland, ninety-five percent of it would have become inert or fallen into the sea. The intent was not to cause an ecological catastrophe but to provoke fear and a violent wave of hatred of America."

"They might not have believed it," said Karpov. "A lot of things could have gone wrong. The executive officer could have been caught alive."

Professor Krilov shook his head. "Rogov had thought of all that. He had worked it out like a chess game. The officer in question would have been told that after pressing the button he had two hours on the timer to drive as far as he could. In fact the timer would have been a sealed unit, set for instant detonation."

Poor Petrofsky, thought Karpov. "And the credibility angle?" he asked.

"On the evening of the same day as the explosion," said Krilov, "a man, who is apparently a covert Soviet agent, would have flown to Prague and held an international press conference. That man is Dr. Nahum Wisser, an Israeli nuclear physicist. It seems he works for us."

General Karpov preserved his deadpan expression. "You amaze me," he said. He was acquainted with Dr. Wisser's file. The scientist had had a son on whom he doted. The youth had been a soldier in the Israeli Army, stationed in Beirut in 1982. When the Phalangists had devastated the Palestinian refugee camps of Sabra and Shatila, the young Lieutenant Wisser had tried to intervene. He had been cut down by a bullet. Carefully constructed evidence had been presented to the grieving father, already a committed opponent of the Likud Party, that it had been an Israeli bullet that had killed his son. In his bitterness and rage, Dr. Wisser had swung a little further left and agreed to work for Russia.

"Anyway," Krilov continued, "Dr. Wisser would have claimed to the world that he had collaborated for years with the Americans, while on exchange visits, in the development of ultra-small nuclear warheads. This, it seems, is true. He would have gone on to say that he had repeatedly warned the Americans that these ultra-small warheads were not stable enough to permit deployment. The Americans had been impatient to deploy these new warheads because their small size permitted space to take on board extra fuel and thus to increase the range of their F-5s.

"It was calculated that these claims, made on the day following the explosion, the fifth before the polling date, would turn the wave of anti-Americanism in Britain into a gale that not even the Conservatives could hope to stem."

Karpov nodded. "Yes, I believe it would have done that. Anything more from the fertile brain of Dr. Rogov?"

"Much more," said Krilov glumly. "He suggested that the American reaction would have been histrionic and violent denial. Thus, on the fourth day before polling, the General Secretary would have announced to the world that if the Americans intended to enter a period of insanity, that was their business. But he, for his part, had no alternative in the protection of the Soviet people but to put all our forces on red alert.

"That evening, one of our friends, a man very close to Mr. Kinnock, would have urged the Labour leader to fly to Moscow, see the General Secretary personally, and intervene for peace. Had there been any hesitation, our own ambassador would have invited him to the embassy for friendly discussions of the crisis. With the cameras on him, it was doubtful he would have resisted.

"Well, he would have been issued a visa within minutes, and flown on Aeroflot the next morning at dawn. The General Secretary would have received him before the cameras of the world's press, and a few hours later they would have parted, both looking extremely grave."

"As, no doubt, he would have been given cause to look," suggested Karpov.

"Precisely. But while he was still airborne on his way back to London in the evening, the General Secretary would have issued a statement to the world: wholly and solely as a result of the plea of the British Labour leader, he, the General Secretary, was standing all Soviet forces down to green status. Mr. Kinnock would have landed in London with the stature of a global statesman.

"The day before polling, he would have made a resounding speech to the British nation on the issue of a final renunciation of the nuclear madness once and for all. It was calculated in Plan Aurora that the events of the previous six days would have shattered the traditional Anglo-American alliance, isolated the United States from all European sympathy, and swung ten percent—the vital ten percent—of the British electorate to vote Labour into office. After that, the Hard Left would have taken over. And that, General, was Plan Aurora."

Karpov rose. "You have been very kind, Professor. And very wise. Remain silent, and I shall, also. As you say, it's all archival now. And your son's file will remain in my safe for a very long time. Good-bye. I do not think I shall be troubling you again."

He leaned back against the cushions as the Chaika swept him away down Komsomolski Prospekt. Oh, yes, it's brilliant, he thought, but is there time?

Like the General Secretary, Karpov, too, knew of the forthcoming election in Britain, slated for that June, nine weeks away. The information to the General Secretary had, after all, come through his rezidentura in the London embassy.

He ran the plan over and over in his mind, seeking the flaws. It's good, he thought at last, damn good. Just so long as it works. . . . The alternative would be catastrophic.

■ "An initiator, my dear man, is a sort of detonator for a bomb," said Dr. Wynne-Evans.

"Oh," said Preston. He felt somewhat deflated. There had been bombs before in Britain. Nasty but local. He had seen quite a few in Ireland. He had heard of detonators, primers, triggers, but never an initiator. Still, it looked as if the Russian, Semyonov, had been carrying in a component for a terrorist group somewhere in Scotland. Which group? Tartan Army? Anarchists? Or an IRA active service unit? The Russian connection was odd; very much worth the trip to Glasgow.

"This . . . er . . . initiator of polonium and lithium—would it be used in an antipersonnel bomb?" he asked.

"Oh, yes, you could say so, boyo," replied the Welshman. "An initiator, you see, is what sets off a nuke."

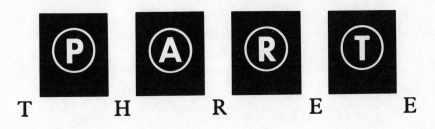

PART

THREE

CHAPTER

B rian Harcourt-Smith listened attentively, leaning back, eyes on the ceiling, fingers toying with a slim gold pencil. "That's it?" he asked when Preston had finished his verbal report.

"Yes," said Preston.

"This Dr. Wynne-Evans, is he prepared to put his deductions in written form?"

"Hardly deductions, Brian. It's a scientific analysis of the metal, coupled with its only two known uses. And yes, he has agreed to put it in the form of a written report. I'll attach it to my own."

"And your own deductions? Or should I say scientific analysis?"

Preston ignored the patronizing tone. "I think it inescapable that Semyonov arrived in Glasgow to deposit his tin and its contents in a dead drop or hand it over to someone he was due to meet," he said. "Either way, that means there is an illegal here, on the ground. I think we could try to find him."

"A charming idea. The trouble is, we haven't a clue where to start. Look, John, let me be frank. You leave me, as so often, in an extremely difficult position. I really do not see how I can take this matter higher unless you can provide me with a little more evidence than a single disk of rare metal taken from a lamentably dead Russian seaman."

"It's been identified as one half of the initiator of a nuclear device," Preston pointed out. "It's hardly just a bit of metal."

"Very well. One half of what might be the trigger of what might be a device—which might have been destined for a Soviet illegal who might be resident in Britain. Believe me, John, when you submit your full report I shall, as ever, consider it with the greatest gravity."

"And then NFA it?" asked Preston.

Harcourt-Smith's smile was unfaltering and dangerous. "Not necessarily. Any report from you will be treated on its merits, like anyone else's. Now I suggest you try to find for me at least some corroborative evidence to support your evident predilection for the conspiracy theory. Make that your next priority."

"All right," said Preston as he rose. "I'll get right on it."

"You do that," said Harcourt-Smith.

When Preston had gone, the Deputy Director-General consulted a list of in-house phone numbers and called the head of Personnel.

■ On the following day, Wednesday, April 15, a British Midland Airways flight from Paris touched down about noon at Birmingham's West Midlands Airport. Among the passengers was a young man with a Danish passport.

The name on the passport was also Danish, and had anyone been so curious as to address him in Danish, he would have responded fluently. He had in fact had a Danish mother, from whom he had acquired his basic grasp of the language, now honed to perfection in several language schools and on visits to Denmark.

His father, however, had been a German, and the young man, born well after the Second World War, originated from Erfurt, where he had been raised. That made him an East German. He also happened to be a staff officer in the East German SSD intelligence service.

He had no idea of the significance of his mission in Britain, nor did he care to find out. His instructions were simple and he followed them to the letter. Passing without difficulty through customs and immigration, he hailed a cab and asked to be taken to the Midland

Hotel on New Street. Throughout the journey, and during the check-in procedures, he was careful to favor his left arm, which was encased in a plaster cast. He had been warned, if warning had been necessary, that under no circumstances was he to attempt to pick up his suitcase with the "broken" arm.

Once in his room, he locked the door and went to work on the plaster cast with the tough steel cutters tucked at the bottom of his shaving kit, carefully snipping down the inside of the forearm, along the line of tiny indentations that marked the cutting path.

When the incision was complete, he prised the cast open half an inch and withdrew his arm, wrist, and hand. The empty cast he dropped into the plastic shopping bag he brought with him.

He spent the entire afternoon in his room so that the day staff at the reception desk should not see him with the cast off, and left the hotel only late at night, when a different staff was on duty.

The newspaper kiosk at New Street Station was where they had said the rendezvous would take place, and at the appointed hour a figure in black leather motorcycle clothing approached him. The muttered exchange of identification took seconds, the shopping bag changed hands, and the figure in leather was gone. Neither of them had attracted a passing glance.

At the hour of dawn, when the night staff at the hotel was still on duty, the Dane checked out, took the early train to Manchester, and flew out from that airport, where no one had ever seen him before, with or without a plaster cast. By sundown, via Hamburg, he was back in Berlin, where as a Dane he went through the Wall at Checkpoint Charlie. His own people met him on the other side, heard his report, and spirited him away. Courier Three had delivered.

■ John Preston was annoyed and not in the best of humors. The week he had arranged to take off work to be with Tommy was being ruined. Tuesday had been partly taken up with his verbal report to Harcourt-Smith, and Tommy had had to spend the day reading or watching television.

Preston had insisted on keeping their date to go to Madame Tussaud's waxwork museum on Wednesday morning, but had come into the office in the afternoon to finish his written report. The letter from Crichton in Personnel was on his desk. He read it with something close to disbelief.

It was couched, as ever, in the friendliest terms. A glance at the files had shown that Preston was owed four weeks' leave; he would be, of course, aware of the rules of the service; backlogging of leave was not encouraged for obvious reasons; necessity to keep all vacation time up to date, blah, blah, blah. In short, he would be required to take his accumulated leave forthwith—that is, as of the following morning.

"Bloody idiots," he called to the office in general, "some of them couldn't find their way to the can without a Labrador."

He called Personnel and insisted on speaking to Crichton personally.

"Tim, it's me, John Preston. Look, what's this letter doing on my desk? I can't take leave now; I'm on a case, right in the middle of it. . . . Yes, I know it's important not to backlog leave, but this case is also important, a damn sight more so, actually."

He heard out the bureaucrat's explanation concerning the disruption caused to the system if staffers accumulated too much vacation time, then cut in. "Look, Tim, let's keep it short. All you have to do is call Brian Harcourt-Smith. He'll vouch for the importance of the case I'm on. I can take the time in the summer."

"John," said Tim Crichton gently, "that letter was written at the express orders of Brian."

Preston stared at the receiver for several moments. "I see," he said finally, and put it down.

"Where are you going?" asked Bright as he headed for the door.

"To get a stiff drink," said Preston.

It was well after the lunch hour and the bar was almost empty. The late-lunch crowd had not yet been replaced by the early-evening thirst-quenchers. There was a couple over from Charles Street having a head-to-head in one corner, so Preston took a stool at the bar. He wanted to be alone. "Whisky," he said, "a large one."

"Same for me," said a voice at his elbow. "And it's my round."

Preston turned to see Barry Banks of K7.

"Hello, John," said Banks, "saw you scooting down here as I was crossing the lobby. Just wanted to say I have something for you. The Master was most grateful."

"Oh, yes, that. Not at all."

"I'll bring it to your office tomorrow," said Banks.

"Don't bother," said Preston angrily. "We are down here to celebrate my four weeks of leave. Beginning as of tomorrow. Enforced. Cheers."

"Don't knock it," said Banks gently. "Most people can't wait to get away from the place." He had already noticed that Preston was nursing a grudge of some kind and intended to ease the reason for it from his MI5 colleague. What he was not able to tell Preston was that he had been asked by Sir Nigel Irvine to cultivate Harcourt-Smith's black sheep and to report back on what he had learned.

An hour and three whiskies later, Preston was still sunk in gloom. "I'm thinking of quitting," he said suddenly.

Banks, a good listener who interrupted only to extract information, was concerned. "Pretty drastic," he said. "Are things that bad?"

"Look, Barry, I don't mind free-falling from twenty thousand feet. I don't even mind people taking potshots at me when the chute opens. But I get bloody annoyed when the flak's coming from my own side. Is that unreasonable?"

"Sounds perfectly justified to me," said Banks. "So who's shooting?"

"The whiz kid upstairs," growled Preston. "Just put in another report he didn't seem to like."

"NFA'ed again?"

Preston shrugged. "It will be."

The door opened to admit a crowd from Five. Brian Harcourt-Smith was at the center of it, several of his heads of section around him.

Preston drained his glass. "Well, I must love you and leave you. Taking my boy to the movies tonight."

When Preston had gone, Barry Banks finished his drink, avoided an invitation to join the group at the bar, and went to his office. From there he made a long phone call to C in his office in Sentinel House.

■ It was not until the small hours of Thursday that Major Petrofsky arrived back at Cherryhayes Close. The black leathers and visored mask were with the BMW in their garage at Thetford. When he drove his little Ford quietly onto the hard pad in front of his garage and let himself into the house, he was in a sober suit and light rain-coat. No one noticed him or the plastic shopping bag in his hand.

With the door firmly locked behind him, he went upstairs and pulled open the bottom drawer of the clothes chest. Inside was a Sony transistor radio. Beside it he laid the empty plaster cast.

He did not interfere with either item. He did not know what they contained, nor did he wish to find out. That would be for the assembler, who would not arrive to perform his task until the complete list of required components had been safely received.

Before sleeping, Petrofsky made himself a cup of tea. There were nine couriers in all. That meant nine first rendezvous and nine back-ups in case of a no-show at the first meeting. He had memorized them all, plus another six that represented the three extra couriers to be used as replacements if necessary.

One of those would now have to be called on, as Courier Two had failed to show. Petrofsky had no idea why that rendezvous had failed. Far away in Moscow, Major Volkov knew. Moscow had had a complete report from the Glasgow consul, who had assured his government that the dead seaman's effects were locked up in Partick police station and would remain there until further notice.

Petrofsky checked his mental list. Courier Four was due in four days, and the meet was to be in the West End of London. It was dawn of the sixteenth when he slept. As he drifted off, he could hear the whine of a milk truck entering the street and the clatter of the day's first deliveries.

■ This time, Banks was more open. He was waiting for Preston in the lobby of his apartment building when the MI5 man drove up on Friday afternoon with Tommy in the passenger seat.

The pair of them had been out at the Hendon Aircraft Museum, where the boy, enthused by the fighter planes of bygone ages, had announced he intended to be a pilot when he grew up. His father knew he had decided on at least six careers in the past, and would have changed his mind again before the year was out. It had been a good afternoon.

Banks seemed surprised to see the boy; he had evidently not expected his presence. He nodded and smiled, and Preston introduced him to Tommy as "someone from the office."

"What is it this time?" asked Preston.

"A colleague of mine wants another word with you," said Banks carefully.

"Will Monday do?" asked Preston. On Sunday his week with Tommy would be over and he would drive the boy to Mayfair to hand him over to Julia.

"Actually, he's waiting for you now."

"Back seat of a car again?" asked Preston.

"Er . . . no. Small flat we keep in Chelsea."

Preston sighed. "Give me the address. I'll go, and you take Tommy up the street for an ice cream."

"I'll have to check," said Banks.

He went into a nearby phone booth and made a call. Preston and his son waited on the sidewalk. Banks came back and nodded.

"It's all right," he said, and gave Preston a piece of paper. Preston drove off while Tommy showed Banks the way to his favorite ice-cream parlor.

The flat was small and discreet, in a modern building off Chelsea Manor Street. Sir Nigel answered the door himself. He was, as usual, full of Old World courtesy. "My dear John, how good of you to come." If someone had been brought into his presence trussed like a chicken and borne by four heavies, he still would have said: "How good of you to come."

When they were seated in the small sitting room, the Master held out the original Preston report. "My sincere thanks. Extremely interesting."

"But not believable, apparently."

Sir Nigel glanced at the younger man sharply but chose his words with care. "I would not necessarily agree to that." Then he smiled quickly and changed the subject. "Now, please don't think ill of Barry, but I asked him to keep an eye on you. It appears you are not too happy in your work at present."

"I'm not in work at present, sir. I'm on compulsory leave."

"So I gather. Something that happened in Glasgow, was it?"

"You haven't received a report yet on the Glasgow incident of last week? It concerned a Russian seaman, a man I believe was a courier. Surely that involves Six?"

"Doubtless it will be on its way before long," said Sir Nigel carefully. "Would you be kind enough to tell me about it?"

Preston started at the beginning and told the tale through to the end, so far as he knew it. Sir Nigel sat as if lost in thought, which he was: taking in every word with part of his mind and calculating with the rest.

They would not really try it, would they? he was thinking. Not breach the Fourth Protocol? Or would they? Desperate men sometimes take desperate measures, and he had several reasons to know that in a number of areas—food production, the economy, the war in Afghanistan—the USSR was in desperate waters. He noted that Preston had stopped talking. "Do forgive me," he said. "What do you deduce from it all?"

"I believe Semyonov was not a merchant navy deckhand, but a courier. That conclusion seems to me unavoidable. I do not believe he would have gone to those lengths to protect what he was carrying, or to end his life to avoid what he must have thought would be interrogation by us, unless he had been instructed his mission was of crucial importance."

"Fair enough," conceded Sir Nigel. "And so?"

"And so I believe there was an intended recipient of that disk of polonium, either directly through a rendezvous or indirectly by dead drop. That means there's an illegal here, on the ground. I think we should try to find him."

Sir Nigel pursed his lips. "If he's a top illegal, finding him will be a needle-in-a-haystack affair," he murmured.

"Yes, I know that."

"If you had not been sent on compulsory leave, what would you have sought authority to do?"

"I think, Sir Nigel, that one disk of polonium is of no use to anybody. Whatever the illegal is up to, there must be other components. Now, it seems that whoever mounted the Semyonov incursion has taken a policy decision not to use the Soviet Embassy's diplomatic bag. I don't know why—it would have been much easier

to ship a small, lead-lined package into Britain in the embassy bag
and have one of their Line N people leave it at a dead drop for collection by the man on the ground. So I ask myself why they didn't
just do that. And the short answer is, I don't know."

"Right," conceded Sir Nigel, "and so?"

"So if there has been one consignment—useless in itself—there
must be others. Some may have already arrived. On the law of av-
erages, there must be more yet to come. And apparently they are
coming in via 'mules,' who pose as harmless seamen and God knows
what else besides."

"And you would want to do—what?" asked Sir Nigel.

Preston took a deep breath. "I would have wanted"—he stressed
the conditional—"to check back on all entrants from the Soviet
Union over the past forty, fifty, even one hundred days. We could
not count on another mugging by hooligans, but there might have
been some other incident. I would have tightened up controls on all
entrants from the USSR, and even from the whole East Bloc, to see
if we could intercept another component. As head of C5(C) I could
have done that."

"And you think now that you won't get the chance?"

Preston shook his head. "Even if I were allowed to go back to
work tomorrow, I'm pretty certain I would be off the case. Apparently I'm an alarmist and I make waves."

Sir Nigel nodded pensively. "Poaching between the services is not
regarded as terribly good form," he said, as if thinking aloud.
"When I asked you to go down to South Africa for me, it was Sir
Bernard who sanctioned it. Later I learned that the assignment,
however temporary, had caused—how shall I put it?—some hostility in certain quarters at Charles Street.

"Now, I don't need an open quarrel with my sister service. On the
other hand, I take a view, shared by yourself, that there might be
more to this iceberg than the tip. In short, you have four weeks'
leave. Would you be prepared to spend that time working on this
case?"

"For whom?" asked Preston, bewildered.

"For me," said Sir Nigel. "You couldn't come to Sentinel. You'd
be seen. Word would get around."

"Then where would I work?"

"Here," said C. "It's small but comfortable. I have the authority to ask for exactly the same information as you would if you were at your desk. Any incident involving a Soviet or East Bloc arrival will have been recorded, either on paper or in a computer. Since you cannot get to the files or the computer, I can arrange for the files and printouts to be brought to you. What do you say?"

"If Charles Street finds out, I'm finished at Five," said Preston. He was thinking of his salary, of his pension, of the chances of getting another job at his age, of Tommy.

"How much longer do you think you have got at Charles under its present management?" asked Sir Nigel.

Preston laughed shortly. "Not long," he said. "All right, sir, I'll do it. I want to stay on this case. There's something buried in there somewhere."

Sir Nigel nodded approvingly. "You're a tenacious man, John. I like tenacity. It usually yields results. Be here on Monday at nine. I'll have two of my own lads waiting for you. Ask them for what you want, and they'll get it."

■ On Monday morning, April 20, as Preston started work in the Chelsea flat, an internationally famous Czech concert pianist arrived at Heathrow Airport from Prague, en route to his Wigmore Hall concert the following evening.

The airport authorities had been alerted, and in deference to the musician's venerability, customs and immigration formalities were as little onerous as possible. The elderly pianist was met after the customs hall by a representative of the sponsoring organization and, with his small entourage, was whisked off to his suite at the Cumberland Hotel.

His retinue consisted of his dresser, who looked after his clothes and other personal effects with dedicated devotion; a female secretary who handled his fan mail and correspondence; and his personal aide, a tall, lugubrious man named Lichka, who took care of finances and negotiations with host organizations, and seemed to live on a diet of antacid tablets.

That Monday, Lichka was working his way through an abnormally large number of his pills. He had not wanted to do what was required of him, but the men from the StB had been extremely persuasive. No one in his right mind deliberately affronted the men of the StB, Czechoslovakia's secret police and intelligence organization, or wished to be invited for further discussions at their headquarters, the dreaded "Monastery." The men had made plain that Lichka's granddaughter's admission to the university would be so much easier to arrange if he were prepared to help them—a polite way of saying the girl did not stand a chance of entering if he failed them.

When they had given him back his shoes, he could find no trace of interference, and according to instructions had worn them on the flight and straight through Heathrow Airport.

That evening, a man walked up to the reception desk and politely asked the number of Lichka's room. Equally politely he was given it. Five minutes later, at the precise hour Lichka had been briefed to expect it, there was a soft knock at his door. A piece of paper was pushed under it. He checked the identification code, opened the door five inches, and passed out a plastic bag containing his shoes. Unseen hands took the bag and Lichka closed the door. When he had flushed the scrap of paper down the toilet, he sighed with relief. It had been easier than he had expected. Now, he thought, we can get on with the business of making music.

Before midnight, in a backwater of Ipswich, the shoes joined the plaster cast and the radio in a bottom drawer. Courier Four had delivered.

■ Sir Nigel Irvine visited Preston at the Chelsea apartment on Friday afternoon. The MI5 man was looking exhausted, and the flat was awash with files and computer printout paper.

He had spent five days and had come up with nothing. He had started with every entry into Britain from the USSR over the past forty days. There had been hundreds: trade delegates, industrial buyers, journalists, trade-union stooges, a choir group from Georgia, a dance troupe of Cossacks, ten athletes and all their entourage, and a team of doctors for a medical conference in Manchester. And those were just the Russians.

Also entering from the Soviet Union were the returning tourists:

the culture-vultures who had been admiring the Hermitage Museum in Leningrad, the school party that had been singing in Kiev, and the "peace" delegation that had been providing rich fodder for the Soviet propaganda machine by condemning its own country at press conferences in Moscow and Kharkov.

Even that list did not include the Aeroflot crews who had been shuttling in and out as part of the normal air traffic, so First Officer Romanov hardly rated a mention.

There was, of course, no reference to a Dane coming into Birmingham from Paris and leaving through Manchester.

By Wednesday, Preston had had two options; stay with entrants from the USSR but go back sixty days, or widen the net to take in *all* entrants from any East Bloc country. That meant thousands and thousands of arrivals. He had decided to stay with his forty-day time scale but to include the non-Soviet Communist states. The paperwork began to get waist-high.

Customs had been most helpful. There had been some confiscations, but always for an excess of the duty-free allowance. Nothing of inexplicable character had been seized. Immigration had come up with no "bent" passports, but that was to be expected. The weird and wonderful bits of paperwork sometimes proffered at passport control by people from the Third World were never produced by people from the Communist bloc. Not even time-expired passports, the usual reason for an immigration officer's stopping a visitor from entry. In Communist countries a traveler's passport was so thoroughly checked before departure that there was little chance of his being detained at the British end.

"And that," said Preston gloomily, "still leaves the uncheckables—the merchant seamen, entering without controls at more than twenty commercial ports; the crews from the fishing factory ships now riding off Scotland; the commercial aircrews, who are hardly checked at all; and those with diplomatic cover."

"As I thought," said Sir Nigel. "Not easy. Have you any idea what you are looking for?"

"Yes, sir. I had one of your lads spend Monday out at Aldermaston with the people in nuclear engineering. It seems that disk of polonium would be suitable for a device that was small, crude, basic in design, and not very powerful—if one can describe any atomic bomb as 'not very powerful.' " He handed Sir Nigel a list of items. "Those are, at a guess, something like what we are looking for."

C studied the list of artifacts. "Is that all it takes?" he asked at length.

"In kit form, apparently, yes. I'd no idea they could be made so basic. Apart from the fissionable core and the steel tamper, that stuff could be hidden almost anywhere and excite no attention."

"All right, John, where do you go now?"

"I'm looking for a pattern, Sir Nigel. It's all I *can* look for. A pattern of entries and exits by the same passport number. If one or two couriers are being used, they would have to come in and out frequently, using different entry and exit points, probably different departure points abroad; but if a pattern shows up, we could put out an all-nation alert for a limited group of passport numbers. It's not much, but it's all I have."

Sir Nigel rose. "Keep at it, John. I'll get you access to anything you ask for. Let's just pray whoever we are dealing with slips up, just once, by using the same courier twice or three times."

■ But Major Volkov was more efficient than that. He did not slip up. He had no idea what the components were or what they were to be used for. He simply knew he had been ordered to ensure their entry into Britain in time for a series of rendezvous, that each courier would have memorized his primary and backup meets, and that nothing was to pass through the KGB rezidentura in the London embassy.

He had nine cargoes to infiltrate and twelve couriers prepared. Some, he knew, were not professionals, but where their cover was impeccable and their journey had been arranged weeks or months earlier, as in the case of Lichka the Czech, he had homed in on them.

In order not to alert Major General Borisov by stripping him of a further twelve illegals and their legends, he had cast his net wider than the USSR by calling on three of the sister services: the StB of Czechoslovakia, the SB of Poland, and, most of all, the obedient and unquestioning Haupt Verwaltung Aufklärung (HVA) of East Germany.

The East Germans were particularly good. While there are Polish

and Czech communities in West Germany, France, and Britain, the
East Germans had one great advantage. Because of the ethnic iden-
ticality of East and West Germans, and the fact that millions of former Easterners had already fled to West Germany, the HVA, from
its East Berlin base, ran by far a greater number of in-place illegals
in the West than any other East Bloc service.

Volkov had decided to use only two Russians, and they would be
the first to go in. He had no way of knowing that one would be
mugged by street thugs, nor was he aware that the false seaman's
consignment was no longer locked up in a Glasgow police station.
He just took treble precautions because that was his nature and his
training.

For his remaining seven cargoes he was using one courier supplied
by the Poles, two by the Czechs (including Lichka), and four by the
East Germans. The tenth courier, replacing the dead Courier Two,
would also come from the Poles. For the structural alterations that
he needed to make to two motor vehicles, Volkov was even using a
garage and workshop run by the HVA in Brunswick, West Germany.

Only the two Russians and the Czech, Lichka, would have East
Bloc departure points; plus, now, the tenth, who would have to
come from the Polish Airline, LOT.

Volkov was simply not allowing the appearance of any of the patterns Preston now sought in his sea of paperwork in Chelsea.

■ Sir Nigel Irvine, like so many who have to work in central London, tried to get away at the weekends for a breath of fresh air. He
and Lady Irvine stayed in London during the week but kept a small,
rustic cottage in southeast Dorset, on the Isle of Purbeck, at a village
called Langton Matravers.

That Sunday C had donned a tweed coat and hat, taken a thick ash
stick, and walked down the lanes and tracks to the cliffs above Chap-
man's Pool at St. Alban's Head. The sun was bright but the wind
chilly. It blew the silver wisps of hair that escaped his hat away over
his ears like small wings. He took the cliff path and walked deep in

thought, occasionally pausing to stare out over the tossed whitecaps of the English Channel.

He was thinking of the conclusions of Preston's original report and of the remarkable concurrence of Sweeting in his Oxford reclusiveness. Coincidence? Straws in the wind? Grounds for conviction? Or just a lot of nonsense from a too-imaginative civil servant and a fanciful academic?

And if it was all true, could there be any link with a small disk of polonium from Leningrad that had arrived uninvited in a Glasgow police station?

If the metal disk was what Wynne-Evans had said, what did that signify? Could it possibly mean that someone, far out over those tossing waves, was really trying to breach the Fourth Protocol?

And if that was true, who could that someone be? Chebrikov and Kryuchkov of the KGB? They would never dare act except under the orders of the General Secretary. And if the General Secretary was behind it all—why?

And why not use the diplomatic bag? So much simpler, easier, safer. To this last question, he thought he could discern an answer. Using the embassy bag would mean using the KGB rezidentura inside the embassy. Better than Chebrikov, Kryuchkov, or the General Secretary, C knew that the rezidentura had been penetrated. He had his source Andreyev inside it.

The General Secretary, C suspected, had good reason to be shaken by the recent spate of defections from the KGB. All the evidence coming across was that the disillusionment at every level in Russia had become so profound that it was even affecting the elite of elites. Apart from the defections, starting in the late 1970s and growing through the 1980s there had been mass expulsions of Soviet diplomats across the world, caused in part by their own desperation to recruit agents, but leading to even further desperation as the diplomatic controllers were compelled to leave and the networks fell into disarray. Even Third World countries that, a decade ago, had danced to the Soviet tune were now asserting themselves and expelling Soviet agents for grossly undiplomatic conduct.

Yes, a major operation conducted outside the auspices of the KGB made sense. Sir Nigel had heard on good authority that the General

Secretary was becoming paranoid about the level of Western penetration of the KGB itself. For every traitor who runs over, went the
adage in the intelligence community, you can bet there's another one
still in place.

So, there was a man out there, running couriers and their cargoes
into Britain, dangerous cargoes, bringing anarchy and chaos in a
manner that C could not yet discern but was ceasing to doubt, even
as he walked. And that man worked for another man, very high, who
had no love for this small island.

"But you won't find them, John," he murmured to the unheeding
wind. "You're good, but they are better. And they hold the aces."

Sir Nigel Irvine was one of the last of the old grandees, one of a
passing breed, being replaced at every level of his society by new
men of a different type, even at the highest stratum of the civil service, where continuity of style and type was something of a household god.

So he gazed out at the Channel, as so many Englishmen had done
before him, and made his decision. He was not convinced of the existence of a threat to the land of his forefathers, only of the possibility
of such a menace. But that was enough.

■ Farther along the coast, on the downs above the small Sussex port
of Newhaven, another man gazed at the tossing waves of the English
Channel.

He was dressed in black leather, his helmet on the seat of his
parked BMW motorcycle. A few Sunday strollers walked with their
children across the downs, but they took no notice of him.

He was watching the approach of a ferry, well over the horizon
and beating her way toward the shelter of the harbor mole. The *Cornouailles* would arrive from Dieppe in thirty minutes. Somewhere on
board should be Courier Five.

In fact, Courier Five was on the foredeck, watching the approach
of the English coast. He was one of those who had no car, but his
ticket was for the boat train right through to London.

Anton Zelewski, his passport said, and it was perfectly accurate.
A West German passport, the immigration officer noted, but there

was nothing odd in that. Hundreds of thousands of West Germans have Polish-sounding names. He was passed through.

Customs examined his suitcase and his bag with the duty-free allowance, bought on board the ship. His bottle of gin and his twenty-five cigars in an unopened box were within the permitted limits. The customs officer nodded him through and turned his attention to someone else.

Zelewski had indeed bought a box of twenty-five good cigars in the duty-free shop on the *Cornouailles*. He had then retired to a bathroom, locked himself in, and eased the identifying duty-free labels off the newly bought box, only to stick them on an identical box he had brought with him. The other went overboard into the waiting sea.

On the train to London, Zelewski sought out the first-class carriage next to the engine, selected the required window seat, and waited. Just before Lewes, the door opened and a man in black leather stood there. A glance confirmed that the compartment was empty except for the German.

"Does this train go straight to London?" he asked in unaccented English.

"I believe it also stops at Lewes," Zelewski replied.

The man held out his hand. Zelewski passed him the flat box of cigars. The man stuffed it under his jacket, nodded, and left. When the train started out of Lewes, Zelewski saw the man once again, on the opposite platform, waiting for a train back to Newhaven.

Before midnight the cigars joined the radio, plaster cast, and shoes in Ipswich. Courier Five had delivered.

CHAPTER

S ir Nigel was right. By Thursday, the last day of April, the reams of computer printout had shown up no pattern at all of East Bloc citizens, from whatever point of departure, entering Britain on repeated occasions over the previous forty days. Nor was there a pattern of persons of any particular nationality entering the country from the East over the same period.

A number of passports containing various irregularities had shown up, but that was par for the course. Each had been checked, its bearer strip-searched, but the answer was still a big zero. Three passports on the "stop" list had appeared; two were previous deportees seeking reentry, and one was an American underworld figure connected to gambling and narcotics. These three were also searched before being put on the next plane out, but there was not an iota of evidence that they had been couriers for Moscow.

If they're using West Bloc citizens, or in-place illegals with impeccable documentation as West Bloc citizens, I'll never find them, thought Preston.

Sir Nigel had again relied on his long friendship with Sir Bernard Hemmings to secure the cooperation of Five. "I have reason to believe the Center is going to try to slip an important illegal into the country in the next few weeks," he had said. "The trouble is, Bernard, I don't have an identity, description, or place of entry. Still, any help your contacts at the points of entry could give us would be highly appreciated."

Sir Bernard had made the request a Five operation, and the other arms of the state—customs, immigration, Special Branch, and docks police—had agreed to keep more than the usual weather eye open either for a foreigner trying to slip past the controls or for an odd or unexplainable item being carried in as luggage.

The explanation was plausible enough, and not even Brian Harcourt-Smith linked it to the report by John Preston on the polonium disk; the report was still in his pending tray while he considered what to do with it.

■ The camper van arrived on May Day. It had West German registration and came in to Dover on the ferry from Calais. The owner and driver, whose papers were in perfect order, was Helmut Dorn, and he had with him his wife, Lisa, and their two small children, Uwe, a flaxen-haired boy of five, and Brigitte, their seven-year-old daughter.

When they had passed immigration, the van rolled toward the nothing-to-declare green zone of customs, but one of the waiting officers gestured it to stop. After reexamining the papers, the customs official asked to look in the back. Herr Dorn complied.

The two children were playing in the living area and stopped when the uniformed customs man entered. He nodded and smiled at them; they giggled. He glanced around the neat and tidy interior, then began to look into the cupboards. If Herr Dorn was nervous, he hid it well.

Most of the cupboards contained the usual bric-a-brac of a family on a camping holiday—clothes, cooking utensils, and so forth. The customs man flicked up the bench seats, beneath which lockers served as extra storage space. One of them was apparently the children's toy locker. It contained two dolls, a teddy bear, and a collection of soft rubber balls, brightly painted with large, gaudy disks in different colors.

The little girl, overcoming her shyness, delved into the locker and pulled out one of the dolls. She babbled excitedly at the customs man in German. He did not understand, but he nodded and smiled.

"Very nice, love," he said. Then he stepped out of the back door and turned to Herr Dorn. "Very well, sir. Enjoy your holiday."

The camper van rolled with the rest of the vehicles out of the sheds and onto the road to the town of Dover and the highways leading to the rest of Kent and to London.

"*Gott sei dank*," breathed Dorn to his wife, "*wir sind durch.*"

She did the map-reading, but it was simple enough. The main M20 to London was so clearly marked no one could miss it. Dorn checked his watch several times. He was a bit late, but his orders were under no circumstances to exceed the speed limit.

They found the village of Charing, lying to one side of the main road, without difficulty, and just to the north of it the Happy Eater cafeteria on the left. Dorn swung into the parking lot and stopped. Lisa Dorn took the children into the café for a snack. Dorn, according to orders, raised the engine cover and buried his head beneath it. Several seconds later he felt a presence beside him and looked up. A young Englishman in black motorcycle leathers stood there.

"Having a little trouble?" he asked.

"I think it must be the carburetor," Dorn answered.

"No," said the motorcyclist gravely, "I suspect it comes from the distributor. Also, you are late."

"I'm sorry, it was the ferry. And customs. I have the package in the back."

Inside the van, the motorcyclist produced a canvas bag from under his jacket, while Dorn, grunting and straining, lifted one of the children's balls out of the toy locker.

It was only five inches in diameter, but it weighed a mite over twenty kilograms, or forty-four pounds. Pure uranium-235 is, after all, twice as heavy as lead.

Carrying the canvas bag across the parking lot, to his motorcycle, Valeri Petrofsky had to use his considerable strength to hold the bag one-handed, as though it contained nothing of note. No one noticed him, anyway. Dorn closed the van's hood and joined his family in the café. The motorcycle, with its cargo in the box behind the pillion, roared away toward London, the Dartford Tunnel, and Suffolk. Courier Six had delivered.

■ By May 4 Preston had realized he was up a blind alley. After two weeks he still had nothing to show for his ferreting other than a single disk of polonium that had fallen into his hands by a pure fluke. He knew it was out of the question to ask for the strip-searching of every visitor entering Britain. All he could do was request increased surveillance on all East Bloc citizens coming in, plus an immediate alert to himself in the case of any suspect passport. There was one other, last chance.

From what the experts in nuclear engineering at Aldermaston had reported, three of the items required for even the most basic nuclear bomb would have to be extremely heavy. One would be a block of pure uranium-235; one would be a tamper, cylindrical or globular in shape, made of high-tensile hardened one-inch-thick steel; and the third would be a steel tube, also high-tensile and hardened, one inch thick, about eighteen inches long, and weighing thirty pounds.

He estimated these three, at least, would have to be brought into the country in vehicles, and asked for an intensification of searches of foreign vehicles with an eye on cargoes resembling a ball, a globe, and a tube of extreme heaviness.

He knew the catchment area was vast. There was a constant stream of motorcycles, cars, vans, and trucks flowing in and out of the country every day of the year. The jamming of commercial traffic alone, if every truck were stopped and stripped, would almost bring the country to a halt. He was looking for the proverbial needle in the haystack, and he did not even have a magnet.

■ The strain was beginning to tell on George Berenson. His wife had left him and returned to her brother's stately home in Yorkshire. He had completed twelve sessions with the team from the ministry and identified for them every single document he had ever passed to Jan Marais. He knew he was under surveillance, and that did not help his nerves, either.

Nor did the daily routine of going to the ministry fully aware that the Permanent Under Secretary, Sir Peregrine Jones, knew about his treachery. The final strain upon him was caused by the fact that he still had to pass occasional packages of apparently purloined documents from the ministry to Marais, for transmission to Moscow.

He had managed to avoid actually meeting Marais since he had learned the South African was a Soviet agent. But he was required to read the material he was passing to Moscow via Marais, just in case Marais called him for a clarification of something already sent.

Every time he read the papers he was to pass on, he was impressed by the skill of the forgers. Each document was based on a real paper that had come across his desk, but with changes so subtle that no individual detail could arouse suspicion. Yet the cumulative effect was to give a quite false impression of Britain's and NATO's strength and preparedness.

On Wednesday, May 6, he received and read a batch of seven papers referring to recent decisions, proposals, briefings, and queries supposed to have reached his desk over the previous fortnight. All were marked either TOP SECRET or COSMIC, and one of them caused him to raise his eyebrows. He passed them to the Benotti ice-cream parlor that evening and received his coded call of acknowledgment of safe receipt twenty-four hours later.

■ That Sunday, May 10, in the seclusion of his bedroom at Cherryhayes Close, Valeri Petrofsky crouched over his powerful portable radio set and listened to the stream of signals in Morse coming over the Moscow Radio commercial band he had been allocated.

His set was not a transmitter; Moscow would never allow a valuable illegal to endanger himself by sending his own messages, not with British and American direction-finding countermeasures as good as they were. What he had was a huge Braun radio, purchasable in any good electronics shop, that would pick up almost any channel in the world.

Petrofsky was tense. It had been a month since he had used the Poplar transmitter to alert Moscow that he had lost a courier and his cargo and to ask for a replacement. Each second evening and on alternate mornings, whenever he was not out on his motorcycle making collections, he had listened for a reply. So far, it had not come.

At ten past ten that evening, he heard his own call sign coming over the airwaves. He already had his pad and pencil ready. After a pause, the message began. He jotted down the letters, a jumble of undecipherable figures, straight from Morse into English. The Germans, British, and Americans would be recording the same letters in their various listening posts.

When the transmission ended, he switched off the set, sat at his dressing table, selected the appropriate one-time pad, and began to decipher. He had it in fifteen minutes: *Firebird Ten replacing Two RVT*. It was repeated three times.

He knew Rendezvous T. It was one of the alternates, to be used only if the occasion demanded, as indeed it now had. And it was in an airport hotel. He preferred wayside cafés or railway stations, but knew that although he was the kingpin of the operation, there were some couriers who for professional reasons had only a few hours in London and could not leave the city.

There was one other problem. They were slotting Courier Ten between two other meets, and perilously close to the rendezvous with Courier Seven.

Ten had to be met at the hour of breakfast in the Post House, Heathrow; Seven would be waiting in a hotel parking lot outside Colchester that same morning at eleven. It would mean hard riding, but he could do it.

■ Late in the evening of Tuesday, May 12, the lights were still burning in 10 Downing Street, office and residence of the British premier. Mrs. Margaret Thatcher had called a strategy conference of her closest advisers and inner cabinet. The only issue on the agenda was that of the forthcoming general election; the meeting was to formalize the decision and decide the timing.

As usual, she made her own view plain from the outset. She believed she would be right to go for a third four-year administration, even though the constitution allowed her to govern until June 1988. There were several who at once doubted the wisdom of going to the country so soon, though on previous evidence they doubted they would get very far. When the British Prime Minister had a gut feeling for something, it took some very powerful counterarguments to dissuade her. On this issue, statistics seemed to support her.

The Conservative Party chairman had all the public-opinion-poll findings at his fingertips. The Liberal/Social Democrat alliance, these showed, seemed stuck at about twenty percent of the support of the national electorate. Under the British system, this would give them between fifteen and twenty seats in Parliament. That left the electoral fight looking like the traditional struggle between the Conservative and Labour parties.

As for the timing, the indicators seemed to support the Prime Minister in her wish for an early election. Since June 1983, with its newfound image of tolerance, unity, and moderation, the Labour Party had hauled itself back a full ten percentage points in the polls, and stood only four percent behind the Conservatives. Moreover, the gap could well be closing. The Hard Left was almost mute, the Labour manifesto moderated, and public television appearances confined to members of Labour's centrist wing. In short, the British public had almost completely regained its confidence in Labour as an alternative party of government.

There was general agreement by midnight that it had to be the summer of 1987, or not until June 1988. Mrs. Thatcher pressed for 1987 and won her point. On the question of the length of the election campaign, she urged a short, three-week snap campaign as against the more traditional four weeks. Again, she won her argument.

Finally, it was agreed; she would seek an audience with the Queen on Thursday, May 28, and ask for a dissolution of Parliament. In accordance with tradition she would return to Downing Street immediately afterward to make a public statement. From that moment the election campaign would be on. Polling day would be Thursday, June 18.

■ While the ministers still slept in the hour before dawn, the BMW cruised toward London from the northeast. Petrofsky rode out to the Post House Hotel at Heathrow Airport, parked, locked the machine, and shut away his crash helmet in the box behind the pillion.

He eased off his black leather jacket and zip-sided trousers. Beneath the leather trousers he wore an ordinary pair of gray flannels, creased but passable. He dropped his jackboots into one of the saddlebags, from which he had taken a pair of shoes. The leathers went into the other bag, from which came a nondescript tweed jacket and tan raincoat. When he left the parking lot and walked into the hotel reception area, he was just an ordinary man in an ordinary mackintosh.

■ Karel Wosniak had not slept well. For one thing, he had been given the shock of his life the previous evening. Normally the aircrews of the Polish LOT airlines, for which he was a senior steward, passed through customs and immigration almost as a formality. This time they had been searched, really searched. When the British officer attending to him had started to rummage through his shaving kit he had nearly been sick from worry. When the man extracted the electric razor the SB people had given him in Warsaw before takeoff, he had thought he would faint. Fortunately it was not a battery-operated or rechargeable model. There had been no available electric plug to turn it on. The officer had put it back and completed his search, to no avail. Wosniak supposed that if someone *had* turned the shaver on, it would not have worked. After all, there must be *something* in it apart from the usual motor. Why else should he be required to bring it to London?

At eight precisely, he entered the men's room just off the reception area on the hotel's ground floor. A nondescript-looking man in a tan raincoat was washing his hands. Damn, thought Wosniak, when the contact shows up, we'll have to wait until this Englishman leaves. Then the man spoke to him, in English.

" 'Morning. Is that the Yugoslav airline uniform?"

Wosniak sighed with relief. "No, I am from the Polish national airline."

"Lovely country, Poland," said the stranger, wiping his hands. He seemed completely at ease. Wosniak was new to this—and he had promised himself this would be the first and last time. He just stood on the tiled floor, holding his razor. "I have spent many happy times in your country," the stranger continued.

That's it, thought Wosniak. "Many happy times . . ." the phrase of identification.

He held out the razor. The Englishman scowled and glanced at one of the booth doors. With a start, Wosniak realized the door was closed; there was someone in there. The stranger nodded to the shelf above the washbasins. Wosniak put the razor on it. Then the Englishman nodded toward the urinals. Hastily Wosniak unzipped his fly and stood in front of one. "Thank you," he burbled. "I, too, think it is beautiful."

The man in the tan raincoat pocketed the razor, held up five fingers to indicate that Wosniak should stay there for five minutes, and left.

An hour later, Petrofsky and his motorcycle were clearing the suburbs where northeast London borders the county of Essex. The M12 motorway opened up in front of him. It was nine o'clock.

■ At that hour the *Tor Britannia* ferry of the DFDS line from Gothenburg was easing herself alongside the Parkstone Quay at Harwich, eighty miles away on the Essex coast. The passengers, when they came off, were the usual crowd of tourists, students, and commercial visitors. Among the latter was Mr. Stig Lundqvist, who was driving his big Saab sedan.

His papers said he was a Swedish businessman and they did not lie. He was indeed Swedish, and had been all his life. The papers omitted to mention that he was also a longtime Communist agent who worked, like Herr Helmut Dorn, for the redoubtable General Marcus Wolf, the Jewish head of foreign operations for the East German HVA intelligence service.

Lundqvist was asked to step out of his car and bring his suitcases to the examination bench. This he did with a courteous smile. A customs officer lifted the Saab's hood and glanced at the engine. He was looking for a globe the size of a small football or a rodlike tube that might be secreted within the compartment. There was nothing like that. He glanced under the frame of the car and finally into the trunk. He sighed. These demands from London were a pain in the neck. The trunk contained nothing but the usual toolkit, a jack strapped to one side, and a fire extinguisher banded to the other. The Swede stood at his side, his suitcases in his hand.

"Please," said the Swede, "is all right?"

"Yes, thank you, sir. Enjoy your stay."

An hour later, just before eleven, the Saab rolled into the parking lot of the Kings Ford Park hotel in the village of Layer de la Haye, just south of Colchester. Lundqvist got out and stretched. It was the midmorning coffee hour and there were several cars in the lot, all unattended. He glanced at his watch—five minutes to rendezvous time. Close, but he knew he would have had the extra hour of waiting time had he been late, then a backup rendezvous somewhere else. He wondered if and when the contact would show. There was no one around except a young man tinkering with the engine of a BMW motorcycle. Lundqvist had no idea what his contact would look like. He lit a cigarette, got back into his car, and sat there.

At eleven, there was a tap on the window. The motorcyclist stood outside. Lundqvist pressed the button and the window hissed down. "Yes?"

"Does the *S* on your license plate stand for Sweden or Switzerland?" asked the Englishman. Lundqvist smiled with relief. He had stopped on the road and detached the fire extinguisher, which now reposed in a burlap bag on the passenger seat.

"It stands for Sweden," he said. "I have just arrived from Gothenburg."

"Never been there," said the man. Then, without a change of inflection, he added, "Got something for me?"

"Yes," said the Swede, "it's in the bag beside me."

"There are windows looking onto the parking lot," said the motorcyclist. "Drive around the car lot, swing past the motorcycle, and drop the bag to me out of the driver's window. Keep the car between me and the windows. Five minutes from now."

He sauntered back to his machine and went on tinkering. Five minutes later the Saab swung past him, the bag slipped to the ground; Petrofsky had picked it up and dropped it into his open saddlebag before the Saab cleared the hotel windows. He never saw the Saab again, nor did he want to.

One hour later he was in his garage in Thetford, exchanging motorcycle for family sedan and stowing his two cargoes in the trunk. He had no idea what they contained. That was not his job.

In the early afternoon he was home in Ipswich, the two consignments stored in his bedroom. Couriers Ten and Seven had delivered.

■ John Preston had been due back at work at Gordon Street on May 13.

"I know it's frustrating, but I'd like you to stay on," said Sir Nigel Irvine on one of his visits. "You'll have to call in with a bad dose of flu. If you need a doctor's chit, let me know. I have a couple who'll oblige."

By the sixteenth, Preston knew he was up a blind alley. Without a major national alert, customs and immigration had done all they could. The sheer volume of human traffic prevented intensive searching of every visitor. It had been five weeks since the mugging of the Russian seaman in Glasgow, and Preston was convinced he had missed the rest of the couriers. Perhaps they had all been in the country before Semyonov, and the deckhand had been the last. Perhaps . . .

With growing desperation he realized he did not know if he had a deadline at all, or, if he did, when it was.

■ On Thursday, May 21, the ferry from Ostende berthed at Folkestone and discharged its habitual contents of tourists on foot, others in cars, and the grunting stream of trucks that haul the freight of the European Economic Community from one end of the Continent to the other.

Seven of the trucks were of German registration, Ostende being a favored port on the Britain run for firms operating in north Germany. The big Hanomag articulated rig with its containerized cargo on the trailer behind was no different from all the others. The fat sheaf of paperwork that took an hour to clear was in good order and there was no reason to believe the driver worked for anyone other than the haulage contractor whose name was painted on the side of the cab. Nor was there any reason to think the rig contained anything other than its prescribed delivery of German coffeemakers for the British breakfast table.

Behind the cab, two big vertical exhaust pipes jutted toward the sky, carrying the fumes from the diesel engine up and away from other road users. It was already evening, the day shift was drawing to a weary close, and the truck was waved forward on the road to Ashford and London.

No one at Folkestone could be expected to know that one of those vertical exhaust tubes, belching dark fumes as it left the customs shed, had a bypass pipe inside it to carry the fumes, or, amid the roar of starting engines, that the sound baffles had been removed to create extra space.

Long after dark, in the parking area of a roadhouse near Lenham, in Kent, the driver climbed to the top of his cab, unbolted that exhaust pipe, and withdrew from it an eighteen-inch-long package wrapped in heatproof cladding. He never opened it; he just handed it to a black-clothed motorcyclist who sped off into the darkness. Courier Eight had delivered.

■ "It's no good, Sir Nigel," John Preston told the Chief of the SIS on Friday evening. "I don't know what the hell's going on. I fear the worst, but I can't prove it. I've tried to find just one more of those couriers I believe have come into this country, and I've failed. I think I should go back to Gordon on Monday."

"I know how you feel, John," said Sir Nigel. "I feel much the same. Please give me just one more week."

"I can't see the point," said Preston. "What more can we do?"

"Pray, I suppose," said C gently.

"One break," said Preston angrily. "All I need is just one small break."

CHAPTER

John Preston got his break the following Monday afternoon, May 25.

At just after four o'clock, an Austrian Airlines flight came into Heathrow from Vienna. One of the travelers aboard, who presented himself at the passport desk for non-UK and non-EEC citizens, offered a perfectly authentic Austrian passport that proclaimed its bearer to be one Franz Winkler.

The immigration officer examined the familiar green, plastic-covered *Reisepass*, fronted by the emblematic gold eagle, with the usual apparent indifference of his profession. It was of current issue, dotted with half a dozen other European entry and exit stamps, and included a valid UK visa.

Beneath his desk the officer's left hand tapped out the passport number, perforated through every page of the booklet. He glanced at the display screen, closed the passport, and handed it back with a brief smile. "Thank you, sir. And the next, please."

As Herr Winkler picked up his suitcase and moved through, the officer raised his eyes to a small window twenty feet away. At the same time, his right foot pressed an "alert" button near the floor.

From the office window, one of the resident Special Branch men caught his gaze. The immigration officer looked in the direction of Herr Winkler's back and nodded. The face of the Special Branch detective withdrew from the window and seconds later he and a colleague were slipping quietly after the Austrian. Another Special Branch man was rustling up a car in front of the concourse.

Winkler had no heavy luggage, so he ignored the carousels in the baggage hall and went straight through the green channel of customs. In the concourse he spent some time at the Midland Bank changing traveler's checks into sterling currency, during which time one of the Special Branch men got a good photograph of him from an upper balcony.

When the Austrian took a cab from the rank in front of Number Two Building, the Special Branch officers piled into their own unmarked car and were right behind him. The driver concentrated on following the taxi; the senior Special Branch detective used the radio to inform Scotland Yard, whence, according to procedure, the information went also to Charles Street. There was a standing order to the effect that Six was also interested in any visitor carrying a "bent" passport, so the tip-off was passed by Charles Street to Sentinel House.

Winkler took his cab as far as Bayswater and paid the driver at the junction of Edgware Road and Sussex Gardens. Then he walked, suitcase in hand, down Sussex Gardens, one side of which is almost entirely taken up with modest bed-and-breakfast boardinghouses of the type favored by commercial travelers and by late arrivals from nearby Paddington Station on modest budgets.

It seemed to the Special Branch officers watching from their car across the street that Winkler had no reservation, for he ambled down the street until he came to a boardinghouse with a VACANCIES sign in the window and went in. He must have got a room because he did not emerge.

It was one hour after Winkler's cab had left Heathrow, and at that time the phone rang in Preston's Chelsea flat. His contact man at Sentinel, the one ordered by Sir Nigel to liaise with Preston, was on the line.

"There's a Joe just came in at Heathrow," said the MI6 man. "It may be nothing, but his passport number came up little red lights on the computer. Name of Franz Winkler, Austrian, off the Vienna flight."

"They didn't pick him up, I hope?" said Preston. He was thinking that Austria is conveniently close to Czechoslovakia and Hungary. Being neutral, it is also a good jumping-off point for Sovbloc illegals.

"No," said the man at Sentinel. "According to our standing request they tailed him. . . . Hold on. . . ." He came back on the line a few seconds later. "They've just 'housed' him at a small B-and-B hotel in Paddington."

"Can you pass me over to C?" asked Preston.

Sir Nigel was in conference, which he left to return to his private office. "Yes, John."

When Preston had related the basic facts to the Chief of the SIS, Sir Nigel asked, "Do you think he's the man you've been waiting for?"

"He could be a courier," said Preston. "He's as good as we've had in the past six weeks."

"What do you want, John?"

"I'd like Six to ask for the watchers to take over. All reports reaching the watchers' controller at Cork to be monitored by one of your people as and when they come in; same to be fed at once to Sentinel and then to me. If he makes a meet, I'd like both men tailed."

"All right," said Sir Nigel. "I'll ask for the watchers. Barry Banks will sit in at the Cork radio room and pass the developments down the line as they come in."

The Chief himself called the director of K Branch and made his request. The head of K contacted his colleagues at A Branch and a standby team of watchers headed for Sussex Gardens. They happened to be led by Harry Burkinshaw.

Preston paced the small apartment in a rage of frustration. He wanted to be out on the streets, or at least at the center of the operation, not tucked away like a deep-cover man in his own country, the pawn in a power game being conducted at a level far above his head.

By seven that evening, Burkinshaw's men had moved in, taking over the watch from the Special Branch men, who happily went off duty. It was a warm and pleasant evening; the four watchers who formed the "box" took up their unobtrusive stations around the hotel—one up the street, one down, one across, and one in back. The two cars positioned themselves amid scores of others parked along Sussex Gardens, ready to move if Chummy took flight. All six men were in contact via their own communicator sets, and Burkinshaw with head office, the radio room in the basement at Cork. Barry Banks was in Cork also, since this was an operation requested by Six, and they all waited for Winkler to make contact.

The trouble was, he did not. He did nothing. He just sat in his hotel room behind the net curtains and lay low. At eight-thirty he came out, walked to a restaurant on Edgware Road, had a simple supper, and went back again. He made no drop, picked up no instructions, left nothing at his table, spoke to no one in the street.

But he did two things of interest. He stopped sharply in Edgware Road on his way to the restaurant, stared in a shop window for several seconds, then headed back the way he had come. It's one of the oldest tricks for trying to spot a tail, and not a very good one. On leaving the restaurant he paused at the curb, waited for a gap in the surging traffic, then sprinted across. On the far side he paused again and scanned the street to see if anyone else had hurried across after him. No one had. All Winkler had done was join Burkinshaw's fourth watcher, who had been on the other side of Edgware Road all the time. While Winkler scanned the traffic to see who might be risking life and limb to pursue him, the watcher was a few feet away, pretending to hail a cab.

"He's 'bent,' all right," Burkinshaw told Cork. "He's surveillance-conscious, and not very good."

Burkinshaw's judgment reached Preston in his Chelsea hideout. He nodded in relief. It was beginning to look better.

After his gyrations on Edgware Road, Winkler returned to his boardinghouse and spent the rest of the night inside.

■ Meanwhile, another small operation was taking its inspired course in the basement at Sentinel House. The photos of Winkler taken by the Special Branch men in Heathrow Airport, together with others taken on the street in Bayswater, had been developed and were being placed reverentially before the gaze of the legendary Miss Blodwyn.

Identification of foreign agents, or of foreigners who might possibly be agents, forms a major part of any intelligence organization. To assist in this task, every year hundreds of thousands of pictures are taken by all the services of people who may, or may not, be working for their rivals. Even allies are not excluded from the snapshot albums. Foreign diplomats, members of trade, scientific, and cultural delegations: all are photographed as a matter of course—particularly, but not always, if they come from Communist or sympathizer countries. The archives grow and grow. The portraits often include twenty shots of the same man or woman, taken at different times and in different places. They are never thrown away. What they are used for is to get a "make."

If a Russian with the name of Ivanov shows up accompanying a Soviet trade delegation to Canada, his photographed face will almost certainly be passed by the Royal Canadian Mounted Police to their colleagues in Washington, London, and the other NATO capitals. It may well be that the same face, calling itself Kozlov, was snapped five years earlier as a visiting journalist covering the independence celebrations of an African republic. If there is any question as to Ivanov's real profession as he takes in the beauties of Ottawa, a make like that will dispel all doubts. It tags him as a full-time KGB hood.

The exchange of such photos among the allied intelligence arms —and these include the brilliant Israeli Mossad—is continuous and comprehensive. Very few Sovbloc visitors to the West, or even to the Third World, do not end up gazing from an album of photographs in at least twenty different democratic capitals. Of course, no one enters the Soviet Union without winding up in the Center's own master gallery of happy snaps.

It is the almost hilarious case, but perfectly true, that while the CIA "cousins" use banks of computers in which are stored millions and millions of facial features to try to match up the incoming daily flow of photographs, Britain uses Blodwyn.

An elderly and often ill-used lady, forever harassed by her younger male colleagues for a quick identification, Blodwyn has been in the job forty years and works underneath Sentinel House, where she presides over the huge archive of pictures that make up

MI6's "mug book." Not a book at all, it is in fact a cavernous vault where are stored rows and rows of volumes of photographs, of which Blodwyn alone possesses an encyclopedic knowledge.

Her mind is something like the CIA's computer bank, which she can occasionally defeat. In her memory is stored not the tiniest detail of the Thirty Years' War or even the Wall Street stock prices; her mind stores faces. Shapes of noses, lines of jaws, casts of eyes; the sag of a cheek, the curve of a lip, the way a glass or cigarette is held, the glint of a capped tooth in a smile taken in an Australian pub and showing up years later in a London supermarket—all are grist to the mill of her remarkable memory.

That night, while Bayswater slept and Burkinshaw's men hugged the shadows, Blodwyn sat and stared at the face of Franz Winkler. Two silent younger men from Six waited. After an hour she simply said, "Far East," and went off along the rows of her albums. She had her make in the small hours of Tuesday, May 26.

It wasn't a good photograph and it was five years old. The hair had been darker then, the waist slimmer. The man was attending a reception at the Indian Embassy, standing beside his own ambassador and smiling deferentially.

One of the younger men stared at the two photographs doubtfully. "Are you sure, Blodwyn?"

If looks could cripple, he would have needed to invest in a wheelchair. He backed away hastily and made for a telephone. "There's a make," he said. "He's a Czech. Five years ago he was a low-level gofer in the Czech Embassy in Tokyo. Name: Jiri Hayek."

Preston was woken by the telephone at three in the morning. He listened, thanked the caller, and replaced the phone. He smiled happily. "Gotcha," he said.

■ At ten in the morning, Winkler was still inside his hotel. Control of the operation at Cork Street had been taken over by Simon Margery, from K2(B), the Soviet Satellites/Czechoslovakia (Operations) desk. After all, a Czech was their affair. Barry Banks, who had slept in the office, was with him, passing developments down the line to Sentinel House.

At the same hour, John Preston made a call to the legal counselor at the American Embassy, a personal contact. The legal counselor at Grosvenor Square is always the London representative of the FBI. Preston made his request and was told he would be called back as soon as the answer came from Washington, probably in five to six hours, bearing in mind the time difference.

At eleven, Winkler emerged from the boardinghouse. He walked to Edgware Road again, hailed a cab, and set off toward Park Lane. At Hyde Park Corner, the cab, tailed by two cars containing the watcher team, went down Piccadilly. Winkler dismissed it in Piccadilly, close to the Circus end, and tried another few basic maneuvers to throw off a tail he had not even spotted.

"Here we go again," Len Stewart muttered into his lapel. He had read Burkinshaw's log and expected something similar. Suddenly Winkler shot down an arcade at a near-run, emerged at the other end, scuttled down the sidewalk, and turned to watch the entrance to the arcade from which he had just emerged. No one came out. No one needed to. There was already a watcher at the southern end of the arcade, anyway.

The watchers know London better than any policeman or cabdriver. They know how many exits every major building has, where the arcades and underpasses go, where the narrow passageways are located and where they lead to. Wherever a Joe tries to scuttle, there will always be one man there ahead of him, one coming slowly behind, and two flankers. The "box" never shatters, and it is a very clever Joe who can spot it.

Satisfied he had no tail, Winkler entered the British Rail Travel Center on Lower Regent Street. There he inquired as to the times of trains to Sheffield. The scarved Scottish football fan standing a few feet away and trying to get back to Motherwell was one of the watchers. Winkler paid cash for a second-class round-trip ticket to Sheffield, noted that the last train of the night left St. Pancras Station at nine-twenty-five, thanked the clerk, and left. He had lunch at a café nearby, returned to Sussex Gardens, and stayed there all afternoon.

Preston received the news about the train ticket to Sheffield at just after one o'clock. He caught Sir Nigel Irvine just as C was about to leave for lunch at his club.

"It may be a blind, but it looks as if he's going out of town," Preston reported. "He may be heading for his rendezvous. It could be on the train or in Sheffield. Maybe he's delayed so long because he was early. The point is, sir, if he leaves London we will need a field controller to go with the watcher team. I want to be that controller."

"Yes, see what you mean. Not easy. Still, I'll see what I can do."

Sir Nigel sighed. Bang goes lunch, he thought. He summoned his aide. "Cancel my lunch at White's. Get my car ready. And take a cable. In that order."

While the aide tackled the first two tasks, C called Sir Bernard Hemmings at his home number near Farnham, in Surrey. "Sorry to trouble you, Bernard. Something's cropped up that I'd like your advice on. . . . No, better face-to-face. Would you mind if I came down? Lovely day, after all. . . . Yes, right, about three, then."

"The cable?" asked his aide, entering the office.

"Yes."

"To whom?"

"Myself."

"Certainly. From?"

"Head of station, Vienna."

"Shall I alert him, sir?"

"No need to bother him. Just arrange with the cipher room for me to receive his cable in three minutes."

"Of course. And the text?"

Sir Nigel dictated it. Sending himself an urgent message to justify what he wanted to do anyway was an old trick that he had picked up from his onetime mentor, the late Sir Maurice Oldfield. When the cipher room sent it back up in the form in which it would have been received from Vienna, the old mandarin put it in his pocket and went down to his car.

■ He found Sir Bernard in his garden, enjoying the warm May sunshine, a blanket around his knees.

"Meant to come in today," said the Director-General of Five with well-feigned joviality. "Be in tomorrow, no doubt."

"Of course, of course."

"Now, how can I help?"

"Ticklish," said Sir Nigel. "Someone has just flown into London from Vienna. Apparent Austrian businessman. But he's a phony.

We got a make on him last night. Czech agent, one of the StB boys. Low-level. We think he's a courier."

Sir Bernard nodded. "Yes, I keep in touch, even from here. Heard all about it. My chaps are on top of him, aren't they?"

"Very much so. The thing is, it looks as if he may be leaving London tonight. For the north. Five will need a field controller to go with the watcher team."

"Of course. We'll have one. Brian can handle it."

"Yes. It's your operation, of course. Still . . . You remember the Berenson affair? We never did discover two things. Does Marais communicate through the rezidentura here in London, or does he use couriers sent in from outside? And was Berenson the only man in the ring run by Marais, or were there others?"

"I recall. We were going to put those questions on ice until we could get a few answers out of Marais."

"That's right. Then today I got this message from my head of station in Vienna."

He proffered the cable. Sir Bernard read it and his eyebrows rose. "Linked? Could they be?"

"Possible. Winkler, a.k.a. Hayek, seems to be a courier of some kind. Vienna confirms he's nominally StB but actually working for the KGB itself. We know that Marais went to Vienna twice in the past two years, while he was running Berenson. Each time on cultural jaunts, but—"

"The missing link?"

Sir Nigel shrugged. Never oversell.

"What's he going to Sheffield for?"

"Who knows, Bernard? Is there another ring up there in Yorkshire? Could Winkler be a bagman for more than one ring?"

"What do you want from Five? More watchers?"

"No, John Preston. You'll recall he tracked down Berenson first, then Marais. I liked his style. He's been on leave for a while. Then he had a dose of the flu, so they tell me. But he's due to return to work tomorrow. He's been off so long, he'll probably have no current cases, anyway. Technically, he's ports and airports, C5(C). But you know how the K boys are always worked off their feet. If he could just have a temporary attachment to K2(B), you could designate him field controller for this one."

"Well, I don't know, Nigel. This is really up to Brian. . . ."

"I'd be awfully grateful, Bernard. Let's face it, Preston was on the Berenson hunt from the start. If Winkler is part of it all, Preston might even see a face he's seen before."

"All right," said Sir Bernard. "You've got it. I'll issue the instruction from here."

"I could take it back if you like," said C. "Save you the trouble. Send my driver up to Charles Street with the chit. . . ."

Sir Nigel left with his "chit," a written order from Sir Bernard Hemmings putting John Preston on temporary assignment to K Branch and naming him field controller of the Winkler operation once it left the metropolis.

Sir Nigel had two copies made, one for him and one for John Preston. The original went to Charles Street. Brian Harcourt-Smith was out of the office, so the order was left on his desk.

■ At 7:00 p.m. John Preston left the Chelsea apartment for the last time. He was out in the open again and loved it.

At Sussex Gardens he slipped up behind Harry Burkinshaw. "Hello, Harry."

"Good Lord. John Preston. What are you doing here?"

"Taking a breath of air."

"Well, don't make yourself visible. We've got a Joe holed up there across the way."

"I know. I gather he's due to leave for Sheffield on the nine-twenty-five."

"How did you know that?"

Preston produced his copy of Sir Bernard's instruction. Burkinshaw studied it. "Wow. From the DG himself. Join the party, then. Just stay out of sight."

"Got an extra radio?"

Burkinshaw nodded down the street. "Round the corner, on Radnor Place. Brown Cortina. There's a spare in the glove compartment."

"I'll wait in the car," said Preston.

Burkinshaw was puzzled. No one had told him that Preston was joining them as field controller. He had not even known that Preston was in Czech Section. Still, the DG's signature carried a lot of weight. For his part, he would just get on with his job. He shrugged, popped another mint, and went on watching.

At 8:30 Winkler left the hotel. He was carrying his suitcase. He hailed a passing cab and gave his instructions to the driver.

When Winkler stepped out of the doorway, Burkinshaw called in his team and his two cars. He jumped in the first one and they were a hundred yards behind the cab across Edgware Road. Preston was in the second car. Ten minutes later they knew they were heading east, toward the station. Burkinshaw reported this.

Simon Margery's voice came back from Cork. "Okay, Harry, our field controller is on his way."

"We've already got a field controller," said Burkinshaw. "He's with us."

This was news to Margery. He asked the controller's name. When he heard it, he thought there had been a mistake. "He's not even with K2(B)," he protested.

"He is now," said Burkinshaw, unfazed. "I've seen the chit. Signed by the DG."

Margery called Charles Street. As the cavalcade cruised east through the dusk, a flap ensued at Charles. The instruction from Sir Bernard was traced and confirmed. Margery threw up his hands in exasperation. "Why can't the buggers up there in Charles ever make up their minds?" he asked an uncaring world. He called off the colleague he had designated to take over at St. Pancras Station. Then he tried to trace Brian Harcourt-Smith to complain.

Winkler paid off his cab, headed through the brick archway into the vaulted dome of the Victorian railway station, and consulted the departure board. Around him the four watchers and Preston vaporized into the throng of passengers in the brick-and-cast-iron concourse.

The 9:25, calling at Leicester, Derby, Chesterfield, and Sheffield, was at platform two. Having found his train, Winkler walked up the length of it, past the three first-class carriages and the buffet car, to the three blue-upholstered second-class carriages near the front end. He selected the middle one, hefted his suitcase onto the rack, and sat quietly awaiting the train's departure.

After a few minutes, a young black man with earphones over his head and a Walkman clipped to his belt came in and sat three rows away. Once seated, the man nodded his head in time to the apparent reggae blasting into his ears, closed his eyes, and enjoyed his music. One of Burkinshaw's team was in place; the earphones were silent of reggae music but were picking up Harry's instruction on strength five.

One of Burkinshaw's team took the front carriage, and Harry himself and John Preston the third, so that Winkler was boxed. The fourth man took a first-class seat in the last car in case Winkler did a "runner" down the train to shake off what he thought was a tail.

At 9:25 on the dot the Inter-City 125 hissed out of St. Pancras and headed north. At 9:30 Brian Harcourt-Smith was traced to the dining room of his club and called to the phone. It was Simon Margery. What he heard caused the Deputy Director-General of Five to hasten outside, grab a taxi, and race the two miles across the West End to Charles Street. On his desk he found the order written out earlier that afternoon by Sir Bernard Hemmings. He went quite pale with rage.

He was a highly self-disciplined man, and after thinking the matter over for several minutes, he picked up the phone and in his usual courteous manner asked the operator to get the service's legal adviser at his home. The legal adviser is the man who does most of the liaison between the service and the Special Branch. While the call was going through, Harcourt-Smith checked train times to Sheffield. The legal adviser was plucked from his seat in front of the television in Camberley and came on the line.

"I need Special Branch to make an arrest," said Harcourt-Smith. "I have reason to believe an illegal immigrant suspected of being a Soviet agent may escape surveillance. Name: Franz Winkler; supposed Austrian citizen. Holding charge: suspected false passport. He'll be arriving by train from London at Sheffield at eleven-fifty-nine. Yes, I know it's short notice. That's why it's urgent. Yes, please get on to the commander of Special Branch at the Yard and ask him to alert his Sheffield operation to make the arrest when the train arrives at Sheffield."

He put down the phone grimly. John Preston might have been sicced on him as field director of the surveillance team, but an arrest of a suspect was a policy matter, and that was his department.

■ The train was almost empty. Two carriages instead of six would have amply accommodated the sixty passengers on board. Barney, the watcher in the front carriage, shared the space with ten others, all innocent passengers. He was facing aft, so that he could see the top of Winkler's head through the window in the intercarriage door.

Ginger, the young black with the headphones who was with Winkler in the second carriage, had five other passengers in there with him. There were a dozen sharing sixty seats with Preston and Burkinshaw in the third. For an hour and a quarter, Winkler did nothing. He had no reading matter; he just stared out of the window at the dark countryside beyond.

At 10:45, when the train slowed for Leicester, he moved. He took his suitcase off the rack, walked up the carriage, passed out to the toilet area, and pulled down the window of the door giving onto the platform. Ginger informed the rest, who prepared to move at short notice if they had to.

Another passenger pushed past Winkler as the train stopped. "Excuse, please, is this Sheffield?" Winkler asked.

"No, it's Leicester," the man said, and descended to the platform.

"Ah, so. Thank you," said Winkler. He put down his suitcase, but stayed at the open window, looking up and down the platform during the brief stopover. As the train pulled out, he returned to his seat and put his suitcase back on the rack.

At 11:12 he did it again at Derby. This time he asked a porter on the platform of the cavernous concrete hall that forms Derby Station.

"Derby," sang out the porter. "Sheffield is the one after next."

Again, Winkler spent the stopover gazing out of the open window, then returned to his seat and tossed his suitcase onto the rack. Preston was watching him through the intercarriage door.

At 11:43 they rolled into Chesterfield, a Victorian station that is beautifully maintained with bright paintwork and hanging baskets of flowers. This time Winkler left his suitcase where it was, but went to lean out of the window as two or three passengers left the train and hurried through the ticket barrier. The platform was empty before the train began to roll. When it did, Winkler snapped open the door, jumped to the concrete, and slammed the door closed with a backward movement of his arm.

Burkinshaw was very rarely caught off balance by a Joe, but he later admitted that Winkler had got him cold. All four of the watchers could easily have made the platform, but there was not an iota of cover on that strip of stone. Winkler would have seen them and aborted his rendezvous, wherever it was.

Preston and Burkinshaw ran forward to the boarding platform, where they were joined by Ginger from the carriage in front. The window was still open. Preston stuck his head out and looked back. Winkler, satisfied at last that he had no tail, was striding briskly down the platform with his back to the train.

"Harry, get back here with the team by car," shouted Preston. "Get me on the radio when you're in range. Ginger, close the door after me." Then he shoved the door open, stepped to the running board, dropped into the paratrooper's landing position, and jumped.

Paratroopers hit the deck at about eleven miles per hour; sideways speed depends on the wind. The train was doing thirty when Preston slammed into the embankment, praying he would not hit a concrete post or a large stone. He was lucky. The thick May grass took some of the shock; then he was rolling, knees together, elbows in, head down. Harry told him later he couldn't watch. Ginger said he was bouncing like a toy along the embankment and down toward the spinning wheels. When he finally stopped, he was lying in the gully between the grass and the roadbed. He hauled himself to his feet, turned, and began to jog back toward the lights of the station.

When he appeared at the ticket barrier, the guard was closing for the night. He looked with amazement at the grazed apparition in the torn coat.

"The last man through here," gasped Preston, "short, stocky, gray mackintosh. Where did he go?"

The guard nodded toward the front of the station, and Preston ran. Too late, the guard realized he had not collected the ticket. At the same time, Preston was watching the taillights of a taxi sweeping out of the station and toward the town. It was the last taxi. He could, he knew, get the local police to trace the driver and ask where he had taken that fare, but he had no doubt Winkler would dismiss the cab short of his ultimate destination and walk the rest. A few feet away, a railway porter was kick-starting his moped.

"I need to borrow your bike," said Preston.

"Bog off," said the porter. There was no time for identification or argument; the lights of the taxi were passing under the new ring road and out of sight. So Preston hit him—just once—on the jaw. The porter crashed over. Preston caught the falling moped, jerked it free of the man's legs, straddled it, and rode off.

He was lucky with the traffic lights. The cab had gone up Corporation Street, and Preston would never have caught it on his tiny-engined putt-putt except that the lights outside the central library were red. When the taxi rolled down Holywell Street and into Saltergate, he was a hundred yards behind, and then he lost more ground as the bigger engine outpaced him for the straight half mile of that highway. If Winkler had been taken out into the countryside due west of Chesterfield, Preston could never have caught him.

Fortunately the taxi's brakelights flashed on when it was a speck in the distance. Winkler was paying the driver where Saltergate becomes Ashgate Road. As Preston closed the gap, he could see Winkler beside the cab, looking up and down the street. There was no other traffic; Preston realized there was nothing for it but to keep going. He puttered past the halted taxi like a late homegoer about his business, swerved into Foljambe Road, and stopped.

Winkler crossed the road on foot; Preston followed. Winkler never looked back again. He just strolled around the boundary wall of Chesterfield's football stadium and entered Compton Street. Here he approached a house and knocked on the door. Moving between patches of shadow, Preston had reached the corner of the street and was hidden behind a bush in the garden of the corner house.

Up the street he saw lights come on in a darkened house. The door opened, there was a brief conversation on the doorstep, and Winkler went inside. Preston sighed and settled behind his bush for a night-long vigil. He could not read the number of the house Winkler had entered, nor could he watch the rear of the place as well, but he could see the towering wall of the football stadium behind the house, so perhaps there was no feasible exit on that side.

At two in the morning, he heard the faint noise of his communi-

cator as Burkinshaw came back into range. He identified himself and
gave his position. At half past two he heard the soft pad of footsteps
and hissed to give his location. Burkinshaw joined him in the shrub-
bery.

"You all right, John?"

"Yes. He's housed up there, second beyond the tree, with a light
behind the curtain."

"Got it. John, there was a reception party at Sheffield. Two Special Branch and three uniformed. Drummed up by London. Did
you want an arrest?"

"Absolutely not. Winkler's a courier. I want the big fish. He
might be inside that house. What happened to the Sheffield party?"

Burkinshaw laughed. "Thank God for the British police. Sheffield is Yorkshire; this is Derbyshire. They're going to have to sort
it out between their chief constables in the morning. It gives you
time."

"Yeah. Where are the others?"

"Down the street. We came back by taxi and dismissed it. John,
we've got no wheels. Also, come the dawn, this street's got no
cover."

"Put two at the top of the street and two down here," said Preston. "I'm going back into the town to find the police station and ask
for a bit of backup. If Chummy leaves, tell me. But shadow him with
two of the team—keep two on that house."

He left the garden and walked back into central Chesterfield looking for the police station, which he found on Beetwell Street. As he
walked, a thought kept repeating itself in his head. There was something about Winkler's performance that did not make sense.

CHAPTER

Superintendent Robin King was not pleased to be woken at three in the morning, but on hearing there was an officer from MI5 at his police station seeking assistance, he agreed to come at once, and was there, unshaven and uncombed, twenty minutes later. He listened attentively while Preston explained the gist of the story: that a foreigner believed to be a Soviet agent had been tailed from London, had jumped train at Chesterfield, and had been followed to a house on Compton Street, number as yet unknown.

"I do not know who lives in that house, or why our suspect has visited it. I intend to find out, but for the moment I do not want an arrest. I want to watch the house. Later this morning, we can sort out a fuller authority through the chief constable for Derbyshire; for the moment the problem is more urgent. I have four men from our watcher service on that street, but come the daylight they'll stick out like sore thumbs. So I need some assistance now."

"What, exactly, can I do for you, Mr. Preston?" the senior police officer asked.

"Have you got an unmarked van, for instance?"

"No. Several police cars, unmarked, and a couple of vans, but with police insignia on the side."

"Can we get hold of an unmarked van and park it on that street with my men inside, just as a temporary measure?"

The superintendent called the duty sergeant on the phone. He put the same question and listened for a while. "Raise him on the phone and ask him to call me right now," he said. To Preston: "One of our men has a van. It's pretty battered—he's always having his leg pulled about it."

Thirty minutes later the sleepy police constable had made rendezvous with the watcher team outside the football stadium's main entrance. Burkinshaw and his men piled inside and the van was driven to Compton Street and parked opposite the suspect house. On instructions, the policeman climbed out, stretched, and walked away down the road, for all the world like a man coming home after working the night shift.

Burkinshaw peered from the van's rear windows and came on the radio to Preston. "That's better," he said, "we've got a great view of the house across the street. By the way, it's Number Fifty-nine."

"Hold on there for a while," said Preston. "I'm trying to fix something better. Meanwhile, if Winkler leaves on foot, tail him with two men and leave two to stay with the house. If he leaves by car, follow in the van." He turned to Superintendent King. "We may have to stake out that house for a longer period. That means taking over an upstairs room of a house across the way. Can we find anyone in Compton Street who might let us do that?"

The police chief was thoughtful. "I do know someone who lives on Compton Street," he said. "We're both Masons, members of the same lodge. That's how I know him. He's a former chief petty officer in the navy, retired now. He's at Number Sixty-eight. I don't know where it's located on the street, though."

Burkinshaw confirmed that 68 Compton Street was across from the suspect house and two buildings up. The second-floor-front window, probably a bedroom, would provide a perfect view of the target. Superintendent King rang his friend from the station.

At Preston's suggestion the policeman told the sleepy householder, a Mr. Sam Royston, that this was an official operation—they wished to watch a possible suspect who had taken refuge across the street. When he had gathered his wits, Royston rose to the occasion. As a law-abiding citizen he would certainly allow the police to use his front room.

The van was quietly driven around the block into West Street; Burkinshaw and his team slipped between the houses there, over the garden fences, and entered Royston's house on Compton Street from the back garden. Just before the sun flooded the street, the watcher team settled down in the Roystons' bedroom behind the lace curtains, through which they could see No. 59 across the way.

Royston, ramrod-stiff in camel dressing gown and bristling with the self-importance of a patriot asked to assist the Queen's officers, glowered through the curtains to the house almost opposite. "Bank robbers, are they? Drug traffickers?"

"Something like that," assented Burkinshaw.

"Foreigners," growled Royston. "Never did like 'em. Should never have let 'em all into the country."

Ginger, whose parents had come from Jamaica, stared stolidly through the curtains. Mungo, the Scot, was bringing a pair of chairs up from below.

Mrs. Royston emerged like a mouse from some secret hiding place, having removed her curlers and hairpins. "Would anyone," she inquired, "like a nice cup of tea?"

Barney, who was young and handsome, flashed his most winning smile. "That would be lovely, ma'am."

It made her day. She began to prepare the first of what turned out to be an endless relay of cups of tea, a brew upon which she appeared to live without any visible recourse to solid foods.

At the police station the desk sergeant had also established the identity of the inhabitants of 59 Compton Street.

"Two Greek Cypriots, sir," he reported to Superintendent King. "Brothers and both bachelors, Andreas and Spiridon Stephanides. Been here about four years, according to the constable on that beat. Seems they run a Greek kebab and take-away joint at Holywell Cross."

Preston had spent half an hour on the phone to London. First he raised the duty officer at Sentinel, who put him through to Banks. "Barry, I want you to contact C wherever he is and ask him to call me back."

Sir Nigel Irvine came on the line five minutes later, as calm and lucid as if he had not been asleep at all. Preston informed him of the night's events.

"Sir, there was a reception party at Sheffield. Two Special Branch and three uniformed, authorized to make an arrest."

"I don't think that was part of the arrangement, John."

"Not as far as I was concerned."

"All right, John, I'll handle it at this end. You've got the house. Are you going to move in now?"

"I've got *a* house," corrected Preston. "I don't want to move in because I don't think it's the end of the trail. One other thing, sir. If Winkler leaves and heads for home, I want him to be allowed to go in peace. If he is a courier, or message carrier, or just checking up, his people will be expecting him back in Vienna. If he fails to show, they'll switch off the cutouts from top to bottom."

"Yes," said Sir Nigel carefully. "I'll have a word with Sir Bernard about that. Do you want to stay with the operation up there or come back to London?"

"I'd like to stay up here, if possible."

"All right. I'll make it a top-level request from Six that what you want is accorded to you. Now, cover yourself and make your operational report to Charles Street."

When he put the phone down, Sir Nigel called Sir Bernard Hemmings at his home. The Director-General of Five agreed to meet him for breakfast at the Guards Club at eight.

■ "So you see, Bernard, it really may be that the Center is mounting quite a large operation inside this country at the moment," said C as he buttered his second piece of toast.

Sir Bernard Hemmings was deeply disturbed. He sat with his food untouched in front of him. "Brian should have told me about the Glasgow incident," he said. "What the hell's that report still sitting on his desk for?"

"We all make errors of judgment from time to time. *Errare humanum est*, and all that," murmured Sir Nigel. "After all, my Vienna people thought Winkler was a bagman for a longstanding ring of agents, and I deduced Jan Marais might be one of that ring. Now it appears there could be two separate operations, after all."

He refrained from admitting that he himself had written the Vienna cable of the previous day in order to obtain what he wanted from his colleague—Preston's inclusion as field controller in the Winkler operation. For C there was a time for candor and a time for discreet silence.

"And the second operation, the one linked to the intercept in Glasgow?" asked Sir Bernard.

Sir Nigel shrugged. "I just don't know, Bernard. We're all feeling our way in the dark. Brian evidently does not believe it. He may be right. In which case I'm the one with egg all over his face. And yet, the Glasgow affair, the mysterious transmitter in the Midlands, the arrival of Winkler . . . That man Winkler was a lucky break, maybe the last we'll get."

"Then what are your conclusions, Nigel?"

C smiled apologetically. It was the question he had been waiting for. "No conclusions, Bernard. A few tentative deductions. If Winkler is a courier, I'd expect him to make his contact and hand over his package, or to pick up the package he came to collect, at some public place. A parking lot, river embankment, garden bench, seat by a pond . . . If there is a big operation going down here, there must be a top-level illegal in on the ground. The man running the show. If you were he, would you want the couriers turning up at your doorstep? Of course not. You'd have one cutout, maybe two. Do have some coffee."

"All right, agreed." Sir Bernard waited as his colleague poured him a cup.

"Therefore, Bernard, it occurs to me that Winkler cannot be the big fish. He's small potatoes—a bagman, a courier, or something else. Same goes for the two Cypriots in a small house in Chesterfield. Sleepers, wouldn't you say?"

"Yes," agreed Sir Bernard, "low-level sleepers."

"It begins to look, therefore, as if the Chesterfield house might be a depository for incoming packages, a mail drop, a safe house, or maybe the home of the transmitter. After all, it's in the right area; the two squirts intercepted by GCHQ were from the Derbyshire

Peak District and the hills north of Sheffield, an easy drive from Chesterfield."

"And Winkler?"

"What can one think, Bernard? A technician sent in to repair the transmitter if it develops problems? A supervisor to check on progress? Either way, I think we should let him report back that everything is in order."

"And the big fish—do you think he might show up?"

Sir Nigel shrugged again. His own fear was that Brian Harcourt-Smith, balked of his intended arrest at Sheffield, would try to engineer the storming of the Chesterfield house. For Sir Nigel, this would be wholly premature. "I should have thought there has to be a contact there somewhere. Either he comes to the Greeks or they go to him," he said.

"You know, Nigel, I think we should stake out that house in Chesterfield, at least for a while."

The Chief of the SIS looked grave. "Bernard, old friend, I happen to agree with you. But young Brian seems very gung-ho to move in and make a few arrests. He tried last night at Sheffield. Of course, arrests look good for a while, but—"

"You leave Harcourt-Smith to me, Nigel," said Sir Bernard grimly. "I may be pegging out, but there's a bark left in the old dog yet. You know, I'm going to take over the direction of this operation personally."

Sir Nigel leaned forward and placed his hand on Sir Bernard's forearm. "I really wish you would, Bernard."

■ Winkler left the house on Compton Street at half past nine, on foot. Mungo and Barney slipped out of the rear of the Royston house, through the garden, and picked up the Czech on the corner of Ashgate Road. Winkler went back to the station, took the London train, and was picked up at St. Pancras by a fresh team. Mungo and Barney went back to Derbyshire.

Winkler never returned to his boardinghouse. Whatever he had left there he abandoned, as he had the suitcase with pajamas and shirt on the train, and went straight to Heathrow. He caught the afternoon flight to Vienna. Irvine's head of station there later reported that Winkler was met on his arrival in Austria by two men from the Soviet Embassy.

■ Preston spent the rest of the day closeted in the police station attending to the wealth of administrative detail involved in a stakeout in the provinces. The bureaucratic machinery ground into action; Charles Street jacked up the Home Office, which authorized the chief constable of Derbyshire to instruct Superintendent King to afford Preston and his men every cooperation. King was happy to do so, anyway, but the paperwork had to be in order.

Len Stewart came up by car with a second team, and they were billeted in police bachelor quarters. Photos were taken with a long lens of the Stephanides brothers as they left Compton Street for their restaurant at Holywell Cross just before noon, and dispatched by motorcycle to London. Other experts came in from Manchester, went into the local telephone exchange, and put a tap on both their phones, at the house and at the restaurant. A direction-finder bleeper was slipped into their car.

By late afternoon London had a make on them. They were not true Cypriots, but they were brothers. Veteran Greek Communists, once active in the ELLAS movement, they had left mainland Greece for Cyprus twenty years earlier. Athens had therefore kindly informed London. Their real name was Costapopoulos. According to Nicosia, they had vanished from Cyprus eight years earlier.

Immigration records at Croydon revealed that the Stephanides brothers had entered Britain five years before as legitimate Cypriot citizens and had been permitted to stay.

Records in Chesterfield showed they had arrived there just three and a half years earlier from London, taken a long lease on the kebab place, and bought the small terrace residence on Compton Street. Since then they had lived as peaceful and law-abiding citizens. Six days a week they opened their restaurant for the lunch trade, which was slack, and stayed open until late, when they did a thriving trade in take-out suppers.

Nobody in the police station except Superintendent King was told the real reason for the stakeout, and only six were told at all. The others were informed that the operation was part of a nationwide drug bust. London people were being brought in only because they knew the faces.

Just after sundown, Preston finished the paperwork at police headquarters and went to join Burkinshaw and his team. Before leaving the police station he thanked Superintendent King profusely for all the latter's assistance to him.

"Are you going to sit in during the stakeout?" asked the police chief.

"Yes, I'll be there," said Preston. "Why do you ask?"

King smiled sadly. "Half of last night we had a very aggrieved railway porter downstairs. Seems someone knocked him off his moped in the station yard and made off with it. We found the moped in Foljambe Road, quite undamaged. Still, he gave us a very clear description of his assailant. You won't be going out much, will you?"

"No, I shouldn't think so."

"How very wise," suggested King.

At his house on Compton Street Mr. Royston had been urged to continue his normal routine, visiting the shops in the morning and the bowling green in the afternoon. Extra food and drink would be brought in after dark, in case neighbors wondered at the Roystons' sudden and vastly increased appetite. A small television set was brought in for what Royston termed "the lads upstairs," and they all settled down to wait and watch.

The Roystons had moved into the back bedroom, and the single bed from that room was brought to the front. It would be shared in shifts by the watchers. Also brought in was a powerful set of binoculars on a tripod, plus a camera with a long lens for daylight shots and an infrared lens for night photography. Two fueled cars were parked close by, and Len Stewart's people were running the communications room at the police station, linking the Royston house, with its handheld sets, and London.

When Preston arrived, the four watchers seemed to have made themselves quite at home. Barney and Mungo were snoozing, one on the bed and the other on the floor; Ginger was sitting in an easy chair sipping a cup of fresh-brewed tea; Harry Burkinshaw was sitting like a Buddha in an armchair behind the lace curtains, gazing across at the empty house.

A man who had spent half his life standing in the rain, Harry was quite content. He was warm, dry, had a large supply of mints, and had his shoes off. There were worse ways of watching, as he well knew. The target house even backed onto a fifteen-foot concrete wall, the football grounds, which meant no one need spend the night crouched in the bushes. Preston took the spare chair beside him, behind the mounted camera, and accepted a cup of tea from Ginger.

"Are you bringing up the covert-entry team?" Harry asked. He meant the skilled burglars that Technical Support maintained for clandestine break-ins.

"No," said Preston. "For one thing, we don't even know whether there is someone else in there as well. For another, there could be a range of warning devices to indicate that an entry has taken place, and we might not spot them all. Finally, what I'm waiting for is another Chummy to show up. When he does, we take the cars and tail him. Len can take over the house."

They settled down in companionable silence. Barney woke up. "Anything on the telly?" he asked.

"Not much," said Ginger. "The evening news. Usual rubbish."

Twenty-four hours later, on Thursday evening at the same hour, the news was quite interesting. On their small screen they saw the Prime Minister standing on the steps of 10 Downing Street in a neat blue suit, facing a horde of press and television crews.

She announced she had just returned from Buckingham Palace, where she had asked for a dissolution of Parliament. In consequence, the country would prepare for a general election, to be held on June 18. The rest of the evening was devoted to the sensation, with the leaders and luminaries of all the parties announcing their confident expectation of victory.

"That's one for the books," Burkinshaw remarked to Preston. He could get no reply.

Lost in thought, Preston was staring at the screen. At last he said, "I think I've got it."

"Well, don't use our loo," said Mungo.

"What's that, John?" asked Harry when the laughter died down. "My deadline," said Preston, but he refused to elaborate.

■ By 1987 very few European-manufactured cars still retained the old-style large round headlights, but one that did was the evergreen Austin Mini. It was a vehicle of this type that was among the many cars to disembark on the evening of June 2 from the Cherbourg ferry arriving at Southampton.

The car had been bought in Austria four weeks earlier, driven to the clandestine garage in Germany, modified there, and driven back to Salzburg. The car had perfect Austrian papers, as did the tourist driving it, though he was in fact a Czech, the second and last of the contributions by the StB to Major Volkov's plan to import into Britain the components Valeri Petrofsky needed.

The Mini was searched at customs, and nothing amiss was discovered. Clearing Southampton docks, the driver followed the directions he had been given until, in the northern suburbs of the port city, he pulled off the road into a large parking lot. It was quite dark already and at the rear of the lot he was out of sight of those still speeding down the main highway. He descended and with a screwdriver began to work on the headlights.

First he removed the chrome ring covering the gap between the headlight unit and the surrounding metal of the car's fender. Using a larger screwdriver he then undid the screws holding the headlight firmly inside the fender. When they came free he eased the entire unit out of its socket, detached the wires that ran from the car's electrical system into the rear of the lamp bowl, and laid the headlight, which appeared exceptionally heavy, in a canvas bag by his side.

It took almost an hour to extract both headlight units. When he had finished, the small car stared sightlessly ahead with empty sockets. In the morning, the agent knew, he would return with freshly purchased headlights from Southampton, fit them, and drive away.

For the moment he hefted the heavy canvas bag, went back to the highway, and walked three hundred yards back toward the port. The bus stop was where they had said it would be. He checked his watch; ten minutes to rendezvous.

Exactly ten minutes later, a man in motorcycle leathers strolled up to the bus stop. There was no one else there. The newcomer glanced down the road and remarked, "It's always a long wait for the last bus of the night."

The Czech sighed with relief. "Yes," he replied, "but, thank God, I should be home by midnight."

They waited in silence until the bus for Southampton arrived. The Czech left the canvas bag on the ground and boarded the bus. As the taillights disappeared toward the port city, the motorcyclist lifted the bag and walked back up the road to where he had left his motorcycle.

At dawn, having ridden to Thetford to change clothes and switch vehicles, he arrived home in Cherryhayes Close, Ipswich, carrying the last of the scheduled list of components he had waited for these long weeks. Courier Nine had delivered.

■ Two days later, the stakeout on the house on Compton Street, Chesterfield, was one week old and had absolutely nothing to report.

The Stephanides brothers lived lives of impeccable uneventfulness. They rose at about nine, busied themselves about their house, where they appeared to do all their own cleaning and dusting, and left in their five-year-old car for their restaurant just before midday. They stayed there until close to midnight, when they returned home to sleep. There were no visitors and few phone calls. What calls there were involved orders for meat and vegetables or other harmless sundries.

Down at the restaurant at Holywell Cross, Len Stewart and his people reported much the same. The telephone was used more frequently, but again the talk was of orders for food, bookings for a table, or deliveries of wine. It was not possible for a watcher to dine there every night; the Greeks were apparently professionals who had spent years in the clandestine life and would have spotted a customer who came too frequently or loitered too long. But Stewart and his team did their best.

For the lads in the Royston house the main problem was boredom. Even Mr. and Mrs. Royston were tiring of the inconvenience caused by their presence after the initial excitement wore off. Royston had agreed to volunteer as a canvasser for the Conservative Party—he resolutely declined to assist anybody else—and the front windows of the house now bore posters in favor of the local Tory candidate.

This enabled more coming and going than usual, since anyone wearing a Conservative rosette seen leaving or entering the house would attract no attention from the neighbors. The ruse enabled Burkinshaw and his team, suitably rosetted, to take an occasional stroll while the Stephanides brothers were at their restaurant. It broke the monotony. The only one who seemed immune from boredom was Harry Burkinshaw.

For the rest, the principal distraction was television, kept at low volume, particularly when the Roystons were out, and the prime topic day and evening was the continuing election campaign. One week into the campaign, three things were becoming clear.

The Liberal/Social Democrat alliance had still failed to surge in the opinion polls and the issue seemed increasingly developing into the traditional race between the Conservatives and the Labour Party. The second factor was that all public-opinion polls indicated that the two main parties were much closer than could have been foreseen four years earlier, in 1983, when the Conservatives won a landslide; further, constituency-level polling indicated that the outcome in the eighty most marginal constituencies would almost certainly decide the color of the country's next government. In every poll it was the "floating vote," varying between ten and twenty percent, that held the balance.

The third development was that despite all the economic and ideological issues involved, and despite the efforts of all parties to make the most of them, the campaign was becoming increasingly dominated by the much more emotive issue of unilateral nuclear disarmament. In more and more polls the nuclear arms race issue was showing as the first or second priority of concern.

The pacifist movements, broadly Left and broadly united for once, were mounting what was in effect a parallel campaign of their own. Huge demonstrations took place on an almost daily basis, rewarded with equally copious coverage by newspapers and television. The movements, while demonstrating no noticeable fund-raising organization, seemed able from their combined resources to hire hundreds of buses at commercial rates to transport their demonstrators hither and thither across the land.

Hard Left luminaries of the Labour Party, agnostics or atheists to a man, shared every public or TV platform with clerics of the trendier wing of the Anglican Church, where the members of one group spent their allocated air time nodding in grave agreement with the points made by the other.

Inevitably, even though the alliance was not unilateralist, the primary target of the disarmers was the Conservative Party, just as their primary ally became the Labour Party. The Party leader, supported by the National Executive, seeing which way the wind was blowing, publicly aligned himself and the Party to every one of the unilateralists' demands.

Another theme that ran through the Left campaign was anti-Americanism. On a hundred platforms it rapidly became impossible for the interviewer or show host to extract from the disarmers' spokesmen a single condemnatory word against Soviet Russia; the constantly reiterated theme was hatred of America, which was portrayed as warmongering, imperialistic, and a threat to world peace.

On Thursday, June 4, the campaign was enlivened by a sudden Soviet offer to "guarantee" to recognize the whole of Western Europe, neutrals and NATO nations alike, as a nuclear-free zone in perpetuity if America would do the same.

An attempt by the British Defense Minister to explain that (a) the removal of European-American defenses was verifiable while Soviet warhead detargeting was not, and (b) the Warsaw Pact had a four-to-one conventional-weapons superiority over NATO's, was howled down twice before lunch, and the minister had to be removed from the grip of the pacifists by bodyguards.

"Anyone would think," grumbled Harry Burkinshaw as he popped another mint, "that this election was a national referendum on nuclear disarmament."

"It is," said Preston sharply.

■ Friday found Major Petrofsky shopping in Ipswich. In an office-equipment shop he acquired a small steel cabinet, thirty inches tall, eighteen wide, and twelve deep, with a door that locked securely.

From a hardware store he bought a light, short-handled, two-wheel dolly of the type used for shifting garbage cans or heavy suitcases. A lumber merchant yielded two ten-foot planks and a variety of laths, rods, and short joists, while a do-it-yourself shop sold him a complete toolbox including a high-speed drill with a selection of bits for steel or wood, plus nails, bolts, nuts, screws, a pair of heavy-duty industrial gloves, and several sheets of foam rubber. He rounded off the morning in an electrical-supply shop with the purchase of four nine-volt batteries and a selection of multicolored electrical wiring. It took two journeys in his hatchback sedan to bring the loads back to Cherryhayes Close, where he stored them in the garage. After dark he brought most of the gear inside the house.

That night the radio told him in Morse the details of the arrival of the assembler, the one event he had not been required to memorize. It would be Rendezvous X and the date Monday, the eighth. Tight, he thought, damn tight, but he would still be on target.

■ While Petrofsky was crouched over his one-time pad deciphering the message and the Stephanides brothers were serving moussaka and shish kebab to a line of people who had just left the nearby bars at closing time, Preston was in the police station, on the phone to Sir Bernard Hemmings.

"The question is, John, how long we can keep going up there in Chesterfield without any results," said Sir Bernard.

"It's only been a week, sir," said Preston. "Stakeouts have lasted a lot longer."

"Yes, I well know that. The thing is, we usually have more to go on. There's a growing move here that advocates crashing in on the Greeks to see what it is they've got stashed away in that house, if anything. Why won't you agree on a clandestine entry while they're at work?"

"Because I think they're top pros and they'd spot they'd been gone over. If that happened, they'd probably have a foolproof way of warning off their controller from ever visiting them again."

"Yes, I suppose you're right. It's all very well your sitting over that house like a tethered goat in India waiting for the tiger to come, but supposing the tiger doesn't show?"

"I believe he will, sooner or later, Sir Bernard," said Preston. "Please, give me a bit more time."

"All right," conceded Hemmings after a pause for a consultation at the other end. "A week, John. Next Friday I'll have to jack up the Special Branch lads to go in there and take the place apart. Let's face it, the man you're looking for could have been inside there all the time."

"I don't believe he is. Winkler would never have visited the lair of the tiger himself. I believe he's still out there somewhere, and that he'll come."

"Very well. One week, John. Friday next, it is."

Sir Bernard hung up. Preston stared at the handset. The election was thirteen days away. He was beginning to feel dejected, that he could have been wrong all along. Nobody else, with the possible exception of Sir Nigel, believed in his hunch. A small disk of polonium and a low-level Czech bagman were not much to go on, and might not even be linked.

"All right, Sir Bernard," he told the buzzing receiver, "one week. After that I'm packing it in, anyway."

■ The Finnair jet from Helsinki arrived the following Monday afternoon, on time, as usual, and its complement of passengers passed through Heathrow without undue problems. One of them was a tall, bearded man of middle age whose Finnish passport claimed him to be Urho Nuutila, and whose fluent command of the language could be partly explained by his Karelian parentage. He was in fact a Russian named Vassiliev, by profession a scientist in nuclear engineering attached to the Soviet Army Artillery, Ordnance Research Directorate. He spoke passable English.

Having cleared customs, he took the airport courtesy bus to the Heathrow Penta Hotel, walked in through the front, kept going right past reception, and emerged at the rear door, which gave onto the parking lot. He waited by that door in the late-afternoon sunshine, unnoticed by anyone, until a small hatchback sedan drew abreast of him. The driver had his window open. "Is this where the buses from the airport drop the passengers?" he asked.

"No," said the traveler. "I think that is around the front."

"Where are you from?" asked the young man.

"Finland, actually," said the bearded one.

"It must be cold in Finland."

"No, at this time of year it is very hot. The main problem is the mosquitoe:."

The young man nodded. Vassiliev walked around the car and climbed in. They drove off.

"Name?" asked Petrofsky.

"Vassiliev."

"That'll do. Nothing more. I'm Ross."

"Far to go?" asked Vassiliev.

"About two hours."

They drove the rest of the way in silence. Petrofsky made three separate maneuvers to detect a tail, had there been one. They arrived at Cherryhayes Close by the last light of day. On the next-door patch of front lawn Petrofsky's neighbor Mr. Armitage was mowing the grass.

"Company?" Armitage asked as Vassiliev descended from the car and walked to the front door.

Petrofsky took his guest's single small suitcase from the back and winked at his neighbor. "Head office," he whispered. "Best behavior. Might get promotion."

"Oh, I should think so, then." Armitage grinned and nodded in encouragement, and went on mowing.

Inside the sitting room, Petrofsky closed the curtains as he always did before putting on the light. Vassiliev stood motionless in the gloom. "Right," he said when the lights went on. "To business. Have you got all nine consignments that were sent to you?"

"Yes. All nine."

"Let's confirm them. One child's ball, weighing about twenty kilograms."

"Check."

"One pair shoes, one box cigars, one plaster cast."

"Check."

"One transistor radio, one electric shaver, one steel tube, extremely heavy."

"That must be this." Petrofsky went to a closet and held up a short length of heavy metal in heat-resistant cladding.

"It is," said Vassiliev. "Finally, one handheld fire extinguisher, unusually heavy, and one pair car headlights, also very heavy."

"Check."

"Well, that's it, then. If you've got the rest of the innocent commercial purchases, I'll start assembling in the morning."

"Why not now?"

"Look, young man. First of all, the sawing and drilling is hardly going to please the neighbors at this hour. Second, I'm tired. With this kind of toy you don't make mistakes. I'll start fresh tomorrow and be finished by sundown."

Petrofsky nodded. "Take the back bedroom. I'll run you to Heathrow on Wednesday in time for the morning flight."

CHAPTER

Vassiliev elected to work in the sitting room, with the curtains closed and by electric light. First he asked for the nine consignments to be assembled.

"We'll need a garbage bag," he said. Petrofsky fetched him one from the kitchen.

"Pass the items to me as I ask for them," said the assembler. "First, the cigar box."

He broke open the seals and lifted the lid. The box contained two layers of cigars, thirteen on the top and twelve below; each cigar was wrapped in an aluminum tube.

"It should be third from the left, bottom row."

It was. He emptied the cigar from its tube and slit it open with a razor. From the sliced tobacco inside he withdrew a slim glass phial with a crimped end and two twisted wires sticking out. An electrical detonator. The waste went into the bag.

"Plaster cast."

The cast had been made in two layers, the first allowed to harden before the second was applied. Between the two layers a sheet of gray, puttylike substance had been rolled flat, encased in polyethylene to prevent adhesion, and wrapped around the arm. Vassiliev prized the two layers of plaster of paris apart, peeled the gray substance from its cavity, pulled away the polyethylene protector sheets, and rolled it back into a ball. Half a pound of plastic explosive.

Given Lichka's shoes, he cut away the heels of both. From one came a steel disk two inches in diameter and one inch thick. Its rim was threaded to turn it into a broad, flat screw, and one surface had a deep cut to take a wide-headed screwdriver. From the other heel came a flatter, two-inch-wide disk of gray metal; it was lithium, an inert metal that, when bonded during the explosion to the polonium, would form the initiator and cause the atomic reaction to reach its full force.

The complementary disk of polonium came from the electric shaver that had so worried Karel Wosniak, and replaced the one lost in Glasgow. There were five of the smuggled consignments left.

The heat-resistant cladding on the exhaust pipe from the Hanomag truck was stripped away to reveal an eighteen-inch-long steel tube weighing twenty kilograms. It had an internal diameter of two inches, external four inches, for the metal's thickness was one inch and it was of hardened steel. One end was flanged and threaded internally, the other capped with steel. The capping had a small hole in the center, capable of allowing the electrical detonator to be passed through it.

From First Officer Romanov's transistor radio Vassiliev extracted the timer device; a flat, sealed steel box, the size of two cigarette packs placed end to end. On one face it had two large round buttons, one red and one yellow; from the other side protruded two colored wires, negative and positive. Each corner had an earlike lug with a hole, for bolting to the outside of the steel cabinet that would contain the bomb.

Taking the fire extinguisher that had arrived in Lundqvist's Saab, the assembler unscrewed the base, which the preparation team had cut open, reassembled, and repainted to hide the seam. Out of the interior came not fire-damping foam but wadding, and last of all a heavy rod of leadlike metal, five inches long and two inches in diameter. Small though it was, it still weighed four and a half kilograms. Vassiliev pulled on the heavy gloves to handle it. It was pure uranium-235.

"Isn't that stuff radioactive?" asked Petrofsky, who was watching in fascination.

"Yes, but not dangerously so. People think that all radioactive materials are dangerous to the same degree. Not so. Luminous watches are radioactive, but we wear them. Uranium is an alpha-emitter, low-level. Now, plutonium—that's really lethal. So is this stuff when it goes critical, as it will just before detonation—but not yet."

The pair of headlights from the Mini took a lot of stripping. Vassiliev took out the glass lamps, the filament inside, and the inner reflector bowl. What he was left with was a pair of extremely heavy semispherical bowls, each of one-inch-thick hardened steel. Each bowl had a flange around its rim, drilled with sixteen holes to take the nuts and bolts. Joined together, they would form a perfect globe.

One of the bowls had at its base a two-inch-wide hole, threaded inside to accept the steel plug from Lichka's left shoe. The other had a short stump of tube sticking out from its base; internally it was two inches wide, and it was flanged and threaded on its outer side to screw into the steel "gun" tube from the Hanomag's exhaust system.

The last item was the child's ball, brought in by the camper van. Vassiliev cut away the bright rubberized skin. A ball of metal gleamed in the light.

"That's lead wrapping," he said. "The ball of uranium, the fissionable core of the nuke, is inside. I'll get it out later. It's also radioactive, like that piece over there."

Having satisfied himself he had his nine components, he started work on the steel cabinet. Turning it on its back, he lifted the lid and with the wooden laths and rods prepared an inner frame in the form of a low cradle, which rested on the floor of the cabinet. This he covered with a thick layer of shock-absorbent foam rubber.

"I'll pack more around the sides and over the top when the bomb's inside," he explained.

Taking the four batteries, he wired them up, terminal to terminal, then lashed them into a block with masking tape. Finally he bored four small holes in the lid of the cabinet and wired the block of batteries inside. It was now midday.

"Right," he said. "Let's put the device together. By the way, have you ever seen a nuke?"

"No," said Petrofsky hoarsely. He was an expert in unarmed combat, unafraid of fists, knives, or guns. But the cold-blooded joviality of Vassiliev as he handled enough destructive power to flatten a town worried him. Like most people, Petrofsky regarded nuclear science as an occult art.

"Once they were very complicated," said the assembler. "Very large, even the low-yield ones, and could be made only under extremely complex laboratory conditions. Today the really sophisticated ones, the multimegaton hydrogen weapons, still are. But the basic atomic bomb today has been simplified to a point where it can be assembled on just about any workbench—given the right parts, of course, and a bit of caution and know-how."

"Great," said Petrofsky. Vassiliev was cutting away the thin lead sheeting around the ball of uranium-235. The lead had been wrapped around cold, like wrapping paper, and its seams sealed with a blowtorch. It came apart quite easily. Inside was the inner ball, five inches in diameter, with a two-inch-wide hole drilled straight through the middle.

"Want to know how it works?" asked Vassiliev.

"Sure."

"This ball is uranium. Weight, fifteen and a half kilograms. Not enough mass to have reached criticality. Uranium goes critical as its mass increases beyond criticality point."

"What do you mean, 'goes critical'?"

"It starts to fizz. Not literally, like soda. I mean fizz in radioactive terms. It passes to the threshold of detonation. This ball is not yet at that stage. See that short rod over there?"

"Yes."

It was the uranium rod from the hollow fire extinguisher.

"That rod will fit exactly into the two-inch hole in the center of this ball. When it does, the whole mass will go critical. The steel tube over there is like a gun barrel, with the uranium rod as the bullet. In detonation the plastic explosive will blast the uranium rod down the tube and into the heart of this ball."

"And it goes bang."

"Not quite. You need the initiator. Left to itself, the uranium would fizz into extinction, create a hell of a lot of radioactivity, but no explosion. To get the bang you have to bombard the critical uranium with a blizzard of neutrons. Those two disks, the lithium and the polonium, form the initiator. Left apart, they are harmless; the polonium is a mild alpha-emitter, the lithium is inert. Smash them together and they do something odd. They start a reaction; they emit that blizzard of neutrons we need. Subjected to this, the uranium tears itself apart in a gigantic release of energy—the destruction of matter. It takes one hundred millionth of a second. The steel tamper is to hold it all together for that tiny period."

"Who drops in the initiator?" asked Petrofsky in an attempt at gallows humor.

Vassiliev grinned. "No one. The two disks are in there already, but held apart. We put the polonium at one end of the hole in the uranium ball, and the lithium on the nose of the incoming uranium projectile. The bullet comes down the tube, into the heart of the ball, and the lithium on its nose is slammed into the polonium waiting at the other end of the tunnel. That's it."

Vassiliev used a drop of Super Glue to stick the polonium disk to one face of the flat steel plug from Lichka's shoe heel. Then he screwed the plug into the hole at the base of one of the steel bowls. Taking the uranium ball, he lowered it into the bowl. The interior of that bowl had four nodules, which slotted into four indentations cast in the uranium. When they met and engaged, the ball was held in place. Vassiliev took a pencil flashlight and peered down the hole through the core of the uranium ball.

"There it is," he said, "waiting at the bottom of the hole."

Then he placed the second steel bowl over the top, to form a perfect globe, and spent an hour tightening the sixteen bolts around the flange to hold the two halves together.

"Now, the gun," he remarked. He pushed the plastic explosive down the eighteen-inch-long steel tube, tamping it firmly but gently with a broom handle from the kitchen until it was packed tightly. Through the small hole in the base of the tube, Petrofsky could make out the plastic explosive bulging up. With the same Super Glue, Vassiliev attached the lithium disk to the flat nose of the uranium rod, wrapped it in a tissue to ensure it could not slip back down the tube from vibration, and rammed the rod down onto the explosive at the bottom. Then he screwed the tube into the globe. It looked like a gray, seven-inch-diameter melon with an eighteen-inch handle sticking out of one end; a sort of oversized stick-grenade.

"Nearly done," said Vassiliev. "The rest is conventional bomb-making."

He took the detonator, separated the wires from its end and insulated each with tape. If they touched each other, there could be a premature detonation. A length of five-amp electrical wiring was twisted onto each wire from the detonator. Then he pressed the detonator through the hole in the far end of the tube until it was embedded in plastic explosive.

He lowered the bomb like a baby onto its foam-rubber cradle, packing more foam rubber all around its sides, and yet more over the top, as if it were going to bed. Only the two wires were kept free. One of these was attached to the positive terminal of the battery block. A third wire went from the negative terminal on the batteries, so Vassiliev still had one of each in his hands. He insulated each exposed end.

"Just in case they touch each other." He grinned. "Now that *would* be bad news."

The single unused component was the timer box. Vassiliev used the drill to bore five holes in the side of the steel cabinet near the top. The center hole was for the wires out of the back of the timer, which he fed through. The other four were for thin bolts with which he fixed the timer to the exterior of the cabinet. This done, he linked the wires from the batteries and detonator to those from the timer, according to their color coding. Petrofsky held his breath.

"Don't worry," said Vassiliev, who had noticed his apprehension. "This timer was repeatedly tested back home. The cutout, or circuit breaker, is inside, and it works."

He stowed the last of the wires, insulated the joins heavily, and lowered the lid of the cabinet, locking it securely and tossing the key to Petrofsky.

"So, Comrade Ross, there it is. You can wheel it on the dolly and put it in the rear of the hatchback, and it will not be damaged. You can drive where you wish—the vibration will not disturb it. One last thing. The yellow button, here, if pushed firmly, will start the timer, but it will not complete the electrical circuit. The timer will do that two hours later. Press this yellow button and you have two hours to get the hell out. The red button is a manual override. Press that and you get instant detonation."

He did not know he was wrong. He really believed what he had been told. Only four men in Moscow knew that both buttons were set for instant detonation. It was now evening.

"Now, friend Ross, I want to eat, drink a little, sleep well, and go home tomorrow morning. If that is all right with you."

"Sure," said Petrofsky. "Let's get the cabinet into the corner here, between the sideboard and the drinks table. Help yourself to a whisky, and I'll rustle up some supper."

■ They set off for Heathrow in Petrofsky's small car at ten the next morning. At a place southwest of Colchester where the dense woods come close to the road, Petrofsky stopped the car and got out to relieve himself. Seconds later, Vassiliev heard a sharp cry of alarm and ran to investigate. The assembler ended his life with an expertly broken neck behind a screen of trees. The body, stripped of all identification, was laid in a shallow ditch and covered with fresh branches. It would probably be discovered in a day or so, maybe later. Police inquiries would eventually involve a photograph in the local papers, which Petrofsky's neighbor Armitage might or might not see, and might or might not recognize. It would be too late, anyway. Petrofsky drove back to Ipswich.

He had no qualms. His orders had been quite clear on the matter of the assembler. How Vassiliev had ever thought he would be allowed to go home, Petrofsky could not imagine. In any case, he had other problems. Everything was ready, but time was short. He had visited Rendlesham Forest and picked his spot; in dense cover but hardly a hundred yards from the perimeter wire of the USAF base at Bentwaters. There would be no one there at four in the morning when he pressed the yellow button to initiate detonation for six o'clock. Fresh branches would cover the cabinet while the minutes ticked away and he drove hard toward London.

The only thing he did not know was which morning it would be. The signal to go operational would, he knew, come on the Radio Moscow English-language-service news at ten o'clock of the preceding evening. It would be in the form of a deliberate word-fluff by the broadcaster in the first news item. But since Vassiliev could not tell them, Petrofsky still had to inform Moscow that all was in readiness. This meant a last message by radio. After that, the Stephanides brothers would be expendable. In the dusk of a warm June evening he left Cherryhayes Close and drove sedately north toward Thetford and his motorcycle. At nine o'clock, having changed clothes and vehicles, he began to ride northwest into the British Midlands.

■ The boredom of an ordinary evening for the watchers in the second-floor-front bedroom of the Royston house was broken at just after ten when Len Stewart came on the air from the police station.

"John, one of my lads was eating in the kebab place just now. The phone rang twice, then the caller hung up. It rang again twice, and he hung up again. Then he did it a third time. The listeners confirm it."

"Did the Greeks try to answer it?"

"They didn't reach it in time the first occasion it rang. After that, they didn't try for it. Just went on serving. . . . Hold on. . . . John, are you there?"

"Yes, of course."

"My people outside report one of the brothers is leaving. Through the back. He's going for his car."

"Two cars and four men to follow," ordered Preston. "Remaining two to stay with the restaurant. The runner may be leaving town."

But he was not. Andreas Stephanides drove back to Compton Street, parked the car, and let himself in. Lights went on behind the curtains. Nothing else happened. At eleven-twenty, earlier than usual, Spiridon closed the restaurant and walked home, arriving at a quarter to twelve.

Preston's tiger came just before the hour of midnight. The street was very quiet. Almost all the lights were out. Preston had scattered his four cars and their crews far and wide, and nobody saw him come. The first they knew, there was a mutter from one of Stewart's men.

"There's a man at the top end of Compton Street, junction of Cross Street."

"Doing?" asked Preston.

"Nothing. Standing motionless in the shadows."

"Wait."

It was pitch-dark in the Roystons' upstairs bedroom. The curtains were back, the men standing away from the window. Mungo crouched behind the camera, which was wearing its infrared lens. Preston held his small radio close to one ear. Stewart's team of six and Burkinshaw's two drivers with their cars were out there somewhere, all linked by radio. A door opened down the street as someone put a cat out. It closed again.

"He's moving," the radio muttered. "Down toward you. Slowly."

"Got him," hissed Ginger, who was at one of the side windows. "Medium height and build. Dark, long raincoat."

"Mungo, can you get him under that streetlight, just before the Greeks' house?" asked Burkinshaw.

Mungo turned the lens a fraction. "I'm focused on the pool of light," he said.

"He's got ten yards to go," said Ginger.

Without a sound the figure in the raincoat entered the glow cast by the streetlamp. Mungo's camera threw off five fast exposures. The man passed out of the light and arrived at the gate to the Stephanides house. He went up the short path and tapped, instead of ringing, at the door. It opened at once. There was no light in the hall. The dark raincoat passed inside. The door closed.

In the Roystons' bedroom the tension broke.

"Mungo, get that film out of there and over to the police lab. I want it developed and passed straight to Scotland Yard. Immediate transmission to Charles and Sentinel. I'll tell them to be ready to try to get a make."

Something was bothering Preston. Something about the way the man had walked. It was a warm night—why a raincoat? To keep dry? The sun had shone all day. To cover something? Pale clothing, distinctive clothing?

"Mungo, what was he wearing? You saw him in close-up."

Mungo was halfway out the door. "A raincoat," he said. "Dark. Long."

"Under that."

Ginger whistled. "Boots. I remember them now. Ten inches of jackboot."

"Shit, he's on a motorcycle," said Preston. He spoke into the radio. "Everyone out on the streets. On foot only. No car engines. Every street in the district except Compton. We're looking for a motorcycle with a warm engine block."

The problem is, he thought, I don't know how long he's going to be in there. Five minutes? Ten? Sixty? He radioed Len Stewart.

"Len, John here. If we get that motorcycle, I want a bleeper in it somewhere. Meanwhile, call up Superintendent King. He'll have to mount the operation. When Chummy leaves, we'll be after him. Harry's team and me. I want you and your boys to stay on the Greeks. When we are all one hour clear, the police can take the house and the Greeks."

Len Stewart, inside the police station, assented and started to phone Superintendent King at home.

It was twenty minutes before one of the roving team found the motorcycle. He reported to Preston, still at the Royston house.

"There's a big BMW, top end of Queen Street. Carrier box behind the pillion, locked. Two saddlebags either side of the rear wheel, unlocked. Engine and exhaust still warm."

"Registration number?"

The number was given him. He passed it to Len Stewart at the police station. Stewart asked for an immediate make on it. It turned out to be a Suffolk number, registered to a Mr. James Duncan Ross of Dorchester.

"It's either a stolen vehicle, a false plate, or a blind address," muttered Preston. Hours later, the Dorchester police established it was the last of the three.

The man who had found the motorcycle was ordered to plant the direction-finder in one of the saddlebags, switch it on, and get well away from the vehicle. The man, Joe, was one of Burkinshaw's two drivers. He went back to his car, effaced himself behind the steering wheel, and confirmed that the bleeper was functioning.

"Okay," said Preston, "we're doing a changeover. All drivers back to their cars. Three of Len Stewart's men, move toward the West Street rear entrance to our observation post and relieve us. One by one, quietly, and now." To the men around him in the room he said, "Harry, pack up. You go first. Take the lead car. I'll ride with you. Barney, Ginger, take the backup car. If Mungo can make it back in time, he'll be with me."

One by one, Stewart's men arrived to replace Burkinshaw's team. Preston prayed that the agent across the road would not move out while the changeover was taking place. He was the last to leave, putting his head around the door of the Roystons' bedroom to thank them for their help and assure them it would all be over by dawn. The whispers that came back were more than a little worried.

Preston slipped through the back garden and into West Street, and five minutes later joined Burkinshaw and Joe, the driver, in their lead car, parked on Foljambe Road. Ginger and Barney reported in from the second car, at the top end of Marsden Street, off the Saltergate.

"Of course," said Burkinshaw gloomily, "if it's not the motorcycle, we're up shit creek without a paddle."

Preston was in the back seat. Beside the driver, Burkinshaw watched the display panel of the console in front of him. Like a small radar screen, it showed a flashing pulse of light at rhythmic intervals, glowing on a quadrant that gave its direction from the end-to-end axis of the car in which they were sitting and its approximate distance from them—half a mile. The second car carried an identical device, enabling the two operators to get a crossbearing if they wished.

"It's got to be the motorcycle," said Preston desperately. "We'd never be able to tail him in these streets, anyway. They're too empty and he's too good."

"He's leaving."

The sudden bark from the radio cut off further talk. Stewart's men in the Roystons' bedroom reported that the man in the raincoat had left the house across the street. They confirmed that he was walking up Compton Street toward Cross Street and in the direction of the BMW. Then he passed out of sight. Two minutes later one of Stewart's drivers, on St. Margaret's Drive, reported that the agent had crossed the top of that street, still heading toward Queen Street. Then nothing. Five minutes went by. Preston prayed.

"He's moving."

Burkinshaw was jumping up and down in the front seat in excitement, most unusual behavior in this phlegmatic watcher. The flashing blip was slowly cruising across the screen as the motorcycle changed the angle between itself and the car.

"Target on the move," the second car confirmed.

"Give him a mile, then take off," said Preston. "Start engines now."

The blip moved south and east through the center of Chesterfield. When it was close to the Lordsmill roundabout the cars began to follow. When they reached the roundabout there was no doubt. The signal from the motorcycle was steady and strong, straight down the A617 to Mansfield and Newark. Range: just over a mile. Even their lights would be out of sight of the motorcyclist ahead. Joe grinned. "Try and shake us now, you bastard," he remarked.

Preston would have been happier if the man ahead had been in a car. Motorcycles were brutes to follow. Fast and maneuverable, they could weave through dense traffic that blocked a tailing car and dive down narrow alleys or between bollards that no car could enter. Even out in the country they could leave the road and ride over grassland where a car would be hard put to follow. The essence was to keep the man ahead unaware that they were following.

The motorcyclist up ahead was good. He stayed within the speed limit, but seldom went below it, taking the curves without slackening speed. He kept to the A617 beneath the sweep of the M1 motorway, through Mansfield, asleep in the small hours of the morning, and on toward Newark. Derbyshire gave way to the fat, rich farmland of Nottinghamshire and he never slackened pace.

Just before Newark he stopped.

"Range closing fast," said Joe suddenly.

"Douse lights, pull over," snapped Preston.

In fact, Petrofsky had swerved into a side road, killed his engine and lights, and now sat at the junction staring back the way he had come. A big truck thundered past him and vanished toward Newark. Nothing else. A mile up the road the two watcher cars held station at the roadside. Petrofsky stayed still for five minutes, then gunned his engine and went off down the road to the southeast. When they saw the flashing light on the console move away, the watchers followed, always keeping at least a mile behind.

The chase ran over the River Trent, where the lights of the huge sugar refinery glowed away to their right, then into Newark itself. It was just short of three o'clock. Inside the town, the signal wavered wildly as the pursuer car swerved through the streets. The blip seemed to settle on the A46 toward Lincoln, and the cars were half a mile up that road before Joe slammed on the brakes.

"He's away to our right," he said. "Distance increasing."

"Turn back," said Preston. They found the turnoff inside Newark; the target had gone down the A17, southeast again, toward Sleaford.

■ In Chesterfield the police operation moved on the Stephanides house at two-fifty-five. There were ten uniformed officers and two Special Branch men in plainclothes. Ten minutes earlier and they would have had the two Soviet agents cold. It was just bad luck. At the moment the Special Branch men approached the door, it opened.

The Stephanides brothers were apparently preparing to leave in their car with their radio to make the transmission that was encoded and recorded inside the transmitter. Andreas was coming out to start their car when he saw the policemen. Spiridon was behind him, carrying the transmitter. Andreas gave a single yell of alarm, stepped back, and slammed the door. The police charged, shoulders first.

When the door came down, Andreas was behind and under it. He came up fighting like an animal in the narrow hallway, and it took two officers to flatten him again.

The Special Branch men stepped over the melee, had a quick glance through the first-floor rooms, called to the two men in the back garden, who had seen no one emerge, and ran up the stairs. The bedrooms were empty. They found Spiridon in the tiny attic beneath the eaves. The transmitter was on the floor; it was plugged into a wall socket, and a small red light on the console glowed. Spiridon came quietly.

■ At Menwith Hill the GCHQ listening post intercepted a single squirt from the covert transmitter and logged it at two-fifty-eight on the morning of Thursday, June 11. Triangulation was immediate and pointed to a spot in the western end of the town of Chesterfield. The police station there was alerted at once and the call was patched through to the car being used by Superintendent Robin King. He took the call and told Menwith Hill, "I know. We've got them."

■ In Moscow, the warrant officer radio operator removed his head-phones and nodded toward the teleprinter. "Faint but clear," he said.

The printer began to chatter, sending out a screed of paper covered with a jumble of meaningless letters. When it fell silent, the officer beside the radio tore off the sheet and fed it through the decoder, already set to the formula of the agreed one-time pad. The decoder absorbed the sheet, its computer ran through the permutations, and it delivered the message in clear. The officer read the text and smiled. He telephoned a number, identified himself, checked the identity of the man he was addressing, and said:

"Aurora is 'go.' "

■ After Newark the countryside flattened and the wind increased. The pursuit entered the gently rolling wolds of Lincolnshire and the arrow-straight roads that lead into the fen country. The flashing blip was steady and strong, leading Preston's two cars down the A17 past Sleaford and toward the Wash and the county of Norfolk.

Southeast of Sleaford, Petrofsky stopped again and scanned the dark horizon behind him for lights. There were none. A mile behind him the pursuers waited in darkened silence. When the blip began to move up the oscilloscope screen, they followed again.

At the village of Sutterton there was another moment of confusion. Two roads led out of the far side of the sleeping township; the A16, due south for Spalding, and the A17, southeast for Long Sutton and King's Lynn, across the border in Norfolk. It took two minutes to discern that the flashing blip was moving down the A17, toward Norfolk. The gap had increased to three miles.

"Close up," ordered Preston, and Joe kept the speedometer needle on ninety until the gap was reduced to a mile and a half.

South of King's Lynn they crossed the spread of the River Ouse, and seconds later the blip took the road due south from the bypass toward Downham Market and Thetford.

"Where the hell's he going?" grumbled Joe.

"He's got a base down there somewhere," said Preston from behind him. "Just keep tracking."

To their left a flush of pink dusted the eastern horizon, and the silhouettes of the passing trees became clearer. Joe went from headlights to sidelights.

■ Far to the south, the lights were also dimmed on the columns of buses that growled on choked roads through the Suffolk market town of Bury St. Edmunds. There were two hundred of them, converging from a variety of different directions across the country, packed to the windows with peace marchers. Other demonstrators came in cars, on motorcycles and bicycles, and on foot. The slow cavalcade, hung with its banners and placards, moved out of the town and up the A143 to come to rest at Ixworth junction. The buses could go no farther down the narrow lanes. They stopped on the verge of the main road close to the junction and discharged their yawning cargoes into the brightening dawn of the Suffolk countryside. The marshals then began to urge and cajole the throng into some semblance of a column while the Suffolk police sat astride their motorcycles and watched.

■ In London, the lights were still burning. Sir Bernard Hemmings had been driven from his home, having been alerted, as he had requested, when the watcher teams in Chesterfield began to follow their man. He was in the basement radio room at Cork Street, with Brian Harcourt-Smith beside him.

Across the city, Sir Nigel Irvine, also roused at his own request, was in his office at Sentinel House. Beneath him, in the basement, Blodwyn had sat for half the night and stared at the face of a man beneath a streetlamp in a small Derbyshire town. She had been driven from her Camden Town home in the small hours, and had agreed to come only at the personal request of Sir Nigel himself. He had greeted her with flowers; for him she would walk over broken glass, but for no one else.

"He's never been here before," Blodwyn had said as soon as she set eyes on the photograph, "and yet . . ."

After an hour it was to the Middle East that she turned her attention, and at four in the morning she had him. It was a contribution from the Israeli Mossad; it was six years old, a bit blurred, and only the one picture. Even the Mossad had not been sure; the accompanying text made plain it was just a suspicion.

One of their men had taken the photograph on the streets of Damascus. The subject had called himself Timothy Donnelly then, and represented himself as a salesman for Waterford crystal. On a hunch the Mossad had snapped him and checked with their people in Dublin. Timothy Donnelly existed, but he was not in Damascus. By the time this was learned, the man in the picture had vanished. He had never surfaced again.

"That's him," Blodwyn said. "The ears prove it. He should have worn a hat."

Sir Nigel called the basement radio room at Cork Street. "We think we have a make, Bernard," he said. "We can run you off a print and send it over."

■ They almost lost him six miles south of King's Lynn. The pursuit cars were heading south to Downham Market when the blip began to drift, imperceptibly at first, then more definitely, toward the east. Preston consulted his road map.

"He turned off back there onto the A134," he said. "Heading for Thetford. Take a left here."

They got on the tail again at Stradsett, and then it was a straight run through the thickening forests of beech, oak, and pine to Thetford. They had reached the top of Gallows Hill and could see the ancient market town spread out ahead of them in the dim light of dawn when Joe slewed to a halt.

"He's stopped again."

Another check for a tail? He had always done that in open countryside before.

"Where is he?"

Joe studied the range indicator and pointed ahead. "Right in the heart of the town, John."

Preston conned the map. Apart from the road they were on, there were five others leading out of Thetford in the configuration of a star. The daylight was growing. It was five o'clock. Preston yawned. "We'll give him ten."

The blip never moved for ten minutes, or another five. Preston sent his second car around the ring road. From four points the second car triangulated with the first; the blip was right in the center of Thetford. Preston picked up the hand mike.

"Okay, I think we have his base. We're moving in."

The two cars closed on the center of town. They converged on Magdalen Street, and at five-twenty-five found the hollow square of garages. Joe maneuvered the nose of the car until it pointed unswervingly at one of the doors. The tension among the men began to mount.

"He's in there," said Joe. Preston climbed out. He was joined by Barney and Ginger from the other car.

"Ginger, can you lose that door handle?"

For answer Ginger took a crowbar from the toolkit in one of the cars, slipped it over the garage door handle and jerked it sharply. There was a crack inside the lock. He looked at Preston, who nodded. Ginger swept the up-and-over garage door open and stood hastily back.

The men in the yard could only stare. The motorcycle was positioned on its stand in the center of the garage. From a hook hung a set of black leathers and a crash helmet. A pair of jackboots stood near the wall. In the dust and oil on the floor were the tracks of automobile tires.

"Oh, Jesus," said Harry Burkinshaw, "it's a switch."

Joe leaned out of his window. "Cork just came on the police network. They say they have a full-face picture. Where do you want it sent?"

"Thetford police station," said Preston. He gazed up at the clear blue sky above him.

"But it's too late," he whispered.

CHAPTER

At just after five that morning, the marchers were finally in a column that was seven men abreast and more than a mile long. The head of the column began to move up the narrow road from Ixworth junction called the A1088, their destination the village of Little Fakenham and thence down the even narrower lane to the Royal Air Force base at Honington.

It was a bright, sunny morning and they were all in good spirits, despite the early hour that had been decreed by the organizers so as to catch the first arrival of the American Galaxy transports bringing in the Cruise missiles. As the head of the column began to surge between the hedgerows flanking the road, the body of the crowd started the ritual chant: "No to Cruise—Yanks out."

Years earlier, RAF Honington had been a base for Tornado strike bombers and had attracted no attention from the nation as a whole. It was left to the villagers of Little Fakenham, Honington, and Sapiston to tolerate the howling of the Tornadoes over their heads. The decision to create at Honington Britain's third Cruise missile base had changed all that.

The Tornadoes had gone to Scotland, but in their place the peace of the rustic neighborhood had been shattered by protesters, mainly

340

female and possessed of strange personal habits, who had infested the fields and set up shanty camps on patches of common land. That had been going on for two years.

There had been marching demonstrations before, but this was to be the biggest. Newsmen and television reporters were in heavy attendance, the cameramen running backward up the road to film the dignitaries in the front rank of the column. These included three members of the Shadow Cabinet, two bishops, a monsignor, various luminaries of the reformed churches, five trade-union leaders, and two noted academics.

Behind them came the pacifists, conscientious objectors, clerics, Quakers, students, pro-Soviet Marxist-Leninists, anti-Soviet Trotskyites, lecturers, and Labour activists, with an admixture of unemployed workers, punks, gays, and bearded ecologists. There were also hundreds of equally concerned housewives, workingmen, teachers, and schoolchildren.

Along the sides of the road were scattered the resident female protesters, most sporting placards and banners, some in anoraks and crewcuts, who held hands with their younger lady friends or applauded the approaching marchers. The whole column was preceded by two policemen on motorcycles.

■ By five-fifteen Valeri Petrofsky was clear of Thetford and as usual was motoring sedately south down the A1088 to pick up the main road to Ipswich and home. He had been up all night and he was tired. But he knew his message must have been sent by three-thirty; by now Moscow would know that he had not let them down.

He crossed the border into Suffolk near Euston Hall and noted a police motorcyclist astride his stationary machine at the side of the road. It was the wrong road and the wrong hour; Petrofsky had driven along this road many times over the previous months and he had never seen a motorcycle patrolman on it.

A mile farther on, at Little Fakenham, all his animal senses went to full alert. Two white Rover police cars were parked on the northern side of the village. Beside them a group of senior officers were in consultation with two more motorcycle patrolmen. They glanced up at him as he drove by, but made no move to stop him.

The move came later, at Ixworth Thorpe. Petrofsky had just

cleared the village itself and was approaching its church on the right-hand side when he saw the motorcycle leaning against the hedge and the figure of the patrolman in the center of the road, a radio held to his mouth and an arm raised to stop him. He began to slow, his right hand dropping to the map pocket inside the door panel where, under a rolled woolen sweater, lay the Finnish automatic.

If it was a trap, he was boxed from behind. But the policeman seemed to be alone. There was no one else nearby. Petrofsky slowed to a halt. The towering figure in black vinyl strolled to the car window and bent down. Petrofsky found himself confronting a ruddy Suffolk face with no hint of guile in it.

"Could I ask you to pull over to the side of the road, please, sir? Just there in front of the church. Then you'll come to no 'arm."

So it *was* a trap. The threat was thinly veiled. But why was there no one else about?

"What seems to be the trouble, Officer?"

" 'Fraid the road's blocked a bit farther down, sir. We'll have it clear directly."

Truth or trick? There *might* be an overturned tractor down there. He decided not to shoot the policeman and make a dash for it. Not yet. He nodded, let in the clutch, and pulled over in front of the church. Then he waited. In his rearview mirror he could see the policeman taking no more notice of him, but signaling another motorist to stop. This could be it, he thought. Counterintelligence. But there was only one man in the other car. It pulled up behind him. The man climbed out.

"What's going on?" he called to the policeman. Petrofsky could hear them through his open window.

"Ain't you 'eard, sir? It's the demonstration. Been in all the papers. And on the telly."

"Oh, hell," said the other driver, "I didn't realize it was this road. Or at this hour."

"They won't take long to pass," said the policeman comfortingly. "No more 'n an hour."

At that moment the head of the column came into sight from around the bend. With disgust and contempt, Petrofsky gazed at the distant banners and heard the faint shouts. He climbed out to watch.

■ The hollow square of tarmac off Magdalen Street with its thirty garages was becoming crowded. Minutes after the discovery of the abandoned motorcycle, Preston had sent Barney and the second car racing up Grove Lane to the police station to ask for help. There had been a duty constable in the front office at that hour, and a sergeant having tea in the back.

Simultaneously Preston had called London on the police network, and even though it was an open circuit and he would normally have used the cover parlance of a car-rental agent, he threw caution to the winds and spoke in clear to Sir Bernard himself.

"I need backup from the police forces of Norfolk and Suffolk," he said. "Also a chopper, sir. Very fast. Or it's all over." He had spent the last twenty minutes studying the large-scale road map of East Anglia, spread on the hood of Joe's car.

After five minutes a Thetford motorcycle patrolman, raised by his station sergeant, drifted into the yard, shut off his engine, and parked his bike. He walked over to Preston, easing off his helmet as he did so. "You the gentlemen from London?" he asked. "Anything I can do to help?"

"Not unless you're a magician," sighed Preston.

Barney arrived back from the police station. "Here's the photograph, John. Came through while I was talking to the duty sergeant."

Preston studied the handsome young face photographed on a Damascus street. "You bastard," he muttered. His words were drowned, so no one else heard. Two American F-111 strike bombers raced across the sky in tight formation, low, heading east. The howl of their engines broke the calm of the waking borough. The policeman did not glance up.

Barney, standing beside Preston, followed their progress out of sight. "Noisy sods," he remarked.

"Ah, they always be coming over Thetford," said the local cop. "Hardly notice them after a while. Come from Lakenheath."

"London Airport's bad enough," said Barney, who lived at Hounslow, "but at least the airliners don't fly that low. Don't think I could live with that for long."

"Don't mind 'em, just so long as they stay up in the air," said the policeman, unwrapping a chocolate bar. "Wouldn't like one to crash, though. They carry atomic bombs, they do. Small, mind."

Preston turned around slowly. "What did you say?" he asked.

■ At Cork Street, MI5 had been working fast. Dispensing with the usual liaison from the legal adviser, Sir Bernard Hemmings had personally called both the assistant commissioners (crime) for the counties of Norfolk and Suffolk. The officer in Norwich was still abed, but in Ipswich his opposite number was already in his office because of the demonstration that was tying up half the Suffolk force.

The assistant commissioner for Norfolk was reached at the same time as the call to him from Thetford police station came through. He authorized complete cooperation; the paperwork could follow later.

Brian Harcourt-Smith was chasing up a helicopter. Britain's two intelligence agencies have access to a special flight of helicopters, which are held at Northolt, outside London. It is possible to call one up in a hurry, but normally advance arrangements are made. The Deputy Director-General's urgent inquiry brought the answer that a chopper could be airborne in forty minutes and could land at Thetford forty minutes after that. Harcourt-Smith asked Northolt to hold on. "Eighty minutes," he reported to Sir Bernard.

The DG happened to be talking to the assistant commissioner for Suffolk, who was in his Ipswich office. "Would you have a police helicopter available? Right now?" he asked the officer.

There was a pause while the ACC for Suffolk consulted his colleague in traffic control on an internal line. "We have one in the air over Bury St. Edmunds," he said.

"Please get it to Thetford and take aboard one of our officers," said Sir Bernard. "It's a matter of national security, I assure you."

"I'll give the order now," said the ACC for Suffolk.

■ Preston beckoned the Thetford policeman over to his car. "Point out the American airbases around here," he said.

The patrolman put a thick finger on the road map. "Well, they're a bit all over, sir. There's Sculthorpe up here in north Norfolk, Lakenheath and Mildenhall out here to the west, Chicksands in Bedfordshire—though I do believe they don't fly out of there anymore. And then there's Bentwaters, here on the Suffolk coast, near Woodbridge."

■ It was six o'clock. The marchers swirled around the two cars parked in front of the Church of All Saints, a tiny but beautiful building, as old as the village, thatched with Norfolk reed and without electric light, so that evensong was still held by candlelight.

Petrofsky stood by his car, arms crossed, his face bland, watching them amble by. His private thoughts were venomous. Across the fields behind him, a traffic control helicopter clattered north, but he failed to hear it for the chanting of the marchers.

The driver of the other car, who turned out to be a biscuit salesman returning home from a seminar on the sales appeal of Butter Osbornes, walked over to him. He nodded toward the marchers. "Arseholes," he muttered above the chant of "No to Cruise—Yanks out." The Russian smiled and nodded. Getting no verbal reaction, the salesman wandered back to his own car, climbed in, and began to read his stack of promotional literature.

If Valeri Petrofsky had had a more developed sense of humor, he might have smiled at his situation. He was standing in front of the church of a God in whom he did not believe, in a country he was seeking to destroy, giving passage to people he heartily despised. And yet, if his mission was successful, all the marchers' demands would be fulfilled. He sighed as he thought of the speedy way his own country's MVD troops would deal with this march before handing over the ringleaders to the lads in the Fifth Chief Directorate for an extended question-and-answer session down at Lefortovo.

■ Preston stared down at the map on which he had circled the five American airbases. If I were an illegal, living in a foreign country under deep cover and on a mission, he thought, I would want to hide myself in a large town or city.

In Norfolk there were King's Lynn, Norwich, and Yarmouth. In Suffolk, Lowestoft, Bury St. Edmunds, Colchester, and Ipswich.

To get back to King's Lynn, close to USAF Sculthorpe, the man he was chasing would have driven back past him on Gallows Hill. No one had. That left four bases, three away to the west and one in the south.

He considered the line of the ride that had brought his quarry from Chesterfield to Thetford. Due southeast, all the way. It would be logical to site the point for switching from motorcycle to car somewhere along the line of travel. From Lakenheath and Mildenhall to the transmitter house at Chesterfield, it would have been more logical to rent a garage in Ely or Peterborough, en route to the Midlands.

He took the line southeast from the Midlands to Thetford and extended it farther southeast. It pointed directly at Ipswich. Twelve miles from Ipswich, in a dense forest and close to the shore, was Bentwaters. He recalled from somewhere that they flew F-5s out of there, modern strike bombers with tactical nukes, designed to halt an onslaught by twenty-nine thousand massed tanks.

Behind him the policeman's radio set crackled into life. The man walked over and answered the call. "There's a helicopter coming up from the south," he reported.

"It's for me," Preston said.

"Oh . . . ah . . . where do you want it to land?"

"Is there a flat area nearby?" asked Preston.

"Place we call the Meadows," said the patrolman. "Down Castle Street by the roundabout. Should be dry enough."

"Tell him to go down there," said Preston. "I'll meet him." He called to his team, some of whom were dozing in the cars. "Everybody in. We're going down to the Meadows."

As they piled into the two cars Preston took his map over to the patrolman. "Tell me. If you were here in Thetford and driving to Ipswich, which way would you go?"

Without hesitation the police motorcyclist pointed to a spot on the map. "I'd take the A1088 straight down to Ixworth, over the junction, and on down to cut into the A45 main road to Ipswich, here at Elmswell village."

Preston nodded. "So would I. Let's hope Chummy thinks the same. I want you to stay here and try to trace any other garage tenant who might have seen the missing man's car. I need that license-plate number."

The light Bell helicopter was waiting in the Meadows, by the roundabout. Preston climbed out of the car, taking a portable radio with him.

"Stay here," he told Harry Burkinshaw. "It's a long shot. He's probably miles away—he's got at least a fifty-minute start. I'll go as far as Ipswich and see if I can spot anything. If not, it's up to that license-plate number. Someone may have seen it. If the Thetford police trace anyone who did, I'll be up there."

He ducked under the whirling rotors and climbed into the narrow cabin, showed his ID card to the pilot, and nodded to the traffic controller, who had squeezed into the back. "That was fast," he shouted to the pilot.

"I was airborne already," the pilot shouted back.

The helicopter lifted off and climbed away from Thetford.

"Where do you want to go?" the pilot asked.

"Down the A1088."

"Want to see the demo, eh?"

"What demo?"

The pilot looked at him as if he had just arrived from Mars. The chopper, nose down, whirled southeast with the line of the A1088 to starboard so that Preston could see the line of marchers.

"The RAF Honington demo," the pilot said. "It's been in all the papers and on TV."

Preston, of course, had seen the news coverage of the projected demonstration against the base. He had spent two weeks watching television in Chesterfield. He had just not realized that the base lay down the A1088 between Thetford and Ixworth. In thirty seconds he could see the real thing.

Away to his right the morning sun glinted on the runways of the airbase. A giant American Galaxy transport was taxiing round the perimeter after landing. Outside the base's several gates were the black lines of Suffolk policemen, hundreds of them, backs to the wire, facing the demonstrators.

From the swelling crowd in front of the police cordon, a dark line of marchers, banners flapping and waving above their heads, ran back down the access lane to the A1088, debouched onto that road, and ran southeast toward Ixworth junction.

Straight below him he could look down at Little Fakenham village, with Honington village swimming into view. He could make out the barns of Honington Hall and the red brick of Malting Row across the road. Here the marchers were at their thickest as they swirled around the entrance to the narrow lane leading to the base. His heart gave a thump.

Up the road from the center of Honington village there was a line of cars backed up for half a mile—all drivers who had not realized that the road would be blocked for part of the early morning, or who had hoped to get through in time. There were more than a hundred vehicles.

Farther down, right in the heart of the marching column, he could see the glint of two or three car roofs; evidently they belonged to drivers who had been allowed through just before the road was closed but who had not made Ixworth junction in time to avoid being trapped. There were some in Ixworth Thorpe village and two parked near a small church farther on.

"I wonder," he whispered.

■ Valeri Petrofsky saw the policeman who had originally stopped him strolling in his direction. The marching column had thinned a bit; it was the tail end that was passing now.

"Sorry it's taken so long, sir. Seems there were more of them than foreseen."

Petrofsky shrugged amiably. "Can't be helped, Officer. I was a fool to try it. Thought I'd get through in time."

"Ah, there's quite a few motorists been caught by it all. Won't be long now. About ten minutes for the marchers, then there's a few big broadcast vans bringing up the tail. Soon as they're past, we'll open the road again."

Across the fields in front of them a police helicopter went past in a wide circle. In its open doorway Petrofsky could see the traffic controller talking into his handset.

■ "Harry, can you hear me? Come in, Harry, it's John." Preston was sitting in the doorway of the chopper over Ixworth Thorpe, trying to raise Burkinshaw.

The watcher's voice came back, scratchy and tinny, from Thetford. "Harry here. Read you, John."

"Harry, there's an anti-Cruise demonstration going on down here. There's a chance, just a chance, that Chummy got caught up in it. Hold on." He turned to the pilot. "How long's that been going on?"

" 'Bout an hour."

"When did they close the road at Ixworth down there?"

From the rear, the traffic officer leaned forward. "Five-twenty," he said.

Preston glanced at his watch. Six-twenty-five. "Harry, get the hell down the A134 to Bury St. Edmunds, pick up the A45, and meet me at the junction of the 1088 and the 45 at Elmswell. Use the cop up at the garages as an outrider. And Harry, tell Joe to drive like never in his life." He tapped the pilot on the shoulder. "Take me to Elmswell and set me down in a field near the road junction."

By air it took only five minutes. As they passed over Ixworth junction, across the A143 Preston could see the long, snaking column of buses parked on the verge, the ones that had brought the bulk of the marchers to this picturesque and sylvan part of the countryside. Two minutes later he could make out the broad A45 running from Bury St. Edmunds to Ipswich.

The pilot banked into a turn, looking for a landing spot. There were meadows near the point where the narrow, lanelike A1088 debouched into the sweep of the A45.

"They could be water meadows," shouted the pilot. "I'll hover. You can jump from a couple of feet."

Preston nodded. He turned to the traffic controller, who was in uniform. "Grab your cap. You're coming with me."

"That's not my job," protested the sergeant, "I'm traffic control."

"That's what I want you for. Come on, let's go."

He jumped the two feet from the step of the Bell into thick, tall grass. The police sergeant, holding his flat cap against the draft of the rotors, followed him. The pilot lifted away and turned toward Ipswich and his base.

With Preston in the lead, the pair plodded across the meadow, climbed the fence, and dropped onto the A1088. A hundred yards away it joined the A45. Across the junction they could see the unending stream of traffic heading toward Ipswich.

"Now what?" asked the police sergeant.

"Now you stand here and stop cars coming south down this road. Ask the drivers if they have been on the road from as far north as Honington. If they joined this road south of Ixworth junction, or at it, let 'em go. Tell me when you get the first one to have come through the demonstration."

Then Preston walked down to the A45 and looked to the right, toward Bury St. Edmunds. "Come on, Harry. Come on."

The cars coming south stopped for the police uniform in their path, but all averred that they had joined the road south of the antinuclear demonstration. Twenty minutes later, Preston saw the Thetford motorcycle patrolman, siren wailing to clear a path, racing toward him, followed by the two watcher cars. They all screeched to a halt at the entrance to the A1088. The policeman raised his visor.

"I hope you know what you're doing, sir. I don't reckon that journey's ever been done faster. There's going to be questions."

Preston thanked him and ordered both his cars a few yards up the narrow secondary road. He pointed to a grassy bank. "Joe, ram it."

"Do what?"

"Ram it. Not hard enough to wreck the car. Just make it look good."

The two policemen stared in amazement as Joe forced his car into the bank by the road. The car's rear end stuck out, blocking half the freeway.

Preston directed the other car to move fifteen yards farther up. "Okay, out," he ordered the driver. "Come on, lads, all together, now. Heave it onto its side."

It took seven shoves before the MI5 car rolled over. Taking a rock from the hedgerow, Preston smashed a side window on Joe's car, scooped up handfuls of the crystalline fragments, and scattered them across the road.

"Ginger, lie on the road, here, near Joe's car. Barney, get a blanket from the trunk and put it over him. Right over. Face and all. Okay, the rest of you, over the hedge, and stay out of sight."

Preston beckoned the two policeman to him. "Sergeant, there's been a nasty pileup. I want you to stand by the body and direct the traffic past it. Officer, park your bike, walk up the road, and slow down oncoming traffic as it approaches."

The two policemen had orders from Ipswich and Norwich, respectively. Cooperate with the men from London. Even if they are maniacs.

Preston sat at the base of the grassy bank, a handkerchief pressed to his face as if to stanch blood from a broken nose.

There is nothing like a body by the roadside to slow down drivers, or cause them to stare through the side window as they crawl past. Preston had made sure Ginger's "body" was on the driver's side for cars coming south down the A1088.

Major Valeri Petrofsky was in the seventeenth car. Like the others before it, the modest family hatchback slowed to the patrolman's flapping hand, then crawled past the crash scene. On the grassy bank, eyes half-closed, the face in the photo in his pocket imprinted on his mind, Preston looked across at the Russian twelve feet away as his sedan swerved slowly past the two cars that almost blocked the road.

From the corner of his eye Preston watched the little hatchback turn left onto the A45, pause for a break in the traffic, and pull into the Ipswich-bound stream. Then he was up and running.

The two drivers and two watchers came back over the hedge at his call. An amazed motorist who was just slowing down saw the "body" leap off the ground and help the others to pull the overturned car back onto its four wheels, where it landed with a crunch.

Joe climbed behind the wheel of his own car and backed it out of the bank. Barney wiped mud and grass off its headlights before climbing in. Harry Burkinshaw took not one but three strong mints and popped the lot.

Preston approached the motorcycle patrolman. "You'd better get back to Thetford, and many, many thanks for all your help." To the sergeant on foot he said, "I'm afraid I'll have to leave you here. Your uniform's too noticeable for you to come with us. But many thanks for your help." Then the two MI5 cars swept away toward the A45 and turned left toward Ipswich.

The bewildered motorist who had seen it all asked the abandoned sergeant, "Are they making a film for the telly?"

"I shouldn't be at all bloody surprised," said the sergeant. "By the way, sir, can you give me a lift into Ipswich?"

■ The commercial and commuter traffic into Ipswich was dense, and became thicker as they approached the town. It provided good cover for the two watcher cars, which constantly shifted position so they could alternately keep the hatchback in view.

They came into town past Whitton, but short of the town center the small car up ahead took a right into Chevallier Street and round the ring to the Handford Bridge, where it crossed the River Orwell. South of the river the quarry followed the Ranelagh Road and then took another right.

"He's heading out of town again," said Joe, holding station five cars behind the suspect. They were entering Belstead Road, which leaves Ipswich heading south.

Quite suddenly the hatchback pulled to the left and entered a small housing development.

"Steady," Preston warned Joe, "he mustn't see us now."

He told the second car to stay at the junction of the access road and Belstead, in case the quarry came around in a circle and back out again. Joe cruised slowly into the complex of seven culs-de-sac that make up The Hayes. They went past the entrance to Cherryhayes Close just in time to see the man they were tailing park in front of a small house halfway up the street. The man was now climbing out of his car. Preston ordered Joe to keep going until out of sight, then stop.

"Harry, give me your hat and see if there's a Conservative rosette in the glove compartment."

There was—left over from the two weeks when the team had used it to enter and leave the Royston house by the front door without arousing suspicion. Preston pinned it to his jacket, stripped off the raincoat he had worn by the roadside where he had first seen Petrofsky face-to-face, donned Harry's porkpie hat, and climbed out.

He walked to Cherryhayes Close and strolled up the walk opposite the house of the Soviet agent. Directly facing No. 12 was No. 9. It had a Social Democratic Party poster in the window. He walked to the front door and knocked.

It was opened by a pretty young woman. Preston could hear a child's voice, then a man's, inside the hourse. It was eight o'clock; the family was at breakfast.

Preston raised his hat. "Good morning, madam."

Seeing his rosette, the woman said, "Oh, I'm so sorry, you're really wasting your time here. We vote Social Democrat."

"I perfectly understand, ma'am. But I have a piece of promotional literature which I would be most grateful if you would show to your husband." He handed her the plastic card that identified him as an officer of MI5.

She did not look at it, but sighed. "Oh, very well. But I'm sure it won't change anything."

She left him standing on the doorstep and withdrew into the house; seconds later, Preston heard a whispered conversation from the kitchen in the back. A man came out and walked down the hall, holding the card. A young business executive in dark trousers, white shirt, striped tie. No jacket; that would come when he left for work. He was holding Preston's card and frowning.

"What on earth's this?" the householder asked.

"What it seems to be, sir. It's the identification card of an officer of MI5."

"It's not a joke?"

"No, it's perfectly genuine."

"I see. Well, what do you want?"

"Would you let me come in and close the door?"

The young man paused for a moment, then nodded. Preston doffed his hat again and stepped over the threshold. He closed the door behind him.

Across the street, Valeri Petrofsky was in his sitting room behind the opaque net curtains. He was tired, and his muscles ached from his long ride. He helped himself to a whisky. Glancing through the

curtains, he could see one of the seemingly endless political canvass-
ers talking to the people at No. 9. He had had three himself over the
past ten days, and another wad of party literature had been on his
doormat when he arrived home. He watched the householder allow
the man into his hallway. Another convert, he thought. Fat lot of
good it will do them.

Preston sighed with relief. The young man watched him doubtfully while his wife stared from the kitchen door. The face of a small
girl of about three appeared around the doorframe at her mother's
knee.

"Are you really from MI5?" asked the man.

"Yes. We don't have two heads and green ears, you know."

For the first time the younger man smiled. "No. Of course not.
It's just a surprise. But what do you want with us?"

"Nothing, of course." Preston grinned. "I don't even know who
you are. My colleagues and I have tailed a man we believe to be a
foreign agent, and he has gone into the house across the way. I would
like to borrow your phone, and perhaps you would allow a couple of
men to observe the suspect from your upstairs bedroom window."

"Foreign agent?" asked the man. "Jim Ross? He's not a foreigner."

"We think he may be. Could I use the phone?"

"Well, yes. I suppose so." He turned toward his family. "Come
on, all back in the kitchen."

Preston rang Charles Street and was put through to Sir Bernard
Hemmings, who was still at Cork. Burkinshaw had already used the
police radio net to inform Cork in guarded language that the "client"
was at his home in Ipswich and that the "taxis" were in the neighborhood and "on call."

"Preston?" said the Director-General when he came on the line.
"John? Where are you, exactly?"

"A small residential cul-de-sac in Ipswich, called Cherryhayes
Close," said Preston. "We've run Chummy to earth. I'm certain this
time it's his base."

"Do you think it's time we moved in?"

"Yes, sir, I do. I fear he may be armed. I think you know what I
mean. I don't think it's one for Special Branch or the local force."

He told his DG what he wanted, then replaced the receiver and put in a call to Sir Nigel at Sentinel House.

"Yes, John, I agree," said C when he had been given the same information. "If he's got with him what we think, it had better be as you ask. The SAS."

CHAPTER

To call in the Special Air Service, Britain's elite and multirole regiment of experts at deep penetration, observation, and (occasionally) urban assault, is not so easy as the more adventurous television dramas might suggest.

The SAS never operates on its own initiative. Under the Constitution it can, like any part of the armed forces, operate inside the United Kingdom only in support of the civil authority—that is, the police. Thus, ostensibly the local police remain in overall command of the operation. In reality, once the SAS men have been given the "go" order, the local police are well advised to step smartly back.

Under the law, it is the chief constable of a county in which an emergency has arisen—an emergency that the local police are deemed not to be able to handle unassisted—who must make a formal request to the Home Office for the SAS to be brought in. It may be that the chief constable is "advised" to make the request, and it is a bold man indeed who refuses to do so if the "advice" comes from high enough.

When the chief constable has made his formal request to the Permanent Under Secretary at the Home Office, the latter passes the request to his opposite number in Defense, who in turn apprises the director of military operations of the request, and the DMO alerts the SAS at its Hereford base camp.

That the procedure can work within minutes is due in part to the fact that it has been rehearsed over and over again and honed to a fine art, and partly to the fact that the British establishment, when required to move fast, contains enough interpersonal relationships to permit a great deal of procedure to be kept at verbal level, with the inevitable paperwork left to catch up later. British bureaucracy may appear slow and cumbersome to the British, but it is greased lightning compared to its European and American counterparts. In any case, most British chief constables have been to Hereford to meet the unit known simply as "the Regiment" and to be shown exactly what kinds of assistance can be put at their disposal if requested. Few have emerged unimpressed.

That morning the chief constable of Suffolk was told from London of the crisis that had been visited on him in the form of a suspected foreign agent, believed to be armed and perhaps with a bomb, who was holed up in Cherryhayes Close, Ipswich. The chief constable contacted Sir Hubert Villiers in Whitehall, where his call was expected. Sir Hubert briefed his minister and his colleague the Cabinet Secretary, who informed the Prime Minister. Downing Street's assent having been obtained, Sir Hubert passed the by now politically cleared request to Sir Peregrine Jones at Defense, who knew it all, anyway, because he had had a chat with Sir Martin Flannery. Within sixty minutes of the first contact between the head of the Suffolk constabulary and the Home Office, the director of military operations was talking on a scrambled line to the commanding officer of the SAS at Hereford.

The fighting arm of the SAS is based on units of four. Four men make up a patrol, four patrols a troop, and four troops a squadron. The four "saber" squadrons are A, B, D, and G. They rotate through the various SAS commitments: Northern Ireland, the Middle East, jungle training, and special projects, apart from the continuing NATO tasks and the maintenance of one squadron on standby at Hereford.

The commitments tend to last from six to nine months, and that month it was B Squadron that was based at Hereford. As usual there was one troop on half-hour standby and another at two-hour readiness. The four troops in each squadron are always the air troop (free-fallers), the boat troop (marines trained in canoe and underwater expertise), the mountain troop (climbers), and the mobile troop (in armed Land-Rovers).

When Brigadier Jeremy Cripps finished his call from London, it was to Seven Troop, the free-fall parachute men of B Squadron, that the task fell of going to Ipswich.

■ "What is your normal routine at this hour?" asked Preston of the Cherryhayes Close householder, whose name was Adrian. The young executive had just finished a phone conversation with the ACC for Suffolk, who was in his office at Ipswich police headquarters. If there had been any lingering doubt in Adrian's mind as to the authenticity of his unexpected guest of half an hour earlier, it had been dispelled. Preston had suggested that Adrian make the call himself, and the young man was now rightly convinced that the Suffolk police were backing the MI5 officer in his sitting room. He had also been told that the man across the street might be armed and dangerous, and that an arrest would have to be made later in the day.

"Well, I drive to work at about quarter to nine—that's in ten minutes. At about ten, Lucinda takes Samantha to playschool. She usually does her shopping, picks up Samantha at midday, and returns home. On foot. I get back from work around six-thirty—by car, of course."

"I'd like you to take the day off work," said Preston. "Ring your office now and say you are not well. But leave the house at the usual time. You will be met at the top of the road, where Belstead Road joins the access to The Hayes, by a police car."

"What about my wife and child?"

"I'd like Mrs. Adrian to wait here until the usual hour, then leave with Samantha and shopping basket, walk up there, and join you. Is there any place you can go for the day?"

"There's my mother at Felixstowe," said Lucinda Adrian nervously.

"Could you spend the day with her? Perhaps even tonight?"

"What about our house?"

"I assure you, Mr. Adrian, nothing will happen to it," said Preston optimistically. He might have added it would either be un-harmed or, if things went wrong, vaporized. "I must ask you to let me and my colleagues use it as an observation post to watch the man across the way. We will come and go via the back. We will do ab-solutely no damage."

"What do you think, darling?" Adrian asked his wife.

She nodded. "I just want to get Samantha out of here," she said.

"In one hour, I promise you," said Preston. "We know that Mr. Ross has been up all night because we have been tailing him. He's probably asleep, and in any case no police move against the house will take place before the afternoon, maybe the early evening."

"All right," said Adrian, "we'll do it."

He made his call to the office to excuse himself for the day, and drove off at eight-forty-five. From his upstairs bedroom window, Valeri Petrofsky saw him go. The Russian was preparing to catch a few hours' sleep. There was nothing unusual going on in the street. Adrian always left for work at this hour.

Preston noted that there was an empty lot behind the Adrians' house. He radioed Harry Burkinshaw and Barney, who came in through the back, nodded to a startled Lucinda Adrian, and went upstairs to adopt again their profession in life—watching. Ginger had found a patch of high ground a quarter of a mile away from which he could see both the estuary of the Orwell, with the docks on its banks, and the small housing development spread out below. With binoculars he could monitor the rear of 12 Cherryhayes Close.

"It backs onto the rear garden of another house, on Bracken-hayes," Ginger told Preston on his radio. "No sign of movement in house or garden. All windows closed—that's odd in this weather."

"Keep watching," said Preston. "I'll be here. If I have to go, Harry will take over."

An hour later, Lucinda and Samantha walked calmly out of the house and away.

■ In the town itself another operation was moving up through the gears. The chief constable, who had risen through the uniformed branch, had handed the details of the pending operation to his as-sistant, Chief Superintendent Peter Low.

Low had dispatched two detectives to the town hall, where they had elicited the information that the target house was owned by a certain Mr. Johnson but that bills were to be sent to Oxborrows, the real-estate agents. A call to Oxborrows revealed that Mr. Johnson was away in Saudi Arabia and the house had been rented to a Mr. James Duncan Ross. A second picture of Ross, alias Timothy Donnelly of the streets of Damascus, was telexed to Ipswich and shown to the agent at Oxborrows, who identified the tenant.

The town hall housing department also came up with the names of the architects who had designed the development called The Hayes, and from this partnership were obtained detailed floor plans of the property at 12 Cherryhayes Close. The architects were even more helpful; other houses, identical in design to the last detail, had been built elsewhere in Ipswich, and one was found to be standing empty. It would be useful for the SAS assault team; they would know the exact geography of the house when they went in.

The other part of Peter Low's duties was to find a "holding area" for the SAS men to use when they arrived. A holding area has to be private, enclosed, and quickly available, with access for vehicles and telephone communication. An empty warehouse down on Eagle Wharf was traced, and the owner agreed to let the police borrow it for a "training exercise."

The warehouse had big sliding doors that could open to admit the vehicle convoy and close to keep out prying eyes, a floor area ample enough to accommodate a mock-up of the house in The Hayes, and a small glass-sided office to use as an operations room.

Just before noon an Army Scout helicopter swished into the far side of Ipswich municipal airport and disgorged three men. One was the commanding officer of the SAS Regiment, Brigadier Cripps; one was the operations officer, a staff major with the Regiment; and the third was the team commander, Captain Julian Lyndhurst. They were all in plainclothes, carried suitcases with their uniforms inside, and were met by an unmarked police car that took them straight to the holding area, where the police were establishing their operational center.

Chief Superintendent Low briefed the three officers to the best of his ability, which was to the limit of what he had been told by London. He had spoken to Preston on the telephone but had not yet met him.

"There's a John Preston, I understand," said Brigadier Cripps, "who is the field controller from MI5. Is he about?"

"I believe he's still up at the observation post," said Low, "the house he has taken over opposite the target dwelling. I can call him and ask him to leave by the back and come here to join us."

"I wonder, sir," said Captain Lyndhurst to his CO, "whether I might not go up there right away. Give me a chance to have a first look at the 'stronghold,' and then I could come back with this Preston chap."

"All right, since a car has to go up, anyway," said the CO.

Fifteen minutes later, the police stationed on the hillside across the estuary from Eagle Wharf pointed out the rear door of No. 9 to Lyndhurst. Still in civilian clothes, the twenty-nine-year-old captain walked across the rough ground, hopped over the garden fence, and went in through the back door. He met Barney in the kitchen, where the watcher was brewing a cup of tea on Mrs. Adrian's stove.

"Lyndhurst," said the officer, "from the Regiment. Is Mr. Preston here?"

"John," Barney called up the stairs in a hoarse whisper, as the house was supposed to be empty, "brown job here to see you."

Lyndhurst mounted to the upstairs bedroom, where he found John Preston and introduced himself. Harry Burkinshaw muttered something about a cup of tea and left. The captain stared across the road at No. 12.

"There still seem to be some gaps in our information," drawled Lyndhurst. "Who exactly do you think is in there?"

"I believe it's a Soviet agent," said Preston, "an illegal, living here under the cover of James Duncan Ross. Mid-thirties, medium height and build, probably very fit, a top pro."

He handed Lyndhurst the photograph taken on the Damascus street. The captain studied it with interest.

"Anyone else in there?"

"Possibly. We don't know. Ross himself, certainly. He might have a helper. We can't talk to the neighbors. In this kind of area we could never stop them gawping. Before they left, the people who live here said they were sure he was living alone. But we can't prove that."

"And according to our briefing, you think he's armed, maybe dangerous. But too much for the local lads, even with handguns, mmmm?"

"Yes, we believe he has a bomb in there with him. He would have to be stopped before he could get to it."

"Bomb, eh?" said Lyndhurst with apparent lack of interest. (He had done two tours in Northern Ireland.) "Big enough to make a mess of the house, or the entire street?"

"A bit bigger than that," said Preston. "If we're right, it's a small nuke."

The tall officer turned his entire gaze from the house across the street, and his pale blue eyes held Preston's. "Bloody hell," he said. "I'm impressed."

"Well, that's a plus," said Preston. "By the way, I want him, and I want him alive."

"Let's go back to the docks and talk to the CO," said Lyndhurst.

■ While Preston and Lyndhurst were getting acquainted at Cherryhayes Close, two more helicopters, a Puma and a Chinook, had arrived at the airport from Hereford. The first bore the assault team, the second their numerous and arcane pieces of equipment.

The team was under the temporary leadership of the deputy team commander, a veteran staff sergeant named Steve Bilbow. He was short, dark, and wiry, tough as old boot leather, with bright, black-button eyes and a ready grin. Like all the senior NCOs in the Regiment, he had been with them a long time—in his case, fifteen years.

The SAS is unusual in this sense also: the officers are almost all on temporary assignment from their "parent" regiments and usually stay two to three years before returning to their own units. Only the Other Ranks stay with the SAS—and not all of them, just the best. Even the commanding officer, though he will probably have served with the Regiment before in his career, serves a short term as CO. Very few officers are long-stay men, and they are all in logistics/supply/technical posts in SAS Group Headquarters.

Steve Bilbow had entered as a trooper from the Parachute Regiment, done his tour, been selected on merit for extension of assignment, and had risen to staff sergeant. He had done two fighting tours in Dhofar, sweated through the jungles of Belize, frozen through the countless nights in ambush in south Armagh, and relaxed in the Cameron Highlands of Malaya. He had helped train the West German GSG-9 teams and worked with Charlie Beckwith's Delta group in America.

In his time he had known the boredom of the endlessly repeated training that brought the men of the SAS to the ultimate peak of fitness and preparation, and the excitement of the high-adrenaline operations: racing under rebel fire for the shelter of a sangar in the hills of Oman, running a covert snatch-squad against Republican gunmen in east Belfast, and doing five hundred parachute jumps, most of them HALO jobs—high altitude, low opening. To his chagrin he had been one of the standby team when colleagues stormed the Iranian Embassy in London in 1981, and he had not been called on.

The rest of the team comprised one photographer, three intelligence collators, eight snipers, and nine assaulters. Steve hoped and prayed he would lead the assault team. Several unmarked police vans had met them at the airport and brought them to the holding area. When Preston and Lyndhurst arrived back at the warehouse, the team had assembled and were spreading their gear on the floor before the bemused gaze of several Ipswich policemen.

"Hello, Steve," said Captain Lyndhurst, "everything okay?"

"Hello, boss. Yes, fine. Just getting sorted."

"I've seen the stronghold. It's a small private house. One occupant known, maybe two. And a bomb. It'll be a small assault, no room for more. I'd like you to be first in."

"Try and stop me, boss," Bilbow answered, grinning.

The accent in the SAS is on self-discipline rather than the externally applied kind. Any man who cannot produce the self-discipline needed to go through what the SAS men must will not be there for long, anyway. Those who can do not need rigid formality in personal relationships, such as are proper in a line regiment.

Thus, officers habitually address those they command, apart from each other, by first names. Other Ranks tend to address their commissioned officers as "boss," although the CO gets a "sir." Among themselves, SAS troopers refer to an officer as "a Rupert."

Staff Sergeant Bilbow caught sight of Preston, and his face lit up in a delighted grin. "Major Preston . . . Good heavens, it's been a long time."

Preston stuck out a hand and smiled back. The last time he had seen Steve Bilbow was when, in the aftermath of the shoot-out in the Bogside, he had taken refuge in a safe house where four SAS men under Bilbow's command had been running a covert snatch-squad. Apart from that, they were both ex-Paras, which always forms a bond.

"I'm with Five now," said Preston, "field controller for this operation, at least from Five's end."

"What have you got for us?" asked Steve.

"Russian. KGB agent. Top pro. Probably done the *spetsnaz* course, so he'll be good, fast, and probably armed."

"Lovely. *Spetsnaz*, eh? We'll see how good they really are."

All three present knew of the *spetsnaz* troops, the crack Russian elite saboteurs who comprised the Soviet equivalent of the SAS.

"Sorry to break up the party, but let's get the briefing under way," said Lyndhurst.

He and Preston mounted the stairs to the upper office, where they met Brigadier Cripps, the major in charge of operations, Chief Superintendent Low, and the SAS intelligence collators. Preston spent an hour giving as thorough a briefing as he could, and the atmosphere grew extremely grave.

"Have you any proof there's a nuclear device in there?" asked Low at length.

"No, sir. We intercepted a component in Glasgow destined for delivery to someone working under cover in this country. The backroom boys say it could have no other use in this world. We know the man in that house is a Soviet illegal—he was made on the streets of Damascus by the Mossad. His associations with the secret transmitter in Chesterfield confirms what he is. So I am left with deductions.

"If the component taken in Glasgow was not for the construction of a small nuclear device inside Britain, then what the hell was it for? On that, I come up with no other feasible explanation. As to Ross, unless there are two major covert operations being mounted in Britain by the KGB, that component was destined for him. Q.E.D."

"Yes," said Brigadier Cripps, "I think we have to go with it. We have to assume it's there. If it's not, we'll have to talk to friend Ross rather earnestly."

Chief Superintendent Low was having a private nightmare. He had to accept the fact that there was no other way but storming the house. What he was trying to envisage was the condition of Ipswich if the device went off. "Couldn't we evacuate?" he asked, with little hope.

"He'd notice," said Preston flatly. "I think if he knows he's ruined, he'll take us all with him."

The soldiers nodded. They knew that, deep inside Soviet Russia, they would have done the same.

The lunch hour was gone and no one had noticed. Food would have been superfluous. The afternoon was spent in reconnaissance and preparation.

Steve Bilbow went back to the airport with the photographer and a policeman. The three took the Scout in one single run down the estuary of the Orwell, well away from The Hayes but on a course from which they could keep it in view. The policeman pointed out the house; the photographer ran off fifty stills while Steve took a long pan-shot on video for screening in the holding area.

The entire assault team, still in civilian clothes, went with the police to see the empty house that had been built by the same architects to the same plans as the one on Cherryhayes Close. By the time they got back to the holding area, they could see the stronghold on video and in close-up still pictures.

They spent the rest of the afternoon inside the holding area, practicing with the mock-up that the policemen had helped build, under SAS supervision, on the warehouse floor. It was a hurried construction, with canvas "walls" dividing the "rooms," but its dimensions were perfect, and it showed up one overriding factor: space inside the house was very limited. It had a narrow front door, a narrow hall, a cramped stairway, and small rooms.

To the eternal grief of the four who were left out, Captain Lyndhurst decided to use only six assaulters. There would also be three snipers—two in the Adrians' upstairs front bedroom and one on the hill overlooking the back garden.

The rear of 12 Cherryhayes Close would be covered by two of Lyndhurst's six assaulters. They would be in full combat gear but their uniforms would be covered by civilian raincoats. They would be driven in an unmarked police car to Brackenhayes Close. Here they would disembark and, without asking permission of the house-holders, would walk through the front garden of the house that backed onto the stronghold, down the side path between house and garage, and into the back garden. Here they would strip off the rain-coats, hop over the garden fence, and take up position in the back garden of the stronghold.

"There may be a trip wire in the garden," warned Lyndhurst. "But probably close to the rear of the house itself. Stand well back. On the signal, I want one stun grenade straight through the window of the rear bedroom and another through the kitchen window. Then unclip the HKs and hold position. Do not fire into the house; Steve and the lads will be coming in the front."

The rear-access men nodded. Captain Lyndhurst knew that he would not be in the assault. Formerly a lieutenant in the King's Dra-goon Guards, he was on his first tour with the SAS and held captain's rank because the SAS have no officers under that grade. He would revert to lieutenant on return to his parent regiment in a year, though he hoped to come back to the SAS later as a squadron com-mander.

He also knew the tradition of the SAS, which is at variance with the convention for the rest of the Army: officers participate in com-bat in desert or jungle but never in an urban environment. Only NCOs and troopers carry out such assaults.

The main attack, Lyndhurst had agreed with his CO and the op-erations officer, would be via the front. A van would draw up quietly and four assaulters would step out. Two would take the front door, one carrying the Wingmaster, the other wielding a seven-pound sledgehammer and/or bolt cutters if necessary.

The instant the door came down, the assault front rank—Steve Bilbow and a corporal—would go in. The door squad would drop their Wingmaster and hammer, rip their HKs off their chests, and enter the hallway as backup for the first pair.

On entering the hallway, Steve would step straight past the stairs to the door to the sitting room on his left. The corporal would race up the stairs to take the front bedroom. Of the backup men, one would follow the corporal up the stairs in case Chummy was in the bathroom, and the other would follow Steve into the sitting room.

The signal for the two men in the back garden to hurl their stun grenades into the two rear rooms, kitchen and back bedroom, would be the crash of the Wingmaster at the front. By the time entry had been made, therefore, anyone in the kitchen or back bedroom should be reeling around, wondering what had hit him.

Preston, who had volunteered to return to the observation post, was allowed to listen to the details of the assault.

He already knew that the SAS was the only regiment in the British Army allowed to choose its weaponry from a worldwide menu. For close assault they had selected the German Heckler and Koch short-barreled nine-millimeter rapid-fire submachine gun—light, easy to handle, and very reliable, with an up-and-over folding stock.

They habitually wore the HK—loaded and cocked—slantwise across the chest; it was held in place by two spring-clips. This left their arms free for opening doors, entering through windows, or throwing stun grenades. When the weapon was needed, a single jerk brought the HK off the chest and into operation in less than half a second.

Practice had shown that to get through doors, it was faster to blast off both hinges rather than take the lock. For this purpose they favored the Remington Wingmaster pump-action repeater shotgun, but with solid heads rather than buckshot in the cartridges.

Apart from these playthings, one of the door squad would need a hammer and bolt cutters in case the door, having lost its hinges, was held on the other side by several bolts and a chain. They also carried stun grenades, designed to blind temporarily by their flash and deafen by their crack, but not to kill. Lastly, each man would have a thirteen-shot nine-millimeter Browning automatic on his hip.

In the assault, Lyndhurst stressed, timing was of the essence. For the hour of the attack he had chosen 9:45 p.m., when dusk would be deep in the Close but it would not yet be darkest night.

Lyndhurst himself would be in the Adrians' house across the way, watching the target house and in radio contact with the van bearing his assaulters. Thus he could monitor the approach of the team. If there were a pedestrian moving down the Close at 9:44, Lyndhurst could tell the van driver to hold until the passerby had cleared the door of the stronghold to be assaulted. The police car bringing the two rear-garden men to position would be on the same wavelength, and would drop those two men ninety seconds before the front door came down.

Lyndhurst planned one last refinement. As the assault van cruised up the Close, he would telephone Ross from the Adrians' house across the road. He already knew that the phone in each of these houses was kept on a small table in the hallway. The ploy was to distance the Soviet agent from his bomb, wherever it was, and to give the assaulters the chance of a fast shot.

Firing, as usual, would come in two fast bursts of two shots each. Although the HK can empty its thirty-round magazine in a couple of seconds, the SAS are accurate enough even in the confused conditions of a terrorist-hostage situation to limit their firing to two-shot bursts, with one repeat. Anyone stopping those four rounds will speedily feel very unwell. Such economy also keeps the hostages alive.

Immediately after the operation the police would move into the Close in strength to calm down the inevitable crowd that would come pouring out of the adjacent houses. A police cordon would be thrown around the front of the target house, and the assaulters would leave through the rear, cross the gardens, and board their van, which by then would be waiting in Brackenhayes Close. As for the interior of the stronghold, the civil authority would take over there as well. A team of six from Aldermaston was due into Ipswich by teatime that evening.

At six, Preston left the holding area and returned to the observation post—the Adrians' house—which he entered, unobserved, by the rear door.

"Lights have just come on," said Harry Burkinshaw when Preston joined him in the upstairs bedroom. Preston could see that the sitting-room curtains of the house opposite were drawn, but there was a light behind them and a reflected glow showing through the panels of the front door.

"I think I saw movement behind the net curtains in the upstairs bedroom just after you left," said Barney. "But he didn't put the light on—well, he wouldn't, of course. It was just after lunch. Anyway, he hasn't come out."

Preston radioed Ginger on his hillside, but the story was the same. No movement at the back, either.

"It'll start getting dark in a couple of hours," Ginger told him over the radio. "Vision will deteriorate after that."

■ Valeri Petrofsky had slept fitfully and not well. Just before one o'clock he awoke fully, propped himself up, and stared across his bedroom, through the net curtains, at the house across the way. After ten minutes he hauled himself off the bed, went to the bathroom, and showered.

He made lunch at two o'clock and ate it at the kitchen table, occasionally glancing into the back garden, where a fine and invisible fishing line ran from side to side, around a small pulley attached by night to the garden fence, and in through his back door. It was tied around the bottom of a column of empty tin cans in the kitchen. He slackened the tension when he was out of the house and tightened it when he was at home. No one had yet brought the tins clattering down.

The afternoon wore on. Not unnaturally, considering what reposed, armed and primed, in his sitting room, he was tense, all his senses at full alert. He tried to read but could not concentrate. Moscow must have had his message for twelve hours by now. He listened to some radio music, then at six settled down in the sitting room. Although he could see the sun reflected in the windows of the houses opposite, his own house faced east, so it was now in shadow. The twilight would deepen in his sitting room from now on. He closed the curtains, as ever, before putting on the reading lamps; then, for want of anything better to do, switched on the television news. As usual, it was dominated by the election campaign.

■ In the warehouse holding area, the tension was mounting. Final preparations were being made to the assaulters' van, a plain gray Volkswagen with a sliding side door. Two men in plainclothes would be in the front, one driving and the other on the radio to Captain

Lyndhurst. They checked those radios over and over again, as they tested every other piece of equipment.

The van would be led to the entrance to The Hayes by an unmarked police car; the driver of the van had memorized the geography of The Hayes and knew where to find Cherryhayes Close. As they entered The Hayes, they would come under the radio control of Captain Lyndhurst in his observation post. The rear of the van had been lined with polystyrene-foam sheeting to prevent the clink of metal on metal.

The assault team was dressing and "tooling up." Over his underwear, each man pulled on the standard one-piece black jump suit of fire-resistant fabric. At the last moment this would be complemented by a treated black fabric balaclava hood. After that came the body armor, lightweight knitted Kevlar designed to absorb a bullet's impact by spreading it outward and sideway from the point of penetration. Behind the Kevlar the men stuffed ceramic "trauma pads" to complete the job of blunting an onrushing projectile even further.

Over all this went the harness to hold the assault weapon, the HK, and to hold the grenades and handgun. On their feet they wore the traditional ankle-high desert boots with thick rubber soles, whose color can only be described as "dirty."

Captain Lyndhurst had a last word with each man, and the longest with his assault leader, Steve Bilbow. There was, of course, no mention of good luck—anything else, but never "Good luck." Then the commander left for the observation post.

He entered the Adrians' house just after 8:00 p.m. Preston could feel the tension emanating from the man. At 8:30 the phone rang. Barney was in the hall, so he took it. There had been several calls that day. Preston had decided it would be fruitless not to answer— someone might come to the house. Each time, the caller had been told that the Adrians were at her mother's for the day and that the speaker was one of the team of painters redoing the sitting room. No caller had refused to accept this explanation. When Barney lifted the receiver, Captain Lyndhurst was coming out of the kitchen with a cup of tea.

"It's for you," Barney told the captain, and went back upstairs.

From 9:00 onward the tension rose steadily. Lyndhurst spent

much time on the radio to the holding area, from which at 9:15 the gray van and its shepherding police car left for The Hayes. At 9:33 the two vehicles had reached the access on Belstead Road, two hundred yards from the target. They had to pause and wait. At 9:41 Mr. Armitage came out to leave four bottles for the milkman. Infuriatingly, he paused in the gathering gloom to inspect the stone bowl of flowers in the center of his front lawn. Then he greeted a neighbor across the road.

"Go back in, you old fool," whispered Lyndhurst, standing in the sitting room and gazing across the road at the lights behind the curtains of the stronghold. At 9:42 the unmarked police car with the two rear-garden men was in position in Brackenhayes and waiting. Ten seconds later Armitage called good night to his neighbor and went back inside.

At 9:43 the gray van entered Gorsehayes, the development's access road. Standing in the hall by the telephone, Preston could hear the chitchat between the van driver and Lyndhurst. The van was cruising slowly and quietly toward the entrance to Cherryhayes.

There were no pedestrians on the street. Lyndhurst ordered the two rear-garden men to leave their police car and start moving.

"Entering Cherryhayes fifteen seconds," muttered the van's co-driver.

"Slow down, thirty seconds to go," replied Lyndhurst. Twenty seconds later he said, "Enter the Close now."

Around the corner came the van, quite slowly, with dimmers on. "Eight seconds," murmured Lyndhurst into the receiver, then a savage whisper to Preston: "Dial now."

The van cruised up the Close, passed the door of No. 12, and stopped in front of Armitage's bowl of flowers. Its position was deliberate—the assaulters wanted to approach the stronghold slantwise. The oiled side door of the van slid back, and into the gloom, in complete silence, stepped four men in black. There was no running, no pounding of feet, no hoarse cries. In rehearsed order they walked calmly across Armitage's lawn, around Ross's parked hatchback, and up to the front door of 12 Cherryhayes Close. The man with the Wingmaster knew which side the hinges would be on. Before he had finished walking, his gun was at his shoulder. He made out the hinge positions and took careful aim. Beside him another figure waited, with a sledgehammer swung back. Behind them were Steve and the corporal, HKs at the ready. . . .

■ In his sitting room, Major Valeri Petrofsky was unquiet. He could not concentrate on the television; his senses picked up too much—the clatter of a man putting out milk bottles, the meow of a cat, the snarl of a motorcycle engine far away, the hoot of a freighter entering the estuary of the Orwell across the valley.

Nine-thirty had produced another current affairs program with yet more interviews with ministers and hopeful ministers-to-be. In exasperation he flicked over to BBC 2, only to find a documentary about birds. He sighed. It was better than politics.

It had been on scarcely ten minutes when he heard Armitage next door putting out his empty milk bottles. Always the same number and always the same time of night, he thought. Then the old fool was calling to someone across the street. Something on the television caught his eye and he stared in amazement. The interviewer was talking to a lanky man in a flat cap about his passion, which appeared to be pigeons. He was holding one up in front of the camera, a sleek creature with a distinctive cast to its beak and head.

Petrofsky sat bolt-upright, concentrating on the bird with almost all of his attention, listening to the interview with the rest. He was sure the bird was identical to one he had seen somewhere before.

"Is this lovely bird for showing in competition?" the interviewer was asking. She was new, a bit too bright, trying to squeeze more from the interview than it merited.

"Good Lord, no," said the flat-cap man. "this isn't a fancy. It's a Westcott."

In a bright flash of recall, Petrofsky saw again the room in the guest suite at the General Secretary's dacha at Usovo. "Found him in the street last winter," the wizened Englishman had said, and the bird had gazed out of its cage with bright, clever eyes.

"Well, it's not the sort we would see about the town," suggested the television interviewer. She was floundering. At that moment the telephone in Petrofsky's hallway rang. . . .

Normally he would have gone to answer it, in case it was a neighbor. To have pretended to be out would have roused suspicions, with the house lights on. And he would not have taken his handgun to the hall. But he stayed and stared at the screen. The phone rang on, insistently. With the television talk, it drowned the soft pad of rubber-soled feet on the pavement.

"I should hope not," replied the flat-cap man cheerfully. "A Westcott ain't a 'streetie,' neither. It's probably one of the finest strains of racer there is. This little beauty will always speed back to the loft where it was raised. That's why they're more commonly known as homers."

Petrofsky came out of his chair with a snarl of rage. The big precision-made Sako target pistol that he had kept close by him since he had entered Britain came up with him from its place down the side of the seat cushion. He uttered one short word in Russian. No one heard him, but the word was *traitor*.

At that moment there was a roar, then another, so close together that they were almost one. With them came the shattering of glass from his front door, two huge bangs from the rear of the house, and the thud of feet in the hall. Petrofsky spun toward the sitting-room door and fired three times. His Sako Triace, made to take three interchangeable barrels, had the heaviest caliber of the three fitted. It also packed five rounds in its magazine. He used only three—he might need the other two for himself. But the three he fired slammed through the flimsy woodwork of the closed door into the hall beyond. . . .

The citizens of Cherryhayes Close will describe that night for the rest of their lives, but none will ever get it quite right.

The roar of the Wingmaster, as it tore the hinges off the door, catapulted them all out of their chairs. The moment he had fired, the gunman stepped sideways and back to give room to his mate. One swing of the sledgehammer and the lock, bolt, and chain on the other side flew in all directions. Then he, too, stepped sideways and back. Both men dropped their weapons and flicked their HKs forward and out.

Steve and the corporal had already gone through the gap. The corporal took three bounds to get up the stairs, with the sledgehammer man following on his heels. Steve ran past the ringing telephone, reached the sitting-room door, turned to face it, and was lifted off his feet. The three slugs that ripped across the hallway hit him with an audible *whap* and blew him against the stairs. The Wingmaster man simply leaned across the still-closed door and fired two two-round bursts. Then he kicked the door open and went in on the roll, coming to his feet at the crouch, well inside the room.

When the shotgun fired, Captain Lyndhurst opened the front door across the street and watched; Preston was behind him. Through the lighted hallway the captain saw his deputy team commander approach the sitting-room door, only to be thrown aside like a rag doll. Lyndhurst started to walk forward; Preston followed.

As the trooper who had fired the two bursts came to his feet and surveyed the inert figure on the carpet, Captain Lyndhurst appeared in the doorway. He took in the scene at a glance, despite the drifting plume of cordite smoke. "Go and help Steve in the hall," he said crisply. The trooper did not argue. The man on the floor began to move. Lyndhurst drew his Browning from beneath his jacket.

The trooper had been good. Petrofsky had taken one slug in the left knee, one in the lower stomach, and one in the right shoulder. His pistol had been flung across the room. Despite the distortion caused by the door's woodwork, the trooper had connected with three out of four slugs. Petrofsky was in hideous pain, but he was alive. He began to crawl. Twelve feet away he could see the gray steel, the flat box on its side, the two buttons, one yellow and one red. Captain Lyndhurst took careful aim and fired once.

John Preston ran past him so fast he jostled the officer's hip. He went down on his knees beside the body on the floor. The Russian was lying on his side, half the back of his head blown away, his mouth still working as if he were a fish on a slab. Preston bent his head to the dying face. Lyndhurst still had his gun at the aim, but the MI5 man was between him and the Russian. He stepped to one side to get a clearer shot, then lowered the Browning. Preston was rising. There was no need for a second shot.

"We'd better get the wallahs from Aldermaston to have a look at *that*," said Lyndhurst, gesturing at the steel cabinet in the corner.

"I wanted him alive," said Preston.

"Sorry, old boy. Couldn't be done," said the captain.

At that moment both men jumped at the sound of a loud click and a voice speaking to them from the sideboard. They saw that the sound had come from a large radio set, which had switched itself on with a timer device. The voice said:

"Good evening. This is Radio Moscow, the English-language service, and here is the ten o'clock news. In Terry . . . I'm sorry, I'll say that again. In Teheran today, the government stated—"

Captain Lyndhurst stepped over and switched the machine off. The man on the floor stared at the carpet with sightless eyes, immune to the coded message meant for him alone.

CHAPTER

The lunch invitation was for one o'clock on Friday, June 19, at Brooks's Club in St. James's. Preston entered the portals at that hour, but even before he could announce himself to the club porter in the booth to his right, Sir Nigel was striding down the marbled hall to meet him. "My dear John, how kind of you to come."

They adjourned to the bar for a pre-lunch drink, and the conversation was informal. Preston was able to tell the Chief that he had just returned from Hereford, where he had visited Steve Bilbow in the hospital. The staff sergeant had had a lucky escape. Only when the flattened slugs from the Russian's gun were removed from his body armor did one of the doctors notice a sticky smear and have it analyzed. The cyanide compound had failed to enter the bloodstream; the SAS man had been saved by the trauma pads. Otherwise he was heavily bruised, slightly dented, but in good shape.

"Excellent," said Sir Nigel with genuine enthusiasm, "one does so hate to lose a good man."

For the rest, most of the bar was discussing the election result and many of those present had been up half the night waiting for the final results in the close-fought contest to come in from the provinces.

At half past the hour they went in to lunch. Sir Nigel had a corner table where they could talk in privacy. On the way in they passed the Cabinet Secretary, Sir Martin Flannery, coming the other way. Although they all knew each other, Sir Martin saw at once that his colleague was "in conference." The mandarins acknowledged each other's presence with an imperceptible inclination of the head, sufficient for two scholars of Oxford. Backslapping is best left to foreigners.

"I really asked you here, John," said C as he spread his linen napkin over his knees, "to offer you my thanks and my congratulations. A remarkable operation and an excellent result. I suggest the rack of lamb, quite delicious at this time of year."

"As to the congratulations, sir, I fear I can hardly accept them," said Preston quietly.

Sir Nigel studied the menu through his half-moon glasses. "Indeed? Are you being admirably modest or not so admirably discourteous? Ah, beans, carrots, and perhaps a roast potato, my dear."

"Simply realistic, I hope," said Preston when the waitress departed. "Might we discuss the man we knew as Franz Winkler?"

"Whom you so brilliantly tailed to Chesterfield."

"Permit me to be frank, Sir Nigel. Winkler could not have shaken off a headache with a box of aspirins. He was an incompetent and a fool."

"I believe he almost lost you all at Chesterfield railway station."

"A fluke," said Preston. "With a bigger watcher operation, we'd have had men at each stop along the line. The point is, his maneuvers were clumsy; they told us he was a pro, and a bad one at that, yet failed to shake us."

"I see. What else about Winkler? Ah, the lamb, and cooked to perfection."

They waited until they were served and the waitress was gone. Preston picked at his food, troubled. Sir Nigel ate with enjoyment.

"Franz Winkler came into Heathrow with a genuine Austrian passport containing a valid British visa."

"So he did, to be sure."

"And we both know, as did the immigration officer, that Austrian citizens do not need a visa to enter Britain. Any consular officer of ours in Vienna would have told Winkler that. It was the visa that prompted the passport control officer at Heathrow to run the passport number through the computer. And it turned out to be false."

"We all make mistakes," murmured Sir Nigel.

"The KGB does not make that kind of mistake, sir. Their documentation is accurate to the point of brilliance."

"Don't overestimate them, John. All large organizations occasionally make a balls-up. More carrots? No? Then, if I may . . ."

"The point is, sir, there were two flaws in that passport. The reason the number caused red lights to flick on was that three years ago another supposed Austrian bearing a passport with the same number was arrested in California by the FBI and is now serving time in Soledad."

"Really? Good Lord, not very clever of the Soviets after all."

"I called up the FBI man here in London and asked what the charge had been. It appears the other agent was trying to blackmail an executive of the Intel Corporation in Silicon Valley into selling him secrets of technology."

"Very naughty."

"Nuclear technology."

"Which gave you the impression . . . ?"

"That Franz Winkler came into this country lit up like a neon sign. And the sign was a message—a message on two legs."

Sir Nigel's face was still wreathed in good humor, but some of the twinkle had faded from his eyes.

"And what did this remarkable message say, John?"

"I think it said: I cannot give you the executive illegal agent because I do not know where he is. But follow this man; he will lead you to the transmitter. And he did. So I staked out the transmitter and the agent came to it at last."

Sir Nigel replaced his knife and fork on the empty plate and dabbed at his mouth with his napkin. "What, exactly, are you trying to say?"

"I believe, sir, that the operation was blown. It seems to me unavoidable to conclude that someone on the other side deliberately blew it away."

"What an extraordinary suggestion. Let me recommend the

strawberry flan. Had some last week. Different batch, of course. Yes? Two, my dear, if you please. Yes, a little fresh cream."

"May I ask a question?" said Preston when the plates had been cleared.

Sir Nigel smiled. "I'm sure you will, anyway."

"Why did the Russian have to die?"

"As I understand it, he was crawling toward a nuclear bomb with every apparent intention of detonating it."

"I was there," said Preston as the strawberry flan arrived. They waited until the cream had been poured.

"The man was wounded in the knee, stomach, and shoulder. Captain Lyndhurst could have stopped him with a kick. There was no need to blow his head off."

"I'm sure the good captain wished to make absolutely sure," suggested the Master.

"With the Russian alive, Sir Nigel, we would have had the Soviet Union bang to rights, caught in the act. Without him, we have nothing that cannot be convincingly denied. In other words, the whole thing now has to be suppressed forever."

"How true," the spymaster replied, masticating thoughtfully on a mouthful of shortcake pastry and strawberries.

"Captain Lyndhurst happens to be the son of Lord Frinton."

"Indeed. Frinton? Does one know him?"

"Apparently. You were at school together."

"Really? There were so many. Hard to recall."

"And I believe Julian Lyndhurst is your godson."

"My dear John, you *do* check up on things, don't you, now?"

Sir Nigel had finished his dessert. He steepled his hands, placed his chin on his knuckles, and regarded the MI5 investigator steadily. The courtesy remained; the good humor was draining away. "Anything else?"

Preston nodded gravely. "An hour before the assault on the house began, Captain Lyndhurst took a call in the hallway of the house across the road. I checked with my colleague who first took the phone. The caller was ringing from a public box."

"No doubt one of his colleagues."

"No, sir. They were using radios. And no one outside that operation knew we were inside the house. No one, that is, but a very few in London."

"May I ask what you are suggesting?"

"Just one more detail, Sir Nigel. Before he died, that Russian whispered one word. He seemed very determined to get that single word out before he went. I had my ear close to his mouth at the time. What he said was: 'Philby.' "

" 'Philby'? Good heavens. I wonder what he could have meant by that."

"I think I know. I think he thought Harold Philby had betrayed him, and I believe he was right."

"I see. And may I be privileged to know of your deductions?"

The Chief's voice was soft, but his tone was devoid of all his earlier bonhomie.

Preston took a deep breath. "I deduce that Philby the traitor was a party to this operation, possibly from the outset. If he was, he would have been in a no-lose situation. Like others, I have heard it whispered that he wants to return home, here to England, to spend his last days.

"If the plan had worked, he could probably have earned his release from his Soviet masters and his entry from a new Hard Left government in London. Perhaps a year from now. Or he could tell London the general outline of the plan, then betray it."

"And which of these two remarkable choices do you suspect he made?"

"The second one, Sir Nigel."

"To what end, pray?"

"To buy his ticket home. From this end. A trade."

"And you think I would be a party to that trade?"

"I don't know what to think, Sir Nigel. I don't know what *else* to think. There has been talk . . . about his old colleagues, the magic circle, the solidarity of the establishment of which he was once a member . . . that sort of thing."

Preston studied his plate, with its half-eaten strawberries. Sir Nigel gazed at the ceiling for a long time before letting out a profound sigh. "You're a remarkable man, John. Tell me, what are you doing a week from today?"

"Nothing, I believe."

"Then please meet me at the door of Sentinel House at eight in the morning of June twenty-sixth. Bring your passport. And now, if you'll forgive me, I suggest we forgo coffee in the library. . . ."

■ The man at the upper window of the safe house in the Geneva back street stood and watched the departure of his visitor. The head and shoulders of the guest appeared below him; the man walked down the short path to the front gate and stepped into the street, where his car waited. The car's driver stepped out, came around the vehicle, and opened the door for the senior man. Then he walked back to the driver's door.

Before he climbed back into the car, Preston raised his gaze to the figure behind the glass in the upper window. When he was behind the steering wheel he asked, "That's him? That's really him? The man from Moscow?"

"Yes, that's him. And now, the airport, if you please," replied Sir Nigel from the rear seat. They drove away.

"Well, John, I promised you an explanation," said Sir Nigel a few moments later. "Ask your questions."

Preston could see the face of the Chief in his rearview mirror. The older man was gazing out at the passing countryside.

"The operation?"

"You were quite right. It was mounted personally by the General Secretary, with the advice and assistance of Philby. It seems it was called Plan Aurora. It *was* betrayed, but not by Philby."

"Why was it blown away?"

Sir Nigel thought for several minutes. "From quite an early stage I believed that you could be right. Both in your tentative conclusions of last December in what is now called the Preston report and in your deductions after the intercept in Glasgow. Even though Harcourt-Smith declined to believe in either. I was not certain the two were linked, but I was not prepared to discount it. The more I looked at it, the more I became convinced that Plan Aurora was not a true KGB operation. It had not the hallmarks, the painstaking care. It looked like a hasty operation mounted by a man or a group who distrusted the KGB. Yet there was little hope of your finding the agent in time."

"I was floundering in the dark, Sir Nigel. And I knew it. There were no patterns of Soviet couriers showing up on any of our immigration controls. Without Winkler I'd never have got to Ipswich in time."

They drove for several minutes in silence. Preston waited for the Master to resume in his own time.

"So, I sent a message to Moscow," said Sir Nigel eventually.

"From yourself?"

"Good Lord, no. That would never have done. Much too obvious. Through another source, one I hoped would be believed. It was not a very truthful message, I'm afraid. Sometimes one must tell untruths in our business. But it went through a channel I hoped would be believed."

"And it was?"

"Thankfully, yes. When Winkler arrived I was sure the message had been received, understood, and, above all, believed as true."

"Winkler was the reply?" asked Preston.

"Yes. Poor man. He believed he was on a routine mission to check on the Stephanides brothers and their transmitter. By the by, he was found drowned in Prague two weeks ago. Knew too much, I suppose."

"And the Russian in Ipswich?"

"His name, I have just learned, was Petrofsky. A first-class professional, and a patriot."

"But he, too, had to die?"

"John, it was a terrible decision. But unavoidable. The arrival of Winkler was an offer, a proposal for a trade-off. No formal agreement, of course. Just a tacit understanding. The man Petrofsky could not be taken alive and interrogated. I had to go along with the unwritten and unspoken trade with the man in the window back there at the safe house."

"If we had got Petrofsky alive, we'd have had the Soviet Union over a barrel."

"Yes, John, indeed we would. We could have subjected them to a huge international humiliation. And to what end? The USSR could not have taken it lying down. They'd have had to reply somewhere else in the world. What would you have wished? A return to the worst aspects of the Cold War?"

"It seems a pity to lose an opportunity to screw them, sir."

"John, they're big and armed and dangerous. The USSR is going to be there tomorrow and next week and next year. Somehow we have to share this planet with them. Better they be ruled by pragmatic and realistic men than hotheads and zealots."

"And that merits a trade with men like the one in the window, Sir Nigel?"

"Sometimes it has to be done. I'm a professional, so is he. There are journalists and writers who would have it that we in our profession live in a dream world. In reality it's the reverse. It is the politicians who dream their dreams—sometimes dangerous dreams, like the General Secretary's dream of changing the face of Europe as his personal monument.

"A top intelligence officer has to be harder-headed than the toughest businessman. One has to trim to the reality, John. When the dreams take command, one ends up with the Bay of Pigs. The first break in the Cuban missiles impasse was suggested by the KGB rezident in New York. It was Khrushchev, not the professionals, who had gone over the top."

"So what happens next, sir?"

The old spymaster sighed. "We leave it to them. There will be some changes made. They will make them in their own inimitable way. The man back there in the house will set them in train. His career will be advanced, those of others broken."

"And Philby?" asked Preston.

"What about Philby?"

"Is he trying to come home?"

Sir Nigel shrugged impatiently. "For years past," he said. "And, yes, he's in touch from time to time, covertly, with my people in our embassy over there. We breed pigeons. . . ."

"Pigeons?"

"Very old-fashioned, I know. And simple. But still surprisingly efficient. That's how he communicates. But *not* about Plan Aurora. And even if he had, so far as I am concerned—"

"So far as you are concerned—?"

"He can rot in hell," said Sir Nigel softly.

They drove for a while in silence.

"What about you, John? Will you stay with Five now?"

"I don't think so, sir. I've had a good run. The DG retires on September first, but he'll take final leave next month. I don't fancy my chances under his successor."

"Can't take you into Six. You know that. We don't take late entrants. Thought of returning to Civvy Street?"

"Not the best time for a man of forty-six with no known skills to get a job nowadays," said Preston.

"I have some friends," mused the Master. "They're in asset protection. They might be able to use a good man. I could have a word."

"Asset protection?"

"Oil wells, mines, deposits, racehorses . . . Things people want kept safe from theft or destruction. Even themselves. It would pay well. Enable you to take full care of that son of yours."

"It seems I'm not the only one who checks up on things," Preston said, grinning.

The older man was staring out of the window, as if at something far away and long ago. "Had a son myself once," he said quietly. "Just the one. Fine lad. Killed in the Falklands. Know how you feel."

Surprised, Preston glanced at the man in the mirror. It had never occurred to him that this urbane and wily spymaster had once played horse-and-rider with a small boy on a sitting-room carpet.

"I'm sorry. Perhaps I'll take you up on that."

They arrived at the airport, turned in the rented car, and flew back to London, as anonymous as they had come.

■ The man in the window of the safe house watched the Britisher's car move away. His own driver would not be there for an hour. He turned back to the room and sat down at the desk to study again the folder he had been brought and which he still held in his hands. He was pleased; it had been a good meeting, and the documents he held would secure his future.

As a professional, Lieutenant General Yevgeni Karpov was sorry about Plan Aurora. It had been good—subtle, low-profile, and effective. But as a professional he also knew that once an operation was well and truly burned there was nothing for it but to cancel and repudiate the whole thing before it was too late. To delay would have been utterly disastrous.

He recalled clearly the batch of documents that his bagman had brought from Jan Marais in London, the product of his agent Hampstead. Six had been the usual stuff, top-rate intelligence material such as only a man of the eminence of George Berenson could have acquired. The seventh had caused him to sit transfixed.

It was a personal memorandum from Berenson to Marais, for transmission to Pretoria. In it the Defense Ministry official had told how, as Deputy Chief of Defense Procurement, with special responsibility for nuclear devices, he had been present at a very restricted briefing by the Director-General of MI5, Sir Bernard Hemmings.

The counterintelligence chief had told the small group that his agency had uncovered the existence and most of the details of a Soviet conspiracy to import in kit form, assemble, and detonate a small atomic device inside Britain. The sting was in the tail: MI5 was closing fast upon the Russian illegal in command of the operation in Britain, and was confident of catching him with all the necessary evidence on him.

Entirely because of its source, General Karpov had believed the report completely. There was an immediate temptation to let the British go ahead; but second thoughts showed this to be disastrous. If the British succeeded alone and unaided, there would be no obligation to suppress the horrendous scandal. To create that obligation, he needed to send a message, and to a man who would understand what had to be done, someone he could deal with across the great divide.

Then there was the question of his personal self-advancement. . . . It was after a long, lonely walk in the spring-green forests of Peredelkino that he had decided to take the most dangerous gamble of his life. He had decided to pay a discreet visit to the private office of Nubar Gevorkovitch Vartanyan.

He had chosen his man with care. The Politburo member from Armenia was believed to be the man who headed the covert faction inside the Politburo that privately thought it was time for a change at the top.

Vartanyan had listened to him without saying a word, secure that he was far too highly placed for his office to be bugged. He just stared at the KGB general with his black lizard's eyes as he listened. When Karpov had finished, he had asked, "You are certain your information is correct, Comrade General?"

"I have the full narrative from Professor Krilov on tape," said Karpov. "The machine was in my briefcase at the time."

"And the information from London?"

"Its source is impeccable. I have run the man personally for nearly three years."

The Armenian power broker stared at him for a long time, as if reflecting on many things, not least how this information could be used to advantage.

"If what you say is true, there has been recklessness and adventurism at the highest level in our country. If such could be proved—of course, one would need the proof—there might have to be changes at the top. Good day to you."

Karpov had understood. When the man on the pinnacle in Soviet Russia fell, all his own men fell with him. If there were changes at the top, there would be a vacant slot as Chairman of the KGB, a slot that Karpov felt would suit him admirably. But to cobble together his alliance of Party forces, Vartanyan would need proof, more proof, solid, irrefutable, documentary proof, that the act of recklessness had almost brought disaster. No one had ever forgotten that Mikhail Suslov had toppled Khrushchev in 1964 on charges of adventurism over the 1962 Cuban missile crisis.

Shortly after the meeting, Karpov had sent in Winkler, the most bumbling agent his files could unearth. His message had been read and understood. Now he held in his hands the proof his Armenian patron needed. He looked through the documents again.

The report of the mythical interrogation and the confession of Major Valeri Petrofsky to the British would need some amendment, but he had people out at Yasyenevo who could accomplish that. The interrogation report forms were absolutely authentic—that was the main thing. Even Preston's reports on his progress, suitably amended to exclude any mention of Winkler, were photocopies of the originals.

The General Secretary would not be able or willing to save the traitor Philby; nor, later, would he be able to save himself. Vartan-yan would see to that, and he would not be ungrateful.

Karpov's car came to take him to Zurich and the Moscow plane. He rose. It had been a good meeting. And as always it had been re-warding to negotiate with Chelsea.

EPILOGUE

S ir Bernard Hemmings formally retired on September 1, 1987,
although he had been on leave since mid-July. He died in No-
vember of that year, his pension rights assured to the benefit
of his wife and stepdaughter.

Brian Harcourt-Smith did not succeed him as Director-General.
The "Wise Men" took their soundings, and though it was agreed
there was nothing in the least sinister in Harcourt-Smith's attempts
to pass the Preston report no further, or to discount the significance
of the Glasgow intercept, one could not avoid concluding that these
constituted two serious errors of judgment. There being no other
discernible successor inside Five, a man was brought in from outside
as Director-General. Harcourt-Smith resigned some months later
and joined the board of a merchant bank in the City.

John Preston retired in early September and joined the staff of the
asset-protection people. His salary was more than doubled, enabling
him to seek his divorce and make a strong case for obtaining custody
of his son, Tommy, whose welfare and education he could now guarantee. Julia abruptly withdrew her objection and custody was
granted to Preston.

Sir Nigel Irvine retired, as scheduled, on the last day of the year, departing his office in time for Christmas. He went to live at his cottage in Langton Matravers, where he joined fully in the life of the village and told anyone who asked that, prior to retirement, he had done "something boring in Whitehall."

Jan Marais was summoned to Pretoria in early December for consultations. As the Boeing 747 of South African Airlines lifted off from Heathrow, two burly NIS agents emerged from the flight crew rest area and put handcuffs on him. He did not enjoy his retirement, the whole of which was spent several feet below ground level assisting teams of large gentlemen with their inquiries.

The arrest of Marais having taken place in public, news of it soon leaked out, which alerted General Karpov that his sleeper had been burned. He was confident that Marais—Frikki Brandt—would not long resist the interrogators, and waited for the arrest of George Berenson and the consequent dismay in the Western Alliance.

In mid-December, Berenson took early retirement from the ministry, but there was no arrest. After the personal intervention of Sir Nigel Irvine, the man was allowed to retire to the British Virgin Islands on a small but adequate pension from his wife.

The news told General Karpov that his top agent had not only been blown, but turned as well. What he did not know was just *when* Berenson had been turned to the service of the British. Then, from inside Karpov's own rezidentura in London, KGB agent Andreyev reported he had heard a rumor to the effect that Berenson had turned to MI5 from the very first approach Jan Marais had ever made to him.

Within a week the analysts at Yasyenevo had to accept that three years of what was actually perfectly good intelligence would have to be junked as suspect from the start.

It was the Master's last stroke.